The Mucker

By Edgar Rice Burroughs

ISBN: 979-8-89718-128-5

All Rights reserved. No part of this book maybe reproduced without written permission from the publishers, except by a reviewer who may quote brief passages in a review to be printed in a newspaper or magazine.

Printed:January 2025

Published and Distributed By:
Lushena Books
607 Country Club Drive, Unit E
Bensenville, IL 60106
www.lushenabks.com

ISBN: 979-8-89718-128-5

Part I

I
BILLY BYRNE

Billy Byrne was a product of the streets and alleys of Chicago's great West Side. From Halsted to Robey, and from Grand Avenue to Lake Street there was scarce a bartender whom Billy knew not by his first name. And, in proportion to their number which was considerably less, he knew the patrolmen and plain clothes men equally as well, but not so pleasantly.

His kindergarten education had commenced in an alley back of a feed-store. Here a gang of older boys and men were wont to congregate at such times as they had naught else to occupy their time, and as the bridewell was the only place in which they ever held a job for more than a day or two, they had considerable time to devote to congregating.

They were pickpockets and second-story men, made and in the making, and all were muckers, ready to insult the first woman who passed, or pick a quarrel with any stranger who did not appear too burly. By night they plied their real vocations. By day they sat in the alley behind the feed-store and drank beer from a battered tin pail.

The question of labor involved in transporting the pail, empty, to the saloon across the street, and returning it, full, to the alley back of the feed-store was solved by the presence of admiring and envious little boys of the neighborhood who hung, wide-eyed and thrilled, about these heroes of their childish lives.

Billy Byrne, at six, was rushing the can for this noble band, and incidentally picking up his knowledge of life and the rudiments of his education. He gloried in the fact that he was personally acquainted with "Eddie" Welch, and that with his own ears he had heard "Eddie" tell the gang how he stuck up a guy on West Lake Street within fifty yards of the Twenty-eighth Precinct Police Station.

The kindergarten period lasted until Billy was ten; then he commenced "swiping" brass faucets from vacant buildings and selling them to a fence who ran a junkshop on Lincoln Street near Kinzie.

From this man he obtained the hint that graduated him to a higher grade, so that at twelve he was robbing freight cars in the yards along Kinzie Street, and it was about this same time that he commenced to find pleasure in the feel of his fist against the jaw of a fellow-man.

He had had his boyish scraps with his fellows off and on ever since he could remember; but his first real fight came when he was twelve. He had had an altercation with an erstwhile pal over the division of the returns from some freight-car booty. The gang was all present, and as words quickly gave place to blows, as they have a habit of doing in certain sections of the West Side, the men and boys formed a rough ring about the contestants.

The battle was a long one. The two were rolling about in the dust of the alley quite as often as they were upon their feet exchanging blows. There was nothing fair, nor decent, nor scientific about their methods. They gouged and bit and tore. They used knees and elbows and feet, and but for the timely presence of a brickbat beneath his fingers at the psychological moment Billy Byrne would have gone down to humiliating defeat. As it was the other boy went down, and for a week Billy remained hidden by one of the gang pending the report from the hospital.

When word came that the patient would live, Billy felt an immense load lifted from his shoulders, for he dreaded arrest and experience with the law that he had learned from childhood to deride and hate. Of course there was the loss of prestige that would naturally have accrued to him could he have been pointed out as the "guy that croaked Sheehan"; but there is always a fly in the ointment, and Billy only sighed and came out of his temporary retirement.

That battle started Billy to thinking, and the result of that mental activity was a determination to learn to handle his mitts scientifically—people of the West Side do not have hands; they are equipped by Nature with mitts and dukes. A few have paws and flippers.

He had no opportunity to realize his new dream for several years; but when he was about seventeen a neighbor's son surprised his little world by suddenly developing from an unknown teamster into a locally famous lightweight.

The young man never had been affiliated with the gang, as his escutcheon was defiled with a record of steady employment. So Billy had known nothing of the sparring lessons his young neighbor had taken, or of the work he had done at the downtown gymnasium of Larry Hilmore.

Now it happened that while the new lightweight was unknown to the charmed circle of the gang, Billy knew him fairly well by reason of the proximity of their respective parental back yards, and so when the glamour of pugilistic success haloed the young man Billy lost no time in basking in the light of reflected glory.

He saw much of his new hero all the following winter. He accompanied him to many mills, and on one glorious occasion occupied a position in the coming champion's corner. When the prize fighter toured, Billy continued to hang around Hilmore's place, running errands and doing odd jobs, the while he picked up pugilistic lore, and absorbed the spirit of the game along with the rudiments and finer points of its science, almost unconsciously. Then his ambition changed. Once he had longed to shine as a gunman; now he was determined to become a prize fighter; but the old gang still saw much of him, and he was a familiar figure about the saloon corners along Grand Avenue and Lake Street.

During this period Billy neglected the box cars on Kinzie Street, partially because he felt that he was fitted for more dignified employment, and as well for the fact that the railroad company had doubled the number of watchmen in the yards; but there were times when he felt the old yearning for excitement and adventure. These times were usually coincident with an acute financial depression in Billy's change pocket, and then he would fare forth in the still watches of the night, with a couple of boon companions and roll a souse, or stick up a saloon.

It was upon an occasion of this nature that an event occurred which was fated later to change the entire course of Billy Byrne's life. Upon the West Side the older gangs are jealous of the sanctity of their own territory. Outsiders do not trespass with impunity. From Halsted to Robey, and from Lake to Grand lay the broad hunting preserve of Kelly's gang, to which Billy had been almost born, one might say. Kelly owned the feed-store back of which the gang had loafed for years, and though himself a respectable businessman his name had been attached to the pack of hoodlums who held forth at his back door as the easiest means of locating and identifying its motley members.

The police and citizenry of this great territory were the natural enemies and prey of Kelly's gang, but as the kings of old protected the deer of their great forests from poachers, so Kelly's gang felt it incumbent upon them to safeguard the lives and property which they considered theirs by divine right. It is doubtful that they thought of the matter in just this way, but the effect was the same.

And so it was that as Billy Byrne wended homeward alone in the wee hours of the morning after emptying the cash drawer of old Schneider's saloon and locking the weeping Schneider in his own ice box, he was deeply grieved and angered to see three rank outsiders from Twelfth Street beating Patrolman Stanley Lasky with his own baton, the while they simultaneously strove to kick in his ribs with their heavy boots.

Now Lasky was no friend of Billy Byrne; but the officer had been born and raised in the district and was attached to the Twenty-eighth Precinct Station on Lake Street near Ashland Avenue, and so was part and parcel of the natural possession of the gang. Billy felt that it was entirely ethical to beat up a cop, provided you confined your efforts to those of your own district; but for a bunch of yaps from south of Twelfth Street to attempt to pull off any such coarse work in *his* bailiwick—why it was unthinkable.

A hero and rescuer of lesser experience than Billy Byrne would have rushed melodramatically into the midst of the fray, and in all probability have had his face pushed completely through the back of his head, for the guys from Twelfth Street were not of the rah-rah-boy type of hoodlum— they were bad men, with an upper case B. So Billy crept stealthily along in the shadows until he was quite close to them, and behind them. On the way he had gathered up a cute little granite paving block, than which there is nothing in the world harder, not even a Twelfth Street skull. He was quite close now to one of the men—he who was wielding the officer's club to such excellent disadvantage to the officer—and then he raised the paving block only to lower it silently and suddenly upon the back of that unsuspecting head—"and then there were two."

Before the man's companions realized what had happened Billy had possessed himself of the fallen club and struck one of them a blinding, staggering blow across the eyes. Then number three pulled his gun and fired point-blank at Billy. The bullet tore through the mucker's left shoulder. It would have sent a more highly organized and nervously inclined man to the pavement; but Billy was neither highly organized nor nervously inclined, so that about the only immediate effect it had upon him was to make him mad—before he had been but peeved—peeved at the rank crust that had permitted these cheapskates from south of Twelfth Street to work his territory.

Thoroughly aroused, Billy was a wonder. From a long line of burly ancestors he had inherited the physique of a prize bull. From earliest childhood he had fought, always unfairly, so that he knew all the tricks of street fighting. During the past year there had been added to Billy's natural fighting ability and instinct a knowledge of the scientific end of the sport. The result was something appalling—to the gink from Twelfth Street.

Before he knew whether his shot had killed Billy his gun had been wrenched from his hand and flung across the street; he was down on the granite with a hand as hard as the paving block scrambling his facial attractions beyond hope of recall.

By this time Patrolman Lasky had staggered to his feet, and most opportunely at that, for the man whom Billy had dazed with the club was recovering. Lasky promptly put him to sleep with the butt of the gun that he had been unable to draw when first attacked, then he turned to assist Billy. But it was not Billy who needed assistance—it was the gentleman from Bohemia. With difficulty Lasky dragged Billy from his prey.

"Leave enough of him for the inquest," pleaded Lasky.

When the wagon arrived Billy had disappeared, but Lasky had recognized him and thereafter the two had nodded pleasantly to each other upon such occasions as they chanced to meet upon the street.

Two years elapsed before the event transpired which proved a crisis in Billy's life. During this period his existence had been much the same as before. He had collected what was coming to him from careless and less muscular citizens. He had helped to stick up a half-dozen saloons. He had robbed the night men in two elevated stations, and for a while had been upon the payroll of a certain union and done strong arm work in all parts of the city for twenty-five dollars a week.

By day he was a general utility man about Larry Hilmore's boxing academy, and time and time again Hilmore urged him to quit drinking and live straight, for he saw in the young giant the makings of a great heavyweight; but Billy couldn't leave the booze alone, and so the best that he got was an occasional five spot for appearing in preliminary bouts with third- and fourth-rate heavies and has-beens; but during the three years that he had hung about Hilmore's he had acquired an enviable knowledge of the manly art of self-defense.

On the night that things really began to happen in the life of Billy Byrne that estimable gentleman was lolling in front of a saloon at the corner of

Lake and Robey. The dips that congregated nightly there under the protection of the powerful politician who owned the place were commencing to assemble. Billy knew them all, and nodded to them as they passed him. He noted surprise in the faces of several as they saw him standing there. He wondered what it was all about, and determined to ask the next man who evinced even mute wonderment at his presence what was eating him.

Then Billy saw a harness bull strolling toward him from the east. It was Lasky. When Lasky saw Billy he too opened his eyes in surprise, and when he came quite close to the mucker he whispered something to him, though he kept his eyes straight ahead as though he had not seen Billy at all.

In deference to the whispered request Billy presently strolled around the corner toward Walnut Street, but at the alley back of the saloon he turned suddenly in. A hundred yards up the alley he found Lasky in the shadow of a telephone pole.

"Wotinell are you doin' around here?" asked the patrolman. "Didn't you know that Sheehan had peached?"

Two nights before old man Schneider, goaded to desperation by the repeated raids upon his cash drawer, had shown fight when he again had been invited to elevate his hands, and the holdup men had shot him through the heart. Sheehan had been arrested on suspicion.

Billy had not been with Sheehan that night. As a matter of fact he never had trained with him, for, since the boyish battle that the two had waged, there had always been ill feeling between them; but with Lasky's words Billy knew what had happened.

"Sheehan says I done it, eh?" he questioned.

"That's what he says."

"I wasn't within a mile of Schneider's that night," protested Billy.

"The Lieut. thinks different," said Lasky. "He'd be only too glad to soak you; for you've always been too slick to get nicked before. Orders is out to get you, and if I were you I'd beat it and beat it quick. I don't have to tell you why I'm handing you this, but it's all I can do for you. Now take my advice and make yourself scarce, though you'll have to go some to make your getaway now—every man on the force has your description by this time."

Billy turned without a word and walked east in the alley toward Lincoln Street. Lasky returned to Robey Street. In Lincoln Street Billy walked north to Kinzie. Here he entered the railroad yards. An hour later he was bumping out of town toward the West on a fast freight. Three weeks later he found himself in San Francisco. He had no money, but the methods that had so often replenished his depleted exchequer at home he felt would serve the same purpose here.

Being unfamiliar with San Francisco, Billy did not know where best to work, but when by accident he stumbled upon a street where there were many saloons whose patrons were obviously seafaring men Billy was distinctly elated. What could be better for his purpose than a drunken sailor?

He entered one of the saloons and stood watching a game of cards, or thus he seemed to be occupied. As a matter of fact his eyes were constantly upon the alert, roving about the room to wherever a man was in the act of paying for a round of drinks that a fat wallet might be located.

Presently one that filled him with longing rewarded his careful watch. The man was sitting at a table a short distance from Billy. Two other men were with him. As he paid the waiter from a well-filled pocketbook he looked up to meet Billy's eyes upon him.

With a drunken smile he beckoned to the mucker to join them. Billy felt that Fate was overkind to him, and he lost no time in heeding her call. A moment later he was sitting at the table with the three sailors, and had ordered a drop of red-eye.

The stranger was very lavish in his entertainment. He scarcely waited for Billy to drain one glass before he ordered another, and once after Billy had left the table for a moment he found a fresh drink awaiting him when he returned—his host had already poured it for him.

It was this last drink that did the business.

II
Shanghaied

When Billy opened his eyes again he could not recall, for the instant, very much of his recent past. At last he remembered with painful regret the drunken sailor it had been his intention to roll. He felt deeply chagrined that his rightful prey should have escaped him. He couldn't understand how it had happened.

"This Frisco booze must be something fierce," thought Billy.

His head ached frightfully and he was very sick. So sick that the room in which he lay seemed to be rising and falling in a horribly realistic manner. Every time it dropped it brought Billy's stomach nearly to his mouth.

Billy shut his eyes. Still the awful sensation. Billy groaned. He never had been so sick in all his life before, and, my, how his poor head did hurt. Finding that it only seemed to make matters worse when he closed his eyes Billy opened them again.

He looked about the room in which he lay. He found it a stuffy hole filled with bunks in tiers three deep around the sides. In the center of the room was a table. Above the table a lamp hung suspended from one of the wooden beams of the ceiling.

The lamp arrested Billy's attention. It was swinging back and forth rather violently. This could not be a hallucination. The room might seem to be rising and falling, but that lamp could not seem to be swinging around in any such manner if it were not really and truly swinging. He couldn't account for it. Again he shut his eyes for a moment. When he opened them to look again at the lamp he found it still swung as before.

Cautiously he slid from his bunk to the floor. It was with difficulty that he kept his feet. Still that might be but the effects of the liquor. At last he reached the table to which he clung for support while he extended one hand toward the lamp.

There was no longer any doubt! The lamp was beating back and forth like the clapper of a great bell. Where was he? Billy sought a window. He found some little round, glass-covered holes near the low ceiling at one side of the room. It was only at the greatest risk to life and limb that he managed to crawl on all fours to one of them.

As he straightened up and glanced through he was appalled at the sight that met his eyes. As far as he could see there was naught but a tumbling waste of water. And then the truth of what had happened to him broke upon his understanding.

"An' I was goin' to roll that guy!" he muttered in helpless bewilderment. "I was a-goin' to roll him, and now look here wot he has done to me!"

At that moment a light appeared above as the hatch was raised, and Billy saw the feet and legs of a large man descending the ladder from above. When the newcomer reached the floor and turned to look about his eyes met Billy's, and Billy saw that it was his host of the previous evening.

"Well, my hearty, how goes it?" asked the stranger.

"You pulled it off pretty slick," said Billy.

"What do you mean?" asked the other with a frown.

"Come off," said Billy; "you know what I mean."

"Look here," replied the other coldly. "Don't you forget that I'm mate of this ship, an' that you want to speak respectful to me if you ain't lookin' for trouble. My name's *Mr.* Ward, an' when you speak to me say *Sir*. Understand?"

Billy scratched his head, and blinked his eyes. He never before had been spoken to in any such fashion—at least not since he had put on the avoirdupois of manhood. His head ached horribly and he was sick to his stomach—frightfully sick. His mind was more upon his physical suffering than upon what the mate was saying, so that quite a perceptible interval of time elapsed before the true dimensions of the affront to his dignity commenced to percolate into the befogged and pain-racked convolutions of his brain.

The mate thought that his bluster had bluffed the new hand. That was what he had come below to accomplish. Experience had taught him that an early lesson in discipline and subordination saved unpleasant encounters in the future. He also had learned that there is no better time to put a bluff of this nature across than when the victim is suffering from the aftereffects of whiskey and a drug—mentality, vitality, and courage are then at their lowest ebb. A brave man often is reduced to the pitiful condition of a yellow dog when nausea sits astride his stomach.

But the mate was not acquainted with Billy Byrne of Kelly's gang. Billy's brain was befuddled, so that it took some time for an idea to wriggle its way through, but his courage was all there, and all to the good. Billy was a mucker, a hoodlum, a gangster, a thug, a tough. When he fought, his methods would have brought a flush of shame to the face of His Satanic Majesty. He had hit oftener from behind than from before. He had always taken every advantage of size and weight and numbers that he could call to his assistance. He was an insulter of girls and women. He was a barroom brawler, and a saloon-corner loafer. He was all that was dirty, and mean, and contemptible, and cowardly in the eyes of a brave man, and yet, notwithstanding all this, Billy Byrne was no coward. He was what he was because of training and environment. He knew no other methods; no other code. Whatever the meager ethics of his kind he would have lived up to them to the death. He never had squealed on a pal, and he never had left a wounded friend to fall into the hands of the enemy—the police.

Nor had he ever let a man speak to him, as the mate had spoken, and get away with it, and so, while he did not act as quickly as would have been his wont had his brain been clear, he did act; but the interval of time had led the mate into an erroneous conception of its cause, and into a further rash show of authority, and had thrown him off his guard as well.

"What you need," said the mate, advancing toward Billy, "is a bash on the beezer. It'll help you remember that you ain't nothin' but a dirty damn landlubber, an' when your betters come around you'll—"

But what Billy would have done in the presence of his betters remained stillborn in the mate's imagination in the face of what Billy really did do to his better as that worthy swung a sudden, vicious blow at the mucker's face.

Billy Byrne had not been scrapping with third- and fourth-rate heavies, and sparring with real, live ones for nothing. The mate's fist whistled through empty air; the blear-eyed hunk of clay that had seemed such easy prey to him was metamorphosed on the instant into an alert, catlike bundle of steel sinews, and Billy Byrne swung that awful right with the pile-driver weight, that even The Big Smoke himself had acknowledged respect for, straight to the short ribs of his antagonist.

With a screech of surprise and pain the mate crumpled in the far corner of the forecastle, rammed halfway beneath a bunk by the force of the terrific blow. Like a tiger Billy Byrne was after him, and dragging the man out into the center of the floor space he beat and mauled him until his victim's bloodcurdling shrieks echoed through the ship from stem to stern.

When the captain, followed by a half-dozen seamen rushed down the companionway, he found Billy sitting astride the prostrate form of the mate. His great fingers circled the man's throat, and with mighty blows he was dashing the fellow's head against the hard floor. Another moment and murder would have been complete.

"Avast there!" cried the captain, and as though to punctuate his remark he swung the heavy stick he usually carried full upon the back of Billy's head. It was that blow that saved the mate's life, for when Billy came to he found himself in a dark and smelly hole, chained and padlocked to a heavy stanchion.

They kept Billy there for a week; but every day the captain visited him in an attempt to show him the error of his way. The medium used by the skipper for impressing his ideas of discipline upon Billy was a large, hard stick. At the end of the week it was necessary to carry Billy above to keep the rats from devouring him, for the continued beatings and starvation had reduced him to little more than an unconscious mass of raw and bleeding meat.

"There," remarked the skipper, as he viewed his work by the light of day, "I guess that fellow'll know his place next time an officer an' a gentleman speaks to him."

That Billy survived is one of the hitherto unrecorded miracles of the power of matter over mind. A man of intellect, of imagination, a being of nerves, would have succumbed to the shock alone; but Billy was not as these. He simply lay still and thoughtless, except for half-formed ideas of revenge, until Nature, unaided, built up what the captain had so ruthlessly torn down.

Ten days after they brought him up from the hold Billy was limping about the deck of the *Halfmoon* doing light manual labor. From the other sailors aboard he learned that he was not the only member of the crew who had been shanghaied. Aside from a half-dozen reckless men from the criminal classes who had signed voluntarily, either because they could not get a berth upon a decent ship, or desired to flit as quietly from the law zone of the United States as possible, not a man was there who had been signed regularly.

They were as tough and vicious a lot as Fate ever had foregathered in one forecastle, and with them Billy Byrne felt perfectly at home. His early threats of awful vengeance to be wreaked upon the mate and skipper had subsided with the rough but sensible advice of his messmates. The mate, for his part, gave no indication of harboring the assault that Billy had made upon him other than to assign the most dangerous or disagreeable duties of the ship to the mucker whenever it was possible to do so; but the result of this was to hasten Billy's nautical education, and keep him in excellent physical trim.

All traces of alcohol had long since vanished from the young man's system. His face showed the effects of his enforced abstemiousness in a marked degree. The red, puffy, blotchy complexion had given way to a clear, tanned skin; bright eyes supplanted the bleary, bloodshot things that had given the bestial expression to his face in the past. His features, always regular and strong, had taken on a peculiarly refined dignity from the salt air, the clean life, and the dangerous occupation of the deep-sea sailor, that would have put Kelly's gang to a pinch to have recognized their erstwhile crony had he suddenly appeared in their midst in the alley back of the feed-store on Grand Avenue.

With the new life Billy found himself taking on a new character. He surprised himself singing at his work—he whose whole life up to now had been devoted to dodging honest labor—whose motto had been: The world owes me a living, and it's up to me to collect it. Also, he was surprised to discover that he liked to work, that he took keen pride in striving to outdo the men who worked with him, and this spirit, despite the suspicion which the captain entertained of Billy since the episode of the forecastle, went far to making his life more endurable on board the *Halfmoon*, for workers such as the mucker developed into are not to be sneezed at, and though he had little idea of subordination it was worth putting up with something to keep him in condition to work. It was this line of reasoning that saved Billy's skull on one or two occasions when his impudence had been sufficient to have provoked the skipper to a personal assault upon him under ordinary conditions; and Mr. Ward, having tasted of Billy's medicine once, had no craving for another encounter with him that would entail personal conflict.

The entire crew was made up of ruffians and unhung murderers, but Skipper Simms had had little experience with seamen of any other ilk, so he handled them roughshod, using his horny fist, and the short, heavy stick that he habitually carried, in lieu of argument; but with the exception of Billy the men all had served before the mast in the past, so that ship's discipline was to some extent ingrained in them all.

Enjoying his work, the life was not an unpleasant one for the mucker. The men of the forecastle were of the kind he had always known—there was no honor among them, no virtue, no kindliness, no decency. With them Billy was at home—he scarcely missed the old gang. He made his friends among them, and his enemies. He picked quarrels, as had been his way since childhood. His science and his great strength, together with his endless stock of underhand tricks brought him out of each encounter with fresh laurels. Presently he found it difficult to pick a fight—his messmates had had enough of him. They left him severely alone.

These ofttimes bloody battles engendered no deep-seated hatred in the hearts of the defeated. They were part of the day's work and play of the half-brutes that Skipper Simms had gathered together. There was only one man aboard whom Billy really hated. That was the passenger, and Billy hated him, not because of anything that the man had said or done to Billy, for he had never even so much as spoken to the mucker, but because of the fine clothes and superior air which marked him plainly to Billy as one of that loathed element of society—a gentleman.

Billy hated everything that was respectable. He had hated the smug, self-satisfied merchants of Grand Avenue. He had writhed in torture at the sight of every shiny, purring automobile that had ever passed him with its load of well-groomed men and women. A clean, stiff collar was to Billy as a red rag to a bull. Cleanliness, success, opulence, decency, spelled but one thing to Billy—physical weakness; and he hated physical weakness. His idea of indicating strength and manliness lay in displaying as much of brutality and uncouthness as possible. To assist a woman over a mud hole would have seemed to Billy an acknowledgement of pusillanimity—to stick out his foot and trip her so that she sprawled full length in it, the hallmark of bluff manliness. And so he hated, with all the strength of a strong nature, the immaculate, courteous, well-bred man who paced the deck each day smoking a fragrant cigar after his meals.

Inwardly he wondered what the dude was doing on board such a vessel as the *Halfmoon*, and marveled that so weak a thing dared venture among real men. Billy's contempt caused him to notice the passenger more than he would have been ready to admit. He saw that the man's face was handsome, but there was an unpleasant shiftiness to his brown eyes; and then, entirely outside of his former reasons for hating him, Billy came to loathe him intuitively, as one who was not to be trusted. Finally his dislike for the man became an obsession. He haunted, when discipline permitted, that part of the vessel where he would be most likely to encounter the object of his wrath, hoping, always hoping, that the "dude" would give him some slight pretext for "pushing in his mush," as Billy would so picturesquely have worded it.

He was loitering about the deck for this purpose one evening when he overheard part of a low-voiced conversation between the object of his wrath and Skipper Simms—just enough to set him to wondering what was doing, and to show him that whatever it might be it was crooked and that the immaculate passenger and Skipper Simms were both "in on it."

He questioned "Bony" Sawyer and "Red" Sanders, but neither had nearly as much information as Billy himself, and so the *Halfmoon* came to Honolulu and lay at anchor some hundred yards from a stanch, trim, white yacht, and none knew, other than the *Halfmoon*'s officers and her single passenger, the real mission of the harmless-looking little brigantine.

III
THE CONSPIRACY

No shore leave was granted the crew of the *Halfmoon* while the vessel lay off Honolulu, and deep and ominous were the grumblings of the men. Only First Officer Ward and the second mate went ashore. Skipper Simms kept the men busy painting and holystoning as a vent for their pent emotions.

Billy Byrne noticed that the passenger had abandoned his daylight strolls on deck. In fact he never once left his cabin while the *Halfmoon* lay at anchor until darkness had fallen; then he would come on deck, often standing for an hour at a time with eyes fastened steadily upon the brave little yacht from the canopied upper deck of which gay laughter and soft music came floating across the still water.

When Mr. Ward and the second mate came to shore a strange thing happened. They entered a third-rate hotel near the water front, engaged a room for a week, paid in advance, were in their room for half an hour and emerged clothed in civilian raiment.

Then they hastened to another hostelry—a first-class one this time, and the second mate walked ahead in frock coat and silk hat while Mr. Ward trailed behind in a neat, blue serge sack suit, carrying both bags.

At the second hotel the second mate registered as Henri Theriere, Count de Cadenet, and servant, France. His first act thereafter was to hand a note to the clerk asking that it be dispatched immediately. The note was addressed to Anthony Harding, Esq., On Board Yacht *Lotus*.

Count de Cadenet and his servant repaired immediately to the count's rooms, there to await an answer to the note. Henri Theriere, the second officer of the *Halfmoon*, in frock coat and silk hat looked every inch a nobleman and a gentleman. What his past had been only he knew, but his polished manners, his knowledge of navigation and seamanship, and his leaning toward the ways of the martinet in his dealings with the men beneath him had led Skipper Simms to assume that he had once held a commission in the French Navy, from which he doubtless had been kicked—in disgrace.

The man was cold, cruel, of a moody disposition, and quick to anger. He had been signed as second officer for this cruise through the intervention of Divine and Clinker. He had sailed with Simms before, but the skipper had found him too hard a customer to deal with, and had been on the point of seeking another second when Divine and Clinker discovered him on board the *Halfmoon* and after ten minutes' conversation with him found that he fitted so perfectly into their scheme of action that they would not hear of Simms' releasing him.

Ward had little use for the Frenchman, whose haughty manner and condescending airs grated on the sensibilities of the uncouth and boorish first officer. The duty which necessitated him acting in the capacity of Theriere's servant was about as distasteful to him as anything could be, and only served to add to his hatred for the inferior, who, in the bottom of his heart, he knew to be in every way, except upon the roster of the *Halfmoon*, his superior; but money can work wonders, and Divine's promise that the officers and crew of the *Halfmoon* would have a cool million United States dollars to divide among them in case of the success of the venture had quite effectually overcome any dislike which Mr. Ward had felt for this particular phase of his duty.

The two officers sat in silence in their room at the hotel awaiting an answer to the note they had dispatched to Anthony Harding, Esq. The parts they were to act had been carefully rehearsed on board the *Halfmoon* many times. Each was occupied with his own thoughts, and as they had nothing in common outside the present rascality that had brought them together, and as that subject was one not well to discuss more than necessary, there seemed no call for conversation.

On board the yacht in the harbor preparations were being made to land a small party that contemplated a motor trip up the Nuuanu Valley when a small boat drew alongside, and a messenger from the hotel handed a sealed note to one of the sailors.

From the deck of the *Halfmoon* Skipper Simms witnessed the transaction, smiling inwardly. Billy Byrne also saw it, but it meant nothing to him. He had been lolling upon the deck of the brigantine glaring at the yacht *Lotus*, hating her and the gay, well-dressed men and women he could see laughing and chatting upon her deck. They represented to him the concentrated essence of all that was pusillanimous, disgusting, loathsome in that other world that was as far separated from him as though he had been a grubworm in the manure pile back of Brady's livery stable.

He saw the note handed by the sailor to a gray-haired, smooth-faced man—a large, sleek, well-groomed man. Billy could imagine the white hands and polished nails of him. The thought was nauseating.

The man who took and opened the note was Anthony Harding, Esq. He read it, and then passed it to a young woman who stood nearby talking with other young people.

"Here, Barbara," he said, "is something of more interest to you than to me. If you wish I'll call upon him and invite him to dinner tonight."

The girl was reading the note.

On Board Yacht *Lotus*,
Honolulu.

ANTHONY HARDING, ESQ.

MY DEAR MR. HARDING:
This will introduce a very dear friend of mine, Count de Cadenet, who expects to be in Honolulu about the time that you are there. The count is traveling for pleasure, and as he is entirely unacquainted upon the islands any courtesies which you may show him will be greatly appreciated.

Cordially,
L. CORTWRITE DIVINE

The girl smiled as she finished perusing the note.

"Larry is always picking up titles and making dear friends of them," she laughed. "I wonder where he found this one."

"Or where this one found him," suggested Mr. Harding. "Well, I suppose that the least we can do is to have him aboard for dinner. We'll be leaving tomorrow, so there won't be much entertaining we can do."

"Let's pick him up on our way through town now," suggested Barbara Harding, "and take him with us for the day. That will be settling our debt to friendship, and dinner tonight can depend upon what sort of person we find the count to be."

"As you will," replied her father, and so it came about that two big touring cars drew up before the Count de Cadenet's hotel half an hour later, and Anthony Harding, Esq., entered and sent up his card.

The "count" came down in person to greet his caller. Harding saw at a glance that the man was a gentleman, and when he had introduced him to the other members of the party it was evident that they appraised him quite as had their host. Barbara Harding seemed particularly taken with the Count de Cadenet, insisting that he join those who occupied her car, and so it was that the second officer of the *Halfmoon* rode out of Honolulu in pleasant conversation with the object of his visit to the island.

Barbara Harding found De Cadenet an interesting man. There was no corner of the globe however remote with which he was not to some degree familiar. He was well read, and possessed the ability to discuss what he had read intelligently and entertainingly. There was no evidence of moodiness in him now. He was the personification of affability, for was he not monopolizing the society of a very beautiful, and very wealthy young lady?

The day's outing had two significant results. It put into the head of the second mate of the *Halfmoon* that which would have caused his skipper and the retiring Mr. Divine acute mental perturbation could they have guessed it; and it put De Cadenet into possession of information which necessitated his refusing the urgent invitation to dine upon the yacht, *Lotus*, that evening—the information that the party would sail the following morning en route to Manila.

"I cannot tell you," he said to Mr. Harding, "how much I regret the circumstance that must rob me of the pleasure of accepting your invitation. Only absolute necessity, I assure you, could prevent me being with you as long as possible," and though he spoke to the girl's father he looked directly into the eyes of Barbara Harding.

A young woman of less experience might have given some outward indication of the effect of this speech upon her, but whether she was pleased or otherwise the Count de Cadenet could not guess, for she merely voiced the smiling regrets that courtesy demanded.

They left De Cadenet at his hotel, and as he bid them farewell the man turned to Barbara Harding with a low aside.

"I shall see you again, Miss Harding," he said, "very, very soon."

She could not guess what was in his mind as he voiced this rather, under the circumstances, unusual statement. Could she have, the girl would have been terror-stricken; but she saw that in his eyes which she could translate, and she wondered many times that evening whether she were pleased or angry with the message it conveyed.

The moment De Cadenet entered the hotel he hurried to the room where the impatient Mr. Ward awaited him.

"Quick!" he cried. "We must bundle out of here posthaste. They sail tomorrow morning. Your duties as valet have been light and short-lived; but I can give you an excellent recommendation should you desire to take service with another gentleman."

"That'll be about all of that, Mr. Theriere," snapped the first officer, coldly. "I did not embark upon this theatrical enterprise for amusement—I see nothing funny in it, and I wish you to remember that I am still your superior officer."

Theriere shrugged. Ward did not chance to catch the ugly look in his companion's eye. Together they gathered up their belongings, descended to the office, paid their bill, and a few moments later were changing back to their sea clothes in the little hotel where they first had engaged accommodations. Half an hour later they stepped to the deck of the *Halfmoon*.

Billy Byrne saw them from where he worked in the vicinity of the cabin. When they were not looking he scowled maliciously at them. They were the personal representatives of authority, and Billy hated authority in whatever guise it might be visited upon him. He hated law and order and discipline.

"I'd like to meet one of dem guys on Green Street some night," he thought.

He saw them enter the captain's cabin with the skipper, and then he saw Mr. Divine join them. Billy noted the haste displayed by the four and it set him to wondering. The scrap of conversation between Divine and Simms that he had overheard returned to him. He wanted to hear more, and as Billy was not handicapped by any overly refined notions of the ethics which frown upon eavesdropping he lost no time in transferring the scene of his labors to a point sufficiently close to one of the cabin ports to permit him to note what took place within.

What the mucker heard of that conversation made him prick up his ears. He saw that something after his own heart was doing—something crooked, and he wondered that so pusillanimous a thing as Divine could have a hand in it. It almost changed his estimate of the passenger of the *Halfmoon*.

The meeting broke up so suddenly that Billy had to drop to his knees to escape the observation of those within the cabin. As it was, Theriere, who had started to leave a second before the others, caught a fleeting glimpse of a face that quickly had been withdrawn from the cabin skylight as though its owner were fearful of detection.

Without a word to his companions the Frenchman left the cabin, but once outside he bounded up the companionway to the deck with the speed of a squirrel. Nor was he an instant too soon, for as he emerged from below he saw the figure of a man disappearing forward.

"Hey there, you!" he cried. "Come back here."

The mucker turned, a sulky scowl upon his lowering countenance, and the second officer saw that it was the fellow who had given Ward such a trimming the first day out.

"Oh, it's you is it, Byrne?" he said in a not unpleasant tone. "Come to my quarters a moment, I want to speak with you," and so saying he wheeled about and retraced his way below, the seaman at his heels.

"My man," said Theriere, once the two were behind the closed door of the officer's cabin, "I needn't ask how much you overheard of the conversation in the captain's cabin. If you hadn't overheard a great deal more than you should you wouldn't have been so keen to escape detection just now. What I wanted to say to you is this. Keep a close tongue in your head and stick by me in what's going to happen in the next few days. This bunch," he jerked his thumb in the direction of the captain's cabin, "are fixing their necks for halters, an' I for one don't intend to poke my head through any noose of another man's making. There's more in this thing if it's handled right, and handled without too many men in on the whack-up than we can get out of it if that man Divine has to be counted in. I've a plan of my own, an' it won't take but three or four of us to put it across.

"You don't like Ward," he continued, "and you may be almighty sure that Mr. Ward ain't losing any sleep nights over love of you. If you stick to that bunch Ward will do you out of your share as sure as you are a foot high, an' the chances are that he'll do you out of a whole lot more besides—as a matter of fact, Byrne, you're a mighty poor life insurance risk right now, with a life expectancy that's pretty near minus as long as Bender Ward is on the same ship with you. Do you understand what I mean?"

"Aw," said Billy Byrne, "I ain't afraid o' that stiff. Let him make any funny crack at me an' I'll cave in a handful of slats for him—the piker."

"That's all right too, Byrne," said Theriere. "Of course you can do it if anybody can, provided you get the chance; but Ward isn't the man to give you any chance. There may be shooting necessary within the next day or so, and there's nothing to prevent Ward letting you have it in the back, purely by accident; and if he don't do it then there'll be all kinds of opportunities for it before any of us ever see a white man's port again. He'll get you, Byrne; he's that kind.

"Now, with my proposition you'll be shut of Ward, Skipper Simms, and Divine. There'll be more money in it for you, an' you won't have to go around expecting a bullet in the small of your back every minute. What do you say? Are you game, or shall I have to go back to Skipper Simms and Ward and tell them that I caught you eavesdropping?"

"Oh, I'm game," said Billy Byrne, "if you'll promise me a square deal on the divvy."

The Frenchman extended his hand.

"Let's shake on it," he said.

Billy took the proffered palm in his.

"That's a go," he said; "but hadn't you better wise me to wot's doin'?"

"Not now," said Theriere, "someone might overhear just as you did. Wait a bit until I have a better opportunity, and I'll tell you all there is to know. In the meantime think over who'd be the best men to let into this with us— we'll need three or four more besides ourselves. Now go on deck about your duties as though nothing had happened, and if I'm a bit rougher than usual with you you'll understand that it's to avert any possible suspicion later."

"I'm next," said Billy Byrne.

IV
Piracy

By dusk the trim little brigantine was scudding away toward the west before a wind that could not have suited her better had it been made to order at the special behest of the devil himself to speed his minions upon their devil's work.

All hands were in the best of humor. The crew had forgotten their recent rancor at not having been permitted shore leave at Honolulu in the expectancy of adventure in the near future, for there was that in the atmosphere of the *Halfmoon* which proclaimed louder than words the proximity of excitement, and the goal toward which they had been sailing since they left San Francisco.

Skipper Simms and Divine were elated at the luck which had brought them to Honolulu in the nick of time, and at the success of Theriere's mission at that port. They had figured upon a week at least there before the second officer of the *Halfmoon* could ingratiate himself sufficiently into the goodwill of the Hardings to learn their plans, and now they were congratulating themselves upon their acumen in selecting so fit an agent as the Frenchman for the work he had handled so expeditiously and so well.

Ward was pleased that he had not been forced to prolong the galling masquerade of valet to his inferior officer. He was hopeful, too, that coming events would bring to the fore an opportunity to satisfy the vengeance he had inwardly sworn against the sailor who had so roughly manhandled him a few weeks past—Theriere had not been in error in his estimate of his fellow-officer.

Billy Byrne, the arduous labor of making sail over for the time, was devoting his energies to the task of piecing out from what Theriere had told him and what he had overheard outside the skipper's cabin some sort of explanation of the work ahead.

As he pondered Theriere's proposition he saw the wisdom of it. It would give those interested a larger amount of the booty for their share. Another feature of it was that it was underhanded and that appealed strongly to the mucker. Now, if he could but devise some scheme for double-crossing Theriere the pleasure and profit of the adventure would be tripled.

It was this proposition that was occupying his attention when he caught sight of "Bony" Sawyer and "Red" Sanders emerging from the forecastle. Billy Byrne hailed them.

When the mucker had explained the possibilities of profit that were to be had by entering the conspiracy aimed at Simms and Ward the two seamen were enthusiastically for it.

"Bony" Sawyer suggested that the black cook, Blanco, was about the only other member of the crew upon whom they could depend, and at Byrne's request "Bony" promised to enlist the cooperation of the giant Ethiopian.

From early morning of the second day out of Honolulu keen eyes scanned the eastern horizon through powerful glasses, until about two bells of the afternoon watch a slight smudge became visible about two points north of east. Immediately the course of the *Halfmoon* was altered so that she bore almost directly north by west in an effort to come safely into the course of the steamer which was seen rising rapidly above the horizon.

The new course of the brigantine was held as long as it seemed reasonably safe without danger of being sighted under full sail by the oncoming vessel, then her head was brought into the wind, and one by one her sails were lowered and furled, as the keen eyes of Second Officer Theriere announced that there was no question but that the white hull in the distance was that of the steam pleasure yacht *Lotus*.

Upon the deck of the unsuspecting vessel a merry party laughed and chatted in happy ignorance of the plotters in their path. It was nearly half an hour after the *Halfmoon* had come to rest, drifting idly under bare poles, that the lookout upon the *Lotus* sighted her.

"Sailin' vessel lyin' to, west half south," he shouted, "flyin' distress signals."

In an instant guests and crew had hurried to points of vantage where they might obtain unobstructed view of the stranger, and take advantage of this break in the monotony of a long sea voyage.

Anthony Harding was on the bridge with the captain, and both men had leveled their glasses upon the distant ship.

"Can you make her out?" asked the owner.

"She's a brigantine," replied the officer, "and all that I can make out from here would indicate that everything was shipshape about her. Her canvas is neatly furled, and she is evidently well manned, for I can see a number of figures above deck apparently engaged in watching us. I'll alter our course and speak to her—we'll see what's wrong, and give her a hand if we can."

"That's right," replied Harding; "do anything you can for them."

A moment later he joined his daughter and their guests to report the meager information he had.

"How exciting," exclaimed Barbara Harding. "Of course it's not a real shipwreck, but maybe it's the next thing to it. The poor souls may have been drifting about here in the center of the Pacific without food or water for goodness knows how many weeks, and now just think how they must be lifting their voices in thanks to God for his infinite mercy in guiding us to them."

"If they've been drifting for any considerable number of weeks without food or water," hazarded Billy Mallory, "about the only things they'll need'll be what we didn't have the foresight to bring along—an undertaker and a preacher."

"Don't be horrid, Billy," returned Miss Harding. "You know perfectly well that I didn't mean weeks—I meant days; and anyway they'll be grateful to us for what we can do for them. I can scarcely wait to hear their story."

Billy Mallory was inspecting the stranger through Mr. Harding's glass. Suddenly he gave an exclamation of dismay.

"By George!" he cried. "It is serious after all. That ship's afire. Look, Mr. Harding," and he passed the glass over to his host.

And sure enough, as the owner of the *Lotus* found the brigantine again in the center of his lens he saw a thin column of black smoke rising amidships; but what he did not see was Mr. Ward upon the opposite side of the *Halfmoon*'s cabin superintending the burning by the black cook of a bundle of oily rags in an iron boiler.

"By Jove!" exclaimed Mr. Harding. "This is terrible. The poor devils are panic-stricken. Look at 'em making for the boats!" and with that he dashed back to the bridge to confer with his captain.

"Yes," said that officer, "I noticed the smoke about the same time you did—funny it wasn't apparent before. I've already signaled full speed ahead, and I've instructed Mr. Foster to have the boats in readiness to lower away if we find that they're short of boats on the brigantine.

"What I can't understand," he added after a moment's silence, "is why they didn't show any signs of excitement about that fire until we came within easy sight of them—it looks funny."

"Well, we'll know in a few minutes more," returned Mr. Harding. "The chances are that the fire is just a recent addition to their predicament, whatever it may be, and that they have only just discovered it themselves."

"Then it can't have gained enough headway," insisted the captain, "to cause them any such immediate terror as would be indicated by the haste with which the whole ship's crew is tumbling into those boats; but as you say, sir, we'll have their story out of them in a few minutes now, so it's idle speculating beforehand."

The officers and men of the *Halfmoon*, in so far as those on board the *Lotus* could guess, had all entered the boats at last, and were pulling frantically away from their own ship toward the rapidly nearing yacht; but what they did not guess and could not know was that Mr. Divine paced nervously to and fro in his cabin, while Second Officer Theriere tended the smoking rags that Ward and Blanco had resigned to him that they might take their places in the boats.

Theriere had been greatly disgusted with the turn events had taken for he had determined upon a line of action that he felt sure would prove highly remunerative to himself. It had been nothing less than a bold resolve to call Blanco, Byrne, "Bony," and "Red" to his side the moment Simms and Ward revealed the true purpose of their ruse to those on board the *Lotus*, and with his henchmen take sides with the men of the yacht against his former companions.

As he had explained it to Billy Byrne the idea was to permit Mr. Harding to believe that Theriere and his companions had been duped by Skipper Simms—that they had had no idea of the work that they were to be called upon to perform until the last moment and that then they had done the only thing they could to protect the passengers and crew of the *Lotus*.

"And then," Theriere had concluded, "when they think we are a band of heroes, and the best friends they have on earth we'll just naturally be in a position to grab the whole lot of them, and collect ransoms on ten or fifteen instead of just one."

"Bully!" exclaimed the mucker. "You sure got some bean, mate."

As a matter of fact Theriere had had no intention of carrying the matter as far as he had intimated to Billy except as a last resort. He had been mightily smitten by the face and fortune of Barbara Harding and had seen in the trend of events a possible opportunity of so deeply obligating her father and herself that when he paid court to her she might fall a willing victim to his wiles. In this case he would be obliged to risk nothing, and could make away with his accomplices by explaining to Mr. Harding that he had been compelled to concoct this other scheme to obtain their assistance against Simms and Ward; then they could throw the three into irons and all would be lovely; but now that fool Ward had upset the whole thing by hitting upon this asinine fire hoax as an excuse for boarding the *Lotus* in force, and had further dampened Theriere's pet scheme by suggesting to Skipper Simms the danger of Theriere being recognized as they were boarding the *Lotus* and bringing suspicion upon them all immediately.

They all knew that a pleasure yacht like the *Lotus* was well supplied with small arms, and that at the first intimation of danger there would be plenty of men aboard to repel assault, and, in all probability, with entire success.

That there were excellent grounds for Theriere's belief that he could win Barbara Harding's hand with such a flying start as his daring plan would have assured him may not be questioned, for the man was cultivated, polished and, in a sinister way, good-looking. The title that he had borne upon the occasion of his visit to the yacht, was, all unknown to his accomplices, his by right of birth, so that there was nothing other than a long-dead scandal in the French Navy that might have proved a bar to an affiance such as he dreamed of. And now to be thwarted at the last moment! It was unendurable. That pig of a Ward had sealed his own death warrant, of that Theriere was convinced.

The boats were now quite close to the yacht, which had slowed down almost to a dead stop. In answer to the query of the *Lotus'* captain Skipper Simms was explaining their trouble.

"I'm Captain Jones," he shouted, "of the brigantine *Clarinda*, Frisco to Yokohama with dynamite. We disabled our rudder yesterday, an' this afternoon fire started in the hold. It's makin' headway fast now, an'll reach the dynamite most any time. You'd better take us aboard, an' get away from here as quick as you can. 'Tain't safe nowhere within five hun'erd fathom of her."

"You'd better make haste, Captain, hadn't you?" suggested Mr. Harding.

"I don't like the looks of things, sir," replied that officer. "She ain't flyin' any dynamite flag, an' if she was an' had a hold full there wouldn't be any particular danger to us, an' anyone that has ever shipped dynamite would know it, or ought to. It's not fire that detonates dynamite, it's concussion. No sir, Mr. Harding, there's something queer here—I don't like the looks of it. Why just take a good look at the faces of those men. Did you ever see such an ugly-looking pack of unhung murderers in your life, sir?"

"I must admit that they're not an overly prepossessing crowd, Norris," replied Mr. Harding. "But it's not always either fair or safe to judge strangers entirely by appearances. I'm afraid that there's nothing else for it in the name of common humanity than to take them aboard, Norris. I'm sure your fears are entirely groundless."

"Then it's your orders, sir, to take them aboard?" asked Captain Norris.

"Yes, Captain, I think you'd better," said Mr. Harding.

"Very good, sir," replied the officer, turning to give the necessary commands.

The officers and men of the *Halfmoon* swarmed up the sides of the *Lotus*, dark-visaged, fierce, and forbidding.

"Reminds me of a boarding party of pirates," remarked Billy Mallory, as he watched Blanco, the last to throw a leg over the rail, reach the deck

"They're not very pretty, are they?" murmured Barbara Harding, instinctively shrinking closer to her companion.

"'Pretty' scarcely describes them, Barbara," said Billy; "and do you know that somehow I am having difficulty in imagining them on their knees giving up thanks to the Lord for their rescue—that was your recent idea of 'em, you will recall."

"If you have purposely set yourself the task of being more than ordinarily disagreeable today, Billy," said Barbara sweetly, "I'm sure it will please you to know that you are succeeding."

"I'm glad I'm successful at something then," laughed the man. "I've certainly been unsuccessful enough in another matter."

"What, for example?" asked Barbara, innocently.

"Why in trying to make myself so agreeable heretofore that you'd finally consent to say 'yes' for a change."

"Now you are going to make it all the worse by being stupid," cried the girl petulantly. "Why can't you be nice, as you used to be before you got this silly notion into your head?"

"I don't think it's a silly notion to be head over heels in love with the sweetest girl on earth," cried Billy.

"Hush! Someone will hear you."

"I don't care if they do. I'd like to advertise it to the whole world. I'm proud of the fact that I love you; and you don't care enough about it to realize how really hard I'm hit—why I'd die for you, Barbara, and welcome the chance; why—My God! What's that?"

"O Billy! What are those men doing?" cried the girl. "They're shooting. They're shooting at papa! Quick, Billy! Do something. For heaven's sake do something."

On the deck below them the "rescued" crew of the "*Clarinda*" had surrounded Mr. Harding, Captain Norris, and most of the crew of the *Lotus*, flashing quick-drawn revolvers from beneath shirts and coats, and firing at two of the yacht's men who showed fight.

"Keep quiet," commanded Skipper Simms, "an' there won't none of you get hurted."

"What do you want of us?" cried Mr. Harding. "If it's money, take what you can find aboard us, and go on your way. No one will hinder you."

Skipper Simms paid no attention to him. His eyes swept aloft to the upper deck. There he saw a wide-eyed girl and a man looking down upon them. He wondered if she was the one they sought. There were other women aboard. He could see them, huddled frightened behind Harding and Norris. Some of them were young and beautiful; but there was something about the girl above him that assured him she could be none other than Barbara Harding. To discover the truth Simms resorted to a ruse, for he knew that were he to ask Harding outright if the girl were his daughter the chances were more than even that the old man would suspect something of the nature of their visit and deny her identity.

"Who is that woman you have on board here?" he cried in an accusing tone of voice. "That's what we're a-here to find out."

"Why she's my daughter, man!" blurted Harding. "Who did you—"

"Thanks," said Skipper Simms, with a self-satisfied grin. "That's what I wanted to be sure of. Hey, you, Byrne! You're nearest the companionway—fetch the girl."

At the command the mucker turned and leaped up the stairway to the upper deck. Billy Mallory had overheard the conversation below and Simms' command to Byrne. Disengaging himself from Barbara Harding who in her terror had clutched his arm, he ran forward to the head of the stairway.

The men of the *Lotus* looked on in mute and helpless rage. All were covered by the guns of the boarding party—the still forms of two of their companions bearing eloquent witness to the slenderness of provocation necessary to tighten the trigger fingers of the beasts standing guard over them.

Billy Byrne never hesitated in his rush for the upper deck. The sight of the man awaiting him above but whetted his appetite for battle. The trim flannels, the white shoes, the natty cap, were to the mucker as sufficient cause for justifiable homicide as is an orange ribbon in certain portions of the West Side of Chicago on St. Patrick's Day. As were "Remember the Alamo," and "Remember the Maine" to the fighting men of the days that they were live things so were the habiliments of gentility to Billy Byrne at all times.

Billy Mallory was an older man than the mucker—twenty-four perhaps— and fully as large. For four years he had played right guard on a great eastern team, and for three he had pulled stroke upon the crew. During the two years since his graduation he had prided himself upon the maintenance of the physical supremacy that had made the name of Mallory famous in collegiate athletics; but in one vital essential he was hopelessly handicapped in combat with such as Billy Byrne, for Mallory was a gentleman.

As the mucker rushed upward toward him Mallory had all the advantage of position and preparedness, and had he done what Billy Byrne would have done under like circumstances he would have planted a kick in the midst of the mucker's facial beauties with all the power and weight and energy at his command; but Billy Mallory could no more have perpetrated a cowardly trick such as this than he could have struck a woman.

Instead, he waited, and as the mucker came on an even footing with him Mallory swung a vicious right for the man's jaw. Byrne ducked beneath the blow, came up inside Mallory's guard, and struck him three times with triphammer velocity and pile-driver effectiveness—once upon the jaw and twice—below the belt!

The girl, clinging to the rail, riveted by the paralysis of fright, saw her champion stagger back and half crumple to the deck. Then she saw him make a brave and desperate rally, as, though torn with agony, he lurched forward in an endeavor to clinch with the brute before him. Again the mucker struck his victim—quick choppy hooks that rocked Mallory's head from side to side, and again the brutal blow below the belt; but with the tenacity of a bulldog the man fought for a hold upon his foe, and at last, notwithstanding Byrne's best efforts, he succeeded in closing with the mucker and dragging him to the deck.

Here the two men rolled and tumbled, Byrne biting, gouging, and kicking while Mallory devoted all of his fast-waning strength to an effort to close his fingers upon the throat of his antagonist. But the terrible punishment which the mucker had inflicted upon him overcame him at last, and as Byrne felt the man's efforts weakening he partially disengaged himself and raising himself upon one arm dealt his now almost unconscious enemy a half-dozen frightful blows upon the face.

With a shriek Barbara Harding turned from the awful sight as Billy Mallory's bloody and swollen eyes rolled up and set, while the mucker threw the inert form roughly from him. Quick to the girl's memory sprang Mallory's recent declaration, which she had thought at the time but the empty, and vainglorious boasting of the man in love—"Why I'd die for you, Barbara, and welcome the chance!"

"Poor boy! How soon, and how terribly has the chance come!" moaned the girl.

Then a rough hand fell upon her arm.

"Here, youse," a coarse voice yelled in her ear. "Come out o' de trance," and at the same time she was jerked roughly toward the companionway.

Instinctively the girl held back, and then the mucker, true to his training, true to himself, gave her arm a sudden twist that wrenched a scream of agony from her white lips.

"Den come along," growled Billy Byrne, "an' quit dis monkey business, or I'll sure twist yer flipper clean off'n yeh."

With an oath, Anthony Harding sprang forward to protect his daughter; but the butt of Ward's pistol brought him unconscious to the deck.

"Go easy there, Byrne," shouted Skipper Simms; "there ain't no call to injure the hussy—a corpse won't be worth nothing to us."

In mute terror the girl now permitted herself to be led to the deck below. Quickly she was lowered into a waiting boat. Then Skipper Simms ordered Ward to search the yacht and remove all firearms, after which he was to engage himself to navigate the vessel with her own crew under armed guard of half a dozen of the *Halfmoon*'s cutthroats.

These things attended to, Skipper Simms with the balance of his own crew and six of the crew of the *Lotus* to take the places upon the brigantine of those left as a prize crew aboard the yacht returned with the girl to the *Halfmoon*.

The sailing vessel's sails were soon hoisted and trimmed, and in half an hour, followed by the *Lotus*, she was scudding briskly southward. For forty-eight hours this course was held until Simms felt assured that they were well out of the lane of regular trans-Pacific traffic.

During this time Barbara Harding had been kept below, locked in a small, untidy cabin. She had seen no one other than a great Negro who brought her meals to her three times daily—meals that she returned scarcely touched.

Now the *Halfmoon* was brought up into the wind where she lay with flapping canvas while Skipper Simms returned to the *Lotus* with the six men of the yacht's crew that he had brought aboard the brigantine with him two days before, and as many more of his own men.

Once aboard the *Lotus* the men were put to work with those already on the yacht. The boat's rudder was unshipped and dropped into the ocean; her fires were put out; her engines were attacked with sledges until they were little better than so much junk, and to make the slender chances of pursuit that remained to her entirely nil every ounce of coal upon her was shoveled into the Pacific. Her extra masts and spare sails followed the way of the coal and the rudder, so that when Skipper Simms and First Officer Ward left her with their own men that had been aboard her she was little better than a drifting derelict.

From her cabin window Barbara Harding had witnessed the wanton wrecking of her father's yacht, and when it was over and the crew of the brigantine had returned to their own ship she presently felt the movement of the vessel as it got under way, and soon the *Lotus* dropped to the stern and beyond the range of her tiny port. With a moan of hopelessness and terror the girl sank prostrate across the hard berth that spanned one end of her prison cell.

How long she lay there she did not know, but finally she was aroused by the opening of her cabin door. As she sprang to her feet ready to defend herself against what she felt might easily be some new form of danger her eyes went wide in astonishment as they rested on the face of the man who stood framed in the doorway of her cabin.

"You?" she cried.

V
LARRY DIVINE UNMASKED

"Yes, Barbara, it is I," said Mr. Divine; "and thank God that I am here to do what little any man may do against this band of murdering pirates."

"But, Larry," cried the girl, in evident bewilderment, "how did you come to be aboard this ship? How did you get here? What are you doing amongst such as these?"

"I am a prisoner," replied the man, "just as are you. I think they intend holding us for ransom. They got me in San Francisco. Slugged me and hustled me aboard the night before they sailed."

"Where are they going to take us?" she asked.

"I do not know," he replied, "although from something I have overheard of their conversations I imagine that they have in mind some distant island far from the beaten track of commerce. There are thousands such in the Pacific that are visited by vessels scarce once in a century. There they will hold us until they can proceed with the ship to some point where they can get into communication with their agents in the States. When the ransom is paid over to these agents they will return for us and land us upon some other island where our friends can find us, or leaving us where we can divulge the location of our whereabouts to those who pay the ransom."

The girl had been looking intently at Mr. Divine during their conversation.

"They cannot have treated you very badly, Larry," she said. "You are as well groomed and well fed, apparently, as ever."

A slight flush mounting to the man's face made the girl wonder a bit though it aroused no suspicion in her mind.

"Oh, no," he hastened to assure her, "they have not treated me at all badly—why should they? If I die they can collect no ransom on me. It is the same with you, Barbara, so I think you need apprehend no harsh treatment."

"I hope you are right, Larry," she said, but the hopelessness of her air rather belied any belief that aught but harm could come from captivity with such as those who officered and manned the *Halfmoon*.

"It seems so remarkable," she went on, "that you should be a prisoner upon the same boat. I cannot understand it. Why only a few days ago we received and entertained a friend of yours who brought a letter from you to papa—the Count de Cadenet."

Again that telltale flush mantled the man's cheek. He cursed himself inwardly for his lack of self-control. The girl would have his whole secret out of him in another half-hour if he were not more careful.

"They made me do that," he said, jerking his thumb in the general direction of Skipper Simms' cabin. "Maybe that accounts for their bringing me along. The 'Count de Cadenet' is a fellow named Theriere, second mate of this ship. They sent him to learn your plans; when you expected sailing from Honolulu and your course. They are all crooks and villains. If I hadn't done as they bid they would have killed me."

The girl made no comment, but Divine saw the contempt in her face.

"I didn't know that they were going to do this. If I had I'd have died before I'd have written that note," he added rather lamely.

The girl was suddenly looking very sad. She was thinking of Billy Mallory who had died in an effort to save her. The mental comparison she was making between him and Mr. Divine was not overly flattering to the latter gentleman.

"They killed poor Billy," she said at last. "He tried to protect me."

Then Mr. Divine understood the trend of her thoughts. He tried to find some excuse for his cowardly act; but with the realization of the true cowardliness and treachery of it that the girl didn't even guess he understood the futility of seeking to extenuate it. He saw that the chances were excellent that after all he would be compelled to resort to force or threats to win her hand at the last.

"Billy would have done better to have bowed to the inevitable as I did," he said. "Living I am able to help you now. Dead I could not have prevented them carrying out their intentions any more than Billy has, nor could I have been here to aid you now any more than he is. I cannot see that his action helped you to any great extent, brave as it was."

"The memory of it and him will always help me," she answered quietly. "They will help me to bear whatever is before me bravely, and, when the time comes, to die bravely; for I shall always feel that upon the other side a true, brave heart is awaiting me."

The man was silent. After a moment the girl spoke again.

"I think I would rather be alone, Larry," she said. "I am very unhappy and nervous. Possibly I could sleep now."

With a bow he turned and left the cabin.

For weeks the *Halfmoon* kept steadily on her course, a little south of west. There was no material change in the relations of those aboard her. Barbara Harding, finding herself unmolested, finally acceded to the repeated pleas of Mr. Divine, to whose society she had been driven by loneliness and fear, and appeared on deck frequently during the daylight watches. Here, one afternoon, she came face to face with Theriere for the first time since her abduction. The officer lifted his cap deferentially; but the girl met his look of expectant recognition with a cold, blank stare that passed through and beyond him as though he had been empty air.

A tinge of color rose to the man's face, and he continued on his way for a moment as though content to accept her rebuff; but after a step or two he turned suddenly and confronted her.

"Miss Harding," he said, respectfully, "I cannot blame you for the feeling of loathing and distrust you must harbor toward me; but in common justice I think you should hear me before finally condemning."

"I cannot imagine," she returned coldly, "what defense there can be for the cowardly act you perpetrated."

"I have been utterly deceived by my employers," said Theriere, hastening to take advantage of the tacit permission to explain which her reply contained. "I was given to understand that the whole thing was to be but a hoax—that I was taking part in a great practical joke that Mr. Divine was to play upon his old friends, the Hardings and their guests. Until they wrecked and deserted the *Lotus* in mid-ocean I had no idea that anything else was contemplated, although I felt that the matter, even before that event, had been carried quite far enough for a joke.

"They explained," he continued, "that before sailing you had expressed the hope that something really exciting and adventurous would befall the party—that you were tired of the monotonous humdrum of twentieth-century existence—that you regretted the decadence of piracy, and the expunging of romance from the seas.

"Mr. Divine, they told me, was a very wealthy young man, to whom you were engaged to be married, and that he could easily afford the great expense of the rather remarkable hoax we were supposed to be perpetrating. I saw no harm in taking part in it, especially as I knew nothing of the supposititious purpose of the cruise until just before we reached Honolulu. Before that I had been led to believe that it was but a pleasure trip to the South Pacific that Mr. Divine intended.

"You see, Miss Harding, that I have been as badly deceived as you. Won't you let me help to atone for my error by being your friend? I can assure you that you will need one whom you can trust amongst this shipload of scoundrels."

"Who am I to believe?" cried the girl. "Mr. Divine assures me that he, too, has been forced into this affair, but by threats of death rather than deception."

The expression on Mr. Theriere's face was eloquent of sarcastic incredulity.

"How about the note of introduction that I carried to your father from Mr. Divine?" asked Theriere.

"He says that he was compelled to write it at the point of a revolver," replied the girl.

"Come with me, Miss Harding," said the officer. "I think that I may be able to convince you that Mr. Divine is not on any such bad terms with Skipper Simms as would be the case were his story to you true."

As he spoke he started toward the companionway leading to the officers' cabins. Barbara Harding hesitated at the top of the stairway.

"Have no fear, Miss Harding," Theriere reassured her. "Remember that I am your friend and that I am merely attempting to prove it to your entire satisfaction. You owe it to yourself to discover as soon as possible who your friends are aboard this ship, and who your enemies."

"Very well," said the girl. "I can be in no more danger one place aboard her than another."

Theriere led her directly to his own cabin, cautioning her to silence with upraised forefinger. Softly, like skulking criminals, they entered the little compartment. Then Theriere turned and closed the door, slipping the bolt noiselessly as he did so. Barbara watched him, her heart beating rapidly with fear and suspicion.

"Here," whispered Theriere, motioning her toward his berth. "I have found it advantageous to know what goes on beyond this partition. You will find a small round hole near the head of the berth, about a foot above the bedding. Put your ear to it and listen—I think Divine is in there now."

The girl, still frightened and fearful of the man's intentions, did, nevertheless, as he bid. At first she could make out nothing beyond the partition but a confused murmur of voices, and the clink of glass, as of the touch of the neck of a bottle against a goblet. For a moment she remained in tense silence, her ear pressed to the tiny aperture. Then, distinctly, she heard the voice of Skipper Simms.

"I'm a-tellin' you, man," he was saying, "that there wan't nothin' else to be done, an' I'm a-gettin' damn sick o' hearin' you finding fault all the time with the way I been a-runnin' o' this little job."

"I'm not finding fault, Simms," returned another voice which the girl recognized immediately as Divine's; "although I do think that it was a mistake to so totally disable the *Lotus* as you did. Why, how on earth are we ever to return to civilization if that boat is lost? Had she been simply damaged a little, in a way that they could themselves have fixed up, the delay would have been sufficient to permit us to escape, and then, when Miss Harding was returned in safety to her father, after our marriage, they would have been so glad to be reunited that he easily could have been persuaded to drop the matter. Then another thing; you intended to demand a ransom for both Miss Harding and myself, to carry out the fiction of my having been stolen also—how can you do that if Mr. Harding be dead? And do you suppose for a moment that Miss Harding will leave a single stone unturned to bring the guilty to justice if any harm has befallen her father or his guests? If so you do not know her as well as I."

The girl turned away from the partition, her face white and drawn, her eyes inexpressibly sad. She rose to her feet, facing Theriere.

"I have heard quite enough, thank you, Mr. Theriere," she said.

"You are convinced then that I am your friend?" he asked.

"I am convinced that Mr. Divine is not," she replied non-committally.

She took a step toward the door. Theriere stood looking at her. She was unquestionably very good to look at. He could not remember ever having seen a more beautiful girl. A great desire to seize her in his arms swept over the man. Theriere had not often made any effort to harness his desires. What he wanted it had been his custom to take—by force if necessary. He took a step toward Barbara Harding. There was a sudden light in his eyes that the girl had not before seen there, and she reached quickly toward the knob of the door.

Theriere was upon her, and then, quickly, he mastered himself, for he recalled his coolly thought-out plan based on what Divine had told him of that clause in the will of the girl's departed grandparent which stipulated that the man who shared the bequest with her must be the choice of both herself and her father. He could afford to bide his time, and play the chivalrous protector before he essayed the role of lover.

Barbara had turned a half-frightened look toward him as he advanced—in doubt as to his intentions.

"Pardon me, Miss Harding," he said; "the door is bolted—let me unlatch it for you," and very gallantly he did so, swinging the portal wide that she might pass out. "I feared interruption," he said, in explanation of the bolt.

In silence they returned to the upper deck. The intoxication of sudden passion now under control, Theriere was again master of himself and ready to play the cold, calculating, waiting game that he had determined upon. Part of his plan was to see just enough of Miss Harding to insure a place in her mind at all times; but not enough to suggest that he was forcing himself upon her. Rightly, he assumed that she would appreciate thoughtful deference to her comfort and safety under the harrowing conditions of her present existence more than a forced companionship that might entail too open devotion on his part. And so he raised his cap and left her, only urging her to call upon him at any time that he might be of service to her.

Left alone the girl became lost in unhappy reflections, and in the harrowing ordeal of attempting to readjust herself to the knowledge that Larry Divine, her lifelong friend, was the instigator of the atrocious villainy that had been perpetrated against her and her father. She found it almost equally difficult to believe that Mr. Theriere was so much more sinned against than sinning as he would have had her believe. And yet, did his story not sound even more plausible than that of Divine which she had accepted before Theriere had made it possible for her to know the truth? Why, then, was it so difficult for her to believe the Frenchman? She could not say, but in the inmost recesses of her heart she knew that she mistrusted and feared the man.

As she stood leaning against the rail, buried deep in thought, Billy Byrne passed close behind her. At sight of her a sneer curled his lip. How he hated her! Not that she ever had done aught to harm him, but rather because she represented to him in concrete form all that he had learned to hate and loathe since early childhood.

Her soft, white skin; her shapely hands and well-cared-for nails; her trim figure and perfectly fitting suit all taunted him with their superiority over him and his kind. He knew that she looked down upon him as an inferior being. She was of the class that addressed those in his walk of life as "my man." Lord, how he hated that appellation!

The intentness of his gaze upon her back had the effect so often noted by the observant, and suddenly aroused from the lethargy of her misery the girl swung around to meet the man's eyes squarely upon her. Instantly she recognized him as the brute who had killed Billy Mallory. If there had been hate in the mucker's eyes as he looked at the girl, it was as nothing by comparison with the loathing and disgust which sprang to hers as they rested upon his sullen face.

So deep was her feeling of contempt for this man, that the sudden appearance of him before her startled a single exclamation from her.

"Coward!" came the one word, involuntarily, from her lips.

The man's scowl deepened menacingly. He took a threatening step toward her.

"Wot's dat?" he growled. "Don't get gay wit me, or I'll black dem lamps fer yeh," and he raised a heavy fist as though to strike her.

The mucker had looked to see the girl cower before his threatened blow—that would have been ample atonement for her insult, and would have appealed greatly to his Kelly-gang sense of humor. Many a time had he threatened women thus, for the keen enjoyment of hearing their screams of fright and seeing them turn and flee in terror. When they had held their ground and opposed him, as some upon the West Side had felt sufficiently muscular to do, the mucker had not hesitated to "hand them one." Thus only might a man uphold his reputation for bravery in the vicinage of Grand Avenue.

He had looked to see this girl of the effete and effeminate upper class swoon with terror before him; but to his intense astonishment she but stood erect and brave before him, her head high held, her eyes cold and level and unafraid. And then she spoke again.

"Coward!" she said.

Billy almost struck her; but something held his hand. What, he could not understand. Could it be that he feared this slender girl? And at this juncture, when the threat of his attitude was the most apparent, Second Officer

Theriere came upon the scene. At a glance he took in the situation, and with a bound had sprung between Billy Byrne and Barbara Harding.

VI
THE MUCKER AT BAY

"What has this man said to you, Miss Harding?" cried Theriere. "Has he offered you harm?"

"I do not think that he would have dared strike me," replied the girl, "though he threatened to do so. He is the coward who murdered poor Mr. Mallory upon the *Lotus*. He might stoop to anything after that."

Theriere turned angrily upon Byrne.

"Go below!" he shouted. "I'll attend to you later. If Miss Harding were not here I'd thrash you within an inch of your life now. And if I ever hear of your speaking to her again, or offering her the slightest indignity I'll put a bullet through you so quick you won't know what has struck you."

"T'ell yeh will!" sneered Billy Byrne. "I got your number, yeh big stiff; an' yeh better not get gay wit me. Dey ain't no guy on board dis man's ship dat can hand Billy Byrne dat kin' o' guff an' get away with it—see?" and before Theriere knew what had happened a heavy fist had caught him upon the point of the chin and lifted him clear off the deck to drop him unconscious at Miss Harding's feet.

"Yeh see wot happens to guys dat get gay wit me?" said the mucker to the girl, and then stooping over the prostrate form of the mate Billy Byrne withdrew a huge revolver from Theriere's hip pocket.

"I guess I'll need dis gat in my business purty soon," he remarked.

Then he planted a vicious kick in the face of the unconscious man and went his way to the forecastle.

"Now maybe she'll tink Billy Byrne's a coward," he thought, as he disappeared below.

Barbara Harding stood speechless with shock at the brutality and ferocity of the unexpected attack upon Theriere. Never in all her life had she dreamed that there could exist upon the face of the earth a thing in human form so devoid of honor, and chivalry, and fair play as the creature that she had just witnessed threatening a defenseless woman, and kicking an unconscious man in the face; but then Barbara Harding had never lived between Grand Avenue and Lake Street, and Halsted and Robey, where standards of masculine bravery are strange and fearful.

When she had recovered her equanimity she hastened to the head of the cabin companionway and called aloud for help. Instantly Skipper Simms and First Officer Ward rushed on deck, each carrying a revolver in readiness for the conflict with their crew that these two worthies were always expecting.

Barbara pointed out the still form of Theriere, quickly explaining what had occurred.

"It was the fellow Byrne who did it," she said. "He has gone into the forecastle now, and he has a revolver that he took from Mr. Theriere after he had fallen."

Several of the crew had now congregated about the prostrate officer.

"Here you," cried Skipper Simms to a couple of them; "you take Mr. Theriere below to his cabin, an' throw cold water in his face. Mr. Ward, get some brandy from my locker, an' try an' bring him to. The rest of you arm yourselves with crowbars and axes, an' see that that son of a sea cook don't get out on deck again alive. Hold him there 'til I get a couple of guns. Then we'll get him, damn him!"

Skipper Simms hastened below while two of the men were carrying Theriere to his cabin and Mr. Ward was fetching the brandy. A moment later Barbara Harding saw the skipper return to the upper deck with a rifle and two revolvers. The sailors whom he had detailed to keep Byrne below were gathered about the hatchway leading to the forecastle. Some of them were exchanging profane and pleasant badinage with the prisoner.

"Yeh better come up an' get killed easy-like," one called down to the mucker. "We're apt to muss yeh all up down there in the dark with these here axes and crowbars, an' then wen we send yeh home yer pore maw won't know her little boy at all."

"Yeh come on down here, an' try mussin' me up," yelled back Billy Byrne. "I can lick de whole gang wit one han' tied behin' me—see?"

"De skipper's gorn to get his barkers, Billy," cried Bony Sawyer. "Yeh better come up an' stan' trial if he gives yeh the chanct."

"Stan' nothin'," sneered Billy. "Swell chanct I'd have wit him an' Squint Eye holdin' court over me. Not on yer life, Bony. I'm here, an' here I stays till I croaks, but yeh better believe me, I'm goin' to croak a few before I goes, so if any of you ginks are me frien's yeh better keep outen here so's

yeh won't get hurted. An' anudder ting I'm goin' to do afore I cashes in—
I'm goin' to put a few of dem ginks in de cabin wise to where dey stands
wit one anudder. If I don't start something before I goes out me name's not
Billy Byrne."

At this juncture Skipper Simms appeared with the three weapons he had
gone to his cabin to fetch. He handed one to Bony Sawyer, another to Red
Sanders and a third to a man by the name of Wison.

"Now, my men," said Skipper Simms, "we will go below and bring
Byrne up. Bring him alive if you can—but bring him."

No one made a move to enter the forecastle.

"Go on now, move quickly," commanded Skipper Simms sharply.

"Thought he said 'we,'" remarked one of the sailors.

Skipper Simms, livid with rage, turned to search out the offender from
the several men behind him.

"Who was that?" he roared. "Show me the blitherin' swab. Jes' show him
to me, I tell you, an I'll learn him. Now you," he yelled at the top of his
voice, turning again to the men he had ordered into the forecastle after Billy
Byrne, "you cowardly landlubbers you, get below there quick afore I kick
you below."

Still no one moved to obey him. From white he went to red, and then
back to white again. He fairly frothed at the mouth as he jumped up and
down, cursing the men, and threatening. But all to no avail. They would not
go.

"Why, Skipper," spoke up Bony Sawyer, "it's sure death for any man as
goes below there. It's easier, an' safer, to starve him out."

"Starve nothin'," shrieked Skipper Simms. "Do you reckon I'm a-goin' to
sit quiet here for a week an' let any blanked wharf rat own that there
fo'c's'le just because I got a lot o' white-livered cowards aboard? No sir!
You're a-goin' down after that would-be bad man an' fetch him up dead or
alive," and with that he started menacingly toward the three who stood near
the hatch, holding their firearms safely out of range of Billy Byrne below.

What would have happened had Skipper Simms completed the
threatening maneuver he had undertaken can never be known, for at this
moment Theriere pushed his way through the circle of men who were
interested spectators of the impending tragedy.

"What's up, sir?" he asked of Simms. "Anything that I can help you
with?"

"Oh!" exclaimed the skipper; "so you ain't dead after all, eh? Well that don't change the looks of things a mite. We gotta get that man outa there an' these flea-bitten imitations of men ain't got the guts to go in after him."

"He's got your gun, sir," spoke up Wison, "an' Gawd knows he be the one as'ud on'y be too glad for the chanct to use it."

"Let me see if I can't handle him, sir," said Theriere to Skipper Simms. "We don't want to lose any men if we can help it."

The skipper was only too glad to welcome this unexpected rescue from the predicament in which he had placed himself. How Theriere was to accomplish the subjugation of the mutinous sailor he could not guess, nor did he care so long as it was done without risk to his own skin.

"Now if you'll go away, sir," said Theriere, "and order the men away I'll see what I can do."

Skipper Simms did as Theriere had requested, so that presently the officer stood alone beside the hatch. Across the deck, amidships, the men had congregated to watch Theriere's operations, while beyond them stood Barbara Harding held fascinated by the grim tragedy that was unfolding before her upon this accursed vessel.

Theriere leaned over the open hatch, in full view of the waiting Byrne, ready below. There was the instant report of a firearm and a bullet whizzed close past Theriere's head.

"Avast there, Byrne!" he shouted. "It's I, Theriere. Don't shoot again, I want to speak to you."

"No monkey business now," growled the mucker in reply. "I won't miss again."

"I want to talk with you, Byrne," said Theriere in a low tone. "I'm coming down there."

"No you ain't, cul," returned Byrne; "leastways yeh ain't a-comin' down here alive."

"Yes I am, Byrne," replied Theriere, "and you don't want to be foolish about it. I'm unarmed. You can cover me with your gun until you have satisfied yourself as to that. I'm the only man on the ship that can save your life—the only man that has any reason to want to; but we've got to talk it over and we can't talk this way where there's a chance of being overheard. I'll be on the square with you if you will with me, and if we can't come to terms I'll come above again and you won't be any worse off than you are now. Here I come," and without waiting for an acceptance of his proposition the second officer of the *Halfmoon* slipped over the edge of the hatchway and disappeared from the sight of the watchers above.

That he was a brave man even Billy Byrne had to admit, and those above who knew nothing of the relations existing between the second mate and the sailor, who had so recently felled him, thought that his courage was little short of marvelous. Theriere's stock went up by leaps and bounds in the estimation of the sailors of the *Halfmoon*, for degraded though they were they could understand and appreciate physical courage of this sort, while to Barbara Harding the man's act seemed unparalleled in its utter disregard of the consequences of life and death to himself that it entailed. She suddenly was sorry that she had entertained any suspicions against Theriere—so brave a man could not be other than the soul of honor, she argued.

Once below Theriere found himself covered by his own revolver in the hands of a very desperate and a very unprincipled man. He smiled at Byrne as the latter eyed him suspiciously.

"See here, Byrne," said Theriere. "It would be foolish for me to say that I am doing this for love of you. The fact is that I need you. We cannot succeed, either one of us, alone. I think you made a fool play when you hit me today. You know that our understanding was that I was to be even a little rougher with you than usual, in order to avoid suspicion being attached to any seeming familiarity between us, should we be caught conferring together. I had the chance to bawl you out today, and I thought that you would understand that I was but taking advantage of the opportunity which it afforded to make it plain to Miss Harding that there could be nothing other than hatred between us—it might have come in pretty handy later to have her believe that.

"If I'd had any idea that you really intended hitting me you'd have been a dead man before your fist reached me, Byrne. You took me entirely by surprise; but that's all in the past—I'm willing to let bygones be bygones, and help you out of the pretty pickle you've got yourself into. Then we can go ahead with our work as though nothing had happened. What do you say?"

"I didn't know yeh was kiddin," replied the mucker, "or I wouldn't have hit yeh. Yeh acted like yeh meant it."

"Very well, that part's understood," said Theriere. "Now will you come out if I can square the thing with the skipper so's you won't get more than a day or so in irons—he'll have to give you something to save his own face; but I promise that you'll get your food regularly and that you won't be beaten up the way you were before when he had you below. If he won't agree to what I propose I give you my word to tell you so."

"Go ahead," said Billy Byrne; "I don't trust nobody wen I don't have to; but I'll be dinged if I see any other way out of it."

Theriere returned to the deck and seeking out the skipper drew him to one side.

"I can get him up peaceably if I can assure him that he'll only get a day or so in the cooler, with full rations and no beatings. I think, sir, that that will be the easiest way out of it. We cannot spare a man now—if we want to get the fellow later we can always find some pretext."

"Very well, Mr. Theriere," replied the skipper, "I'll leave the matter entirely in your hands—you can do what you want with the fellow; it's you as had your face punched."

Theriere returned immediately to the forecastle, from which he presently emerged with the erstwhile recalcitrant Byrne, and for two days the latter languished in durance vile, and that was the end of the episode, though its effects were manifold. For one thing it implanted in the heart of Theriere a personal hatred for the mucker, so that while heretofore his intention of ridding himself of the man when he no longer needed him was due purely to a matter of policy, it was now reinforced by a keen desire for personal revenge. The occurrence had also had its influence upon Barbara Harding, in that it had shown her Mr. Theriere in a new light—one that reflected credit upon him. She had thought his magnanimous treatment of the sailor little short of heroic; and it had deepened the girl's horror of Billy Byrne until it now amounted to little short of an obsession. So vivid an impression had his brutality made upon her that she would start from deep slumber, dreaming that she was menaced by him.

After Billy was released for duty following his imprisonment, he several times passed the girl upon deck. He noticed that she shrank from him in disgust and terror; but what surprised him was that instead of the thrill of pride which he formerly would have felt at this acknowledgment of his toughness, for Billy prided himself on being a tough, he now felt a singular resentment against the girl for her attitude, so that he came to hate her even more than he had before hated. Formerly he had hated her for the things she stood for, now he hated her for herself.

Theriere was often with her now, and, less frequently, Divine; for at the second officer's suggestion Barbara had not acquainted that gentleman with the fact that she was aware of his duplicity.

"It is just as well not to let him know," said Theriere. "It gives you an advantage that would be wanting should he suspect the truth, so that now you are always in a position to be warned in plenty of time against any ulterior suggestion he may make. Keep me posted as to all he tells you of his plans, and in this way we can defeat him much more easily than as though you followed your natural inclinations and refused to hold communication of any sort with him. It might be well, Miss Harding, even to encourage him in the hope that you will wed him voluntarily. I think that that would throw him entirely off his guard, and pave the way for your early release."

"Oh, I doubt if I could do that, Mr. Theriere," exclaimed the girl. "You cannot imagine how I loathe the man now that I know him in his true colors. For years he has importuned me to marry him, and though I never cared for him in that way at all, and never could, I felt that he was a very good friend and that his constancy demanded some return on my part—my friendship and sympathy at least; but now I shiver whenever he is near me, just as I would were I to find a snake coiled close beside me. I cannot abide treachery."

"Nor I, Miss Harding," agreed Theriere glibly. "The man deserves nothing but your contempt, though for policy's sake I hope that you will find it possible to lead him on until his very treachery proves the means of your salvation, for believe me, if he has been false to you how much more quickly will he be false to Simms and Ward! He would ditch them in a minute if the opportunity presented itself for him to win you without their aid. I had thought it might be feasible to lead him into attempting to take the ship by force, and return you to San Francisco, or, better still possibly, to the nearest civilized port.

"You might, with propriety suggest this to him, telling him that you believe that I would stand ready to assist in the undertaking. I can promise you the support of several of the men—quite a sufficient number with Divine and myself, easily to take the *Halfmoon* away from her present officers."

"I will think over your suggestion, Mr. Theriere," replied Barbara, "and I thank you for the generous impulse that has prompted you to befriend me—

heaven knows how badly I need a friend now among so many enemies. What is it, Mr. Theriere? What is the matter?"

The officer had turned his eyes casually toward the southeast as the girl spoke, and just now he had given a sudden exclamation of surprise and alarm.

"That cloud, Miss Harding," he answered. "We're in for a bad blow, and it'll be on us in a minute," and with that he started forward on a run, calling back over his shoulder, "you'd better go below at once."

VII
THE TYPHOON

The storm that struck the *Halfmoon* took her entirely unaware. It had sprung, apparently, out of a perfectly clear sky. Both the lookout and the man at the wheel were ready to take oath that they had scanned the horizon not a half-minute before Second Mate Theriere had come racing forward bellowing for all hands on deck and ordering a sailor below to report the menacing conditions to Captain Simms.

Before that officer reached the deck Theriere had the entire crew aloft taking in sail; but though they worked with the desperation of doomed men they were only partially successful in their efforts.

The sky and sea had assumed a sickly yellowish color, except for the mighty black cloud that raced toward them, low over the water. The low moaning sound that had followed the first appearance of the storm, gave place to a sullen roar, and then, of a sudden, the thing struck the *Halfmoon*, ripping her remaining canvas from her as if it had been wrought from tissue paper, and with the flying canvas, spars, and cordage went the mainmast, snapping ten feet above the deck, and crashing over the starboard bow with a noise and jar that rose above the bellowing of the typhoon.

Fully half the crew of the *Halfmoon* either went down with the falling rigging or were crushed by the crashing weight of the mast as it hurtled against the deck. Skipper Simms rushed back and forth screaming out curses that no one heeded, and orders that there was none to fill.

Theriere, on his own responsibility, looked to the hatches. Ward with a handful of men armed with axes attempted to chop away the wreckage, for the jagged butt of the fallen mast was dashing against the ship's side with such vicious blows that it seemed but a matter of seconds ere it would stave a hole in her.

With the utmost difficulty a sea anchor was rigged and tumbled over the *Halfmoon*'s pitching bow into the angry sea, that was rising to more gigantic proportions with each succeeding minute. This frail makeshift which at best could but keep the vessel's bow into the wind, saving her from instant engulfment in the sea's trough, seemed to Theriere but a sorry means of prolonging the agony of suspense preceding the inevitable end. That nothing could save them was the second officer's firm belief, nor was he alone in his conviction. Not only Simms and Ward, but every experienced sailor on the ship felt that the life of the *Halfmoon* was now but a matter of hours, possibly minutes, while those of lesser experience were equally positive that each succeeding wave must mark the termination of the lives of the vessel and her company.

The deck, washed now almost continuously by hurtling tons of stormmad water, as one mountainous wave followed another the length of the ship, had become entirely impossible. With difficulty the men were attempting to get below between waves. All semblance of discipline had vanished. For the most part they were a pack of howling, cursing, terrorridden beasts, fighting at the hatches with those who would have held them closed against the danger of each new assault of the sea.

Ward and Skipper Simms had been among the first to seek the precarious safety below deck. Theriere alone of the officers had remained on duty until the last, and now he was exerting his every faculty in the effort to save as many of the men as possible without losing the ship in the doing of it. Only between waves was the entrance to the main cabins negotiable, while the forecastle hatch had been abandoned entirely after it had with difficulty been replaced following the retreat of three of the crew to that part of the ship.

The mucker stood beside Theriere as the latter beat back the men when the seas threatened. It was the man's first experience of the kind. Never had he faced death in the courage-blighting form which the grim harvester assumes when he calls unbridled Nature to do his ghastly bidding. The mucker saw the rough, brawling bullies of the forecastle reduced to whitefaced, gibbering cowards, clawing and fighting to climb over one another toward the lesser danger of the cabins, while the mate fought them off, except as he found it expedient to let them pass him; he alone cool and fearless.

Byrne stood as one apart from the dangers and hysteric strivings of his fellows. Once when Theriere happened to glance in his direction the Frenchman mentally ascribed the mucker's seeming lethargy to the paralysis of abject cowardice. "The fellow is in a blue funk," thought the second mate; "I did not misjudge him—like all his kind he is a coward at heart."

Then a great wave came, following unexpectedly close upon the heels of a lesser one. It took Theriere off his guard, threw him down and hurtled him roughly across the deck, landing him in the scuppers, bleeding and stunned. The next wave would carry him overboard.

Released from surveillance the balance of the crew pushed and fought their way into the cabin—only the mucker remained without, staring first at the prostrate form of the mate and then at the open cabin hatch. Had one been watching him he might reasonably have thought that the man's mind was in a muddle of confused thoughts and fears; but such was far from the case. Billy was waiting to see if the mate would revive sufficiently to return across the deck before the next wave swept the ship. It was very interesting—he wondered what odds O'Leary would have laid against the man.

In another moment the wave would come. Billy glanced at the open cabin hatch. That would never do—the cabin would be flooded with tons of water should the next wave find the hatch still open. Billy closed it. Then he looked again toward Theriere. The man was just recovering consciousness—and the wave was coming.

Something stirred within Billy Byrne. It gripped him and made him act quickly as though by instinct to do something that no one, Billy himself least of all, would have suspected that the Grand Avenue mucker would have been capable of.

Across the deck Theriere was dragging himself painfully to his hands and knees, as though to attempt the impossible feat of crawling back to the cabin hatch. The wave was almost upon Billy. In a moment it would engulf him, and then rush on across him to tear Theriere from the deck and hurl him beyond the ship into the tumbling, watery, chaos of the sea.

The mucker saw all this, and in the instant he launched himself toward the man for whom he had no use, whose kind he hated, reaching him as the great wave broke over them, crushing them to the deck, choking and blinding them.

For a moment they were buried in the swirling maelstrom, and then as the *Halfmoon* rose again, shaking the watery enemy from her back, the two men were disclosed—Theriere half over the ship's side—the mucker clinging to him with one hand, the other clutching desperately at a huge cleat upon the gunwale.

Byrne dragged the mate to the deck, and then slowly and with infinite difficulty across it to the cabin hatch. Through it he pushed the man, tumbling after him and closing the aperture just as another wave swept the *Halfmoon*.

Theriere was conscious and but little the worse for his experience though badly bruised. He looked at the mucker in astonishment as the two faced each other in the cabin.

"I don't know why you did it," said Theriere.

"Neither do I," replied Billy Byrne.

"I shall not forget it, Byrne," said the officer.

"Yeh'd better," answered Billy, turning away.

The mucker was extremely puzzled to account for his act. He did not look upon it at all as a piece of heroism; but rather as a "fool play" which he should be ashamed of. The very idea! Saving the life of a gink who, despite his brutal ways, belonged to the much-despised "highbrow" class. Billy was peeved with himself.

Theriere, for his part, was surprised at the unexpected heroism of the man he had long since rated as a cowardly bully. He was fully determined to repay Byrne in so far as he could the great debt he owed him. All thoughts of revenge for the mucker's former assault upon him were dropped, and he now looked upon the man as a true friend and ally.

For three days the *Halfmoon* plunged helplessly upon the storm-wracked surface of the mad sea. No soul aboard her entertained more than the faintest glimmer of a hope that the ship would ride out the storm; but during the third night the wind died down, and by morning the sea had fallen sufficiently to make it safe for the men of the *Halfmoon* to venture upon deck.

There they found the brigantine clean-swept from stem to stern. To the north of them was land at a league or two, perhaps. Had the storm continued during the night they would have been dashed upon the coast. God-fearing men would have given thanks for their miraculous rescue; but not so these. Instead, the fear of death removed, they assumed their former bravado.

Skipper Simms boasted of the seamanship that had saved the *Halfmoon*—his own seamanship of course. Ward was cursing the luck that had disabled the ship at so crucial a period of her adventure, and revolving in his evil mind various possible schemes for turning the misfortune to his own advantage. Billy Byrne, sitting upon the corner of the galley table, hobnobbed with Blanco. These choice representatives of the ship's company were planning a raid on the skipper's brandy chest during the disembarkation which the sight of land had rendered not improbable.

The *Halfmoon*, with the wind down, wallowed heavily in the trough of the sea, but even so Barbara Harding, wearied with days of confinement in her stuffy cabin below, ventured above deck for a breath of sweet, clean air.

Scarce had she emerged from below than Theriere espied her, and hastened to her side.

"Well, Miss Harding," he exclaimed, "it seems good to see you on deck again. I can't tell you how sorry I have felt for you cooped up alone in your cabin without a single woman for companionship, and all those frightful days of danger, for there was scarce one of us that thought the old hooker would weather so long and hard a blow. We were mighty fortunate to come through it so handily."

"Handily?" queried Barbara Harding, with a wry smile, glancing about the deck of the *Halfmoon*. "I cannot see that we are either through it handily or through it at all. We have no masts, no canvas, no boats; and though I am not much of a sailor, I can see that there is little likelihood of our effecting a landing on the shore ahead either with or without boats—it looks most forbidding. Then the wind has gone down, and when it comes up again it is possible that it will carry us away from the land, or if it takes us toward it, dash us to pieces at the foot of those frightful cliffs."

"I see you are too good a sailor by far to be cheered by any questionable hopes," laughed Theriere; "but you must take the will into consideration—I only wished to give you a ray of hope that might lighten your burden of apprehension. However, honestly, I do think that we may find a way to make a safe landing if the sea continues to go down as it has in the past two hours. We are not more than a league from shore, and with the jury mast and sail that the men are setting under Mr. Ward now we can work in comparative safety with a light breeze, which we should have during the afternoon. There are few coasts, however rugged they may appear at a distance, that do not offer some foothold for the wrecked mariner, and I doubt not but that we shall find this no exception to the rule."

"I hope you are right, Mr. Theriere," said the girl, "and yet I cannot but feel that my position will be less safe on land than it has been upon the *Halfmoon*. Once free from the restraints of discipline which tradition, custom, and law enforce upon the high seas there is no telling what atrocities these men will commit. To be quite candid, Mr. Theriere, I dread a landing worse than I dreaded the dangers of the storm through which we have just passed."

"I think you have little to fear on that score, Miss Harding," said the Frenchman. "I intend making it quite plain that I consider myself your protector once we have left the *Halfmoon*, and I can count on several of the men to support me. Even Mr. Divine will not dare do otherwise. Then we can set up a camp of our own apart from Skipper Simms and his faction where you will be constantly guarded until succor may be obtained."

Barbara Harding had been watching the man's face as he spoke. The memory of his consideration and respectful treatment of her during the trying weeks of her captivity had done much to erase the intuitive feeling of distrust that had tinged her thoughts of him earlier in their acquaintance, while his heroic act in descending into the forecastle in the face of the armed and desperate Byrne had thrown a glamour of romance about him that could not help but tend to fascinate a girl of Barbara Harding's type. Then there was the look she had seen in his eyes for a brief instant when she had found herself locked in his cabin on the occasion that he had revealed to her Larry Divine's duplicity. That expression no red-blooded girl could mistake, and the fact that he had subdued his passion spoke eloquently to the girl of the fineness and chivalry of his nature, so now it was with a feeling of utter trustfulness that she gladly gave herself into the keeping of Henri Theriere, Count de Cadenet, Second Officer of the *Halfmoon*.

"O Mr. Theriere," she cried, "if you only can but arrange it so, how relieved and almost happy I shall be. How can I ever repay you for all that you have done for me?"

Again she saw the light leap to the man's eyes—the light of a love that would not be denied much longer other than through the agency of a mighty will. Love she thought it; but the eye-light of love and lust are twin lights between which it takes much worldly wisdom to differentiate, and Barbara Harding was not worldly-wise in the ways of sin.

"Miss Harding," said Theriere, in a voice that he evidently found it difficult to control, "do not ask me now how you may repay me; I—;" but what he would have said he checked, and with an effort of will that was almost appreciable to the eye he took a fresh grip upon himself, and continued: "I am amply repaid by being able to serve you, and thus to retrieve myself in your estimation—I know that you have doubted me; that you have questioned the integrity of my acts that helped to lead up to the unfortunate affair of the *Lotus*. When you tell me that you no longer doubt—that you accept me as the friend I would wish to be, I shall be more than amply repaid for anything which it may have been my good fortune to have been able to accomplish for your comfort and safety."

"Then I may partially repay you at once," exclaimed the girl with a smile, "for I can assure you that you possess my friendship to the fullest, and with it, of course, my entire confidence. It is true that I doubted you at first—I doubted everyone connected with the *Halfmoon*. Why shouldn't I? But now I think that I am able to draw a very clear line between my friends and my enemies. There is but one upon the right side of that line—you, my friend," and with an impulsive little gesture Barbara Harding extended her hand to Theriere.

It was with almost a sheepish expression that the Frenchman took the proffered fingers, for there had been that in the frank avowal of confidence and friendship which smote upon a chord of honor in the man's soul that had not vibrated in response to a chivalrous impulse for so many long years that it had near atrophied from disuse.

Then, of a sudden, the second officer of the *Halfmoon* straightened to his full height. His head went high, and he took the small hand of the girl in his own strong, brown one.

"Miss Harding," he said, "I have led a hard, bitter life. I have not always done those things of which I might be most proud; but there have been times when I have remembered that I am the grandson of one of Napoleon's greatest field marshals, and that I bear a name that has been honored by a mighty nation. What you have just said to me recalls these facts most vividly to my mind—I hope, Miss Harding, that you will never regret having spoken them," and to the bottom of his heart the man meant what he said, at the moment; for inherent chivalry is as difficult to suppress or uproot as is inherent viciousness.

The girl let her hand rest in his for a moment, and as their eyes met she saw in his a truth and honesty and cleanness which revealed what Theriere might have been had Fate ordained his young manhood to different channels. And in that moment a question sprang, all unbidden and unforeseen to her mind; a question which caused her to withdraw her hand quickly from his, and which sent a slow crimson to her cheek.

Billy Byrne, slouching by, cast a bitter look of hatred upon the two. The fact that he had saved Theriere's life had not increased his love for that gentleman. He was still much puzzled to account for the strange idiocy that had prompted him to that act; and two of his fellows had felt the weight of his mighty fist when they had spoken words of rough praise for his heroism—Billy had thought that they were kidding him.

To Billy the knocking out of Theriere, and the subsequent kick which he had planted in the unconscious man's face, were true indications of manliness. He gauged such matters by standards purely Grand Avenuesque and now it enraged him to see that the girl before whose very eyes he had demonstrated his superiority over Theriere should so look with favor upon the officer.

It did not occur to Billy that he would care to have the girl look with favor upon him. Such a thought would have sent him into a berserker rage; but the fact remained that Billy felt a strong desire to cut out Theriere's heart when he saw him now in close converse with Barbara Harding—just why he felt so Billy could not have said. The truth of the matter is that Billy was far from introspective; in fact he did very little thinking. His mind had never been trained to it, as his muscles had been trained to fighting. Billy reacted more quickly to instinct than to the processes of reasoning, and on this account it was difficult for him to explain any great number of his acts or moods—it is to be doubted, however, that Billy Byrne had ever attempted to get at the bottom of his soul, if he possessed one.

Be that as it may, had Theriere known it he was very near death that moment when a summons from Skipper Simms called him aft and saved his life. Then the mucker, unseen by the officer, approached the girl. In his heart were rage and hatred, and as the girl turned at the sound of his step behind her she saw them mirrored in his dark, scowling face.

VIII

THE WRECK OF THE *HALFMOON*

Instantly Barbara Harding looked into the face of the mucker she read her danger. Why the man should hate her so she could not guess; but that he did was evidenced by the malevolent expression of his surly countenance. For a moment he stood glaring at her, and then he spoke.

"I'm wise to wot youse an' dat guy was chinnin' about," he growled, "an' I'm right here to tell youse dat you don't wanta try an' put nothin' over on me, see? Youse ain't a-goin' to double-cross Billy Byrne. I gotta good notion to han' youse wot's comin' to you. If it hadn't been fer youse I wouldn't have been here now on dis Gawd-forsaken wreck. Youse is de cause of all de trouble. Wot youse ought to get is croaked an' den dere wouldn't be nothin' to bother any of us. You an' yer bunch of kale, dey give me a swift pain. Fer half a cent I'd soak youse a wallop to de solar plexus dat would put youse to sleep fer de long count, you—you;" but here words failed Billy.

To his surprise the girl showed not the slightest indication of fear. Her head was high, and her level gaze never wavered from his own eyes. Presently a sneer of contempt curled her lip.

"You coward!" she said quietly. "To insult and threaten a woman! You are nothing but an insufferable bully, and a cowardly murderer. You murdered a man on the *Lotus* whose little finger held more true manhood, bravery, and worth than the whole of your great, hulking carcass. You are only fit to strike from behind, or when your victim is unsuspecting, as you did Mr. Theriere that other day. Do you think I fear a *thing* such as you—a beast without honor that kicks an unconscious man in the face? I know that you can kill me. I know that you are coward enough to do it because I am a defenseless woman; and though you may kill me, you never can make me show fear for you. That is what you wish to do—that is your idea of manliness. I had never imagined that such a thing as you lived in the guise of man; but I have read you, Mr. Byrne, since I have had occasion to notice you, and I know now that you are what is known in the great cities as a mucker. The term never meant much to me before, but I see now that it fits your kind perfectly, for in it is all the loathing and contempt that a real man—a gentleman—must feel for such as you."

As she spoke Billy Byrne's eyes narrowed; but not with the cunning of premeditated attack. He was thinking. For the first time in his life he was thinking of how he appeared in the eyes of another. Never had any human being told Billy Byrne thus coolly and succinctly what sort of person he seemed to them. In the heat of anger men of his own stamp had applied vile epithets to him, describing him luridly as such that by the simplest laws of nature he could not possibly be; but this girl had spoken coolly, and her descriptions had been explicit—backed by illustrations. She had given real reasons for her contempt, and somehow it had made that contempt seem very tangible.

One who had known Billy would have expected him to fly into a rage and attack the girl brutally after her scathing diatribe. Billy did nothing of the sort. Barbara Harding's words seemed to have taken all the fight out of him. He stood looking at her for a moment—it was one of the strange contradictions of Billy Byrne's personality that he could hold his eyes quite steady and level, meeting the gaze of another unwaveringly—and in that moment something happened to Billy Byrne's perceptive faculties. It was as though scales which had dimmed his mental vision had partially dropped away, for suddenly he saw what he had not before seen—a very beautiful girl, brave and unflinching before the brutal menace of his attitude, and though the mucker thought that he still hated her, the realization came to him that he must not raise a hand against her—that for the life of him he could not, nor ever again against any other woman. Why this change, Billy did not know, he simply knew that it was so, and with an ugly grunt he turned his back upon her and walked away.

A slight breeze had risen from the southwest since Theriere had left Barbara Harding and now all hands were busily engaged in completing the jury rigging that the *Halfmoon* might take advantage of the wind and make the shore that rose abruptly from the bosom of the ocean but a league away.

Before the work was completed the wind increased rapidly, so that when the tiny bit of canvas was hoisted into position it bellied bravely, and the *Halfmoon* moved heavily forward toward the land.

"We gotta make a mighty quick run of it," said Skipper Simms to Ward, "or we'll go to pieces on them rocks afore ever we find a landing."

"That we will if this wind rises much more," replied Ward; "and 's far as I can see there ain't no more chance to make a landing there than there would be on the side of a house."

And indeed as the *Halfmoon* neared the towering cliffs it seemed utterly hopeless that aught else than a fly could find a foothold upon that sheer and rocky face that rose abruptly from the ocean's surface.

Some two hundred yards from the shore it became evident that there was no landing to be made directly before them, and so the course of the ship was altered to carry them along parallel to the shore in an effort to locate a cove, or beach where a landing might safely be effected.

The wind, increasing steadily, was now whipping the sea into angry breakers that dashed resoundingly against the rocky barrier of the island. To drift within reach of those frightful destroyers would mean the instant annihilation of the *Halfmoon* and all her company, yet this was precisely what the almost unmanageable hulk was doing at the wheel under the profane direction of Skipper Simms, while Ward and Theriere with a handful of men altered the meager sail from time to time in an effort to keep the ship off the rocks for a few moments longer.

The *Halfmoon* was almost upon the cliff's base when a narrow opening showed some hundred fathoms before her nose, an opening through which the sea ran in long, surging sweeps, rolling back upon itself in angry breakers that filled the aperture with swirling water and high-flung spume. To have attempted to drive the ship into such a place would have been the height of madness under ordinary circumstances. No man knew what lay beyond, nor whether the opening carried sufficient water to float the *Halfmoon*, though the long, powerful sweep of the sea as it entered the opening denoted considerable depth.

Skipper Simms, seeing the grim rocks rising close beside his vessel, realized that naught could keep her from them now. He saw death peering close to his face. He felt the icy breath of the Grim Reaper upon his brow. A coward at heart, he lost every vestige of his nerve at this crucial moment of his life. Leaping from the wheelhouse to the deck he ran backward and forward shrieking at the top of his lungs begging and entreating someone to save him, and offering fabulous rewards to the man who carried him safely to the shore.

The sight of their captain in a blue funk had its effect upon the majority of the crew, so that in a moment a pack of screaming, terror-ridden men had supplanted the bravos and bullies of the *Halfmoon*.

From the cabin companionway Barbara Harding looked upon the disgusting scene. Her lip curled in scorn at the sight of these men weeping and moaning in their fright. She saw Ward busy about one of the hatches. It was evident that he intended making a futile attempt to utilize it as a means of escape after the *Halfmoon* struck, for he was attaching ropes to it and dragging it toward the port side of the ship, away from the shore. Larry Divine crouched beside the cabin and wept.

When Simms gave up the ship Barbara Harding saw the wheelmen, there had been two of them, desert their post, and almost instantly the nose of the *Halfmoon* turned toward the rocks; but scarcely had the men reached the deck than Theriere leaped to their place at the wheel.

Unassisted he could do little with the heavy helm. Barbara saw that he alone of all the officers and men of the brigantine was making an attempt to save the vessel. However futile the effort might be, it at least bespoke the coolness and courage of the man. With the sight of him there wrestling with death in a hopeless struggle a little wave of pride surged through the girl. Here indeed was a man! And he loved her—that she knew. Whether or no she returned his love her place was beside him now, to give what encouragement and physical aid lay in her power.

Quickly she ran to the wheelhouse. Theriere saw her and smiled.

"There's no hope, I'm afraid," he said; "but, by George, I intend to go down fighting, and not like those miserable yellow curs."

Barbara did not reply, but she grasped the spokes of the heavy wheel and tugged as he tugged. Theriere made no effort to dissuade her from the strenuous labor—every ounce of weight would help so much, and the man had a wild, mad idea that he was attempting to put into effect.

"What do you hope to do?" asked the girl. "Make that opening in the cliffs?"

Theriere nodded.

"Do you think me crazy?" he asked.

"It is such a chance as only a brave man would dare to take," she replied. "Do you think that we can get her to take it?"

"I doubt it," he answered. "With another man at the wheel we might, though."

Below them the crew of the *Halfmoon* ran hither and thither along the deck on the side away from the breakers. They fought with one another for useless bits of planking and cordage. The giant figure of the black cook, Blanco, rose above the others. In his hand was a huge butcher knife. When he saw a piece of wood he coveted in the hands of another he rushed upon his helpless victim with wild, bestial howls, menacing him with his gleaming weapon. Thus he was rapidly accumulating the material for a life raft.

But there was a single figure upon the deck that did not seem mad with terror. A huge fellow he was who stood leaning against the capstan watching the wild antics of his fellows with a certain wondering expression of incredulity, the while a contemptuous smile curled his lips. As Barbara Harding chanced to look in his direction he also chanced to turn his eyes toward the wheelhouse. It was the mucker.

The girl was surprised that he, the greatest coward of them all, should be showing no signs of cowardice now—probably he was paralyzed with fright. The moment that the man saw the two who were in the wheelhouse and the work that they were doing he sprang quickly toward them. At his approach the girl shrank closer to Theriere.

What new outrage did the fellow contemplate? Now he was beside her. The habitual dark scowl blackened his expression. He laid a heavy hand on Barbara Harding's arm.

"Come out o' dat," he bellowed. "Dat's no kind o' job fer a broiler."

And before either she or Theriere could guess his intention the mucker had pushed Barbara aside and taken her place at the wheel.

"Good for you, Byrne!" cried Theriere. "I needed you badly."

"Why didn't yeh say so den?" growled the man.

With the aid of Byrne's Herculean muscles and great weight the bow of the *Halfmoon* commenced to come slowly around so that presently she almost paralleled the cliffs again, but now she was much closer in than when Skipper Simms had deserted her to her fate—so close that Theriere had little hope of being able to carry out his plan of taking her opposite the opening and then turning and running her before the wind straight into the swirling waters of the inlet.

Now they were almost opposite the aperture and between the giant cliffs that rose on either side of the narrow entrance a sight was revealed that filled their hearts with renewed hope and rejoicing, for a tiny cove was seen to lie beyond the fissure—a cove with a long, wide, sandy beach up which the waves, broken at the entrance to the little haven, rolled with much diminished violence.

"Can you hold her alone for a second, Byrne?" asked Theriere. "We must make the turn in another moment and I've got to let out sail. The instant that you see me cut her loose put your helm hard to starboard. She'll come around easy enough I imagine, and then hold her nose straight for that opening. It's one chance in a thousand; but it's the only one. Are you game?"

"You know it, cul—go to 't," was Billy Byrne's laconic rejoinder.

As Theriere left the wheel Barbara Harding stepped to the mucker's side.

"Let me help you," she said. "We need every hand that we can get for the next few moments."

"Beat it," growled the man. "I don't want no skirts in my way."

With a flush, the girl drew back, and then turning watched Theriere where he stood ready to cut loose the sail at the proper instant. The vessel was now opposite the cleft in the cliffs. Theriere had lashed a new sheet in position. Now he cut the old one. The sail swung around until caught in position by the stout line. The mucker threw the helm hard to starboard. The nose of the brigantine swung quickly toward the rocks. The sail filled, and an instant later the ship was dashing to what seemed her inevitable doom.

Skipper Simms, seeing what Theriere had done after it was too late to prevent it, dashed madly across the deck toward his junior.

"You fool!" he shrieked. "You fool! What are you doing? Driving us straight for the rocks—murdering the whole lot of us!" and with that he sprang upon the Frenchman with maniacal fury, bearing him to the deck beneath him.

Barbara Harding saw the attack of the fear-demented man, but she was powerless to prevent it. The mucker saw it too, and grinned—he hoped that it would be a good fight; there was nothing that he enjoyed more. He was sorry that he could not take a hand in it, but the wheel demanded all his attention now, so that he was even forced to take his eyes from the combatants that he might rivet them upon the narrow entrance to the cove toward which the *Halfmoon* was now plowing her way at constantly increasing speed.

The other members of the ship's company, all unmindful of the battle that at another time would have commanded their undivided attention, stood with eyes glued upon the wild channel toward which the brigantine's nose was pointed. They saw now what Skipper Simms had failed to see—the little cove beyond, and the chance for safety that the bold stroke offered if it proved successful.

With steady muscles and giant sinews the mucker stood by the wheel—nursing the erratic wreck as no one might have supposed it was in him to do. Behind him Barbara Harding watched first Theriere and Simms, and then Byrne and the swirling waters toward which he was heading the ship.

Even the strain of the moment did not prevent her from wondering at the strange contradictions of the burly young ruffian who could at one moment show such traits of cowardliness and the next rise so coolly to the highest pinnacles of courage. As she watched him occasionally now she noted for the first time the leonine contour of his head, and she was surprised to note that his features were regular and fine, and then she recalled Billy Mallory and the cowardly kick that she had seen delivered in the face of the unconscious Theriere—with a little shudder of disgust she turned away from the man at the wheel.

Theriere by this time had managed to get on top of Skipper Simms, but that worthy still clung to him with the desperation of a drowning man. The *Halfmoon* was rising on a great wave that would bear her well into the maelstrom of the cove's entrance. The wind had increased to the proportions of a gale, so that the brigantine was fairly racing either to her doom or her salvation—who could tell which?

Halfway through the entrance the wave dropped the ship, and with a mighty crash that threw Barbara Harding to her feet the vessel struck full amidships upon a sunken reef. Like a thing of glass she broke in two with the terrific impact, and in another instant the waters about her were filled with screaming men.

Barbara Harding felt herself hurtled from the deck as though shot from a catapult. The swirling waters engulfed her. She knew that her end had come, only the most powerful of swimmers might hope to win through that lashing hell of waters to the beach beyond. For a girl to do it was too hopeless even to contemplate; but she recalled Theriere's words of so short a time ago: "There's no hope, I'm afraid; but, by George, I intend to go down fighting," and with the recollection came a like resolve on her part—to go down fighting, and so she struck out against the powerful waters that swirled her hither and thither, now perilously close to the rocky sides of the entrance, and now into the mad chaos of the channel's center. Would to heaven that Theriere were near her, she thought, for if any could save her it would be he.

Since she had come to believe in the man's friendship and sincerity Barbara Harding had felt renewed hope of eventual salvation, and with the hope had come a desire to live which had almost been lacking for the greater part of her detention upon the *Halfmoon*.

Bravely she battled now against the awful odds of the mighty Pacific, but soon she felt her strength waning. More and more ineffective became her puny efforts, and at last she ceased almost entirely the futile struggle.

And then she felt a strong hand grasp her arm, and with a sudden surge she was swung over a broad shoulder. Quickly she grasped the rough shirt that covered the back of her would-be rescuer, and then commenced a battle with the waves that for many minutes, that seemed hours to the frightened girl, hung in the balance; but at last the swimmer beneath her forged steadily and persistently toward the sandy beach to flounder out at last with an unconscious burden in his mighty arms.

As the man staggered up out of reach of the water Barbara Harding opened her eyes to look in astonishment into the face of the mucker.

IX
ODA YORIMOTO

Only four men of the *Halfmoon*'s crew were lost in the wreck of the vessel. All had been crowded in the bow when the ship broke in two, and being far-flung by the forward part of the brigantine as it lunged toward the cove on the wave following the one which had dropped the craft upon the reef, with the exception of the four who had perished beneath the wreckage they had been able to swim safely to the beach.

Larry Divine, who had sat weeping upon the deck of the doomed ship during the time that hope had been at its lowest, had recovered his poise. Skipper Simms, subdued for the moment, soon commenced to regain his bluster. He took Theriere to task for the loss of the *Halfmoon*.

"An' ever we make a civilized port," he shouted, "I'll prefer charges ag'in' you, you swab you; a-losin' of the finest bark as ever weathered a storm. Ef it hadn't o' been fer you a-mutinyin' agin' me I'd a-brought her through in safety an' never lost a bloomin' soul."

"Stow it!" admonished Theriere at last; "your foolish bluster can't hide the bald fact that you deserted your post in time of danger. We're ashore now, remember, and there is no more ship for you to command, so were I you I'd be mighty careful how I talked to my betters."

"What's that!" screamed the skipper. "My betters! You frog-eatin' greaser you, I'll teach you. Here, some of you, clap this swab into irons. I'll learn him that I'm still captain of this here bunch."

Theriere laughed in the man's face; but Ward and a couple of hands who had been shown favoritism by the skipper and first mate closed menacingly toward the second officer.

The Frenchman took in the situation at a glance. They were ashore now, where they didn't think that they needed him further and the process of elimination had commenced. Well, it might as well come to a showdown now as later.

"Just a moment," said Theriere, raising his hand. "You're not going to take me alive, and I have no idea that you want to anyhow, and if you start anything in the killing line some of you are going to Davy Jones' locker along with me. The best thing for all concerned is to divide up this party now once and for all."

As he finished speaking he turned toward Billy Byrne.

"Are you and the others with me, or against me?" he asked.

"I'm ag'in' Simms," replied the mucker non-committally.

Bony Sawyer, Red Sanders, Blanco, Wison, and two others drew in behind Billy Byrne.

"We all's wid Billy," announced Blanco.

Divine and Barbara Harding stood a little apart. Both were alarmed at the sudden, hostile turn events had taken. Simms, Ward, and Theriere were the only members of the party armed. Each wore a revolver strapped about his hips. All were still dripping from their recent plunge in the ocean.

Five men stood behind Skipper Simms and Ward, but there were two revolvers upon that side of the argument. Suddenly Ward turned toward Divine.

"Are you armed, Mr. Divine?" he asked.

Divine nodded affirmatively.

"Then you'd better come over with us—it looks like we might need you to help put down this mutiny," said Ward.

Divine hesitated. He did not know which side was more likely to be victorious, and he wanted to be sure to be on the winning side. Suddenly an inspiration came to him.

"This is purely a matter to be settled by the ship's officers," he said. "I am only a prisoner, call me a passenger if you like—I have no interest whatever in the matter, and shall not take sides."

"Yes you will," said Mr. Ward, in a low, but menacing tone. "You're in too deep to try to ditch us now. If you don't stand by us we'll treat you as one of the mutineers when we're through with them, and you can come pretty near a-guessin' what they'll get."

Divine was about to reply, and the nature of his answer was suggested by the fact that he had already taken a few steps in the direction of Simms' faction, when he was stopped by the low voice of the girl behind him.

"Larry," she said, "I know all—your entire connection with this plot. If you have a spark of honor or manhood left you will do what little you can to retrieve the terrible wrong you have done me, and my father. You can never marry me. I give you my word of honor that I shall take my own life if that is the only way to thwart your plans in that direction, and so as the fortune can never be yours it seems to me that the next best thing would be to try and save me from the terrible predicament in which your cupidity has placed me. You can make the start now, Larry, by walking over and placing yourself at Mr. Theriere's disposal. He has promised to help and protect me."

A deep flush mounted to the man's neck and face. He did not turn about to face the girl he had so grievously wronged—for the life of him he could not have met her eyes. Slowly he turned, and with gaze bent upon the ground walked quickly toward Theriere.

Ward was quick to recognize the turn events had taken, and to see that it gave Theriere the balance of power, with two guns and nine men in his party against their two guns and seven men. It also was evident to him that to the other party the girl would naturally gravitate since Divine, an old acquaintance, had cast his lot with it; nor had the growing intimacy between Miss Harding and Theriere been lost upon him.

Ward knew that Simms was an arrant coward, nor was he himself overly keen for an upstanding, man-to-man encounter such as must quickly follow any attempt upon his part to uphold the authority of Simms, or their claim upon the custody of the girl.

Intrigue and trickery were more to Mr. Ward's liking, and so he was quick to alter his plan of campaign the instant that it became evident that Divine had elected to join forces with the opposing faction.

"I reckon," he said, directing his remarks toward no one in particular, "that we've all been rather hasty in this matter, being het up as we were with the strain of what we been through an' so it seems to me, takin' into consideration that Mr. Theriere really done his best to save the ship, an' that as a matter of fact we was all mighty lucky to come out of it alive, that we'd better let bygones be bygones, for the time bein' at least, an' all of us pitch in to save what we can from the wreckage, hunt water, rig up a camp, an' get things sort o' shipshape here instid o' squabblin' amongst ourselves."

"Suit yourself," said Theriere, "it's all the same to us," and his use of the objective pronoun seemed definitely to establish the existence of his faction as a separate and distinct party.

Simms, from years of experience with his astute mate, was wont to acquiesce in anything that Ward proposed, though he had not the brains always to appreciate the purposes that prompted Ward's suggestions. Now, therefore, he nodded his approval of Squint Eye's proposal, feeling that whatever was in Ward's mind would be more likely to work out to Skipper Simms' interests than some unadvised act of Skipper Simms himself.

"Supposin'," continued Ward, "that we let two o' your men an' two o' ourn under Mr. Divine, shin up them cliffs back o' the cove an' search fer water an' a site fer camp—the rest o' us'll have our hands full with the salvage."

"Good," agreed Theriere. "Miller, you and Swenson will accompany Mr. Divine."

Ward detailed two of his men, and the party of five began the difficult ascent of the cliffs, while far above them a little brown man with beady, black eyes set in narrow fleshy slits watched them from behind a clump of bushes. Strange, medieval armor and two wicked-looking swords gave him a most warlike appearance. His temples were shaved, and a broad strip on the top of his head to just beyond the crown. His remaining hair was drawn into an unbraided queue, tied tightly at the back, and the queue then brought forward to the top of the forehead. His helmet lay in the grass at his feet. At the nearer approach of the party to the cliff top the watcher turned and melted into the forest at his back. He was Oda Yorimoto, descendant of a powerful daimio of the Ashikaga Dynasty of shoguns who had fled Japan with his faithful samurai nearly three hundred and fifty years before upon the overthrow of the Ashikaga Dynasty.

Upon this unfrequented and distant Japanese isle the exiles had retained all of their medieval military savagery, to which had been added the aboriginal ferocity of the head-hunting natives they had found there and with whom they had intermarried. The little colony, far from making any advances in arts or letters had, on the contrary, relapsed into primeval ignorance as deep as that of the natives with whom they had cast their lot— only in their arms and armor, their military training and discipline did they show any of the influence of their civilized progenitors. They were cruel, crafty, resourceful wild men trapped in the habiliments of a dead past, and armed with the keen weapons of their forbears. They had not even the crude religion of the Malaysians they had absorbed unless a highly exaggerated propensity for head-hunting might be dignified by the name of religion. To the tender mercies of such as these were the castaways of the *Halfmoon* likely to be consigned, for what might sixteen men with but four revolvers among them accomplish against near a thousand savage samurai?

Theriere, Ward, Simms, and the remaining sailors at the beach busied themselves with the task of retrieving such of the wreckage and the salvage of the *Halfmoon* as the waves had deposited in the shallows of the beach. There were casks of fresh water, kegs of biscuit, clothing, tinned meats, and a similar heterogeneous mass of flotsam. This arduous labor consumed the best part of the afternoon, and it was not until it had been completed that Divine and his party returned to the beach.

They reported that they had discovered a spring of fresh water some three miles east of the cove and about half a mile inland, but it was decided that no attempt be made to transport the salvage of the party to the new camp site until the following morning.

Theriere and Divine erected a rude shelter for Barbara Harding close under the foot of the cliff, as far from the water as possible, while above them Oda Yorimoto watched their proceedings with beady, glittering eyes. This time a half-dozen of his fierce samurai crouched at his side. Besides their two swords these latter bore the primitive spears of their mothers' savage tribe.

Oda Yorimoto watched the white men upon the beach. Also, he watched the white girl—even more, possibly, than he watched the men. He saw the shelter that was being built, and when it was complete he saw the girl enter it, and he knew that it was for her alone. Oda Yorimoto sucked in his lips and his eyes narrowed even more than nature had intended that they should.

A fire burned before the rude domicile that Barbara Harding was to occupy, and another, larger fire roared a hundred yards to the west where the men were congregated about Blanco, who was attempting to evolve a meal from the miscellany of his larder that had been cast up by the sea. There seemed now but little to indicate that the party was divided into two bitter factions, but when the meal was over Theriere called his men to a point midway between Barbara's shelter and the main camp fire. Here he directed them to dispose themselves for the night as best they could, building a fire of their own if they chose, for with the coming of darkness the chill of the tropical night would render a fire more than acceptable.

All were thoroughly tired and exhausted, so that darkness had scarce fallen ere the entire camp seemed wrapped in slumber. And still Oda Yorimoto sat with his samurai upon the cliff's summit, beady eyes fixed upon his intended prey.

For an hour he sat thus in silence, until, assured that all were asleep before him, he arose and with a few whispered instructions commenced the descent of the cliff toward the cove below. Scarce had he started, however, with his men stringing in single file behind him, than he came to a sudden halt, for below him in the camp that lay between the girl's shelter and the westerly camp a figure had arisen stealthily from among his fellows.

It was Theriere. Cautiously he moved to a sleeper nearby whom he shook gently until he had awakened him.

"Hush, Byrne," cautioned the Frenchman. "It is I, Theriere. Help me awaken the others—see that there is no noise."

"Wot's doin'?" queried the mucker.

"We are going to break camp, and occupy the new location before that bunch of pirates can beat us to it," whispered Theriere in reply; "and," he added, "we're going to take the salvage and the girl with us."

The mucker grinned.

"Gee!" he said. "Won't dey be a sore bunch in de mornin'?"

The work of awakening the balance of the party required but a few minutes and when the plan was explained to them, all seemed delighted with the prospect of discomfiting Skipper Simms and Squint Eye. It was decided that only the eatables be carried away on the first trip, and that if a second trip was possible before dawn the clothing, canvas, and cordage that had been taken from the water might then be purloined.

Miller and Swenson were detailed to bring up the rear with Miss Harding, assisting her up the steep side of the cliff. Divine was to act as guide to the new camp, lending a hand wherever necessary in the scaling of the heights with the loot.

Cautiously the party, with the exception of Divine, Miller, and Swenson, crept toward the little pile of supplies that were heaped fifty or sixty feet from the sleeping members of Simms' faction. The three left behind walked in silence to Barbara Harding's shelter. Here Divine scratched at the piece of sail cloth which served as a door until he had succeeded in awakening the sleeper within. And from above Oda Yorimoto watched the activity in the little cove with intent and unwavering eyes.

The girl, roused from a fitful slumber, came to the doorway of her primitive abode, alarmed by this nocturnal summons.

"It is I, Larry," whispered the man. "Are you dressed?"

"Yes," replied the girl, stepping out into the moonlight. "What do you want? What has happened?"

"We are going to take you away from Simms—Theriere and I," replied the man, "and establish a safe camp of our own where they cannot molest you. Theriere and the others have gone for the supplies now and as soon as they return we shall commence the ascent of the cliffs. If you have any further preparations to make, Barbara, please make haste, as we must get away from here as quickly as possible. Should any of Simms' people awaken there is sure to be a fight."

The girl turned back into the shelter to gather together a handful of wraps that had been saved from the wreck.

Down by the salvage Theriere, Byrne, Bony Sawyer, Red Sanders, Blanco, and Wison were selecting the goods that they wished to carry with them. It was found that two trips would be necessary to carry off the bulk of the rations, so Theriere sent the mucker to summon Miller and Swenson.

"We'll carry all that eight of us can to the top of the cliffs," he said; "hide it there and then come back for the balance. We may be able to get it later if we are unable to make two trips to the camp tonight."

While they were waiting for Byrne to return with the two recruits one of the sleepers in Simms' camp stirred. Instantly the five marauders dropped stealthily to the ground behind the boxes and casks. Only Theriere kept his eyes above the level of the top of their shelter that he might watch the movements of the enemy.

The figure sat up and looked about. It was Ward. Slowly he arose and approached the pile of salvage. Theriere drew his revolver, holding it in readiness for an emergency. Should the first mate look in the direction of Barbara Harding's shelter he must certainly see the four figures waiting there in the moonlight. Theriere turned his own head in the direction of the shelter that he might see how plainly the men there were visible. To his delight he saw that no one was in sight. Either they had seen Ward, or for the sake of greater safety from detection had moved to the opposite side of the shelter.

Ward was quite close to the boxes upon the other side of which crouched the night raiders. Theriere's finger found the trigger of his revolver. He was convinced that the mate had been disturbed by the movement in camp and was investigating. The Frenchman knew that the search would not end upon the opposite side of the salvage—in a moment Ward would be upon them.

He was sorry—not for Ward, but because he had planned to carry the work out quietly and he hated to have to muss things up with a killing, especially on Barbara's account.

Ward stopped at one of the water casks. He tipped it up, filling a tin cup with water, took a long drink, set the cup back on top of the cask, and, turning, retraced his steps to his blanket. Theriere could have hugged himself. The man had suspected nothing. He merely had been thirsty and come over for a drink—in another moment he would be fast asleep once more. Sure enough, before Byrne returned with Miller and Swenson Theriere could bear the snores of the first mate.

On the first trip to the cliff top eight men carried heavy burdens, Divine alone remaining to guard Barbara Harding. The second trip was made with equal dispatch and safety. No sound or movement came from the camp of the enemy, other than that of sleeping men. On the second trip Divine and Theriere each carried a burden up the cliffs, Miller and Swenson following with Barbara Harding, and as they came Oda Yorimoto and his samurai slunk back into the shadows that their prey might pass unobserving.

Theriere had the bulk of the loot hidden in a rocky crevice just beyond the cliff's summit. Brush torn from the mass of luxuriant tropical vegetation that covered the ground was strewn over the cache. All had been accomplished in safety and without detection. The camp beneath them still lay wrapped in silence.

The march toward the new camp, under the guidance of Divine, was immediately undertaken. On the return trip after the search for water Divine had discovered a well-marked trail along the edge of the cliffs to a point opposite the spring, and another leading from the main trail directly to the water. In his ignorance he had thought these the runways of animals, whereas they were the age-old highways of the headhunters.

Now they presented a comparatively quick and easy approach to the destination of the mutineers, but so narrow a one as soon to convince Theriere that it was not feasible for him to move back and forth along the flank of his column. He had tried it once, but it so greatly inconvenienced and retarded the heavily laden men that he abandoned the effort, remaining near the center of the cavalcade until the new camp was reached.

Here he found a fair-sized space about a clear and plentiful spring of cold water. Only a few low bushes dotted the grassy clearing which was almost completely surrounded by dense and impenetrable jungle. The men had deposited their burdens, and still Theriere stood waiting for the balance of his party—Miller and Swenson with Barbara Harding.

But they did not come, and when, in alarm, the entire party started back in search of them they retraced their steps to the very brink of the declivity leading to the cove before they could believe the testimony of their own perceptions—Barbara Harding and the two sailors had disappeared.

X
BARBARA CAPTURED BY HEADHUNTERS

When Barbara Harding, with Miller before and Swenson behind her, had taken up the march behind the loot-laden party seven dusky, noiseless shadows had emerged from the forest to follow close behind.

For half a mile the party moved along the narrow trail unmolested. Theriere had come back to exchange a half-dozen words with the girl and had again moved forward toward the head of the column. Miller was not more than twenty-five feet behind the first man ahead of him, and Miss Harding and Swenson followed at intervals of but three or four yards.

Suddenly, without warning, Swenson and Miller fell, pierced with savage spears, and at the same instant sinewy fingers gripped Barbara Harding, and a silencing hand was clapped over her mouth. There had been no sound above the muffled tread of the seamen. It had all been accomplished so quickly and so easily that the girl did not comprehend what had befallen her for several minutes.

In the darkness of the forest she could not clearly distinguish the forms or features of her abductors, though she reasoned, as was only natural, that Skipper Simms' party had become aware of the plot against them and had taken this means of thwarting a part of it; but when her captors turned directly into the mazes of the jungle, away from the coast, she began first to wonder and then to doubt, so that presently when a small clearing let the moonlight full upon them she was not surprised to discover that none of the members of the *Halfmoon*'s company was among her guard.

Barbara Harding had not circled the globe half a dozen times for nothing. There were few races or nations with whose history, past and present, she was not fairly familiar, and so the sight that greeted her eyes was well suited to fill her with astonishment, for she found herself in the hands of what appeared to be a party of Japanese warriors of the fifteenth or sixteenth century. She recognized the medieval arms and armor, the ancient helmets, the hairdressing of the two-sworded men of old Japan. At the belts of two of her captors dangled grisly trophies of the hunt. In the moonlight she saw that they were the heads of Miller and Swenson.

The girl was horrified. She had thought her lot before as bad as it could be, but to be in the clutches of these strange, fierce warriors of a long-dead age was unthinkably worse. That she could ever have wished to be back upon the *Halfmoon* would have seemed, a few days since, incredible; yet that was precisely what she longed for now.

On through the night marched the little, brown men—grim and silent—until at last they came to a small village in a valley away from the coast—a valley that lay nestled high among lofty mountains. Here were cavelike dwellings burrowed half under ground, the upper walls and thatched roofs rising scarce four feet above the level. Granaries on stilts were dotted here and there among the dwellings.

Into one of the filthy dens Barbara Harding was dragged. She found a single room in which several native and half-caste women were sleeping, about them stretched and curled and perched a motley throng of dirty yellow children, dogs, pigs, and chickens. It was the palace of Daimio Oda Yorimoto, Lord of Yoka, as his ancestors had christened their new island home.

Once within the warren the two samurai who had guarded Barbara upon the march turned and withdrew—she was alone with Oda Yorimoto and his family. From the center of the room depended a swinging shelf upon which a great pile of grinning skulls rested. At the back of the room was a door which Barbara had not at first noticed—evidently there was another apartment to the dwelling.

The girl was given little opportunity to examine her new prison, for scarce had the guards withdrawn than Oda Yorimoto approached and grasped her by the arm.

"Come!" he said, in Japanese that was sufficiently similar to modern Nippon to be easily understood by Barbara Harding. With the word he drew her toward a sleeping mat on a raised platform at one side of the room.

One of the women awoke at the sound of the man's voice. She looked up at Barbara in sullen hatred—otherwise she gave no indication that she saw anything unusual transpiring. It was as though an exquisite American belle were a daily visitor at the Oda Yorimoto home.

"What do you want of me?" cried the frightened girl, in Japanese.

Oda Yorimoto looked at her in astonishment. Where had this white girl learned to speak his tongue?

"I am the daimio, Oda Yorimoto," he said. "These are my wives. Now you are one of them. Come!"

"Not yet—not here!" cried the girl clutching at a straw. "Wait. Give me time to think. If you do not harm me my father will reward you fabulously. Ten thousand koku he would gladly give to have me returned to him safely."

Oda Yorimoto but shook his head.

"Twenty thousand koku!" cried the girl.

Still the daimio shook his head negatively.

"A hundred thousand—name your own price, if you will but not harm me."

"Silence!" growled the man. "What are even a million koku to me who only know the word from the legends of my ancestors. We have no need for koku here, and had we, my hills are full of the yellow metal which measures its value. No! you are my woman. Come!"

"Not here! Not here!" pleaded the girl. "There is another room—away from all these women," and she turned her eyes toward the door at the opposite side of the chamber.

Oda Yorimoto shrugged his shoulders. That would be easier than a fight, he argued, and so he led the girl toward the doorway that she had indicated. Within the room all was dark, but the daimio moved as one accustomed to the place, and as he moved through the blackness the girl at his side felt with stealthy fingers at the man's belt.

At last Oda Yorimoto reached the far side of the long chamber.

"Here!" he said, and took her by the shoulders.

"Here!" answered the girl in a low, tense voice, and at the instant that she spoke Oda Yorimoto, Lord of Yoka, felt a quick tug at his belt, and before he guessed what was to happen his own short sword had pierced his breast.

A single shriek broke from the lips of the daimio; but it was so high and shrill and like the shriek of a woman in mortal terror that the woman in the next room who heard it but smiled a crooked, wicked smile of hate and turned once more upon her pallet to sleep.

Again and again Barbara Harding plunged the sword of the brown man into the still heart, until she knew beyond peradventure of a doubt that her enemy was forevermore powerless to injure her. Then she sank, exhausted and trembling, upon the dirt floor beside the corpse.

When Theriere came to the realization that Barbara Harding was gone he jumped to the natural conclusion that Ward and Simms had discovered the ruse that he had worked upon them just in time to permit them to intercept Miller and Swenson with the girl, and carry her back to the main camp.

The others were prone to agree with him, though the mucker grumbled that "it listened fishy." However, all hands returned cautiously down the face of the cliff, expecting momentarily to be attacked by the guards which they felt sure Ward would post in expectation of a return of the mutineers, the moment they discovered that the girl had been taken from them; but to the surprise of all they reached the cove without molestation, and when they had crept cautiously to the vicinity of the sleepers they discovered that all were there, in peaceful slumber, just as they had left them a few hours before.

Silently the party retraced its steps up the cliff. Theriere and Billy Byrne brought up the rear.

"What do you make of it anyway, Byrne?" asked the Frenchman.

"If you wanta get it straight, cul," replied the mucker, "I tink youse know a whole lot more about it dan you'd like to have de rest of us tink."

"What do you mean, Byrne?" cried Theriere. "Out with it now!"

"Sure I'll out wid it. You didn't tink I was bashful didja? Wot fer did you detail dem two pikers, Miller and Swenson, to guard de skirt fer if it wasn't fer some special frame-up of yer own? Dey never been in our gang, and dats just wot you wanted 'em fer. It was easy to tip dem off to hike out wid de squab, and de first chanct you get you'll hike after dem, while we hold de bag. Tought you'd double-cross us easy, didn't yeh? Yeh cheapskate!"

"Byrne," said Theriere, and it was easy to see that only through the strength of his willpower did he keep his temper, "you may have cause to suspect the motives of everyone connected with this outfit. I can't say that I blame you; but I want you to remember what I say to you now. There was a time when I fully intended to 'double-cross' you, as you say—that was before you saved my life. Since then I have been on the square with you not only in deed but in thought as well. I give you the word of a man whose word once meant something—I am playing square with you now except in one thing, and I shall tell you what that is at once. I do not know where Miss Harding is, or what has happened to her, and Miller, and Swenson. That is God's truth. Now for the one thing that I just mentioned. Recently I changed my intentions relative to Miss Harding. I was after the money the same as the rest—that I am free to admit; but now I don't give a rap for it, and I had intended taking advantage of the first opportunity to return Miss Harding to civilization unharmed and without the payment of a penny to anyone. The reason for my change of heart is my own affair. In all probability you wouldn't believe the sincerity or honesty of my motives should I disclose them. I am only telling you these things because you have accused me of double dealing, and I do not want the man who saved my life at the risk of his own to have the slightest grounds to doubt my honesty with him. I've been a fairly bad egg, Byrne, for a great many years; but, by George! I'm not entirely rotten yet."

Byrne was silent for a few moments. He, too, had recently come to the conclusion that possibly he was not entirely rotten either, and had in a vague and half-formed sort of way wished for the opportunity to demonstrate the fact, so he was willing to concede to another that which he craved for himself.

"Yeh listen all right, cul," he said at last; "an' I'm willin' to take yeh at yer own say-so until I learn different."

"Thanks," said Theriere tersely. "Now we can work together in the search for Miss Harding; but where, in the name of all that's holy, are we to start?"

"Why, where we seen her last, of course," replied the mucker. "Right here on top of dese bluffs."

"Then we can't do anything until daylight," said the Frenchman.

"Not a ting, and at daylight we'll most likely have a scrap on our hands from below," and the mucker jerked his thumb in the direction of the cove.

"I think," said Theriere, "that we had better spend an hour arming ourselves with sticks and stones. We've a mighty good position up here. One that we can defend splendidly from an assault from below, and if we are prepared for them we can stave 'em off for a while if we need the time to search about up here for clues to Miss Harding's whereabouts."

And so the party set to work to cut stout bludgeons from the trees about them, and pile loose fragments of rock in handy places near the cliff top. Theriere even went so far as to throw up a low breastwork across the top of the trail up which the enemy must climb to reach the summit of the cliff. When they had completed their preparations three men could have held the place against ten times their own number.

Then they lay down to sleep, leaving Blanco and Divine on guard, for it had been decided that these two, with Bony Sawyer, should be left behind on the morrow to hold the cliff top while the others were searching for clues to the whereabouts of Barbara Harding. They were to relieve each other at guard duty during the balance of the night.

Scarce had the first suggestion of dawn lightened the eastern sky than Divine, who was again on guard, awakened Theriere. In a moment the others were aroused, and a hasty raid on the cached provisions made. The lack of water was keenly felt by all, but it was too far to the spring to chance taking the time necessary to fetch the much-craved fluid and those who were to forge into the jungle in search of Barbara Harding hoped to find water farther inland, while it was decided to dispatch Bony Sawyer to the spring for water for those who were to remain on guard at the cliff top.

A hurried breakfast was made on water-soaked ship's biscuit. Theriere and his searching party stuffed their pockets full of them, and a moment later the search was on. First the men traversed the trail toward the spring, looking for indications of the spot where Barbara Harding had ceased to follow them. The girl had worn heelless buckskin shoes at the time she was taken from the *Lotus*, and these left little or no spoor in the well-tramped earth of the narrow path; but a careful and minute examination on the part of Theriere finally resulted in the detection of a single small footprint a hundred yards from the point they had struck the trail after ascending the cliffs. This far at least she had been with them.

The men now spread out upon either side of the track—Theriere and Red Sanders upon one side, Byrne and Wison upon the other. Occasionally Theriere would return to the trail to search for further indications of the spoor they sought.

The party had proceeded in this fashion for nearly half a mile when suddenly they were attracted by a low exclamation from the mucker.

"Here!" he called. "Here's Miller an' the Swede, an' they sure have mussed 'em up turrible."

The others hastened in the direction of his voice, to come to a horrified halt at the sides of the headless trunks of the two sailors.

"*Mon Dieu!*" exclaimed the Frenchman, reverting to his mother tongue as he never did except under the stress of great excitement.

"Who done it?" queried Red Sanders, looking suspiciously at the mucker.

"Headhunters," said Theriere. "God! What an awful fate for that poor girl!"

Billy Byrne went white.

"Yeh don't mean dat dey've lopped off her block?" he whispered in an awed voice. Something strange rose in the mucker's breast at the thought he had just voiced. He did not attempt to analyze the sensation; but it was far from joy at the suggestion that the woman he so hated had met a horrible and disgusting death at the hands of savages.

"I'm afraid not, Byrne," said Theriere, in a voice that none there would have recognized as that of the harsh and masterful second officer of the *Halfmoon*.

"Yer afraid not!" echoed Billy Byrne, in amazement.

"For her sake I hope that they did," said Theriere; "for such as she it would have been a far less horrible fate than the one I fear they have reserved her for."

"You mean—" queried Byrne, and then he stopped, for the realization of just what Theriere did mean swept over him quite suddenly.

There was no particular reason why Billy Byrne should have felt toward women the finer sentiments which are so cherished a possession of those men who have been gently born and raised, even after they have learned that all women are not as was the feminine ideal of their boyhood.

Billy's mother, always foul-mouthed and quarrelsome, had been a veritable demon when drunk, and drunk she had been whenever she could, by hook or crook, raise the price of whiskey. Never, to Billy's recollection, had she spoken a word of endearment to him; and so terribly had she abused him that even while he was yet a little boy, scarce out of babyhood, he had learned to view her with a hatred as deep-rooted as is the affection of most little children for their mothers.

When he had come to man's estate he had defended himself from the woman's brutal assaults as he would have defended himself from another man—when she had struck, Billy had struck back; the only thing to his credit being that he never had struck her except in self-defense. Chastity in woman was to him a thing to joke of—he did not believe that it existed; for he judged other women by the one he knew best—his mother. And as he hated her, so he hated them all. He had doubly hated Barbara Harding since she not only was a woman, but a woman of the class he loathed.

And so it was strange and inexplicable that the suggestion of the girl's probable fate should have affected Billy Byrne as it did. He did not stop to reason about it at all—he simply knew that he felt a mad and unreasoning rage against the creatures that had borne the girl away. Outwardly Billy showed no indication of the turmoil that raged within his breast.

"We gotta find her, bo," he said to Theriere. "We gotta find the skirt."

Ordinarily Billy would have blustered about the terrible things he would do to the objects of his wrath when once he had them in his power; but now he was strangely quiet—only the firm set of his strong chin, and the steely glitter of his gray eyes gave token of the iron resolution within.

Theriere, who had been walking slowly to and fro about the dead men, now called the others to him.

"Here's their trail," he said. "If it's as plain as that all the way we won't be long in overhauling them. Come along."

Before he had the words half out of his mouth the mucker was forging ahead through the jungle along the well-marked spoor of the samurai.

"Wot kind of men do you suppose they are?" asked Red Sanders.

"Malaysian headhunters, unquestionably," replied Theriere.

Red Sanders shuddered inwardly. The appellation had a most gruesome sound.

"Come on!" cried Theriere, and started off after the mucker, who already was out of sight in the thick forest.

Red Sanders and Wison took a few steps after the Frenchman. Theriere turned once to see that they were following him, and then a turn in the trail hid them from his view. Red Sanders stopped.

"Damme if I'm goin' to get my coconut hacked off on any such wild-goose chase as this," he said to Wison.

"The girl's more'n likely dead long ago," said the other.

"Sure she is," returned Red Sanders, "an' if we go buttin' into that there thicket we'll be dead too. Ugh! Poor Miller. Poor Swenson. It's orful. Did you see wot they done to 'em beside cuttin' off their heads?"

"Yes," whispered Wison, looking suddenly behind him.

Red Sanders gave a little start, peering in the direction that his companion had looked.

"Wot was it?" he whimpered. "Wot did you do that fer?"

"I thought I seen something move there," replied Wison. "Fer Gawd's sake let's get outen this," and without waiting for a word of assent from his companion the sailor turned and ran at breakneck speed along the little path toward the spot where Divine, Blanco, and Bony Sawyer were stationed. When they arrived Bony was just on the point of setting out for the spring to fetch water, but at sight of the frightened, breathless men he returned to hear their story.

"What's up?" shouted Divine. "You men look as though you'd seen a ghost. Where are the others?"

"They're all murdered, and their heads cut off," cried Red Sanders. "We found the bunch that got Miller, Swenson, and the girl. They'd killed 'em all and was eatin' of 'em when we jumps 'em. Before we knew wot had happened about a thousand more of the devils came runnin' up. They got us separated, and when we seen Theriere and Byrne kilt we jest natch'rally beat it. Gawd, but it was orful."

"Do you think they will follow you?" asked Divine.

At the suggestion every head turned toward the trail down which the two panic-stricken men had just come. At the same moment a hoarse shout arose from the cove below and the five looked down to see a scene of wild activity upon the beach. The defection of Theriere's party had been discovered, as well as the absence of the girl and the theft of the provisions.

Skipper Simms was dancing about like a madman. His bellowed oaths rolled up the cliffs like thunder. Presently Ward caught a glimpse of the men at the top of the cliff above him.

"There they are!" he cried.

Skipper Simms looked up.

"The swabs!" he shrieked. "A-stealin' of our grub, an' abductin' of that there pore girl. The swabs! Lemme to 'em, I say; jest lemme to 'em."

"We'd all better go to 'em," said Ward. "We've got a fight on here sure. Gather up some rocks, men, an' come along. Skipper, you're too fat to do any fightin' on that there hillside, so you better stay here an' let one o' the men take your gun," for Ward knew so well the mettle of his superior that he much preferred his absence to his presence in the face of real fighting, and with the gun in the hands of a braver man it would be vastly more effective.

Ward himself was no lover of a fight, but he saw now that starvation might stare them in the face with their food gone; and everything be lost with the loss of the girl. For food and money a much more cowardly man than Bender Ward would fight to the death.

Up the face of the cliff they hurried, expecting momentarily to be either challenged or fired upon by those above them. Divine and his party looked down with mixed emotions upon those who were ascending in so threatening a manner. They found themselves truly between the devil and the deep sea.

Ward and his men were halfway up the cliff, yet Divine had made no move to repel them. He glanced timorously toward the dark forest behind from which he momentarily expected to see the savage, snarling faces of the headhunters appear.

"Surrender! You swabs," called Ward from below, "or we'll string the last mother's son of you to the yardarm."

For reply Blanco hurled a heavy fragment of rock at the assaulters. It grazed perilously close to Ward, against whom Blanco cherished a keen hatred. Instantly Ward's revolver barked, the bullet whistling close by Divine's head. L. Cortwrite Divine, cotillion leader, ducked behind Theriere's breastwork, where he lay sprawled upon his belly, trembling in terror.

Bony Sawyer and Red Sanders followed the example of their commander. Blanco and Wison alone made any attempt to repel the assault. The big Negro ran to Divine's side and snatched the terror-stricken man's revolver from his belt. Then turning he fired at Ward. The bullet, missing its intended victim, pierced the heart of a sailor directly behind him, and as the man crumpled to the ground, rolling down the steep declivity, his fellows sought cover.

Wison followed up the advantage with a shower of well-aimed missiles, and then hostilities ceased temporarily.

"Have they gone?" queried Divine, with trembling lips, noticing the quiet that followed the shot.

"Gone nothin', yo big cowahd," replied Blanco. "Do yo done suppose dat two men is a-gwine to stan' off five? Ef yo white-livered skunks 'ud git up an' fight we might have a chanct. I'se a good min' to cut out yo cowahdly heart fer yo, das wot I has—a-lyin' der on yo belly settin' dat kin' o' example to yo men!"

Divine's terror had placed him beyond the reach of contumely or reproach.

"What's the use of fighting them?" he whimpered. "We should never have left them. It's all the fault of that fool Theriere. What can we do against the savages of this awful island if we divide our forces? They will pick us off a few at a time just as they picked off Miller and Swenson, Theriere and Byrne. We ought to tell Ward about it, and call this foolish battle off."

"Now you're talkin'," cried Bony Sawyer. "I'm not a-goin' to squat up here any longer with my friends a-shootin' at me from below an' a lot of wild heathen creeping down on me from above to cut off my bloomin' head."

"Same here!" chimed in Red Sanders.

Blanco looked toward Wison. For his own part the Negro would not have been averse to returning to the fold could the thing be accomplished without danger of reprisal on the part of Skipper Simms and Ward; but he knew the men so well that he feared to trust them even should they seemingly acquiesce to any such proposal. On the other hand, he reasoned, it would be as much to their advantage to have the deserters return to them as it would to the deserters themselves, for when they had heard the story told by Red Sanders and Wison of the murder of the others of the party they too would realize the necessity for maintaining the strength of the little company to its fullest.

"I don't see that we're goin' to gain nothin' by fightin' 'em," said Wison. "There ain't nothin' in it any more nohow for nobody since the girl's gorn. Let's chuck it, an' see wot terms we can make with Squint Eye."

"Well," grumbled the Negro, "I can't fight 'em alone. What yo doin' dere, Bony?"

During the conversation Bony Sawyer had been busy with a stick and a piece of rag, and now as he turned toward his companions once more they saw that he had rigged a white flag of surrender. None interfered as he raised it above the edge of the breastwork.

Immediately there was a hail from below. It was Ward's voice.

"Surrenderin', eh? Comin' to your senses, are you?" he shouted.

Divine, feeling that immediate danger from bullets was past, raised his head above the edge of the earthwork.

"We have something to communicate, Mr. Ward," he called.

"Spit it out, then; I'm a-listenin'," called back the mate.

"Miss Harding, Mr. Theriere, Byrne, Miller, and Swenson have been captured and killed by native headhunters," said Divine.

Ward's eyes went wide, and he blew out his cheeks in surprise. Then his face went black with an angry scowl.

"You see what you done now, you blitherin' fools, you!" he cried, "with your funny business? You gone an' killed the goose what laid the golden eggs. Thought you'd get it all, didn't you? and now nobody won't get nothin', unless it is the halter. Nice lot o' numbskulls you be, an' whimperin' 'round now expectin' of us to take you back—well, I reckon not, not on your measly lives," and with that he raised his revolver to fire again at Divine.

The society man toppled over backward into the pit behind the breastwork before Ward had a chance to pull the trigger.

"Hol' on there mate!" cried Bony Sawyer; "there ain't no call now fer gettin' excited. Wait until you hear all we gotta say. You can't blame us pore sailormen. It was this here fool dude and that scoundrel Theriere that put us up to it. They told us that you an' Skipper Simms was a-fixin' to double-cross us all an' leave us here to starve on this Gawd-forsaken islan'.

Theriere said that he was with you when you planned it. That you wanted to git rid o' as many of us as you could so that you'd have more of the ransom to divide. So all we done was in self-defense, as it were.

"Why not let bygones be bygones, an' all of us join forces ag'in' these murderin' heathen? There won't be any too many of us at best—Red an' Wison seen more'n two thousan' of the man-eatin' devils. They're a-creepin' up on us from behin' right this minute, an' you can lay to that; an' the chances are that they got some special kind o' route into that there cove, an' maybe they're a-watchin' of you right now!"

Ward turned an apprehensive glance to either side. There was logic in Bony's proposal. They couldn't spare a man now. Later he could punish the offenders at his leisure—when he didn't need them any further.

"Will you swear on the Book to do your duty by Skipper Simms an' me if we take you back?" asked Ward.

"You bet," answered Bony Sawyer.

The others nodded their heads, and Divine sprang up and started down toward Ward.

"Hol' on you!" commanded the mate. "This here arrangement don' include you—it's jes' between Skipper Simms an' his sailors. You're a rank outsider, an' you butts in an' starts a mutiny. Ef you come back you gotta stand trial fer that—see?"

"You better duck, mister," advised Red Sanders; "they'll hang you sure."

Divine went white. To face trial before two such men as Simms and Ward meant death, of that he was positive. To flee into the forest meant death, almost equally certain, and much more horrible. The man went to his knees, lifting supplicating hands to the mate.

"For God's sake, Mr. Ward," he cried, "be merciful. I was led into this by Theriere. He lied to me just as he did to the men. You can't kill me—it would be murder—they'd hang you for it."

"We'll hang for this muss you got us into anyway, if we're ever caught," growled the mate. "Ef you hadn't a-carried the girl off to be murdered we might have had enough ransom money to have got clear some way, but now you gone and cooked the whole goose fer the lot of us."

"You can collect ransom on me," cried Divine, clutching at a straw. "I'll pay a hundred thousand myself the day you set me down in a civilized port, safe and free."

Ward laughed in his face.

"You ain't got a cent, you four-flusher," he cried. "Clinker put us next to that long before we sailed from Frisco."

"Clinker lies," cried Divine. "He doesn't know anything about it—I'm rich."

"Wot's de use ob chewin' de rag 'bout all dis," cried Blanco, seeing where he might square himself with Ward and Simms easily. "Does yo' take back all us sailormen, Mr. Ward, an' promise not t' punish none o' us, ef we swear to stick by yo' all in de future?"

"Yes," replied the mate.

Blanco took a step toward Divine.

"Den yo come along too as a prisoner, white man," and the burly black grasped Divine by the scruff of the neck and forced him before him down the steep trail toward the cove, and so the mutineers returned to the command of Skipper Simms, and L. Cortwrite Divine went with them as a prisoner, charged with a crime the punishment for which has been death since men sailed the seas.

XI
THE VILLAGE OF YOKA

For several minutes Barbara Harding lay where she had collapsed after the keen short sword of the daimio had freed her from the menace of his lust.

She was in a half-stupor that took cognizance only of a freezing terror and exhaustion. Presently, however, she became aware of her contact with the corpse beside her, and with a stifled cry she shrank away from it.

Slowly the girl regained her self-control and with it came the realization of the extremity of her danger. She rose to a sitting posture and turned her wide eyes toward the doorway to the adjoining room—the women and children seemed yet wrapped in slumber. It was evident that the man's scream had not disturbed them.

Barbara gained her feet and moved softly to the doorway. She wondered if she could cross the intervening space to the outer exit without detection. Once in the open she could flee to the jungle, and then there was a chance at least that she might find her way to the coast and Theriere.

She gripped the short sword which she still held, and took a step into the larger room. One of the women turned and half roused from sleep. The girl shrank back into the darkness of the chamber she had just quitted. The woman sat up and looked around. Then she rose and threw some sticks upon the fire that burned at one side of the dwelling. She crossed to a shelf and took down a cooking utensil. Barbara saw that she was about to commence the preparation of breakfast.

All hope of escape was thus ended, and the girl cautiously closed the door between the two rooms. Then she felt about the smaller apartment for some heavy object with which to barricade herself; but her search was fruitless. Finally she bethought herself of the corpse. That would hold the door against the accident of a child or dog pushing it open—it would be better than nothing, but could she bring herself to touch the loathsome thing?

The instinct of self-preservation will work wonders even with a frail and delicate woman. Barbara Harding steeled herself to the task, and after several moments of effort she succeeded in rolling the dead man against the door. The scraping sound of the body as she dragged it into position had sent cold shivers running up her spine.

She had removed the man's long sword and armor before attempting to move him, and now she crouched beside the corpse with both the swords beside her—she would sell her life dearly. Theriere's words came back to her now as they had when she was struggling in the water after the wreck of the *Halfmoon*: "but, by George, I intend to go down fighting." Well, she could do no less.

She could hear the movement of several persons in the next room now. The voices of women and children came to her distinctly. Many of the words were Japanese, but others were of a tongue with which she was not familiar.

Presently her own chamber began to lighten. She looked over her shoulder and saw the first faint rays of dawn showing through a small aperture near the roof and at the opposite end of the room. She rose and moved quickly toward it. By standing on tiptoe and pulling herself up a trifle with her hands upon the sill she was able to raise her eyes above the bottom of the window frame.

Beyond she saw the forest, not a hundred yards away; but when she attempted to crawl through the opening she discovered to her chagrin that it was too small to permit the passage of her body. And then there came a knocking on the door she had just quitted, and a woman's voice calling her lord and master to his morning meal.

Barbara ran quickly across the chamber to the door, the long sword raised above her head in both hands. Again the woman knocked, this time much louder, and raised her voice as she called again upon Oda Yorimoto to come out.

The girl within was panic-stricken. What should she do? With but a little respite she might enlarge the window sufficiently to permit her to escape into the forest, but the woman at the door evidently would not be denied. Suddenly an inspiration came to her. It was a forlorn hope, but well worth putting to the test.

"Hush!" she hissed through the closed door. "Oda Yorimoto sleeps. It is his wish that he be not disturbed."

For a moment there was silence beyond the door, and then the woman grunted, and Barbara heard her turn back, muttering to herself. The girl breathed a deep sigh of relief—she had received a brief reprieve from death. Again she turned to the window, where, with the short sword, she commenced her labor of enlarging it to permit the passage of her body. The work was necessarily slow because of the fact that it must proceed with utter noiselessness.

For an hour she worked, and then again came an interruption at the door. This time it was a man.

"Oda Yorimoto still sleeps," whispered the girl. "Go away and do not disturb him. He will be very angry if you awaken him."

But the man would not be put off so easily as had the woman. He still insisted.

"The daimio has ordered that there shall be a great hunt today for the heads of the *sei-yo-jin* who have landed upon Yoka," persisted the man. "He will be angry indeed if we do not call him in time to accomplish the task today. Let me speak with him, woman. I do not believe that Oda Yorimoto still sleeps. Why should I believe one of the *sei-yo-jin*? It may be that you have bewitched the daimio," and with that he pushed against the door.

The corpse gave a little, and the man glued his eyes to the aperture. Barbara held the sword behind her, and with her shoulder against the door attempted to reclose it.

"Go away!" she cried. "I shall be killed if you awaken Oda Yorimoto, and, if you enter, you, too, shall be killed."

The man stepped back from the door, and Barbara could hear him in low converse with some of the women of the household. A moment later he returned, and without a word of warning threw his whole weight against the portal. The corpse slipped back enough to permit the entrance of the man's body, and as he stumbled into the room the long sword of the Lord of Yoka fell full and keen across the back of his brown neck.

Without a sound he lunged to the floor, dead; but the women without had caught a fleeting glimpse of what had taken place within the little chamber, even before Barbara Harding could slam the door again, and with shrieks of rage and fright they rushed into the main street of the village shouting at the tops of their voices that Oda Yorimoto and Hawa Nisho had been slain by the woman of the *sei-yo-jin*.

Instantly, the village swarmed with samurai, women, children, and dogs. They rushed toward the hut of Oda Yorimoto, filling the outer chamber where they jabbered excitedly for several minutes, the warriors attempting to obtain a coherent story from the moaning women of the daimio's household.

Barbara Harding crouched close to the door, listening. She knew that the crucial moment was at hand; that there were at best but a few moments for her to live. A silent prayer rose from her parted lips. She placed the sharp point of Oda Yorimoto's short sword against her breast, and waited—waited for the coming of the men from the room beyond, snatching a few brief seconds from eternity ere she drove the weapon into her heart.

Theriere plunged through the jungle at a run for several minutes before he caught sight of the mucker.

"Are you still on the trail?" he called to the man before him.

"Sure," replied Byrne. "It's dead easy. They must o' been at least a dozen of 'em. Even a mutt like me couldn't miss it."

"We want to go carefully, Byrne," cautioned Theriere. "I've had experience with these fellows before, and I can tell you that you never know when one of 'em is near you till you feel a spear in your back, unless you're almighty watchful. We've got to make all the haste we can, of course, but it won't help Miss Harding any if we rush into an ambush and get our heads lopped off."

Byrne saw the wisdom of his companion's advice and tried to profit by it; but something which seemed to dominate him today carried him ahead at reckless, breakneck speed—the flight of an eagle would have been all too slow to meet the requirements of his unaccountable haste.

Once he found himself wondering why he was risking his life to avenge or rescue this girl whom he hated so. He tried to think that it was for the ransom—yes, that was it, the ransom. If he found her alive, and rescued her he should claim the lion's share of the booty.

Theriere too wondered why Byrne, of all the other men upon the *Halfmoon* the last that he should have expected to risk a thing for the sake of Miss Harding, should be the foremost in pursuit of her captors.

"I wonder how far behind Sanders and Wison are," he remarked to Byrne after they had been on the trail for the better part of an hour. "Hadn't we better wait for them to catch up with us? Four can do a whole lot more than two."

"Not wen Billy Byrne's one of de two," replied the mucker, and continued doggedly along the trail.

Another half-hour brought them suddenly in sight of a native village, and Billy Byrne was for dashing straight into the center of it and "cleaning it up," as he put it, but Theriere put his foot down firmly on that proposition, and finally Byrne saw that the other was right.

"The trail leads straight toward that place," said Theriere, "so I suppose here is where they brought her, but which of the huts she's in now we ought to try to determine before we make any attempt to rescue her. Well, by George! Now what do you think of that?"

"Tink o' wot?" asked the mucker. "Wot's eatin' yeh?"

"See those three men down there in the village, Byrne?" asked the Frenchman. "They're no more aboriginal headhunters than I am—they're Japs, man. There must be something wrong with our trailing, for it's as certain as fate itself that Japs are not headhunters."

"There ain't been nothin' fony about our trailin', bo," insisted Byrne, "an' whether Japs are bean collectors or not here's where de ginks dat copped de doll hiked fer, an if dey ain't dere now it's because dey went t'rough an' out de odder side, see."

"Hush, Byrne," whispered Theriere. "Drop down behind this bush. Someone is coming along this other trail to the right of us," and as he spoke he dragged the mucker down beside him.

For a moment they crouched, breathless and expectant, and then the slim figure of an almost nude boy emerged from the foliage close beside and entered the trail toward the village. Upon his head he bore a bundle of firewood.

When he was directly opposite the watchers Theriere sprang suddenly upon him, clapping a silencing hand over the boy's mouth. In Japanese he whispered a command for silence.

"We shall not harm you if you keep still," he said, "and answer our questions truthfully. What village is that?"

"It is the chief city of Oda Yorimoto, Lord of Yoka," replied the youth. "I am Oda Iseka, his son."

"And the large hut in the center of the village street is the palace of Oda Yorimoto?" guessed Theriere shrewdly.

"It is."

The Frenchman was not unversed in the ways of orientals, and he guessed also that if the white girl were still alive in the village she would be in no other hut than that of the most powerful chief; but he wished to verify his deductions if possible. He knew that a direct question as to the whereabouts of the girl would call forth either a clever oriental evasion or an equally clever oriental lie.

"Does Oda Yorimoto intend slaying the white woman that was brought to his house last night?" asked Theriere.

"How should the son know the intentions of his father?" replied the boy.

"Is she still alive?" continued Theriere.

"How should I know, who was asleep when she was brought, and only heard the womenfolk this morning whispering that Oda Yorimoto had brought home a new woman the night before."

"Could you not see her with your own eyes?" asked Theriere.

"My eyes cannot pass through the door of the little room behind, in which they still were when I left to gather firewood a half hour since," retorted the youth.

"Wot's de Chink sayin'?" asked Billy Byrne, impatient of the conversation, no word of which was intelligible to him.

"He says, in substance," replied Theriere, with a grin, "that Miss Harding is still alive, and in the back room of that largest hut in the center of the village street; but," and his face clouded, "Oda Yorimoto, the chief of the tribe, is with her."

The mucker sprang to his feet with an oath, and would have bolted for the village had not Theriere laid a detaining hand upon his shoulder.

"It is too late, my friend," he said sadly, "to make haste now. We may, if we are cautious, be able to save her life, and later, possibly, avenge her wrong. Let us act coolly, and after some manner of plan, so that we may work together, and not throw our lives away uselessly. The chance is that neither of us will come out of that village alive, but we must minimize that chance to the utmost if we are to serve Miss Harding."

"Well, wot's de word?" asked the mucker, for he saw that Theriere was right.

"The jungle approaches the village most closely on the opposite side— the side in rear of the chief's hut," pointed out Theriere. "We must circle about until we can reach that point undetected, then we may formulate further plans from what our observations there develop."

"An' dis?" Byrne shoved a thumb at Oda Iseka.

"We'll take him with us—it wouldn't be safe to let him go now."

"Why not croak him?" suggested Byrne.

"Not unless we have to," replied Theriere; "he's just a boy—we'll doubtless have all the killing we want among the men before we get out of this."

"I never did have no use fer Chinks," said the mucker, as though in extenuation of his suggestion that they murder the youth. For some unaccountable reason he had felt a sudden compunction because of his thoughtless remark. What in the world was coming over him, he wondered. He'd be wearing white pants and playing lawn tennis presently if he continued to grow much softer and more unmanly.

So the three set out through the jungle, following a trail which led around to the north of the village. Theriere walked ahead with the boy's arm in his grasp. Byrne followed closely behind. They reached their destination in the rear of Oda Yorimoto's "palace" without interruption or detection. Here they reconnoitered through the thick foliage.

"Dere's a little winder in de back of de house," said Byrne. "Dat must be where dem guys cooped up de little broiler."

"Yes," said Theriere, "it would be in the back room which the boy described. First let's tie and gag this young heathen, and then we can proceed to business without fear of alarm from him," and the Frenchman stripped a long, grass rope from about the waist of his prisoner, with which he was securely trussed up, a piece of his loin cloth being forced into his mouth as a gag, and secured there by another strip, torn from the same garment, which was passed around the back of the boy's head.

"Rather uncomfortable, I imagine," commented Theriere; "but not particularly painful or dangerous—and now to business!"

"I'm goin' to make a break fer dat winder," announced the mucker, "and youse squat here in de tall grass wid yer gat an' pick off any fresh guys dat get gay in back here. Den, if I need youse you can come a-runnin' an' open up all over de shop wid de artillery, or if I gets de lizzie outen de jug an' de Chinks push me too clost youse'll be here where yeh can pick 'em off easy-like."

"You'll be taking all the risk that way, Byrne," objected Theriere, "and that's not fair."

"One o' us is pretty sure to get hurted," explained the mucker in defense of his plan, "an, if it's a croak it's a lot better dat it be me than youse, fer the girl wouldn't be crazy about bein' lef' alone wid me—she ain't got no use fer the likes o' me. Now youse are her kin, an' so youse stay here w'ere yeh can help her after I git her out—I don't want nothing to do wid her anyhow. She gives me a swift pain, and," he added as though it were an afterthought, "I ain't got no use fer dat ransom eider—youse can have dat, too."

"Hold on, Byrne," cried Theriere; "I have something to say, too. I do not see how I can expect you to believe me; but under the circumstances, when one of us and maybe both are pretty sure to die before the day is much older, it wouldn't be worth while lying. I do not want that damned ransom any more, either. I only want to do what I can to right the wrong that I have helped to perpetrate against Miss Harding. I—I—Byrne, I love her. I shall never tell her so, for I am not the sort of man a decent girl would care to marry; but I did want the chance to make a clean breast to her of all my connection with the whole dirty business, and get her forgiveness if I could; but first I wanted to prove my repentance by helping her to civilization in safety, and delivering her to her friends without the payment of a cent of money. I may never be able to do that now; but if I die in the attempt, and you don't, I wish that you would tell her what I have just told you. Paint me as black as you can—you couldn't commence to make me as black as I have been—but let her know that for love of her I turned white at the last minute. Byrne, she is the best girl that you or I ever saw—we're not fit to breathe the same air that she breathes. Now you can see why I should like to go first."

"I t'ought youse was soft on her," replied the mucker, "an' dat's de reason w'y youse otter not go first; but wot's de use o' chewin', les flip a coin to see w'ich goes an w'ich stays—got one?"

Theriere felt in his trousers' pocket, fishing out a dime.

"Heads, you go; tails, I go," he said and spun the silver piece in the air, catching it in the flat of his open palm.

"It's heads," said the mucker, grinning. "Gee! Wot's de racket?"

Both men turned toward the village, where a jabbering mob of half-caste Japanese had suddenly appeared in the streets, hurrying toward the hut of Oda Yorimoto.

"Somepin doin', eh?" said the mucker. "Well, here goes—s'long!" And he broke from the cover of the jungle and dashed across the clearing toward the rear of Oda Yorimoto's hut.

XII
The Fight in the Palace

Barbara Harding heard the samurai in the room beyond her prison advancing toward the door that separated them from her. She pressed the point of the daimio's sword close to her heart. A heavy knock fell upon the door and at the same instant the girl was startled by a noise behind her—a noise at the little window at the far end of the room.

Turning to face this new danger, she was startled into a little cry of surprise to see the head and shoulders of the mucker framed in the broken square of the half-demolished window.

The girl did not know whether to feel renewed hope or utter despair. She could not forget the heroism of her rescue by this brutal fellow when the *Halfmoon* had gone to pieces the day before, nor could she banish from her mind his threats of violence toward her, or his brutal treatment of Mallory and Theriere. And the question arose in her mind as to whether she would be any better off in his power than in the clutches of the savage samurai.

Billy Byrne had heard the knock upon the door before which the girl knelt. He had seen the corpses of the dead men at her feet. He had observed the telltale position of the sword which the girl held to her breast and he had read much of the story of the impending tragedy at a glance.

"Cheer up, kid!" he whispered. "I'll be wid youse in a minute, an' Theriere's out here too, to help youse if I can't do it alone."

The girl turned toward the door again.

"Wait," she cried to the samurai upon the other side, "until I move the dead men, then you may come in, their bodies bar the door now."

All that kept the warriors out was the fear that possibly Oda Yorimoto might not be dead after all, and that should they force their way into the room without his permission some of them would suffer for their temerity. Naturally none of them was keen to lose his head for nothing, but the moment that the girl spoke of the dead "men" they knew that Oda Yorimoto had been slain, too, and with one accord they rushed the little door.

The girl threw all her weight against her side, while the dead men, each to the extent of his own weight, aided the woman who had killed them in her effort to repulse their fellows; and behind the three Billy Byrne kicked and tore at the mud wall about the window in a frantic effort to enlarge the aperture sufficiently to permit his huge bulk to pass through into the little room.

The mucker won to the girl's side first, and snatching Oda Yorimoto's long sword from the floor he threw his great weight against the door, and commanded the girl to make for the window and escape to the forest as quickly as she could.

"Theriere is waiting dere," he said. "He will see youse de moment yeh reach de window, and den youse will be safe."

"But you!" cried the girl. "What of you?"

"Never yeh mind me," commanded Billy Byrne. "Youse jes' do as I tells yeh, see? Now, beat it," and he gave her a rough shove toward the window.

And then, between the combined efforts of the samurai upon one side and Billy Byrne of Kelly's gang upon the other the frail door burst from its rotten hinges and fell to one side.

The first of the samurai into the little room was cleft from crown to breast bone with the keen edge of the sword of the Lord of Yoka wielded by the mighty arm of the mucker. The second took the count with a left hook to the jaw, and then all that could crowd through the little door swarmed upon the husky bruiser from Grand Avenue.

Barbara Harding took one look at the carnage behind her and then sprang to the window. At a short distance she saw the jungle and at its edge what she was sure was the figure of a man crouching in the long grass.

"Mr. Theriere!" she cried. "Quick! They are killing Byrne," and then she turned back into the room, and with the short sword which she still grasped in her hand sprang to the side of the mucker who was offering his life to save her.

Byrne cast a horrified glance at the figure fighting by his side.

"Fer de love o' Mike! Beat it!" he cried. "Duck! Git out o' here!"

But the girl only smiled up bravely into his face and kept her place beside him. The mucker tried to push her behind him with one hand while he fought with the other, but she drew away from him to come up again a little farther from him.

The samurai were pushing them closely now. Three men at a time were reaching for the mucker with their long swords. He was bleeding from numerous wounds, but at his feet lay two dead warriors, while a third crawled away with a mortal wound in his abdomen.

Barbara Harding devoted her energies to thrusting and cutting at those who tried to press past the mucker, that they might take him from behind. The battle could not last long, so unequal were the odds. She saw the room beyond filled with surging warriors all trying to force their way within reach of the great white man who battled like some demigod of old in the close, dark, evil warren of the daimio.

She shot a side glance at the man. He was wonderful! The fire of battle had transformed him. No longer was he the sullen, sulky, hulking brute she had first known upon the *Halfmoon*. Instead, huge, muscular, alert, he towered above his pygmy antagonists, his gray eyes gleaming, a half-smile upon his strong lips.

She saw the long sword, wielded awkwardly in his unaccustomed hands, beat down the weapons of his skilled foemen by the very ferocity of its hurtling attack. She saw it pass through a man's shoulder, cleaving bone and muscle as if they had been cheese, until it stopped two-thirds across its victim's body, cutting him almost in two.

She saw a samurai leap past her champion's guard in an attempt to close upon him with a dagger, and when she had rushed forward to thwart the fellow's design she had seen Byrne swing his mighty left to the warrior's face with a blow that might well have felled an ox. Then another leaped into closer quarters and she saw Byrne at the same instant bury his sword in the body of a dark-visaged devil who looked more Malay than Jap, and as the stricken man fell she saw the hilt of the mucker's blade wrenched from his grip by the dead body of his foe. The samurai who had closed upon Byrne at that instant found his enemy unarmed, and with a howl of delight he struck full at the broad chest with his long, thin dagger.

But Billy Byrne was not to be dispatched so easily. With his left forearm he struck up the hand that wielded the menacing blade, and then catching the fellow by the shoulder swung him around, grasped him about the waist and lifting him above his head hurled him full in the faces of the swordsmen who were pressing through the narrow doorway.

Almost simultaneously a spear shot through a tiny opening in the ranks before Billy Byrne, and with a little gasp of dismay the huge fellow pitched forward upon his face. At the same instant a shot rang out behind Barbara Harding, and Theriere leaped past her to stand across the body of the fallen mucker.

With the sound of the shot a samurai sank to the floor, dead, and the others, unaccustomed to firearms, drew back in dismay. Again Theriere fired point-blank into the crowded room, and this time two men fell, struck by the same bullet. Once more the warriors retreated, and with an exultant yell Theriere followed up his advantage by charging menacingly upon them. They stood for a moment, then wavered, turned and fled from the hut.

When Theriere turned back toward Barbara Harding he found her kneeling beside the mucker.

"Is he dead?" asked the Frenchman.

"No. Can we lift him together and get him through that window?"

"It is the only way," replied Theriere, "and we must try it."

They seized upon the huge body and dragged it to the far end of the room, but despite their best efforts the two were not able to lift the great, inert mass of flesh and bone and muscle and pass it through the tiny opening.

"What shall we do?" cried Theriere.

"We must stay here with him," replied Barbara Harding. "I could never desert the man who has fought so noble a fight for me while a breath of life remained in him."

Theriere groaned.

"Nor I," he said; "but you—he has given his life to save yours. Should you render his sacrifice of no avail now?"

"I cannot go alone," she answered simply, "and I know that you will not leave him. There is no other way—we must stay."

At this juncture the mucker opened his eyes.

"Who hit me?" he murmured. "Jes' show me de big stiff."

Theriere could not repress a smile. Barbara Harding again knelt beside the man.

"No one hit you, Mr. Byrne," she said. "You were struck by a spear and are badly wounded."

Billy Byrne opened his eyes a little wider, turning them until they rested on the beautiful face of the girl so close to his.

"*Mr.* Byrne!" he ejaculated in disgust. "Forget it. Wot do youse tink I am, one of dose paper-collar dudes?"

Then he sat up. Blood was flowing from a wound in his chest, saturating his shirt, and running slowly to the earth floor. There were two flesh wounds upon his head—one above the right eye and the other extending entirely across the left cheek from below the eye to the lobe of the ear—but these he had received earlier in the fracas. From crown to heel the man was a mass of blood. Through his crimson mask he looked at the pile of bodies in the far end of the room, and a broad grin cracked the dried blood about his mouth.

"Wot we done to dem Chinks was sure a plenty, kiddo," he remarked to Miss Harding, and then he came to his feet, seemingly as strong as ever, shaking himself like a great bull. "But I guess it's lucky youse butted in when you did, old pot," he added, turning toward Theriere; "dey jest about had me down fer de long count."

Barbara Harding was looking at the man in wide-eyed amazement. A moment before she had been expecting him, momentarily, to breathe his last—now he was standing before her talking as unconcernedly as though he had not received a scratch—he seemed totally unaware of his wounds. At least he was entirely indifferent to them.

"You're pretty badly hurt, old man," said Theriere. "Do you feel able to make the attempt to get to the jungle? The Japs will be back in a moment."

"Sure!" cried Billy Byrne. "Come ahead," and he sprang for the window. "Pass de kid up to me. Quick! Dey're comin' from in back."

Theriere lifted Barbara Harding to the mucker who drew her through the opening. Then Billy extended a hand to the Frenchman, and a moment later the three stood together outside the hut.

A dozen samurai were running toward them from around the end of the "Palace." The jungle lay a hundred yards across the clearing. There was no time to be lost.

"You go first with Miss Harding," cried Theriere. "I'll cover our retreat with my revolver, following close behind you."

The mucker caught the girl in his arms, throwing her across his shoulder. The blood from his wounds smeared her hands and clothing.

"Hang tight, kiddo," he cried, and started at a brisk trot toward the forest.

Theriere kept close behind the two, reserving his fire until it could be effectively delivered. With savage yells the samurai leaped after their escaping quarry. The natives all carried the long, sharp spears of the aboriginal headhunters. Their swords swung in their harness, and their ancient armor clanked as they ran.

It was a strange, weird picture that the oddly contrasted party presented as they raced across the clearing of this forgotten isle toward a jungle as primitive as when "the evening and the morning were the third day." An American girl of the highest social caste borne in the arms of that most vicious of all social pariahs—the criminal mucker of the slums of a great city—and defending them with drawn revolver, a French count and soldier of fortune, while in their wake streamed a yelling pack of half-caste demons clothed in the habiliments of sixteenth century Japan, and wielding the barbarous spears of the savage head-hunting aborigines whose fierce blood coursed in their veins with that of the descendants of Taka-mi-musu-bi-no-kami.

Three-quarters of the distance had been covered in safety before the samurai came within safe spear range of the trio. Theriere, seeing the danger to the girl, dropped back a few paces hoping to hold the brown warriors from her. The foremost of the pursuers raised his weapon aloft, carrying his spear hand back of his shoulder for the throw. Theriere's revolver spoke, and the man pitched forward, rolling over and over before he came to rest.

A howl of rage went up from the samurai, and a half-dozen spears leaped at long range toward Theriere. One of the weapons transfixed his thigh, bringing him to earth. Byrne was at the forest's edge as the Frenchman fell—it was the girl, though, who witnessed the catastrophe.

"Stop!" she cried. "Mr. Theriere is down."

The mucker halted, and turned his head in the direction of the Frenchman, who had raised himself to one elbow and was firing at the advancing enemy. He dropped the girl to her feet.

"Wait here!" he commanded and sprang back toward Theriere.

Before he reached him another spear had caught the man full in the chest, toppling him, unconscious, to the earth. The samurai were rushing rapidly upon the wounded officer—it was a question who would reach him first.

Theriere had been nipped in the act of reloading his revolver. It lay beside him now, the cylinder full of fresh cartridges. The mucker was first to his side, and snatching the weapon from the ground fired coolly and rapidly at the advancing Japanese. Four of them went down before that deadly fusillade; but the mucker cursed beneath his breath because of his two misses.

Byrne's stand checked the brown men momentarily, and in the succeeding lull the man lifted the unconscious Frenchman to his shoulder and bore him back to the forest. In the shelter of the jungle they laid him upon the ground. To the girl it seemed that the frightful wound in his chest must prove fatal within a few moments.

Byrne, apparently unmoved by the seriousness of Theriere's condition, removed the man's cartridge belt and buckled it about his own waist, replacing the six empty shells in the revolver with six fresh ones. Presently he noticed the bound and gagged Oda Iseka lying in the brush behind them where he and Theriere had left him. The samurai were now sneaking cautiously toward their refuge. A sudden inspiration came to the mucker.

"Didn't I hear youse chewin' de rag wit de Chinks wen I hit de dump over dere?" he asked of Barbara.

The girl, oddly, understood him. She nodded her head, affirmatively.

"Youse savvy deyre lingo den, eh?"

"A little."

"Tell dis gazimbat to wise his pals to de fact dat I'll croak 'im, if dey don't beat it, an' let us make our getaway. Theriere says as how he's kink when his ole man croaks, an' his ole man was de guy youse put to sleep in de chicken coop," explained the mucker lucidly; "so dis slob's kink hisself now."

Barbara Harding was quick to see the strength of the man's suggestion. Stepping to the edge of the clearing in full view of the advancing enemy, with the mucker at her side, revolver in hand, she called to them in the language of their forbears to listen to her message. Then she explained that they held the son of Oda Yorimoto prisoner, and that his life would be the price of any further attack upon them.

The samurai conferred together for a moment, then one of them called out that they did not believe her, that Oda Iseka, son of Oda Yorimoto, was safe in the village.

"Wait!" replied the girl. "We will show him to you," and turning to Byrne she asked him to fetch the youth.

When the white man returned with the boy in his arms, a wail of mingled anguish and rage rose from the natives.

"If you molest us no further we shall not harm him," cried Barbara, "and when we leave your island we shall set him free; but renew your attack upon us and this white man who holds him says that he will cut out his heart and feed it to the fox," which was rather a bloodthirsty statement for so gentle a character as Barbara Harding; but she knew enough of the superstitious fears of the ancient Japanese to feel confident that this threat would have considerable weight with the subjects of the young Lord of Yoka.

Again the natives conferred in whispers. Finally he who had acted as spokesman before turned toward the strangers.

"We shall not harm you," he said, "so long as you do not harm Oda Iseka; but we shall watch you always until you leave the island, and if harm befalls him then shall you never leave, for we shall kill you all."

Barbara translated the man's words to the mucker.

"Do youse fall fer dat?" he asked.

"I think they will be careful to make no open assault upon us," replied the girl; "but never for an instant must we cease our watchfulness for at the first opportunity I am sure that they will murder us."

They turned back to Theriere now. The man still lay, unconscious and moaning, where Byrne had deposited him. The mucker removed the gag from Oda Iseka's mouth.

"Which way is water? Ask him," he said to Barbara.

The girl put the question.

"He says that straight up this ravine behind us there is a little spring," translated the girl.

Byrne lifted Theriere in his arms, after loosening Oda Iseka's feet and tethering him to his own belt with the same grass rope; then he motioned the youth up the ravine.

"Walk beside me," he said to Barbara Harding, "an' keep yer lamps peeled behind."

Thus, in silence, the party commenced the ascent of the trail which soon became rough and precipitous, while behind them, under cover of the brush, sneaked four trailing samurai.

After half an hour of the most arduous climbing the mucker commenced to feel the effects of loss of blood from his many wounds. He coughed a little now from the exertion, and when he did the blood spurted anew from the fresh wound in his breast.

Yet there was no wavering or weakness apparent to the girl who marched beside him, and she wondered at the physical endurance of the man. But when at last they came to a clear pool of water, half hidden by overhanging rocks and long masses of depending mosses, in the midst of a natural grotto of enchanting loveliness, and Oda Iseka signaled that their journey was at an end, Byrne laid Theriere gently upon the flower-starred sward, and with a little, choking gasp collapsed, unconscious, beside the Frenchman

Barbara Harding was horror-stricken. She suddenly realized that she had commenced to feel that this giant of the slums was invulnerable, and with the thought came another—that to him she had come to look more than to Theriere for eventual rescue; and now, here she found herself in the center of a savage island, surrounded as she felt confident she was by skulking murderers, with only two dying white men and a brown hostage as companions.

And now Oda Iseka took in the situation, and with a grin of triumph raised his voice in a loud halloo.

"Come quickly, my people!" he cried; "for both the white men are dying," and from the jungle below them came an answering shout.

"We come, Oda Iseka, Lord of Yoka! Your faithful samurai come "

XIII
A Gentleman of France

At the sound of the harsh voices so close upon her Barbara Harding was galvanized into instant action. Springing to Byrne's side she whipped Theriere's revolver from his belt, where it reposed about the fallen mucker's hips, and with it turned like a tigress upon the youth.

"Quick!" she cried. "Tell them to go back—that I shall kill you if they come closer."

The boy shrank back in terror before the fiery eyes and menacing attitude of the white girl, and then with the terror that animated him ringing plainly in his voice he screamed to his henchmen to halt.

Relieved for a moment at least from immediate danger Barbara Harding turned her attention toward the two unconscious men at her feet. From appearances it seemed that either might breathe his last at any moment, and as she looked at Theriere a wave of compassion swept over her, and the tears welled to her eyes; yet it was to the mucker that she first ministered—why, she could not for the life of her have explained.

She dashed cold water from the spring upon his face. She bathed his wrists, and washed his wounds, tearing strips from her skirt to bandage the horrid gash upon his breast in an effort to stanch the flow of lifeblood that welled forth with the man's every breath.

And at last she was rewarded by seeing the flow of blood quelled and signs of returning consciousness appear. The mucker opened his eyes. Close above him bent the radiant vision of Barbara Harding's face. Upon his fevered forehead he felt the soothing strokes of her cool, soft hand. He closed his eyes again to battle with the effeminate realization that he enjoyed this strange, new sensation—the sensation of being ministered to by a gentle woman—and, perish the thought, by a gentlewoman!

With an effort he raised himself to one elbow, scowling at her.

"Gwan," he said; "I ain't no boob dude. Cut out de mush. Lemme be. Beat it!"

Hurt, more than she would have cared to admit, Barbara Harding turned away from her ungrateful and ungracious patient, to repeat her ministrations to the Frenchman. The mucker read in her expression something of the wound his words had inflicted, and he lay thinking upon the matter for some time, watching her deft, white fingers as they worked over the scarce breathing Theriere.

He saw her wash the blood and dirt from the ghastly wound in the man's chest, and as he watched he realized what a world of courage it must require for a woman of her stamp to do gruesome work of this sort. Never before would such a thought have occurred to him. Neither would he have cared at all for the pain his recent words to the girl might have inflicted. Instead he would have felt keen enjoyment of her discomfiture.

And now another strange new emotion took possession of him. It was none other than a desire to atone in some way for his words. What wonderful transformation was taking place in the heart of the Kelly gangster?

"Say!" he blurted out suddenly.

Barbara Harding turned questioning eyes toward him. In them was the cold, haughty aloofness again that had marked her cognizance of him upon the *Halfmoon*—the look that had made his hate of her burn most fiercely. It took the mucker's breath away to witness it, and it made the speech he had contemplated more difficult than ever—nay, almost impossible. He coughed nervously, and the old dark, lowering scowl returned to his brow.

"Did you speak?" asked Miss Harding, icily.

Billy Byrne cleared his throat, and then there blurted from his lips not the speech that he had intended, but a sudden, hateful rush of words which seemed to emanate from another personality, from one whom Billy Byrne once had been.

"Ain't dat boob croaked yet?" he growled.

The shock of that brutal question brought Barbara Harding to her feet. In horror she looked down at the man who had spoken thus of a brave and noble comrade in the face of death itself. Her eyes blazed angrily as hot, bitter words rushed to her lips, and then of a sudden she thought of Byrne's self-sacrificing heroism in returning to Theriere's side in the face of the advancing samurai—of the cool courage he had displayed as he carried the unconscious man back to the jungle—of the devotion, almost superhuman, that had sustained him as he struggled, uncomplaining, up the steep mountain path with the burden of the Frenchman's body the while his own lifeblood left a crimson trail behind him.

Such deeds and these words were incompatible in the same individual. There could be but one explanation—Byrne must be two men, with as totally different characters as though they had possessed separate bodies. And who may say that her hypothesis was not correct—at least it seemed that Billy Byrne was undergoing a metamorphosis, and at the instant there was still a question as to which personality should eventually dominate.

Byrne turned away from the reproach which replaced the horror in the girl's eyes, and with a tired sigh let his head fall upon his outstretched arm. The girl watched him for a moment, a puzzled expression upon her face, and then returned to work above Theriere.

The Frenchman's respiration was scarcely appreciable, yet after a time he opened his eyes and looked up wearily. At sight of the girl he smiled wanly, and tried to speak, but a fit of coughing flecked his lips with bloody foam, and again he closed his eyes. Fainter and fainter came his breathing, until it was with difficulty that the girl detected any movement of his breast whatever. She thought that he was dying, and she was afraid. Wistfully she looked toward the mucker. The man still lay with his head buried in his arm, but whether he were wrapped in thought, in slumber, or in death the girl could not tell. At the final thought she went white with terror.

Slowly she approached the man, and leaning over placed her hand upon his shoulder.

"Mr. Byrne!" she whispered.

The mucker turned his face toward her. It looked tired and haggard.

"Wot is it?" he asked, and his tone was softer than she had ever heard it.

"I think Mr. Theriere is dying," she said, "and I—I—Oh, I am so afraid."

The man flushed to the roots of his hair. All that he could think of were the ugly words he had spoken a short time before—and now Theriere was dying! Byrne would have laughed had anyone suggested that he entertained any other sentiment than hatred toward the second officer of the *Halfmoon*—that is he would have twenty-four hours before; but now, quite unexpectedly, he realized that he didn't want Theriere to die, and then it dawned upon him that a new sentiment had been born within him—a sentiment to which he had been a stranger all his hard life—friendship.

He felt friendship for Theriere! It was unthinkable, and yet the mucker knew that it was so. Painfully he crawled over to the Frenchman's side.

"Theriere!" he whispered in the man's ear.

The officer turned his head wearily.

"Do youse know me, old pal?" asked the mucker, and Barbara Harding knew from the man's voice that there were tears in his eyes; but what she did not know was that they welled there in response to the words the mucker had just spoken—the nearest approach to words of endearment that ever had passed his lips.

Theriere reached up and took Byrne's hand. It was evident that he too had noted the unusual quality of the mucker's voice.

"Yes, old man," he said very faintly, and then "water, please."

Barbara Harding brought him a drink, holding his head against her knee while he drank. The cool liquid seemed to give him new strength for presently he spoke, quite strongly.

"I'm going, Byrne," he said; "but before I go I want to tell you that of all the brave men I ever have known I have learned within the past few days to believe that you are the bravest. A week ago I thought you were a coward— I ask your forgiveness."

"Ferget it," whispered Byrne, "fer a week ago I guess I was a coward. Dere seems to be more'n one kind o' nerve—I'm jest a-learnin' of the right kind, I guess."

"And, Byrne," continued Theriere, "don't forget what I asked of you before we tossed up to see which should enter Oda Yorimoto's house."

"I'll not ferget," said Billy.

"Goodbye, Byrne," whispered Theriere. "Take good care of Miss Harding."

"Goodbye, old pal," said the mucker. His voice broke, and two big tears rolled down the cheeks of "de toughest guy on de Wes' Side."

Barbara Harding stepped to Theriere's side.

"Goodbye, my friend," she said. "God will reward you for your friendship, your bravery, and your devotion. There must be a special honor roll in heaven for such noble men as you."

Theriere smiled sadly.

"Byrne will tell you all," he said, "except who I am—he does not know that."

"Is there any message, my friend," asked the girl, "that you would like to have me deliver?"

Theriere remained silent for a moment as though thinking.

"My name," he said, "is Henri Theriere. I am the Count de Cadenet of France. There is no message, Miss Harding, other than you see fit to deliver to my relatives. They lived in Paris the last I heard of them—my brother, Jacques, was a deputy."

His voice had become so low and weak that the girl could scarce distinguish his words. He gasped once or twice, and then tried to speak again. Barbara leaned closer, her ear almost against his lips.

"Goodbye—dear." The words were almost inaudible, and then the body stiffened with a little convulsive tremor, and Henri Theriere, Count de Cadenet, passed over into the keeping of his noble ancestors.

"He's gone!" whispered the girl, dry-eyed but suffering. She had not loved this man, she realized, but she had learned to think of him as her one true friend in their little world of scoundrels and murderers. She had cared for him very much—it was entirely possible that some day she might have come to return his evident affection for her. She knew nothing of the seamy side of his hard life. She had guessed nothing of the scoundrelly duplicity that had marked his first advances toward her. She thought of him only as a true, brave gentleman, and in that she was right, for whatever Henri Theriere might have been in the past the last few days of his life had revealed him in the true colors that birth and nature had intended him to wear through a brilliant career. In his death he had atoned for many sins.

And in those last few days he had transferred, all unknown to himself or the other man, a measure of the gentility and chivalry that were his birthright, for, unrealizing, Billy Byrne was patterning himself after the man he had hated and had come to love.

After the girl's announcement the mucker had continued to sit with bowed head staring at the ground. Afternoon had deepened into evening, and now the brief twilight of the tropics was upon them—in a few moments it would be dark.

Presently Byrne looked up. His eyes wandered about the tiny clearing. Suddenly he staggered to his feet. Barbara Harding sprang up, startled by the evident alarm in the man's attitude.

"What is it?" she whispered. "What is the matter?"

"De Chink!" he cried. "Where is de Chink?"

And, sure enough, Oda Iseka had disappeared!

The youthful daimio had taken advantage of the preoccupation of his captors during the last moments of Theriere to gnaw in two the grass rope which bound him to the mucker, and with hands still fast bound behind him had slunk into the jungle path that led toward his village.

"They will be upon us again now at any moment," whispered the girl. "What can we do?"

"We better duck," replied the mucker. "I hates to run away from a bunch of Chinks, but I guess it's up to us to beat it."

"But poor Mr. Theriere?" asked the girl.

"I'll have to bury him close by," replied the mucker. "I don't tink I could pack him very fer tonight—I don't feel jest quite fit agin yet. You wouldn't mind much if I buried him here, would you?"

"There is no other way, Mr. Byrne," replied the girl. "You mustn't think of trying to carry him far. We have done all we can for poor Mr. Theriere— you have almost given your life for him already—and it wouldn't do any good to carry his dead body with us."

"I hates to tink o' dem head-huntin' Chinks gettin' him," replied Byrne; "but maybe I kin hide his grave so's dey won't tumble to it."

"You are in no condition to carry him at all," said the girl. "I doubt if you can go far even without any burden."

The mucker grinned.

"Youse don't know me, miss," he said, and stooping he lifted the body of the Frenchman to his broad shoulder, and started up the hillside through the trackless underbrush.

It would have been an impossible feat for an ordinary man in the pink of condition, but the mucker, weak from pain and loss of blood, strode sturdily upward while the marveling girl followed close behind him. A hundred yards above the spring they came upon a little level spot, and here with the two swords of Oda Yorimoto which they still carried they scooped a shallow grave in which they placed all that was mortal of the Count de Cadenet.

Barbara Harding whispered a short prayer above the new-made grave, while the mucker stood with bowed head beside her. Then they turned to their flight again up the wild face of the savage mountain. The moon came up at last to lighten the way for them, but it was a rough and dangerous climb at best. In many places they were forced to walk hand in hand for considerable distances, and twice the mucker had lifted the girl bodily in his arms to bear her across particularly dangerous or difficult stretches.

Shortly after midnight they struck a small mountain stream up which they followed until in a natural cul-de-sac they came upon its source and found their farther progress barred by precipitous cliffs which rose above them, sheer and unscalable.

They had entered the little amphitheater through a narrow, rocky pass in the bottom of which the tiny stream flowed, and now, weak and tired, the mucker was forced to admit that he could go no farther.

"Who'd o' t'ought dat I was such a sissy?" he exclaimed disgustedly.

"I think that you are very wonderful, Mr. Byrne," replied the girl. "Few men could have gone through what you have today and been alive now."

The mucker made a deprecatory gesture.

"I suppose we gotta make de best of it," he said. "Anyhow, dis ought to make a swell joint to defend."

Weak as he was he searched about for some soft grasses which he threw in a pile beneath a stunted tree that grew well back in the hollow.

"Here's yer downy," he said, with an attempt at jocularity. "Now you'd better hit de hay, fer youse must be dead fagged."

"Thanks!" replied the girl. "I *am* nearly dead."

So tired was she that she was asleep almost as soon as she had found a comfortable position in the thick mat of grass, so that she gave no thought to the strange position in which circumstance had placed her.

The sun was well up the following morning before the girl awakened, and it was several minutes before she could readjust herself to her strange surroundings. At first she thought that she was alone, but finally she discerned a giant figure standing at the opening which led from their mountain retreat.

It was the mucker, and at sight of him there swept over the girl the terrible peril of her position—alone in the savage mountains of a savage island with the murderer of Billy Mallory—the beast that had kicked the unconscious Theriere in the face—the mucker who had insulted and threatened to strike her! She shuddered at the thought. And then she recalled the man's other side, and for the life of her she could not tell whether to be afraid of him or not—it all depended upon what mood governed him. It would be best to propitiate him. She called a pleasant good morning.

Byrne turned. She was shocked at the pallor of his haggard face.

"Good morning," he said. "How did yeh sleep?"

"Oh, just splendidly, and you?" she replied.

"So-so," he answered.

She looked at him searchingly as he approached her.

"Why I don't believe that you have slept at all," she cried.

"I didn't feel very sleepy," he replied evasively.

"You sat up all night on guard!" she exclaimed. "You know you did."

"De Chinks might o' been shadowin' us—it wasn't safe to sleep," he admitted; "but I'll tear off a few dis mornin' after we find a feed of some kind."

"What can we find to eat here?" she asked.

"Dis crick is full o' fish," he explained, "an' ef youse got a pin I guess we kin rig up a scheme to hook a couple."

The girl found a pin that he said would answer very nicely, and with a shoe lace for a line and a big locust as bait the mucker set forth to argle in the little mountain torrent. The fish, unwary, and hungry thus early in the morning proved easy prey, and two casts brought forth two splendid specimens.

"I could eat a dozen of dem minnows," announced the mucker, and he cast again and again, until in twenty minutes he had a goodly mess of plump, shiny trout on the grass beside him.

With his pocketknife he cleaned and scaled them, and then between two rocks he built a fire and passing sticks through the bodies of his catch roasted them all. They had neither salt, nor pepper, nor butter, nor any other viand than the fish, but it seemed to the girl that never in her life had she tasted so palatable a meal, nor had it occurred to her until the odor of the cooking fish filled her nostrils that no food had passed her lips since the second day before—no wonder that the two ate ravenously, enjoying every mouthful of their repast.

"An' now," said Billy Byrne, "I tink I'll poun' my ear fer a few. You kin keep yer lamps peeled fer de Chinks, an' de first fony noise youse hears, w'y be sure to wake me up," and with that he rolled over upon the grass, asleep almost on the instant.

The girl, to while away the time, explored their rockbound haven. She found that it had but a single means of ingress, the narrow pass through which the brook found outlet. Beyond the entrance she did not venture, but through it she saw, beneath, a wooded slope, and twice deer passed quite close to her, stopping at the brook to drink.

It was an ideal spot, one whose beauties appealed to her even under the harrowing conditions which had forced her to seek its precarious safety. In another land and with companions of her own kind she could well imagine the joy of a fortnight spent in such a sylvan paradise.

The thought aroused another—how long would the mucker remain a safe companion? She seemed to be continually falling from the frying pan into the fire. So far she had not been burned, but with returning strength, and the knowledge of their utter isolation could she expect this brutal thug to place any check upon his natural desires?

Why there were few men of her own station in life with whom she would have felt safe to spend a fortnight alone upon a savage, uncivilized island! She glanced at the man where he lay stretched in deep slumber. What a huge fellow he was! How helpless would she be were he to turn against her! Yet his very size; yes, and the brutality she feared, were her only salvation against every other danger than he himself. The man was physically a natural protector, for he was able to cope with odds and dangers to which an ordinary man would long since have succumbed. So she found that she was both safer and less safe because the mucker was her companion.

As she pondered the question her eyes roved toward the slope beyond the opening to the amphitheater. With a start she came to her feet, shading her eyes with her hand and peering intently at something that she could have sworn moved among the trees far below. No, she could not be mistaken—it was the figure of a man.

Swiftly she ran to Byrne, shaking him roughly by the shoulder.

"Someone is coming," she cried, in response to his sleepy query.

XIV
THE MUCKER SEES A NEW LIGHT

Together the girl and the mucker approached the entrance to the amphitheater. From behind a shoulder of rock they peered down into the forest below them. For several minutes neither saw any cause for alarm.

"I guess youse must o' been seein' things," said Byrne, drily.

"Yes," said the girl, "and I see them again. Look! Quick! Down there—to the right."

Byrne looked in the direction she indicated.

"Chinks," he commented. "Gee! Look at 'em comin'. Dere must be a hundred of 'em."

He turned a rueful glance back into the amphitheater.

"I dunno as dis place looks as good to me as it did," he remarked. "Dose yaps wid de toad stabbers could hike up on top o' dese cliffs an' make it a case o' 'thence by carriages to Calvary' for ours in about two shakes."

"Yes," said the girl, "I'm afraid it's a regular cul-de-sac."

"I dunno nothin' about dat," replied the mucker; "but I do know dat if we wants to get out o' here we gotta get a hump on ourselves good an' lively. Come ahead," and with his words he ran quickly through the entrance, and turning squarely toward the right skirted the perpendicular cliffs that extended as far as they could see to be lost to view in the forest that ran up to meet them from below.

The trees and underbrush hid them from the headhunters. There had been danger of detection but for the brief instant that they passed through the entrance of the hollow, but at the time they had chosen the enemy had been hidden in a clump of thick brush far down the slope.

For hours the two fugitives continued their flight, passing over the crest of a ridge and downward toward another valley, until by a small brook they paused to rest, hopeful that they had entirely eluded their pursuers.

Again Byrne fished, and again they sat together at a one-course meal. As they ate the man found himself looking at the girl more and more often. For several days the wonder of her beauty had been growing upon him, until now he found it difficult to take his eyes from her. Thrice she surprised him in the act of staring intently at her, and each time he had dropped his eyes guiltily. At length the girl became nervous, and then terribly frightened—was it coming so soon?

The man had talked but little during this meal, and for the life of her Barbara Harding could not think of any topic with which to distract his attention from his thoughts.

"Hadn't we better be moving on?" she asked at last.

Byrne gave a little start as though surprised in some questionable act.

"I suppose so," he said; "this ain't no place to spend the night—it's too open. We gotta find a sort o' hiding place if we can, dat a fellow kin barricade wit something."

Again they took up their seemingly hopeless march—an aimless wandering in search of they knew not what. Away from one danger to possible dangers many fold more terrible. Barbara's heart was very heavy, for again she feared and mistrusted the mucker.

They followed down the little brook now to where it emptied into a river and then down the valley beside the river which grew wider and more turbulent with every mile. Well past mid-afternoon they came opposite a small, rocky island, and as Byrne's eyes fell upon it an exclamation of gratification burst from his lips.

"Jest de place!" he cried. "We orter be able to hide dere forever."

"But how are we to get there?" asked the girl, looking fearfully at the turbulent river.

"It ain't deep," Byrne assured her. "Come ahead; I'll carry yeh acrost," and without waiting for a reply he gathered her in his arms and started down the bank.

What with the thoughts that had occupied his mind off and on during the afternoon the sudden and close contact of the girl's warm young body close to his took Billy Byrne's breath away, and sent the hot blood coursing through his veins. It was with the utmost difficulty that he restrained a mad desire to crush her to him and cover her face with kisses.

And then the fatal thought came to him—why should he restrain himself? What was this girl to him? Had he not always hated her and her kind? Did she not look with loathing and contempt upon him? And to whom did her life belong anyway but to him—had he not saved it twice? What difference would it make? They'd never come out of this savage world alive, and if he didn't take her some monkey-faced Chink would get her.

They were in the middle of the stream now. Byrne's arms already had commenced to tighten upon the girl. With a sudden tug he strove to pull her face down to his; but she put both hands upon his shoulders and held his lips at arms' length. And her wide eyes looked full into the glowing gray ones of the mucker. And each saw in the other's something that held their looks for a full minute.

Barbara saw what she had feared, but she saw too something else that gave her a quick, pulsing hope—a look of honest love, or could she be mistaken? And the mucker saw the true eyes of the woman he loved without knowing that he loved her, and he saw the plea for pity and protection in them.

"Don't," whispered the girl. "Please don't, you frighten me."

A week ago Billy Byrne would have laughed at such a plea. Doubtless, too, he would have struck the girl in the face for her resistance. He did neither now, which spoke volumes for the change that was taking place within him, but neither did he relax his hold upon her, or take his burning eyes from her frightened ones.

Thus he strode through the turbulent, shallow river to clamber up the bank onto the island. In his soul the battle still raged, but he had by no means relinquished his intention to have his way with the girl. Fear, numb, freezing fear, was in the girl's eyes now. The mucker read it there as plain as print, and had she not said that she was frightened? That was what he had wanted to accomplish back there upon the *Halfmoon*—to frighten her. He would have enjoyed the sight, but he had not been able to accomplish the thing. Now she not only showed that she was frightened—she had admitted it, and it gave the mucker no pleasure—on the contrary it made him unaccountably uncomfortable.

And then came the last straw—tears welled to those lovely eyes. A choking sob wracked the girl's frame—"And just when I was learning to trust you so!" she cried.

They had reached the top of the bank, now, and the man, still holding her in his arms, stood upon a mat of jungle grass beneath a great tree. Slowly he lowered her to her feet. The madness of desire still gripped him; but now there was another force at work combating the evil that had predominated before.

Theriere's words came back to him: "Goodbye, Byrne; take good care of Miss Harding," and his admission to the Frenchman during that last conversation with the dying man: "—a week ago I guess I was a coward. Dere seems to be more'n one kind o' nerve—I'm just a-learnin' of the right kind, I guess."

He had been standing with eyes upon the ground, his heavy hand still gripping the girl's arm. He looked into her face again. She was waiting there, her great eyes upon his filled with fear and questioning, like a prisoner before the bar awaiting the sentence of her judge.

As the man looked at Barbara Harding standing there before him he saw her in a strange new light, and a sudden realization of the truth flashed upon him. He saw that he could not harm her now, or ever, for he loved her!

And with the awakening there came to Billy Byrne the withering, numbing knowledge that his love must forever be a hopeless one—that this girl of the aristocracy could never be for such as he.

Barbara Harding, still looking questioningly at him, saw the change that came across his countenance—she saw the swift pain that shot to the man's eyes, and she wondered. His fingers released their grasp upon her arm. His hands fell limply to his sides.

"Don't be afraid," he said. "Please don't be afraid o' me. I couldn't hurt youse if I tried."

A deep sigh of relief broke from the girl's lips—relief and joy; and she realized that its cause was as much that the man had proved true to the new estimate she had recently placed upon him as that the danger to herself had passed.

"Come," said Billy Byrne, "we'd better move in a bit out o' sight o' de mainland, an' look fer a place to make camp. I reckon we'd orter rest here for a few days till we git in shape ag'in. I know youse must be dead beat, an' I sure am, all right, all right."

Together they sought a favorable site for their new home, and it was as though the horrid specter of a few moments before had never risen to menace them, for the girl felt that a great burden of apprehension had been lifted forever from her shoulders, and though a dull ache gnawed at the mucker's heart, still he was happier than he had ever been before—happy to be near the woman he loved.

With the long sword of Oda Yorimoto, Billy Byrne cut saplings and bamboo and the fronds of fan palms, and with long tough grasses bound them together into the semblance of a rude hut. Barbara gathered leaves and grasses with which she covered the floor.

"Number One, Riverside Drive," said the mucker, with a grin, when the work was completed; "an' now I'll go down on de river front an' build de Bowery."

"Oh, are you from New York?" asked the girl.

"Not on yer life," replied Billy Byrne. "I'm from good ol' Chi; but I been to Noo York twict wit de Goose Island Kid, an' so I knows all about it. De roughnecks belongs on de Bowery, so dat's wot we'll call my dump down by de river. You're a highbrow, so youse gotta live on Riverside Drive, see?" and the mucker laughed at his little pleasantry.

But the girl did not laugh with him. Instead she looked troubled.

"Wouldn't you rather be a 'highbrow' too?" she asked, "and live up on Riverside Drive, right across the street from me?"

"I don't belong," said the mucker gruffly.

"Wouldn't you rather belong?" insisted the girl.

All his life Billy had looked with contempt upon the hated, pusillanimous highbrows, and now to be asked if he would not rather be one! It was unthinkable, and yet, strange to relate, he realized an odd longing to be like Theriere, and Billy Mallory; yes, in some respects like Divine, even. He wanted to be more like the men that the woman he loved knew best.

"It's too late fer me ever to belong, now," he said ruefully. "Yeh gotta be borned to it. Gee! Wouldn't I look funny in wite pants, an' one o' dem dinky, little 'Willie-off-de-yacht' lids?"

Even Barbara had to laugh at the picture the man's words raised to her imagination.

"I didn't mean that," she hastened to explain. "I didn't mean that you must necessarily dress like them; but *be* like them—act like them—talk like them, as Mr. Theriere did, you know. He was a gentleman."

"An' I'm not," said Billy.

"Oh, I didn't mean *that*," the girl hastened to explain.

"Well, whether youse meant it or not, it's so," said the mucker. "I ain't no gent—I'm a mucker. I have your word for it, you know—yeh said so that time on de *Halfmoon*, an' I ain't fergot it; but youse was right—I am a mucker. I ain't never learned how to be anything else. I ain't never wanted to be anything else until today. Now, I'd like to be a gent; but it's too late."

"Won't you try?" asked the girl. "For my sake?"

"Go to't," returned the mucker cheerfully; "I'd even wear side whiskers fer youse."

"Horrors!" exclaimed Barbara Harding. "I couldn't look at you if you did."

"Well, then, tell me wot youse do want me to do."

Barbara discovered that her task was to be a difficult one if she were to accomplish it without wounding the man's feelings; but she determined to strike while the iron was hot and risk offending him—why she should be interested in the regeneration of Mr. Billy Byrne it never once occurred to her to ask herself. She hesitated a moment before speaking.

"One of the first things you must do, Mr. Byrne," she said, "is to learn to speak correctly. You mustn't say 'youse' for 'you,' or 'wot' for 'what'—you must try to talk as I talk. No one in the world speaks any language faultlessly, but there are certain more or less obvious irregularities of grammar and pronunciation that are particularly distasteful to people of refinement, and which are easy to guard against if one be careful."

"All right," said Billy Byrne, "youse—you kin pitch in an' learn me wot—whatever you want to an' I'll do me best to talk like a dude—fer your sake."

And so the mucker's education commenced, and as there was little else for the two to do it progressed rapidly, for once started the man grew keenly interested, spurred on by the evident pleasure which his self-appointed tutor took in his progress—further it meant just so much more of close companionship with her.

For three weeks they never left the little island except to gather fruit which grew hard by on the adjacent mainland. Byrne's wounds had troubled him considerably—at times he had been threatened with blood poisoning. His temperature had mounted once to alarming heights, and for a whole night Barbara Harding had sat beside him bathing his forehead and easing his sufferings as far as it lay within her power to do; but at last the wonderful vitality of the man had saved him. He was much weakened though and neither of them had thought it safe to attempt to seek the coast until he had fully regained his old-time strength.

So far but little had occurred to give them alarm. Twice they had seen natives on the mainland—evidently hunting parties; but no sign of pursuit had developed. Those whom they had seen had been pure-blood Malays—

there had been no samurai among them; but their savage, warlike appearance had warned the two against revealing their presence.

They had subsisted upon fish and fruit principally since they had come to the island. Occasionally this diet had been relieved by messes of wild fowl and fox that Byrne had been successful in snaring with a primitive trap of his own invention; but lately the prey had become wary, and even the fish seemed less plentiful. After two days of fruit diet, Byrne announced his intention of undertaking a hunting trip upon the mainland.

"A mess of venison wouldn't taste half bad," he remarked.

"Yes," cried the girl, "I'm nearly famished for meat—it seems as though I could almost eat it raw."

"I know that I could," stated Billy. "Lord help the deer that gets within range of this old gat of Theriere's, and you may not get even a mouthful—I'm that hungry I'll probably eat it all, hoof, hide, and horns, before ever I get any of it back here to you."

"You'd better not," laughed the girl. "Goodbye and good luck; but please don't go very far—I shall be terribly lonely and frightened while you are away."

"Maybe you'd better come along," suggested Billy.

"No, I should be in the way—you can't hunt deer with a gallery, and get any."

"Well, I'll stay within hailing distance, and you can look for me back any time between now and sundown. Goodbye," and he picked his way down the bank into the river, while from behind a bush upon the mainland two wicked, black eyes watched his movements and those of the girl on the shore behind him while a long, sinewy, brown hand closed more tightly upon a heavy war spear, and steel muscles tensed for the savage spring and the swift throw.

The girl watched Billy Byrne forging his way through the swift rapids. What a mighty engine of strength and endurance he was! What a man! Yes, brute! And strange to relate Barbara Harding found herself admiring the very brutality that once had been repellent to her. She saw him leap lightly to the opposite bank, and then she saw a quick movement in a bush close at his side. She did not know what manner of thing had caused it, but her intuition warned her that behind that concealing screen lay mortal danger to the unconscious man.

"Billy!" she cried, the unaccustomed name bursting from her lips involuntarily. "In the bush at your left—look out!"

At the note of warning in her voice Byrne had turned at her first word—it was all that saved his life. He saw the half-naked savage and the outshooting spear arm, and as he would, instinctively, have ducked a right-for-the-head in the squared circle of his other days, he ducked now, side stepping to the right, and the heavy weapon sped harmlessly over his shoulder.

The warrior, with a growl of rage, drew his sharp parang, leaping to close quarters. Barbara Harding saw Byrne whip Theriere's revolver from its holster, and snap it in the face of the savage; but to her horror the cartridge failed to explode, and before he could fire again the warrior was upon him.

The girl saw the white man leap to one side to escape the furious cut aimed at him by his foe, and then she saw him turn with the agility of a panther and spring to close quarters with the wild man. Byrne's left arm went around the Malay's neck, and with his heavy right fist he rained blow after blow upon the brown face.

The savage dropped his useless parang—clawing and biting at the mighty creature in whose power he found himself; but never once did those terrific, relentless blows cease to fall upon his unprotected face.

The sole witness to this battle primeval stood spellbound at the sight of the fierce, brutal ferocity of the white man, and the lion-like strength he exhibited. Slowly but surely he was beating the face of his antagonist into an unrecognizable pulp—with his bare hands he had met and was killing an armed warrior. It was incredible! Not even Theriere or Billy Mallory could have done such a thing. Billy Mallory! And she was gazing with admiration upon his murderer!

XV
THE RESCUE

After Byrne had dropped the lifeless form of his enemy to the ground he turned and retraced his steps toward the island, a broad grin upon his face as he climbed to the girl's side.

"I guess I'd better overhaul this gat," he said, "and stick around home. It isn't safe to leave you alone here—I can see that pretty plainly. Gee, supposin' I'd got out of sight before he showed himself!" And the man shuddered visibly at the thought.

The girl had not spoken and the man looked up suddenly, attracted by her silence. He saw a look of horror in her eyes, such as he had seen there once before when he had kicked the unconscious Theriere that time upon the *Halfmoon*.

"What's the matter?" he asked, alarmed. "What have I done now? I had to croak the stiff—he'd have got me sure if I hadn't, and then he'd have got you, too. I had to do it for your sake—I'm sorry you saw it."

"It isn't that," she said slowly. "That was very brave, and very wonderful. It's Mr. Mallory I'm thinking of. O Billy! How could you do it?"

The man hung his head.

"Please don't," he begged. "I'd give my life to bring him back again, for your sake. I know now that you loved him, and I've tried to do all I could to atone for what I did to him; just as I tried to play white with Theriere when I found that he loved you, and intended to be on the square with you. He was your kind, and I hoped that by helping him to win you fairly it might help to wipe out what I had done to Mallory. I see that nothing ever can wipe that out. I've got to go through life regretting it because you have taught me what a brutal, cowardly thing I did. If it hadn't been for you I'd always have been proud of it—but you and Theriere taught me to look at things in a different way than I ever had learned to before. I'm not sorry for that—I'm glad, for if remorse is a part of my punishment I'll take it gladly and welcome the chance to get a little of what's coming to me. Only please don't look at me that way any more—it's more than I can stand, from you."

It was the first time that the man ever had opened his heart in any such whole-souled way to her, and it touched the girl more than she would have cared to admit.

"It would be silly to tell you that I ever can forget that terrible affair," she said; "but somehow I feel that the man who did that was an entirely different man from the man who has been so brave and chivalrous in his treatment of me during the past few weeks."

"It was me that did it, though," he said; "you can't get away from that. It'll always stick in your memory, so that you can never think of Mr. Mallory without thinking of the damned beast that murdered him—God! and I thought it smart!

"But you have no idea how I was raised, Miss Harding," he went on. "Not that that's any excuse for the thing I did; but it does make it seem a wonder that I ever could have made a start even at being decent. I never was well acquainted with any human being that wasn't a thief, or a pickpocket, or a murderer—and they were all beasts, each in his own particular way, only they weren't as decent as dumb beasts.

"I wasn't as crafty as most of them, so I had to hold my own by brute force, and I did it; but, gad, how I accomplished it. The idea of fighting fair," he laughed at the thought, "was utterly unknown to me. If I'd ever have tried it I'd have seen my finish in a hurry. No one fought fair in my gang, or in any other gang that I ever ran up against. It was an honor to kill a man, and if you accomplished it by kicking him to death when he was unconscious it detracted nothing from the glory of your exploit—it was *what* you did, not *how* you did it, that counted.

"I could have been decent, though, if I'd wanted to. Other fellows who were born and raised near me were decent enough. They got good jobs and stuck to them, and lived straight; but they made me sick—I looked down on them, and spent my time hanging around saloon corners rushing the can and insulting women—I didn't want to be decent—not until I met you, and learned to—to," he hesitated, stammering, and the red blood crept up his neck and across his face, "and learned to want your respect."

It wasn't what he had intended saying and the girl knew it. There sprang into her mind a sudden wish to hear Billy Byrne say the words that he had dared not say; but she promptly checked the desire, and a moment later a qualm of self-disgust came over her because of the weakness that had prompted her to entertain such a wish in connection with a person of this man's station in life.

Days ran into weeks, and still the two remained upon their little island refuge. Byrne found first one excuse and then another to delay the march to the sea. He knew that it must be made sooner or later, and he knew, too, that its commencement would mark the beginning of the end of his association with Miss Harding, and that after that was ended life would be a dreary waste.

Either they would be picked up by a passing vessel or murdered by the natives, but in the latter event his separation from the woman he loved would be no more certain or absolute than in her return to her own people, for Billy Byrne knew that he "didn't belong" in any society that knew Miss Barbara Harding, and he feared that once they had regained civilization there would be a return on the girl's part to the old haughty aloofness, and that again he would be to her only a creature of a lower order, such as she and her kind addressed with a patronizing air as, "my man."

He intended, of course, to make every possible attempt to restore her to her home; but, he argued, was it wrong to snatch a few golden hours of happiness in return for his service, and as partial recompense for the lifetime of lonely misery that must be his when the woman he loved had passed out of his life forever? Billy thought not, and so he tarried on upon "Manhattan Island," as Barbara had christened it, and he lived in the second finest residence in town upon the opposite side of "Riverside Drive" from the palatial home of Miss Harding.

Nearly two months had passed before Billy's stock of excuses and delay ran out, and a definite date was set for the commencement of the journey.

"I believe," Miss Harding had said, "that you do not wish to be rescued at all. Most of your reasons for postponing the trip have been trivial and ridiculous—possibly you are afraid of the dangers that may lie before us," she added, banteringly.

"I'm afraid you've hit it off about right," he replied with a grin. "I don't want to be rescued, and I am very much afraid of what lies before—me."

"Before *you*?"

"I'm going to lose you, any way you look at it, and—and—oh, can't you see that I love you?" he blurted out, despite all his good intentions.

Barbara Harding looked at him for a moment, and then she did the one thing that could have hurt him most—she laughed.

The color mounted to Billy Byrne's face, and then he went very white. The girl started to say something, and at the same instant there came faintly to them from the mainland the sound of hoarse shouting, and of shots.

Byrne turned and started on a run in the direction of the firing, the girl following closely behind. At the island's edge he motioned her to stop.

"Wait here, it will be safer," he said. "There may be white men there—those shots sound like it, but again there may not. I want to find out before they see you, whoever they are."

The sound of firing had ceased now, but loud yelling was distinctly audible from down the river. Byrne took a step down the bank toward the water.

"Wait!" whispered the girl. "Here they come now, we can see them from here in a moment," and she dragged the mucker down behind a bush.

In silence the two watched the approaching party.

"They're the Chinks," announced Byrne, who insisted on using this word to describe the proud and haughty samurai.

"Yes, and there are two white men with them," whispered Barbara Harding, a note of suppressed excitement in her voice.

"Prisoners," said Byrne. "Some of the precious bunch from the *Halfmoon* doubtless."

The samurai were moving straight up the edge of the river. In a few minutes they would pass within a hundred feet of the island. Billy and the girl crouched low behind their shelter.

"I don't recognize them," said the man.

"Why—why—O Mr. Byrne, it can't be possible!" cried the girl with suppressed excitement. "Those two men are Captain Norris and Mr. Foster, mate of the *Lotus*!"

Byrne half rose to his feet. The party was opposite their hiding place now.

"Sit tight," he whispered. "I'm goin' to get 'em," and then, fiercely "for your sake, because I love you—now laugh," and he was gone.

He ran lightly down the river bank unnoticed by the samurai who had already passed the island. In one hand he bore the long war spear of the headhunter he had slain. At his belt hung the long sword of Oda Yorimoto, and in its holster reposed the revolver of the Count de Cadenet.

Barbara Harding watched him as be forded the river, and clambered up the opposite bank. She saw him spring rapidly after the samurai and their prisoners. She saw his spear hand go up, and then from the deep lungs of the man rose a savage yell that would have done credit to a whole tribe of Apaches.

The warriors turned in time to see the heavy spear flying toward them and then, as he dashed into their midst, Billy Byrne drew his revolver and fired to right and left. The two prisoners took advantage of the consternation of their guards to grapple with them and possess themselves of weapons.

There had been but six samurai in the party, two had fallen before Byrne's initial onslaught, but the other four, recovered from their first surprise, turned now to battle with all the terrific ferocity of their kind.

Again, at a crucial moment, had Theriere's revolver missed fire, and in disgust Byrne discarded it, falling back upon the long sword with which he was no match for the samurai. Norris snatched Byrne's spear from the ground, and ran it through the body of one of the Japs who was pressing Byrne too closely. Odds were even now—they fought three against three.

Norris still clung to the spear—it was by far the most effective weapon against the long swords of the samurai. With it he killed his antagonist and then rushed to the assistance of Foster.

Barbara Harding from the island saw that Byrne's foe was pressing him closely. The white man had no chance against the superior swordsmanship of the samurai. She saw that the mucker was trying to get past the Jap's guard and get his hands upon him, but it was evident that the man was too crafty and skilled a fighter to permit of that. There could be but one outcome to that duel unless Byrne had assistance, and that mighty quickly. The girl grasped the short sword that she constantly wore now, and rushed into the river. She had never before crossed it except in Byrne's arms. She found the current swift and strong. It almost swept her off her feet before she was halfway across, but she never for an instant thought of abandoning her effort.

After what seemed an eternity she floundered out upon the main and, and when she reached the top of the bank she saw to her delight that Byrne was still on his feet, fighting. Foster and Norris were pushing their man back— they were in no danger.

Quickly she ran toward Byrne and the samurai. She saw a wicked smile upon the brown face of the little warrior, and then she saw his gleaming sword twist in a sudden feint, and as Byrne lunged out awkwardly to parry the expected blow the keen edge swerved and came down upon his head.

She was an instant too late to save, but just in time to avenge—scarcely had the samurai's sword touched the mucker than the point of Oda Yorimoto's short sword, wielded by the fair hand of Barbara Harding, plunged into his heart. With a shriek he collapsed beside the body of his victim.

Barbara Harding threw herself beside Byrne. Apparently life was extinct. With a little cry of horror the girl put her ear close to the man's lips. She could hear nothing.

"Come back! Come back!" she wailed. "Forgive me that cruel laugh. O Billy! Billy! I love you!" and the daughter of old Anthony Harding, multimillionaire and scion of the oldest aristocracy that America boasts, took the head of the Grand Avenue mucker in her arms and covered the white, bloody face with kisses—and in the midst of it Billy Byrne opened his eyes.

She was caught in the act. There was no escape, and as a crimson flush suffused her face Billy Byrne put his arms about her and drew her down until their lips met, and this time she did not put her hands upon his shoulders and push him away.

"I love you, Billy," she said simply.

"Remember who and what I am," he cautioned, fearful lest this great happiness be stolen away from him because she had forgotten for the moment.

"I love you Billy," she answered, "for what you *are*."

"Forever?"

"Until death do us part!"

And then Norris and Foster, having dispatched their man, came running up.

"Is he badly hurt, madam?" cried Captain Norris.

"I don't know," replied Miss Harding; "I'm just trying to help him up, Captain Norris," she laboriously explained in an effort to account for her arms about Billy's neck.

Norris gave a start of surprise at hearing his name.

"Who are you?" he cried. "How do you know me?" and as the girl turned her face toward him, "Miss Harding! Thank God, Miss Harding, you are safe."

"But where on earth did you come from?" asked Barbara.

"It's a long story, Miss Harding," replied the officer, "and the ending of it is going to be pretty hard on you—you must try to bear up though."

"You don't mean that father is dead?" she asked, a look of terror coming to her eyes.

"Not that—we hope," replied Norris. "He has been taken prisoner by these half-breed devils on the island. I doubt if they have killed him—we were going to his rescue when we ourselves were captured. He and Mr. Mallory were taken three days ago."

"Mallory!" shouted Billy Byrne, who had entirely recovered from the blow that had merely served to stun him for a moment. "Is Mallory alive?"

"He was yesterday," replied Norris; "these fellows from whom you so bravely rescued us told us that much."

"Thank God!" whispered Billy Byrne.

"What made you think he was dead?" inquired the officer, looking closely at Byrne as though trying to place him.

Another man might have attempted to evade the question but the new Billy Byrne was no coward in any department of his moral or physical structure.

"Because I thought that I had killed him," he replied, "the day that we took the *Lotus*."

Captain Norris looked at the speaker in undisguised horror.

"You!" he cried. "You were one of those damned cutthroats! You the man that nearly killed poor Mr. Mallory! Miss Harding, has he offered you any indignities?"

"Don't judge him rashly, Captain Norris," said the girl. "But for him I should have been dead and worse than dead long since. Some day I will tell you of his heroism and his chivalry, and don't forget, Captain, that he has just saved you and Mr. Foster from captivity and probable death."

"That's right," exclaimed the officer, "and I want to thank him; but I don't understand about Mallory."

"Never mind about him now," said Billy Byrne. "If he's alive that's all that counts—I haven't got his blood on my hands. Go on with your story."

"Well, after that gang of pirates left us," continued the captain, "we rigged an extra wireless that they didn't know we had, and it wasn't long before we raised the warship *Alaska*. Her commander put a crew on board the *Lotus* with machinists and everything necessary to patch her up—coaled and provisioned her and then lay by while we got her in running order. It didn't take near as long as you would have imagined. Then we set out in company with the warship to search for the '*Clarinda*,' as your Captain Simms called her. We got on her track through a pirate junk just north of Luzon—he said he'd heard from the natives of a little out-of-the-way island near Formosa that a brigantine had been wrecked there in the recent typhoon, and his description of the vessel led us to believe that it might be the '*Clarinda*,' or *Halfmoon*.

"We made the island, and after considerable search found the survivors. Each of 'em tried to lay the blame on the others, but finally they all agreed that a man by the name of Theriere with a seaman called Byrne, had taken you into the interior, and that they had believed you dead until a few days since they had captured one of the natives and learned that you had all escaped, and were wandering in some part of the island unknown to them.

"Then we set out with a company of marines to find you. Your father, impatient of the seeming slowness of the officer in command, pushed ahead with Mr. Mallory, Mr. Poster, and myself, and two of the men of the *Lotus* whom he had brought along with us.

"Three days ago we were attacked and your father and Mr. Mallory taken prisoners. The rest of us escaped, and endeavored to make our way back to the marines, but we became confused and have been wandering aimlessly about the island ever since until we were surprised by these natives a few moments ago. Both the seamen were killed in this last fight and Mr. Foster and myself taken prisoners—the rest you know."

Byrne was on his feet now. He found his sword and revolver and replaced them in his belt.

"You men stay here on the island and take care of Miss Harding," he said. "If I don't come back the marines will find you sooner or later, or you can make your way to the coast, and work around toward the cove. Goodbye, Miss Harding."

"Where are you going?" cried the girl.

"To get your father—and Mr. Mallory," said the mucker.

XVI
The Supreme Sacrifice

Through the balance of the day and all during the long night Billy Byrne swung along his lonely way, retracing the familiar steps of the journey that had brought Barbara Harding and himself to the little island in the turbulent river.

Just before dawn he came to the edge of the clearing behind the dwelling of the late Oda Yorimoto. Somewhere within the silent village he was sure that the two prisoners lay.

During the long march he had thrashed over again and again all that the success of his rash venture would mean to him. Of all those who might conceivably stand between him and the woman he loved—the woman who had just acknowledged that she loved him—these two men were the most to be feared.

Billy Byrne did not for a moment believe that Anthony Harding would look with favor upon the Grand Avenue mucker as a prospective son-in-law. And then there was Mallory! He was sure that Barbara had loved this man, and now should he be restored to her as from the grave there seemed little doubt but that the old love would be aroused in the girl's breast. The truth of the matter was that Billy Byrne could not conceive the truth of the testimony of his own ears—even now he scarce dared believe that the wonderful Miss Harding loved him—him, the despised mucker!

But the depth of the man's love for the girl, and the genuineness of his newfound character were proven beyond question by the relentless severity with which he put away every thought of himself and the consequences to him in the matter he had undertaken.

For Her Sake! had become his slogan. What though the results sent him to a savage death, or to a life of lonely misery, or to the arms of his beloved! In the face of duty the result was all the same to Billy Byrne.

For a moment he stood looking at the moon-bathed village, listening for any sign of wakefulness or life, then with all the stealth of an Indian, and with the trained wariness of the thief that he had been, the mucker slunk noiselessly across the clearing to the shadows of the nearest hut. He listened beneath the window through which he and Barbara and Theriere had made their escape a few weeks before. There was no sound from within. Cautiously he raised himself to the sill, and a moment later dropped into the inky darkness of the interior.

With groping hands he felt about the room—it was unoccupied. Then he passed to the door at the far end. Cautiously he opened it until a narrow crack gave him a view of the dimly lighted chamber beyond. Within all seemed asleep. The mucker pushed the door still further open and stepped within—so must he search every hut within the village until he had found those he sought?

They were not there, and on silent feet that disturbed not even the lightly slumbering curs the man passed out by the front entrance into the street beyond.

Through a second and third hut he made his precarious way. In the fourth a man stirred as Byrne stood upon the opposite side of the room from the door—with a catlike bound the mucker was beside him. Would the fellow awake? Billy scarce breathed. The samurai turned restlessly, and then, with a start, sat up with wide-open eyes. At the same instant iron fingers closed upon his throat and the long sword of his dead daimio passed through his heart.

Byrne held the corpse until he was positive that life was extinct, then he dropped it quietly back upon its pallet, and departed to search the adjoining dwelling. Here he found a large front room, and a smaller chamber in the rear—an arrangement similar to that in the daimio's house.

The front room revealed no clue to the missing men. Within the smaller, rear room Byrne heard the subdued hum of whispered conversation just as he was about to open the door. Like a graven image he stood in silence, his ear glued to the frail door. For a moment he listened thus and then his heart gave a throb of exultation, and he could have shouted aloud in thanksgiving—the men were conversing in English!

Quietly Byrne pushed open the door far enough to admit his body. Those within ceased speaking immediately. Byrne closed the door behind him, advancing until he felt one of the occupants of the room. The man shrank from his touch.

"I guess we're done for, Mallory," said the man in a low tone; "they've come for us."

"Sh-sh," warned the mucker. "Are you and Mallory alone?"

"Yes—for God's sake who are you and where did you come from?" asked the surprised Mr. Harding.

"Be still," admonished Byrne, feeling for the cords that he knew must bind the captive.

He found them presently and with his jackknife cut them asunder. Then he released Mallory.

"Follow me," he said, "but go quietly. Take off your shoes if you have 'em on, and hang 'em around your neck—tie the ends of the laces together."

The men did as he bid and a moment later he was leading them across the room, filled with sleeping men, women, children, and domestic animals. At the far side stood a rack filled with long swords. Byrne removed two without the faintest suspicion of a noise. He handed one to each of his companions, cautioning them to silence with a gesture.

But neither Anthony Harding nor Billy Mallory had had second-story experience, and the former struck his weapon accidentally against the door frame with a resounding clatter that brought half the inmates of the room, wide-eyed, to sitting postures. The sight that met the natives' eyes had them on their feet, yelling like madmen, and dashing toward their escaping prisoners, in an instant.

"Quick!" shouted Billy Byrne. "Follow me!"

Down the village street the three men ran, but the shouts of the natives had brought armed samurai to every door with a celerity that was uncanny, and in another moment the fugitives found themselves surrounded by a pack of howling warriors who cut at them with long swords from every side, blocking their retreat and hemming them in in every direction.

Byrne called to his companions to close in, back to back, and thus, the gangster in advance, the three slowly fought their way toward the end of the narrow street and the jungle beyond. The mucker fought with his long sword in one hand and Theriere's revolver in the other—hewing a way toward freedom for the two men whom he knew would take his love from him.

Beneath the brilliant tropic moon that lighted the scene almost as brilliantly as might the sun himself the battle waged, and though the odds were painfully uneven the white men moved steadily, though slowly, toward the jungle. It was evident that the natives feared the giant white who led the three. Anthony Harding, familiar with Japanese, could translate sufficient of their jargon to be sure of that, had not the respectful distance most of them kept from Byrne been ample proof.

Out of the village street they came at last into the clearing. The warriors danced about them, yelling threats and taunts the while they made occasional dashes to close quarters that they might deliver a swift sword cut and retreat again before the great white devil could get them with the sword that had been Oda Yorimoto's, or the strange fire stick that spoke in such a terrifying voice.

Fifty feet from the jungle Mallory went down with a spear through the calf of his leg. Byrne saw him fall, and dropping back lifted the man to his feet, supporting him with one arm as the two backed slowly in front of the onpressing natives.

The spears were flying thick and fast now, for the samurai all were upon the same side of the enemy and there was no danger of injuring one of their own number with their flying weapons as there had been when the host entirely surrounded the three men, and when the whites at last entered the tall grasses of the jungle a perfect shower of spears followed them.

With the volley Byrne went down—he had been the principal target for the samurai and three of the heavy shafts had pierced his body. Two were buried in his chest and one in his abdomen.

Anthony Harding was horrified. Both his companions were down, and the savages were pressing closely on toward their hiding place. Mallory sat upon the ground trying to tear the spear from his leg. Finally he was successful. Byrne, still conscious, called to Harding to pull the three shafts from him.

"What are we to do?" cried the older man. "They will get us again as sure as fate."

"They haven't got us yet," said Billy. "Wait, I got a scheme. Can you walk, Mallory?"

Mallory staggered to his feet.

"I'll see," he said, and then: "Yes, I can make it."

"Good," exclaimed Byrne. "Now listen. Almost due north, across this range of hills behind us is a valley. In the center of the valley is a river. It is a good fifteen-hour march for a well man—it will take Mallory and you longer. Follow down the river till you come to a little island—it should be the first one from where you strike the river. On that island you will find Miss Harding, Norris, and Foster. Now hurry."

"But you, man!" exclaimed Mallory. "We can't leave you."

"Never!" said Anthony Harding.

"You'll have to, though," replied Billy. "That's part of the scheme. It won't work any other way." He raised his revolver and fired a single shot in the direction of the howling savages. "That's to let 'em know we're still here," he said. "I'll keep that up, off and on, as long as I can. It'll fool 'em into thinking that we're all here, and cover your escape. See?"

"I won't do it," said Mallory.

"Yes you will," replied the mucker. "It's not any of us that counts—it's Miss Harding. As many as can have got to get back to her just as quick as the Lord'll let us. I can't, so you two'll have to. I'm done for—a blind man could see that. It wouldn't do a bit of good for you two to hang around here and get killed, waitin' for me to die; but it would do a lot of harm, for it might mean that Miss Harding would be lost too."

"You say my daughter is on this island you speak of, with Norris and Foster—is she quite safe and well?" asked Harding.

"Perfectly," said Byrne; "and now beat it—you're wasting a lot of precious time."

"For Barbara's sake it looks like the only way," said Anthony Harding, "but it seems wicked and cowardly to desert a noble fellow like you, sir."

"It is wicked," said Billy Mallory. "There must be some other way. By the way, old man, who are you anyhow, and how did you happen to be here?"

Byrne turned his face upward so that the full moon lighted his features clearly.

"There is no other way, Mallory," he said. "Now take a good look at me—don't you recognize me?"

Mallory gazed intently at the strong face looking into his. He shook his head.

"There is something familiar about your face," he said; "but I cannot place you. Nor does it make any difference who you are—you have risked your life to save ours and I shall not leave you. Let Mr. Harding go—it is not necessary for both to stay."

"You will both go," insisted Byrne; "and you will find that it does make a big difference who I am. I hadn't intended telling you, but I see there is no other way. I'm the mucker that nearly killed you on board the *Lotus*, Mallory. I'm the fellow that manhandled Miss Harding until even that beast of a Simms made me quit, and Miss Harding has been alone with me on this island for weeks—now go!"

He turned away so that they could no longer see his face, with the mental anguish that he knew must be writ large upon it, and commenced firing toward the natives once more.

Anthony Harding stood with white face and clinched hands during Byrne's recital of his identity. At its close he took a threatening step toward the prostrate man, raising his long sword, with a muffled oath. Billy Mallory sprang before him, catching his upraised arm.

"Don't!" he whispered. "Think what we owe him now. Come!" and the two men turned north into the jungle while Billy Byrne lay upon his belly in the tall grass firing from time to time into the direction from which came an occasional spear.

Anthony Harding and Billy Mallory kept on in silence along their dismal way. The crack of the mucker's revolver, growing fainter and fainter, as they drew away from the scene of conflict, apprised the men that their rescuer still lived.

After a time the distant reports ceased. The two walked on in silence for a few minutes.

"He's gone," whispered Mallory.

Anthony Harding made no response. They did not hear any further firing behind them. On and on they trudged. Night turned to day. Day rolled slowly on into night once more. And still they staggered on, footsore and weary. Mallory suffered excruciating agony from his wound. There were times when it seemed that it would be impossible for him to continue another yard; but then the thought that Barbara Harding was somewhere ahead of them, and that in a short time now they must be with her once more kept him doggedly at his painful task.

They had reached the river and were following slowly down its bank. The moon, full and gorgeous, flooded the landscape with silvery light.

"Look!" exclaimed Mallory. "The island!"

"Thank God!" whispered Harding, fervently.

On the bank opposite they stopped and hallooed. Almost instantly three figures rushed from the interior of the island to the shore before them—two men and a woman.

"Barbara!" cried Anthony Harding. "O my daughter! My daughter!"

Norris and Foster hastened through the river and brought the two men to the island. Barbara Harding threw herself into her father's arms. A moment later she had grasped Mallory's outstretched hands, and then she looked beyond them for another.

"Mr. Byrne?" she asked. "Where is Mr. Byrne?"

"He is dead," said Anthony Harding.

The girl looked, wide-eyed and uncomprehending, at her father for a full minute.

"Dead!" she moaned, and fell unconscious at his feet.

XVII
Home Again

Billy Byrne continued to fire intermittently for half an hour after the two men had left him. Then he fired several shots in quick succession, and dragging himself to his hands and knees crawled laboriously and painfully back into the jungle in search of a hiding place where he might die in peace.

He had progressed some hundred yards when he felt the earth give way beneath him. He clutched frantically about for support, but there was none, and with a sickening lunge he plunged downward into Stygian darkness.

His fall was a short one, and he brought up with a painful thud at the bottom of a deer pit—a covered trap which the natives dig to catch their fleet-footed prey.

The pain of his wounds after the fall was excruciating. His head whirled dizzily. He knew that he was dying, and then all went black.

When consciousness returned to the mucker it was daylight. The sky above shone through the ragged hole that his falling body had broken in the pit's covering the night before.

"Gee!" muttered the mucker; "and I thought that I was dead!"

His wounds had ceased to bleed, but he was very weak and stiff and sore.

"I guess I'm too tough to croak!" he thought.

He wondered if the two men would reach Barbara in safety. He hoped so. Mallory loved her, and he was sure that Barbara had loved Mallory. He wanted her to be happy. No thought of jealousy entered his mind. Mallory was her kind. Mallory "belonged." He didn't. He was a mucker. How would he have looked training with her bunch. She would have been ashamed of him, and he couldn't have stood that. No, it was better as it had turned out. He'd squared himself for the beast he'd been to her, and he'd squared himself with Mallory, too. At least they'd have only decent thoughts of him, dead; but alive, that would be an entirely different thing. He would be in the way. He would be a constant embarrassment to them all, for they would feel that they'd have to be nice to him in return for what he had done for them. The thought made the mucker sick.

"I'd rather croak," he murmured.

But he didn't "croak"—instead, he waxed stronger, and toward evening the pangs of hunger and thirst drove him to consider means for escaping from his hiding place, and searching for food and water.

He waited until after dark, and then he crawled, with utmost difficulty, from the deep pit. He had heard nothing of the natives since the night before, and now, in the open, there came to him but the faint sounds of the village life across the clearing.

Byrne dragged himself toward the trail that led to the spring where poor Theriere had died. It took him a long time to reach it, but at last he was successful. The clear, cold water helped to revive and strengthen him. Then he sought food. Some wild fruit partially satisfied him for the moment, and he commenced the laborious task of retracing his steps toward "Manhattan Island."

The trail that he had passed over in fifteen hours as he had hastened to the rescue of Anthony Harding and Billy Mallory required the better part of three days now. Occasionally he wondered why in the world he was traversing it anyway. Hadn't he wanted to die, and leave Barbara free? But life is sweet, and the red blood still flowed strong in the veins of the mucker.

"I can go my own way," he thought, "and not bother her; but I'll be dinged if I want to croak in this Godforsaken hole—Grand Avenue for mine, when it comes to passing in my checks. Gee! but I'd like to hear the rattle of the Lake Street 'L' and see the dolls coming down the station steps by Skidmore's when the crowd comes home from the Loop at night."

Billy Byrne was homesick. And then, too, his heart was very heavy and sad because of the great love he had found—a love which he realized was as hopeless as it was great. He had the memory, though, of the girl's arms about his neck, and her dear lips crushed to his for a brief instant, and her words—ah, those words! They would ring in Billy's head forever: "I love you, Billy, for what you *are*."

And a sudden resolve came into the mucker's mind as he whispered those words over and over again to himself. "I can't have her," he said. "She isn't for the likes of me; but if I can't live with her, I can live for her—as she'd want me to live, and, s'help me, those words'll keep me straight. If she ever hears of Billy Byrne again it won't be anything to make her ashamed that she had her arms around him, kissing him, and telling him that she loved him."

At the river's edge across from the little island Billy came to a halt. He had reached the point near midnight, and hesitated to cross over and disturb the party at that hour. At last, however, he decided to cross quietly, and lie down near *her* hut until morning.

The crossing was most difficult, for he was very weak, but at last he came to the opposite bank and drew himself up to lie panting for a few minutes on the sloping bank. Then he crawled on again up to the top, and staggering to his feet made his way cautiously toward the two huts. All was quiet. He assumed that the party was asleep, and so he lay down near the rude shelter he had constructed for Barbara Harding, and fell asleep.

It was broad daylight when he awoke—the sun was fully three hours high, and yet no one was stirring. For the first time misgivings commenced to assail Billy's mind. Could it be possible? He crossed over to his own hut and entered—it was deserted. Then he ran to Barbara's—it, too, was unoccupied. They had gone!

All during the painful trip from the village to the island Billy had momentarily expected to meet a party of rescuers coming back for him. He had not been exactly disappointed, but a queer little lump had risen to his throat as the days passed and no help had come, and now this was the final blow. They had deserted him! Left him wounded and dying on this savage island without taking the trouble to assure themselves that he really was dead! It was incredible!

"But was it?" thought Billy. "Didn't I tell them that I was dying? I thought so myself, and there is no reason why they shouldn't have thought so too. I suppose I shouldn't blame them, and I don't; but I wouldn't have left them that way and not come back. They had a warship full of blue jackets and marines—there wouldn't have been much danger to them."

Presently it occurred to him that the party may have returned to the coast to get the marines, and that even now they were searching for him. He hastened to return to the mainland, and once more he took up his wearisome journey.

That night he reached the coast. Early the next morning he commenced his search for the man-of-war. By walking entirely around the island he should find her he felt sure.

Shortly after noon he scaled a high promontory which jutted out into the sea. From its summit he had an unobstructed view of the broad Pacific. His heart leaped to his throat, for there but a short distance out were a great battleship and a trim white yacht—the *Alaska* and the *Lotus*! They were steaming slowly out to sea.

He was just in time! Filled with happiness the mucker ran to the point of the promontory and stripping off his shirt waved it high above his head, the while he shouted at the top of his lungs; but the vessels kept on their course, giving no answering signal.

For half an hour the man continued his futile efforts to attract the attention of someone on board either craft, but to his dismay he saw them grow smaller and smaller until in a few hours they passed over the rim of the world, disappearing from his view forever.

Weak, wounded, and despairing, Billy sank to the ground, burying his face in his arms, and there the moon found him when she rose, and he was still there when she passed from the western sky.

For three months Billy Byrne lived his lonely life upon the wild island. The trapping and fishing were good and there was a plentiful supply of good water. He regained his lost strength, recovering entirely from his wounds. The natives did not molest him, for he had stumbled upon a section of the shore which they considered bewitched and to which none of them would come under any circumstances.

One morning, at the beginning of his fourth month of solitude, the mucker saw a smudge of smoke upon the horizon. Slowly it increased in volume and the speck beneath it resolved itself into the hull of a steamer. Closer and closer to the island it came.

Billy gathered together a quantity of dry brush and lighted a signal fire on the lofty point from which he had seen the *Alaska* and the *Lotus* disappear. As it commenced to blaze freely he threw fresh, green boughs upon it until a vertical column of smoke arose high above the island.

In breathless suspense Billy watched the movements of the steamer. At first it seemed that she would pass without taking notice of his signal, but at last he saw that she was changing her course and moving directly toward the island.

Close in she came, for the sea was calm and the water deep, and when Billy was sure that those on board saw him and his frantic waving, he hurried, stumbling and falling, down the steep face of the cliff to the tiny beach at its foot.

Already a boat had been lowered and was putting in for land. Billy waded out to the end of the short shelving beach and waited.

The sight that met the eyes of the rescuers was one that filled them with awe, for they saw before them a huge, giant of a white man, half-naked except for a few tattered rags, who wore the long sword of an ancient samurai at his side, a modern revolver at his hip, and bore in his brawny hand the heavy war spear of a headhunter. Long black hair, and a huge beard covered the man's head and face, but clean gray eyes shone from out of the tangle, and a broad grin welcomed them.

"Oh, you white men!" shouted the mucker. "You certainly do look good to me."

Six months later a big, smooth-faced giant in ill-fitting sea togs strolled up Sixth Avenue. It was Billy Byrne—broke, but happy; Grand Avenue was less than a thousand miles away!

"Gee!" he murmured; "but it's good to be home again!"

There were places in New York where Billy would find acquaintances. One in particular he recalled—a little, third-floor gymnasium not far distant from the Battery. Thither he turned his steps now. As he entered the stuffy room in which two big fellows, stripped to the waist, were sparring, a stout, low-browed man sitting in a back-tilted chair against one wall looked up inquiringly. Billy crossed over to him, with outstretched hand.

"Howdy, Professor!" he said.

"Yeh got me, kid," replied Professor Cassidy, taking the proffered hand.

"I was up here with Larry Hilmore and the Goose Island Kid a year or so ago—my name's Byrne," exclaimed Billy.

"Sure," said the professor; "I gotcha now. You're de guy 'at Larry was a tellin' me about. He said you'd be a great heavy if you'd leave de booze alone."

Billy smiled and nodded.

"You don't look much like a booze fighter now," remarked Cassidy.

"And I ain't," said the mucker. "I've been on the wagon for most a year, and I'm never comin' down."

"That's right, kid," said the professor; "but wots the good word? Wot you doin' in little ol' Noo York?"

"Lookin' for a job," said Billy.

"Strip!" commanded Professor Cassidy. "I'm lookin' for sparrin' partners for a gink dat's goin' to clean up de Big Smoke—if he'll ever come back an' scrap."

"You're on," said Billy, commencing to divest himself of his outer clothing.

Stripped to the waist he displayed as wondrous a set of muscles as even Professor Cassidy had ever seen. The man waxed enthusiastic over them.

"You sure ought to have some wallop up your sleeve," he said, admiringly. He then introduced Billy to the Harlem Hurricane, and Battling Dago Pete. "Pete's de guy I was tellin' you about," explained Professor Cassidy. "He's got such a wallop dat I can't keep no sparrin' partners for him. The Hurricane here's de only bloke wit de guts to stay wit him—he's a fiend for punishment, Hurricane is; he jest natchrly eats it.

"If you're broke I'll give you your keep as long as you stay wit Pete an' don't get cold feet, an' I'll fix up a mill for you now an' then so's you kin pull down a little coin fer yourself. Are you game?"

"You know it," said Billy.

"All to the good then," said the professor gaily; "now you put on the mitts an' spell Hurricane for a couple o' rounds."

Billy slipped his huge hands into the tight-fitting gloves.

"It's been more'n a year since I had these on," he said, "an' I may be a little slow an' stale at first; but after I get warmed up I'll do better."

Cassidy grinned and winked at Hurricane. "He won't never get warmed up," Hurricane confided; "Pete'll knock his block off in about two minutes," and the men settled back to watch the fun with ill-concealed amusement written upon their faces.

What happened within the next few minutes in the stuffy little room of Professor Cassidy's third-floor "gymnasium" marks an epoch in the professor's life—he still talks of it, and doubtless shall until the Great Referee counts him out in the Last Round.

The two men sparred for a moment, gaging one another. Then Battling Dago Pete swung a vicious left that landed square on Billy's face. It was a blow that might have felled an ox; but Billy only shook his head—it scarce seemed to jar him. Pete had half lowered his hands as he recovered from the blow, so sure he was that it would finish his new sparring partner, and now before he could regain his guard the mucker tore into him like a whirlwind. That single blow to the face seemed to have brought back to Billy Byrne all that he ever had known of the manly art of self-defense.

Battling Dago Pete landed a few more before the fight was over, but as any old fighter will tell you there is nothing more discouraging than to discover that your most effective blows do not feeze your opponent, and only the knowledge of what a defeat at the hands of a new sparring partner would mean to his future, kept him plugging away at the hopeless task of attempting to knock out this mountain of bone and muscle.

For a few minutes Billy Byrne played with his man, hitting him when and where he would. He fought, crouching, much as Jeffries used to fight, and in his size and strength was much that reminded Cassidy of the fallen idol that in his heart of hearts he still worshiped.

And then, like a panther, the mucker sprang in with a vicious left hook to the jaw, followed, with lightning rapidity, by a right upper cut to the chin that lifted Battling Dago Pete a foot from the floor to drop him, unconscious, against the foot of the further wall.

It was a clean knockout, and when Cassidy and Hurricane got through ministering to the fallen man, and indications of returning consciousness were apparent, the professor turned to Billy.

"Got any more 'hopes' lyin' around loose?" asked the mucker with a grin. "I guess the big dinge's safe for a while yet."

"Not if you'll keep on stayin' away from the booze, kid," said Professor Cassidy, "an' let me handle you."

"I gotcha Steve," said Billy; "go to it; but first, stake me to a feed. The front side of my stomach's wrapped around my back bone."

XVIII
THE GULF BETWEEN

For three months Billy met has-beens, and third- and fourth-rate fighters from New York and its environs. He thrashed them all—usually by the knockout route and finally local sports commenced talking about him a bit, and he was matched up with second-raters from other cities.

These men he cleaned up as handily as he had the others, so that it was apparent to fight fandom that the big, quiet "unknown" was a comer; and pretty soon Professor Cassidy received an offer from another trainer-manager to match Billy against a real "hope" who stood in the forefront of hopedom.

This other manager stated that he thought the mill would prove excellent practice for his man who was having difficulty in finding opponents. Professor Cassidy thought so too, and grinned for two hours straight after reading the challenge.

The details of the fight were quickly arranged. In accordance with the state regulations it was to be a ten round, no decision bout—the weight of the gloves was prescribed by law.

The name of the "white hope" against whom Billy was to go was sufficient to draw a fair house, and there were some there who had seen Billy in other fights and looked for a good mill. When the "coming champion," as Billy's opponent was introduced, stepped into the ring he received a hearty round of applause, whereas there was but a scattered ripple of handclapping to greet the mucker. It was the first time he ever had stepped into a ring with a first-rate fighter, and as he saw the huge muscles of his antagonist and recalled the stories he had heard of his prowess and science, Billy, for the first time in his life, felt a tremor of nervousness.

His eyes wandered across the ropes to the sea of faces turned up toward him, and all of a sudden Billy Byrne went into a blue funk. Professor Cassidy, shrewd and experienced, saw it even as soon as Billy realized it— he saw the fading of his high hopes—he saw his castles in Spain tumbling in ruins about his ears—he saw his huge giant lying prone within that squared circle as the hand of the referee rose and fell in cadence to the ticking of seconds that would count his man out.

"Here," he whispered, "take a swig o' this," and he pressed a bottle toward Billy's lips.

Billy shook his head. The stuff had kept him down all his life—he had sworn never to touch another drop of it, and he never would, whether he lost this and every other fight he ever fought. He had sworn to leave it alone for *her* sake! And then the gong called him to the center of the ring.

Billy knew that he was afraid—he thought that he was afraid of the big, trained fighter who faced him; but Cassidy knew that it was a plain case of stage fright that had gripped his man. He knew, too, that it would be enough to defeat Billy's every chance for victory, and after the big "white hope" had felled Billy twice in the first minute of the first round Cassidy knew that it was all over but the shouting.

The fans, many of them, were laughing, and yelling derogatory remarks at Billy.

"Stan' up an' fight, yeh big stiff!" and "Back to de farm fer youse!" and then, high above the others a shrill voice cried "Coward! Coward!"

The word penetrated Billy's hopeless, muddled brain. Coward! *She* had called him that once, and then she had changed her mind. Theriere had thought him a coward, yet as he died he had said that he was the bravest man he ever had known. Billy recalled the yelling samurai with their keen swords and terrible spears. He saw the little room in the "palace" of Oda Yorimoto, and again he faced the brown devils who had hacked and hewed and stabbed at him that day as he fought to save the woman he loved. Coward! What was there in this padded ring for a man to fear who had faced death as Billy had faced it, and without an instant's consciousness of the meaning of the word fear? What was wrong with him, and then the shouts and curses and taunts of the crowd smote upon his ears, and he knew. It was the crowd! Again the heavy fist of the "coming champion" brought Billy to the mat, and then, before further damage could be done him, the gong saved him.

It was a surprised and chastened mucker that walked with bent head to his corner after the first round. The "white hope" was grinning and confident, and so he returned to the center of the ring for the second round. During the short interval Billy had thrashed the whole thing out. The crowd had gotten on his nerves. He was trying to fight the whole crowd instead of just one man—he would do better in this round; but the first thing that happened after he faced his opponent sent the fans into delirious ecstasies of shouting and hooting.

Billy swung his right for his foe's jaw—a terrible blow that would have ended the fight had it landed—but the man sidestepped it, and Billy's momentum carried him sprawling upon his face. When he regained his feet the "white hope" was waiting for him, and Billy went down again to lie there, quite still, while the hand of the referee marked the seconds: One. Two. Three. Four. Five. Six. Billy opened his eyes. Seven. Billy sat up. Eight. The meaning of that monotonous count finally percolated to the mucker's numbed perceptive faculties. He was being counted out! Nine! Like a flash he was on his feet. He had forgotten the crowd. Rage—cool, calculating rage possessed him—not the feverish, hysterical variety that takes its victim's brains away.

They had been counting out the man whom Barbara Harding had once loved!—the man she had thought the bravest in the world!—they were making a monkey and a coward of him! He'd show them!

The "white hope" was waiting for him. Billy was scarce off his knees before the man rushed at him wickedly, a smile playing about his lips. It was to be the last of that smile, however. Billy met the rush with his old familiar crouch, and stopped his man with a straight to the body.

Cassidy saw it and almost smiled. He didn't think that Billy could come back—but at least he was fighting for a minute in his old form.

The surprised "hope" rushed in to punish his presuming foe. The crowd was silent. Billy ducked beneath a vicious left swing and put a right to the side of the "hope's" head that sent the man to his knees. Then came the gong.

In the third round Billy fought carefully. He had made up his mind that he would show this bunch of pikers that he knew how to box, so that none might say that he had won with a lucky punch, for Billy intended to win.

The round was one which might fill with delight the soul of the fan who knows the finer points of the game. And when it was over, while little damage had been done on either side, it left no shadow of a doubt in the minds of those who knew that the unknown fighter was the more skilful boxer.

Then came the fourth round. Of course there was no question in the minds of the majority of the spectators as to who would win the fight. The stranger had merely shown one of those sudden and ephemeral bursts of form that occasionally are witnessed in every branch of sport; but he couldn't last against such a man as the "white hope"!—they looked for a knockout any minute now. Nor did they look in vain.

Billy was quite satisfied with the work he had done in the preceding round. Now he would show them another style of fighting! And he did. From the tap of the gong he rushed his opponent about the ring at will. He hit him when and where he pleased. The man was absolutely helpless before him. With left and right hooks Billy rocked the "coming champion's" head from side to side. He landed upon the swelling optics of his victim as he listed.

Thrice he rushed him to the ropes, and once the man fell through them into the laps of the hooting spectators—only now they were not hooting Billy. Until the gong Billy played with his man as a cat might play with a mouse; yet not once had he landed a knockout blow.

"Why didn't you finish him?" cried Professor Cassidy, as Billy returned to his corner after the round. "You had 'im goin' man—why in the world didn't yeh finish him?"

"I didn't want to," said Billy; "not in that round. I'm reserving the finish for the fifth round, and if you want to win some money you can take the hunch!"

"Do you mean it?" asked Cassidy.

"Sure," said Billy. "You might make more by laying that I'd make him take the count in the first minute of the round—you can place a hundred of mine on that, if you will, please."

Cassidy took the hunch, and a moment later as the two men faced each other he regretted his act, for to his surprise the "white hope" came up for the fifth round smiling and confident once more.

"Someone's been handin' him an earful," grumbled Cassidy, "an' it might be all he needed to take 'im through the first minute of the round, and maybe the whole round—I've seen that did lots o' times."

As the two men met the "white hope" was the aggressor. He rushed in to close quarters aiming a stinging blow at Billy's face, and then to Cassidy's chagrin and the crowd's wonder, the mucker lowered his guard and took the wallop full on the jaw. The blow seemed never to jar him the least. The "hope" swung again, and there stood Billy Byrne, like a huge bronze statue taking blow after blow that would have put an ordinary man down for the count.

The fans saw and appreciated the spectacular bravado of the act, and they went wild. Cheer on cheer rose, hoarse and deafening, to the rafters. The "white hope" lost his self-control and what little remained of his short temper, and deliberately struck Billy a foul blow, but before the referee could interfere the mucker swung another just such blow as he had missed and fallen with in the second round; but this time he did not miss—his mighty fist caught the "coming champion" on the point of the chin, lifted him off his feet and landed him halfway through the ropes. There he lay while the referee tolled off the count of ten, and as the official took Billy's hand in his and raised it aloft in signal that he had won the fight the fickle crowd cheered and screamed in a delirium of joy.

Cassidy crawled through the ropes and threw his arms around Billy.

"I knew youse could do it, kid!" he screamed. "You're as good as made now, an' you're de next champ, or I never seen one."

The following morning the sporting sheets hailed "Sailor" Byrne as the greatest "white hope" of them all. Flashlights of him filled a quarter of a page. There were interviews with him. Interviews with the man he had defeated. Interviews with Cassidy. Interviews with the referee. Interviews with everybody, and all were agreed that he was the most likely heavy since Jeffries. Corbett admitted that, while in his prime he could doubtless have bested the new wonder, he would have found him a tough customer.

Everyone said that Byrne's future was assured. There was not a man in sight who could touch him, and none who had seen him fight the night before but would have staked his last dollar on him in a mill with the black champion.

Cassidy wired a challenge to the Negro's manager, and received an answer that was most favorable. The terms were, as usual, rather one-sided but Cassidy accepted them, and it seemed before noon that a fight was assured.

Billy was more nearly happy again than he had been since the day he had renounced Barbara Harding to the man he thought she loved. He read and reread the accounts in the papers, and then searching for more references to himself off the sporting page he ran upon the very name that had been constantly in his thoughts for all these months—Harding.

Persistent rumor has it that the engagement of the beautiful Miss Harding to Wm. J. Mallory has been broken. Miss Harding could not be seen at her father's home up to a late hour last night. Mr. Mallory refused to discuss the matter, but would not deny the rumor.

There was more, but that was all that Billy Byrne read. The paper dropped from his hand. Battles and championships faded from his thoughts. He sat with his eyes bent upon the floor, and his mind was thousands of miles away across the broad Pacific upon a little island in the midst of a turbulent stream.

And far uptown another sat with the same paper in her hand. Barbara Harding was glancing through the sporting sheet in search of the scores of yesterday's woman's golf tournament. And as she searched her eyes suddenly became riveted upon the picture of a giant man, and she forgot about tournaments and low scores. Hastily she searched the heads and text until she came upon the name—"'Sailor' Byrne!"

Yes! It must be he. Greedily she read and reread all that had been written about him. Yes, she, Barbara Harding, scion of an aristocratic house—ultra-society girl, read and reread the accounts of a brutal prize fight.

A half hour later a messenger boy found "Sailor" Byrne the center of an admiring throng in Professor Cassidy's third-floor gymnasium. With worshiping eyes taking in his new hero from head to foot the youth handed Byrne a note.

He stood staring at the heavy weight until he had perused it.

"Any answer?" he asked.

"No answer, kid," replied Byrne, "that I can't take myself," and he tossed a dollar to the worshiping boy.

An hour later Billy Byrne was ascending the broad, white steps that led to the entrance of Anthony Harding's New York house. The servant who answered his ring eyed him suspiciously, for Billy Byrne still dressed like a teamster on holiday. He had no card!

"Tell Miss Harding that Mr. Byrne has come," he said.

The servant left him standing in the hallway, and started to ascend the great staircase, but halfway up he met Miss Harding coming down.

"Never mind, Smith," she said. "I am expecting Mr. Byrne," and then seeing that the fellow had not seated her visitor she added, "He is a very dear friend." Smith faded quickly from the scene.

"Billy!" cried the girl, rushing toward him with outstretched hands. "O Billy, we thought you were dead. How long have you been here? Why haven't you been to see me?"

Byrne hesitated.

A great, mad hope had been surging through his being since he had read of the broken engagement and received the girl's note. And now in her eyes, in her whole attitude, he could read, as unmistakably as though her lips had formed the words that he had not hoped in vain.

But some strange influence had seemed suddenly to come to work upon him. Even in the brief moment of his entrance into the magnificence of Anthony Harding's home he had felt a strange little stricture of the throat—a choking, half-suffocating sensation.

The attitude of the servant, the splendor of the furnishings, the stateliness of the great hall, and the apartments opening upon it—all had whispered to him that he did not "belong."

And now Barbara, clothed in some wondrous foreign creation, belied by her very appearance the expression that suffused her eyes.

No, Billy Byrne, the mucker, did not belong there. Nor ever could he belong, more than Barbara ever could have "belonged" on Grand Avenue. And Billy Byrne knew it now. His heart went cold. The bottom seemed suddenly to have dropped out of his life.

Bravely he had battled to forget this wonderful creature, or, rather, his hopeless love for her—her he could never forget. But the note from her, and the sight of her had but served to rekindle the old fire within his breast.

He thought quickly. His own life or happiness did not count. Nothing counted now but Barbara. He had seen the lovelight in her eyes. He thanked God that he had realized what it all would have meant, before he let her see that he had seen it.

"I've been back several months," he said presently, in answer to her question; "but I got sense enough to stay where I belong. Gee! Wouldn't I look great comin' up here buttin' in, wit youse bunch of highlifes?"

Billy slapped his thigh resoundingly and laughed in stentorian tones that caused the eyebrows of the sensitive Smith on the floor above to elevate in shocked horror.

"Den dere was de mills. I couldn't break away from me work, could I, to chase a bunch of skirts?"

Barbara felt a qualm of keen disappointment that Billy had fallen again into the old dialect that she had all but eradicated during those days upon distant "Manhattan Island."

"I wouldn't o' come up atal," he went on, "if I hadn't o' read in de poiper how youse an' Mallory had busted. I t'ought I'd breeze in an' see wot de trouble was."

His eyes had been averted, mostly, as he talked. Now he swung suddenly upon her.

"He's on de square, ain't he?" he demanded.

"Yes," said Barbara. She was not quite sure whether to feel offended, or not. But the memory of Billy's antecedents came to his rescue. Of course he didn't know that it was such terribly bad form to broach such a subject to her, she thought.

"Well, then," continued the mucker, "wot's up? Mallory's de guy fer youse. Youse loved him or youse wouldn't have got engaged to him."

The statement was almost an interrogation.

Barbara nodded affirmatively.

"You see, Billy," she started, "I have always known Mr. Mallory, and always thought that I loved him until—until—" There was no answering light in Billy's eyes—no encouragement for the words that were on her lips. She halted lamely. "Then," she went on presently, "we became engaged after we reached New York. We all thought you dead," she concluded simply.

"Do you think as much of him now as you did when you promised to marry him?" he asked, ignoring her reference to himself and all that it implied.

Barbara nodded.

"What is at the bottom of this row?" persisted Billy. He had fallen back into the decent pronunciation that Barbara had taught him, but neither noticed the change. For a moment he had forgotten that he was playing a part. Then he recollected.

"Nothing much," replied the girl. "I couldn't rid myself of the feeling that they had murdered you, by leaving you back there alone and wounded. I began to think 'coward' every time I saw Mr. Mallory. I couldn't marry him, feeling that way toward him, and, Billy, I really never *loved* him as—as—" Again she stumbled, but the mucker made no attempt to grasp the opportunity opened before him.

Instead he crossed the library to the telephone. Running through the book he came presently upon the number he sought. A moment later he had his connection.

"Is this Mallory?" he asked.

"I'm Byrne—Billy Byrne. De guy dat cracked your puss fer youse on de *Lotus*."

"Dead, hell! Not me. Say, I'm up here at Barbara's."

"Yes, dat's wot I said. She wants youse to beat it up here's swift as youse kin beat it."

Barbara Harding stepped forward. Her eyes were blazing.

"How dare you?" she cried, attempting to seize the telephone from Billy's grasp.

He turned his huge frame between her and the instrument. "Git a move!" he shouted into the mouthpiece. "Goodbye!" and he hung up.

Then he turned back toward the angry girl.

"Look here," he said. "Once youse was strong on de sob stuff wit me, tellin' me how noble I was, an' all de different tings youse would do fer me to repay all I done fer youse. Now youse got de chanct."

"What do you mean?" asked the girl, puzzled. "What can I do for you?"

"Youse kin do dis fer me. When Mallory gits here youse kin tell him dat de engagement is all on again—see!"

In the wide eyes of the girl Billy read a deeper hurt than he had dreamed of. He had thought that it would not be difficult for her to turn back from the vulgar mucker to the polished gentleman. And when he saw that she was suffering, and guessed that it was because he had tried to crush her love by brute force he could carry the game no further.

"O Barbara," he cried, "can't you see that Mallory is your kind—that *he* is a fit mate for you. I have learned since I came into this house a few minutes ago the unbridgeable chasm that stretches between Billy Byrne, the mucker, and such as you. Once I aspired; but now I know just as you must have always known, that a single lifetime is far too short for a man to cover the distance from Grand Avenue to Riverside Drive.

"I want you to be happy, Barbara, just as I intend to be. Back there in Chicago there are plenty of girls on Grand Avenue as straight and clean and fine as they make 'em on Riverside Drive. Girls of my own kind, they are, and I'm going back there to find the one that God intended for me. You've taught me what a good girl can do toward making a man of a beast. You've taught me pride and self-respect. You've taught me so much that I'd rather that I'd died back there beneath the spears of Oda Iseka's warriors than live here beneath the sneers and contempt of servants, and the pity and condescension of your friends.

"I want you to be happy, Barbara, and so I want you to promise me that you'll marry Billy Mallory. There isn't any man on earth quite good enough for you; but Mallory comes nearer to it than anyone I know. I've heard 'em talking about him around town since I came back—and there isn't a rotten story chalked up against him nowhere, and that's a lot more than you can say for ninety-nine of a hundred New Yorkers that are talked about at all.

"And Mallory's a man, too—the kind that every woman ought to have, only they ain't enough of 'em to go 'round. Do you remember how he stood up there on the deck of the *Lotus* and fought fair against my dirty tricks? He's a man and a gentleman, Barbara—the sort you can be proud of, and that's the sort you got to have. You see I know you.

"And he fought against those fellows of Yoka in the street of Oda Iseka's village like a man should fight. There ain't any yellow in him, Barbara, and he didn't leave me until there seemed no other way, even in the face of the things I told them to make them go. Don't harbor that against him—I only wonder that he didn't croak me; your dad wanted to, and Mallory wouldn't let him."

"They never told me that," said Barbara.

The bell rang.

"Here he is now," said Billy. "Goodbye—I'd rather not see him. Smith'll let me out the servants' door. Guess that'll make him feel better. You'll do as I ask, Barbara?"

He had paused at the door, turning toward her as he asked the final question.

The girl stood facing him. Her eyes were dim with unshed tears. Billy Byrne swam before them in a hazy mist.

"You'll do as I ask, Barbara!" he repeated, but this time it was a command.

As Mallory entered the room Barbara heard the door of the servants' entrance slam behind Billy Byrne.

PART II

I
THE MURDER TRIAL

Billy Byrne squared his broad shoulders and filled his deep lungs with the familiar medium which is known as air in Chicago. He was standing upon the platform of a New York Central train that was pulling into the La Salle Street Station, and though the young man was far from happy something in the nature of content pervaded his being, for he was coming home.

After something more than a year of world wandering and strange adventure Billy Byrne was coming back to the great West Side and Grand Avenue.

Now there is not much upon either side or down the center of long and tortuous Grand Avenue to arouse enthusiasm, nor was Billy particularly enthusiastic about that more or less squalid thoroughfare.

The thing that exalted Billy was the idea that he was coming back to *show them*. He had left under a cloud and with a reputation for genuine toughness and rowdyism that has seen few parallels even in the ungentle district of his birth and upbringing.

A girl had changed him. She was as far removed from Billy's sphere as the stars themselves; but Billy had loved her and learned from her, and in trying to become more as he knew the men of her class were he had sloughed off much of the uncouthness that had always been a part of him, and all of the rowdyism. Billy Byrne was no longer the mucker.

He had given her up because he imagined the gulf between Grand Avenue and Riverside Drive to be unbridgeable; but he still clung to the ideals she had awakened in him. He still sought to be all that she might wish him to be, even though he realized that he never should see her again.

Grand Avenue would be the easiest place to forget his sorrow—her he could never forget. And then, his newly awakened pride urged him back to the haunts of his former life that he might, as he would put it himself, show them. He wanted the gang to see that he, Billy Byrne, wasn't afraid to be decent. He wanted some of the neighbors to realize that he could work steadily and earn an honest living, and he looked forward with delight to the pleasure and satisfaction of rubbing it in to some of the saloon keepers and bartenders who had helped keep him drunk some five days out of seven, for Billy didn't drink any more.

But most of all he wanted to vindicate himself in the eyes of the once-hated law. He wanted to clear his record of the unjust charge of murder which had sent him scurrying out of Chicago over a year before, that night that Patrolman Stanley Lasky of the Lake Street Station had tipped him off that Sheehan had implicated him in the murder of old man Schneider.

Now Billy Byrne had not killed Schneider. He had been nowhere near the old fellow's saloon at the time of the holdup; but Sheehan, who had been arrested and charged with the crime, was an old enemy of Billy's, and Sheehan had seen a chance to divert some of the suspicion from himself and square accounts with Byrne at the same time.

The new Billy Byrne was ready to accept at face value everything which seemed to belong in any way to the environment of that exalted realm where dwelt the girl he loved. Law, order, and justice appeared to Billy in a new light since he had rubbed elbows with the cultured and refined.

He no longer distrusted or feared them. They would give him what he sought—a square deal.

It seemed odd to Billy that he should be seeking anything from the law or its minions. For years he had waged a perpetual battle with both. Now he was coming back voluntarily to give himself up, with every conviction that he should be exonerated quickly. Billy, knowing his own innocence, realizing his own integrity, assumed that others must immediately appreciate both.

"First," thought Billy, "I'll go take a look at little old Grand Ave., then I'll give myself up. The trial may take a long time, an' if it does I want to see some of the old bunch first."

So Billy entered an "L" coach and leaning on the sill of an open window watched grimy Chicago rattle past until the guard's "Granavenoo" announced the end of his journey.

Maggie Shane was sitting on the upper step of the long flight of stairs which lean precariously against the scarred face of the frame residence upon the second floor front of which the lares and penates of the Shane family are crowded into three ill-smelling rooms.

It was Saturday and Maggie was off. She sat there rather disconsolate for there was a dearth of beaux for Maggie, none having arisen to fill the aching void left by the sudden departure of "Coke" Sheehan since that worthy gentleman had sought a more salubrious clime—to the consternation of both Maggie Shane and Mr. Sheehan's bondsmen.

Maggie scowled down upon the frowsy street filled with frowsy women and frowsy children. She scowled upon the street cars rumbling by with their frowsy loads. Occasionally she varied the monotony by drawing out her chewing gum to wondrous lengths, holding one end between a thumb and finger and the other between her teeth.

Presently Maggie spied a rather pleasing figure sauntering up the sidewalk upon her side of the street. The man was too far away for her to recognize his features, but his size and bearing and general appearance appealed to the lonesome Maggie. She hoped it was someone she knew, or with whom she might easily become acquainted, for Maggie was bored to death.

She patted the hair at the back of her head and righted the mop which hung over one eye. Then she rearranged her skirts and waited. As the man approached she saw that he was better looking than she had even dared to hope, and that there was something extremely familiar about his appearance. It was not, though, until he was almost in front of the house that he looked up at the girl and she recognized him.

Then Maggie Shane gasped and clutched the handrail at her side An instant later the man was past and continuing his way along the sidewalk.

Maggie Shane glared after him for a minute, then she ran quickly down the stairs and into a grocery store a few doors west, where she asked if she might use the telephone.

"Gimme West 2063," she demanded of the operator, and a moment later: "Is this Lake Street?"

"Well say, Billy Byrne's back. I just see him."

"Yes an' never mind who I am; but if youse guys want him he's walkin' west on Grand Avenoo right now. I just this minute seen him near Lincoln," and she smashed the receiver back into its hook.

Billy Byrne thought that he would look in on his mother, not that he expected to be welcomed even though she might happen to be sober, or not that he cared to see her; but Billy's whole manner of thought had altered within the year, and something now seemed to tell him that it was his duty to do the thing he contemplated. Maybe he might even be of help to her.

But when he reached the gloomy neighborhood in which his childhood had been spent it was to learn that his mother was dead and that another family occupied the tumble-down cottage that had been his home.

If Billy Byrne felt any sorrow because of his mother's death he did not reveal it outwardly. He owed her nothing but for kicks and cuffs received, and for the surroundings and influences that had started him upon a life of crime at an age when most boys are just entering grammar school.

Really the man was relieved that he had not had to see her, and it was with a lighter step that he turned back to retrace his way along Grand Avenue. No one of the few he had met who recognized him had seemed particularly delighted at his return. The whole affair had been something of a disappointment. Therefore Billy determined to go at once to the Lake Street Station and learn the status of the Schneider murder case. Possibly they had discovered the real murderer, and if that was the case Billy would be permitted to go his way; but if not then he could give himself up and ask for a trial, that he might be exonerated.

As he neared Wood Street two men who had been watching his approach stepped into the doorway of a saloon, and as he passed they stepped out again behind him. One upon either side they seized him.

Billy turned to remonstrate.

"Come easy now, Byrne," admonished one of the men, "an' don't make no fuss."

"Oh," said Billy, "it's you, is it? Well, I was just goin' over to the station to give myself up."

Both men laughed, skeptically. "We'll just save you the trouble," said one of them. "We'll take you over. You might lose your way if you tried to go alone."

Billy went along in silence the rest of the way to where the patrol waited at another corner. He saw there was nothing to be gained by talking to these detectives; but he found the lieutenant equally inclined to doubt his intentions. He, too, only laughed when Billy assured him that he was on his way to the station at the very instant of arrest.

As the weeks dragged along, and Billy Byrne found no friendly interest in himself or his desire to live on the square, and no belief in his protestations that he had had naught to do with the killing of Schneider he began to have his doubts as to the wisdom of his act.

He also commenced to entertain some of his former opinions of the police, and of the law of which they are supposed to be the guardians. A cell-mate told him that the papers had scored the department heavily for their failure to apprehend the murderer of the inoffensive old Schneider, and that public opinion had been so aroused that a general police shakeup had followed.

The result was that the police were keen to fasten the guilt upon someone—they did not care whom, so long as it was someone who was in their custody.

"You may not o' done it," ventured the cell-mate; "but they'll send you up for it, if they can't hang you. They're goin' to try to get the death sentence. They hain't got no love for you, Byrne. You caused 'em a lot o' throuble in your day an' they haven't forgot it. I'd hate to be in your boots."

Billy Byrne shrugged. Where were his dreams of justice? They seemed to have faded back into the old distrust and hatred. He shook himself and conjured in his mind the vision of a beautiful girl who had believed in him and trusted him—who had inculcated within him a love for all that was finest and best in true manhood, for the very things that he had most hated all the years of his life before she had come into his existence to alter it and him.

And then Billy would believe again—believe that in the end justice would triumph and that it would all come out right, just the way he had pictured it.

With the coming of the last day of the trial Billy found it more and more difficult to adhere to his regard for law, order, and justice. The prosecution had shown conclusively that Billy was a hard customer. The police had brought witnesses who did not hesitate to perjure themselves in their testimony—testimony which it seemed to Billy the densest of jurymen could plainly see had been framed up and learned by rote until it was letter-perfect.

These witnesses could recall with startling accuracy every detail that had occurred between seventeen minutes after eight and twenty-one minutes past nine on the night of September 23 over a year before; but where they had been and what they had done ten minutes earlier or ten minutes later, or where they were at nine o'clock in the evening last Friday they couldn't for the lives of them remember.

And Billy was practically without witnesses.

The result was a foregone conclusion. Even Billy had to admit it, and when the prosecuting attorney demanded the death penalty the prisoner had an uncanny sensation as of the tightening of a hempen rope about his neck. As he waited for the jury to return its verdict Billy sat in his cell trying to read a newspaper which a kindly guard had given him. But his eyes persisted in boring through the white paper and the black type to scenes that were not in any paper. He saw a turbulent river tumbling through a savage world, and in the swirl of the water lay a little island. And he saw a man there upon the island, and a girl. The girl was teaching the man to speak the language of the cultured, and to view life as people of refinement view it.

She taught him what honor meant among her class, and that it was better to lose any other possession rather than lose honor. Billy realized that it had been these lessons that had spurred him on to the mad scheme that was to end now with the verdict of "Guilty"—he had wished to vindicate his honor. A hard laugh broke from his lips; but instantly he sobered and his face softened.

It had been for her sake after all, and what mattered it if they did send him to the gallows? He had not sacrificed his honor—he had done his best to assert it. He was innocent. They could kill him but they couldn't make him guilty. A thousand juries pronouncing him so could not make it true that he had killed Schneider.

But it would be hard, after all his hopes, after all the plans he had made to live square, to *show them*. His eyes still boring through the paper suddenly found themselves attracted by something in the text before them—a name, Harding.

Billy Byrne shook himself and commenced to read:

> The marriage of Barbara, daughter of Anthony Harding, the multimillionaire, to William Mallory will take place on the twenty-fifth of June.

The article was dated New York. There was more, but Billy did not read it. He had read enough. It is true that he had urged her to marry Mallory; but now, in his lonesomeness and friendlessness, he felt almost as though she had been untrue to him.

"Come along, Byrne," a bailiff interrupted his thoughts, "the jury's reached a verdict."

The judge was emerging from his chambers as Billy was led into the courtroom. Presently the jury filed in and took their seats. The foreman handed the clerk a bit of paper. Even before it was read Billy knew that he had been found guilty. He did not care any longer, so he told himself. He hoped that the judge would send him to the gallows. There was nothing more in life for him now anyway. He wanted to die. But instead he was sentenced to life imprisonment in the penitentiary at Joliet.

This was infinitely worse than death. Billy Byrne was appalled at the thought of remaining for life within the grim stone walls of a prison. Once more there swept over him all the old, unreasoning hatred of the law and all that pertained to it. He would like to close his steel fingers about the fat neck of the red-faced judge. The smug jurymen roused within him the lust to kill. Justice! Billy Byrne laughed aloud.

A bailiff rapped for order. One of the jurymen leaned close to a neighbor and whispered. "A hardened criminal," he said. "Society will be safer when he is behind the bars."

The next day they took Billy aboard a train bound for Joliet. He was handcuffed to a deputy sheriff. Billy was calm outwardly; but inwardly he was a raging volcano of hate.

In a certain very beautiful home on Riverside Drive, New York City, a young lady, comfortably backed by downy pillows, sat in her bed and alternated her attention between coffee and rolls, and a morning paper.

On the inside of the main sheet a heading claimed her languid attention: CHICAGO MURDERER GIVEN LIFE SENTENCE. Of late Chicago had aroused in Barbara Harding a greater proportion of interest than ever it had in the past, and so it was that she now permitted her eyes to wander casually down the printed column.

> Murderer of harmless old saloon keeper is finally brought to justice. The notorious West Side rowdy, "Billy" Byrne, apprehended after more than a year as fugitive from justice, is sent to Joliet for life.

Barbara Harding sat stony-eyed and cold for what seemed many minutes. Then with a stifled sob she turned and buried her face in the pillows.

The train bearing Billy Byrne and the deputy sheriff toward Joliet had covered perhaps half the distance between Chicago and Billy's permanent destination when it occurred to the deputy sheriff that he should like to go into the smoker and enjoy a cigar.

Now, from the moment that he had been sentenced Billy Byrne's mind had been centered upon one thought—escape. He knew that there probably would be not the slightest chance for escape; but nevertheless the idea was always uppermost in his thoughts.

His whole being revolted, not alone against the injustice which had sent him into life imprisonment, but at the thought of the long years of awful monotony which lay ahead of him.

He could not endure them. He would not! The deputy sheriff rose, and motioning his prisoner ahead of him, started for the smoker. It was two cars ahead. The train was vestibuled. The first platform they crossed was tightly enclosed; but at the second Billy saw that a careless porter had left one of the doors open. The train was slowing down for some reason—it was going, perhaps, twenty miles an hour.

Billy was the first upon the platform. He was the first to see the open door. It meant one of two things—a chance to escape, or, death. Even the latter was to be preferred to life imprisonment.

Billy did not hesitate an instant. Even before the deputy sheriff realized that the door was open, his prisoner had leaped from the moving train dragging his guard after him.

II
THE ESCAPE

Byrne had no time to pick any particular spot to jump for. When he did jump he might have been directly over a picket fence, or a bottomless pit—he did not know. Nor did he care.

As it happened he was over neither. The platform chanced to be passing across a culvert at the instant. Beneath the culvert was a slimy pool. Into this the two men plunged, alighting unharmed.

Byrne was the first to regain his feet. He dragged the deputy sheriff to his knees, and before that frightened and astonished officer of the law could gather his wits together he had been relieved of his revolver and found himself looking into its cold and businesslike muzzle.

Then Billy Byrne waded ashore, prodding the deputy sheriff in the ribs with cold steel, and warning him to silence. Above the pool stood a little wood, thick with tangled wildwood. Into this Byrne forced his prisoner.

When they had come deep enough into the concealment of the foliage to make discovery from the outside improbable Byrne halted.

"Now say yer prayers," he commanded. "I'm a-going to croak yeh."

The deputy sheriff looked up at him in wild-eyed terror.

"My God!" he cried. "I ain't done nothin' to you, Byrne. Haven't I always been your friend? What've I ever done to you? For God's sake Byrne you ain't goin' to murder me, are you? They'll get you, sure."

Billy Byrne let a rather unpleasant smile curl his lips.

"No," he said, "youse ain't done nothin' to me; but you stand for the law, damn it, and I'm going to croak everything I meet that stands for the law. They wanted to send me up for life—me, an innocent man. Your kind done it—the cops. You ain't no cop; but you're just as rotten. Now say yer prayers."

He leveled the revolver at his victim's head. The deputy sheriff slumped to his knees and tried to embrace Billy Byrne's legs as he pleaded for his life.

"Cut it out, you poor boob," admonished Billy. "You've gotta die and if you was half a man you'd wanna die like one."

The deputy sheriff slipped to the ground. His terror had overcome him, leaving him in happy unconsciousness. Byrne stood looking down upon the man for a moment. His wrist was chained to that of the other, and the pull of the deputy's body was irritating.

Byrne stooped and placed the muzzle of the revolver back of the man's ear. "Justice!" he muttered, scornfully, and his finger tightened upon the trigger.

Then, conjured from nothing, there rose between himself and the unconscious man beside him the figure of a beautiful girl. Her face was brave and smiling, and in her eyes was trust and pride—whole worlds of them. Trust and pride in Billy Byrne.

Billy closed his eyes tight as though in physical pain. He brushed his hand quickly across his face.

"Gawd!" he muttered. "I can't do it—but I came awful close to it."

Dropping the revolver into his side pocket he kneeled beside the deputy sheriff and commenced to go through the man's clothes. After a moment he came upon what he sought—a key ring confining several keys.

Billy found the one he wished and presently he was free. He still stood looking at the deputy sheriff.

"I ought to croak you," he murmured. "I'll never make my getaway if I don't; but *she* won't let me—God bless her."

Suddenly a thought came to Billy Byrne. If he could have a start he might escape. It wouldn't hurt the man any to stay here for a few hours, or even for a day. Billy removed the deputy's coat and tore it into strips. With these he bound the man to a tree. Then he fastened a gag in his mouth.

During the operation the deputy regained consciousness. He looked questioningly at Billy.

"I decided not to croak you," explained the young man. "I'm just a-goin' to leave you here for a while. They'll be lookin' all along the right o' way in a few hours—it won't be long afore they find you. Now so long, and take care of yerself, bo," and Billy Byrne had gone.

A mistake that proved fortunate for Billy Byrne caused the penitentiary authorities to expect him and his guard by a later train, so no suspicion was aroused when they failed to come upon the train they really had started upon. This gave Billy a good two hours' start that he would not otherwise have had—an opportunity of which he made good use.

Wherefore it was that by the time the authorities awoke to the fact that something had happened Billy Byrne was fifty miles west of Joliet, bowling along aboard a fast Santa Fe freight. Shortly after night had fallen the train crossed the Mississippi. Billy Byrne was hungry and thirsty, and as the train slowed down and came to a stop out in the midst of a dark solitude of silent, sweet-smelling country, Billy opened the door of his box car and dropped lightly to the ground.

So far no one had seen Billy since he had passed from the ken of the trussed deputy sheriff, and as Billy had no desire to be seen he slipped over the edge of the embankment into a dry ditch, where he squatted upon his haunches waiting for the train to depart. The stop out there in the dark night was one of those mysterious stops which trains are prone to make, unexplained and doubtless unexplainable by any other than a higher intelligence which directs the movements of men and rolling stock. There was no town, and not even a switch light. Presently two staccato blasts broke from the engine's whistle, there was a progressive jerking at coupling pins, which started up at the big locomotive and ran rapidly down the length of the train, there was the squeaking of brake shoes against wheels, and the train moved slowly forward again upon its long journey toward the coast, gaining momentum moment by moment until finally the way-car rolled rapidly past the hidden fugitive and the freight rumbled away to be swallowed up in the darkness.

When it had gone Billy rose and climbed back upon the track, along which he plodded in the wake of the departing train. Somewhere a road would presently cut across the track, and along the road there would be farmhouses or a village where food and drink might be found.

Billy was penniless, yet he had no doubt but that he should eat when he had discovered food. He was thinking of this as he walked briskly toward the west, and what he thought of induced a doubt in his mind as to whether it was, after all, going to be so easy to steal food.

"Shaw!" he exclaimed, half aloud, "she wouldn't think it wrong for a guy to swipe a little grub when he was starvin'. It ain't like I was goin' to stick a guy up for his roll. Sure she wouldn't see nothin' wrong for me to get something to eat. I ain't got no money. They took it all away from me, an' I got a right to live—but, somehow, I hate to do it. I wisht there was some other way. Gee, but she's made a sissy out o' me! Funny how a feller can change. Why I almost like bein' a sissy," and Billy Byrne grinned at the almost inconceivable idea.

Before Billy came to a road he saw a light down in a little depression at one side of the track. It was not such a light as a lamp shining beyond a window makes. It rose and fell, winking and flaring close to the ground. It looked much like a camp fire, and as Billy drew nearer he saw that such it was, and he heard a voice, too. Billy approached more carefully. He must be careful always to see before being seen. The little fire burned upon the bank of a stream which the track bridged upon a concrete arch.

Billy dropped once more from the right of way, and climbed a fence into a thin wood. Through this he approached the camp fire with small chance of being observed. As he neared it the voice resolved itself into articulate words, and presently Billy leaned against a tree close behind the speaker and listened.

There was but a single figure beside the small fire—that of a man squatting upon his haunches roasting something above the flames. At one edge of the fire was an empty tin can from which steam arose, and an aroma that was now and again wafted to Billy's nostrils.

Coffee! My, how good it smelled. Billy's mouth watered. But the voice—that interested Billy almost as much as the preparations for the coming meal.

> We'll dance a merry saraband from here to drowsy Samarcand.
> Along the sea, across the land, the birds are flying South,
> And you, my sweet Penelope, out there somewhere you wait
>   for me,
> With buds of roses in your hair and kisses on your mouth.

The words took hold of Billy somewhere and made him forget his hunger. Like a sweet incense which induces pleasant daydreams they were wafted in upon him through the rich, mellow voice of the solitary camper, and the lilt of the meter entered his blood.

But the voice. It was the voice of such as Billy Byrne always had loathed and ridiculed until he had sat at the feet of Barbara Harding and learned many things, including love. It was the voice of culture and refinement. Billy strained his eyes through the darkness to have a closer look at the man. The light of the camp fire fell upon frayed and bagging clothes, and upon the back of a head covered by a shapeless, and disreputable soft hat.

Obviously the man was a hobo. The coffee boiling in a discarded tin can would have been proof positive of this without other evidence; but there seemed plenty more. Yes, the man was a hobo. Billy continued to stand listening.

> The mountains are all hid in mist; the valley is like amethyst;
> The poplar leaves they turn and twist; oh, silver, silver green!
> Out there somewhere along the sea a ship is waiting patiently,
> While up the beach the bubbles slip with white afloat between.

"Gee!" thought Billy Byrne; "but that's great stuff. I wonder where he gets it. It makes me want to hike until I find that place he's singin' about."

Billy's thoughts were interrupted by a sound in the wood to one side of him. As he turned his eyes in the direction of the slight noise which had attracted him he saw two men step quietly out and cross toward the man at the camp fire.

These, too, were evidently hobos. Doubtless pals of the poetical one. The latter did not hear them until they were directly behind him. Then he turned slowly and rose as they halted beside his fire.

"Evenin', bo," said one of the newcomers.

"Good evening, gentlemen," replied the camper, "welcome to my humble home. Have you dined?"

"Naw," replied the first speaker, "we ain't; but we're goin' to. Now can the chatter an' duck. There ain't enough fer one here, let alone three. Beat it!" and the man, who was big and burly, assumed a menacing attitude and took a truculent step nearer the solitary camper.

The latter was short and slender. The larger man looked as though he might have eaten him at a single mouthful; but the camper did not flinch.

"You pain me," he said. "You induce within me a severe and highly localized pain, and furthermore I don't like your whiskers."

With which apparently irrelevant remark he seized the matted beard of the larger tramp and struck the fellow a quick, sharp blow in the face. Instantly the fellow's companion was upon him; but the camper retained his death grip upon the beard of the now yelling bully and continued to rain blow after blow upon head and face.

Billy Byrne was an interested spectator. He enjoyed a good fight as he enjoyed little else; but presently when the first tramp succeeded in tangling his legs about the legs of his chastiser and dragging him to the ground, and the second tramp seized a heavy stick and ran forward to dash the man's brains out, Billy thought it time to interfere.

Stepping forward he called aloud as he came: "Cut it out, boes! You can't pull off any rough stuff like that with this here sweet singer. Can it! Can it!" as the second tramp raised his stick to strike the now prostrate camper.

As he spoke Billy Byrne broke into a run, and as the stick fell he reached the man's side and swung a blow to the tramp's jaw that sent the fellow spinning backward to the river's brim, where he tottered drunkenly for a moment and then plunged backward into the shallow water.

Then Billy seized the other attacker by the shoulder and dragged him to his feet.

"Do you want some, too, you big stiff?" he inquired.

The man spluttered and tried to break away, striking at Billy as he did so; but a sudden punch, such a punch as Billy Byrne had once handed the surprised Harlem Hurricane, removed from the mind of the tramp the last vestige of any thought he might have harbored to do the newcomer bodily injury, and with it removed all else from the man's mind, temporarily.

As the fellow slumped, unconscious, to the ground, the camper rose to his feet.

"Some wallop you have concealed in your sleeve, my friend," he said; "place it there!" and he extended a slender, shapely hand.

Billy took it and shook it.

"It don't get under the ribs like those verses of yours, though, bo," he returned.

"It seems to have insinuated itself beneath this guy's thick skull," replied the poetical one, "and it's a cinch my verses, nor any other would ever get there."

The tramp who had plumbed the depths of the creek's foot of water and two feet of soft mud was crawling ashore.

"Whadda *you* want now?" inquired Billy Byrne. "A piece o' soap?"

"I'll get youse yet," spluttered the moist one through his watery whiskers.

"Ferget it," admonished Billy, "an' hit the trail." He pointed toward the railroad right of way. "An' you, too, John L," he added turning to the other victim of his artistic execution, who was now sitting up. "Hike!"

Mumbling and growling the two unwashed shuffled away, and were presently lost to view along the vanishing track.

The solitary camper had returned to his culinary effort, as unruffled and unconcerned, apparently, as though naught had occurred to disturb his peaceful solitude.

"Sit down," he said after a moment, looking up at Billy, "and have a bite to eat with me. Take that leather easy chair. The Louis Quatorze is too small and spindle-legged for comfort." He waved his hand invitingly toward the sward beside the fire.

For a moment he was entirely absorbed in the roasting fowl impaled upon a sharp stick which he held in his right hand. Then he presently broke again into verse.

> Around the world and back again; we saw it all. The mist and rain
> In England and the hot old plain from Needles to Berdoo.
> We kept a-rambling all the time. I rustled grub, he rustled rhyme—
> Blind-baggage, hoof it, ride or climb—we always put it through.

"You're a good sort," he broke off, suddenly. "There ain't many boes that would have done as much for a fellow."

"It was two against one," replied Billy, "an' I don't like them odds. Besides I like your poetry. Where d'ye get it—make it up?"

"Lord, no," laughed the other. "If I could do that I wouldn't be panhandling. A guy by the name of Henry Herbert Knibbs did them. Great, ain't they?"

"They sure is. They get me right where I live," and then, after a pause; "sure you got enough fer two, bo?"

"I have enough for you, old top," replied the host, "even if I only had half as much as I have. Here, take first crack at the ambrosia. Sorry I have but a single cup; but James has broken the others. James is very careless. Sometimes I almost feel that I shall have to let him go."

"Who's James?" asked Billy.

"James? Oh, James is my man," replied the other.

Billy looked up at his companion quizzically, then he tasted the dark, thick concoction in the tin can.

"This is coffee," he announced. "I thought you said it was ambrose."

"I only wished to see if you would recognize it, my friend," replied the poetical one politely. "I am highly complimented that you can guess what it is from its taste."

For several minutes the two ate in silence, passing the tin can back and forth, and slicing—hacking would be more nearly correct—pieces of meat from the half-roasted fowl. It was Billy who broke the silence.

"I think," said he, "that you been stringin' me—'bout James and ambrose."

The other laughed good-naturedly.

"You are not offended, I hope," said he. "This is a sad old world, you know, and we're all looking for amusement. If a guy has no money to buy it with, he has to manufacture it."

"Sure, I ain't sore," Billy assured him. "Say, spiel that part again 'bout Penelope with the kisses on her mouth, an' you can kid me till the cows come home."

The camper by the creek did as Billy asked him, while the latter sat with his eyes upon the fire seeing in the sputtering little flames the oval face of her who was Penelope to him.

When the verse was completed he reached forth his hand and took the tin can in his strong fingers, raising it before his face.

"Here's to—to his Knibbs!" he said, and drank, passing the battered thing over to his new friend.

"Yes," said the other; "here's to his Knibbs, and—Penelope!"

"Drink hearty," returned Billy Byrne.

The poetical one drew a sack of tobacco from his hip pocket and a rumpled package of papers from the pocket of his shirt, extending both toward Billy.

"Want the makings?" he asked.

"I ain't stuck on sponging," said Billy; "but maybe I can get even some day, and I sure do want a smoke. You see I was frisked. I ain't got nothin'—they didn't leave me a sou markee."

Billy reached across one end of the fire for the tobacco and cigarette papers. As he did so the movement bared his wrist, and as the firelight fell upon it the marks of the steel bracelet showed vividly. In the fall from the train the metal had bitten into the flesh.

His companion's eyes happened to fall upon the telltale mark. There was an almost imperceptible raising of the man's eyebrows; but he said nothing to indicate that he had noticed anything out of the ordinary.

The two smoked on for many minutes without indulging in conversation. The camper quoted snatches from Service and Kipling, then he came back to Knibbs, who was evidently his favorite. Billy listened and thought.

"Goin' anywheres in particular?" he asked during a momentary lull in the recitation.

"Oh, south or west," replied the other. "Nowhere in particular—any place suits me just so it isn't north or east."

"That's me," said Billy.

"Let's travel double, then," said the poetical one. "My name's Bridge."

"And mine's Billy. Here, shake," and Byrne extended his hand.

"Until one of us gets wearied of the other's company," said Bridge.

"You're on," replied Billy. "Let's turn in."

"Good," exclaimed Bridge. "I wonder what's keeping James. He should have been here long since to turn down my bed and fix my bath."

Billy grinned and rolled over on his side, his head uphill and his feet toward the fire. A couple of feet away Bridge paralleled him, and in five minutes both were breathing deeply in healthy slumber.

III
"Five Hundred Dollars Reward"

"'We kept a-rambling all the time. I rustled grub, he rustled rhyme,'" quoted Billy Byrne, sitting up and stretching himself.

His companion roused and came to one elbow. The sun was topping the scant wood behind them, glinting on the surface of the little creek. A robin hopped about the sward quite close to them, and from the branch of a tree a hundred yards away came the sweet piping of a song bird. Farther off were the distance-subdued noises of an awakening farm. The lowing of cows, the crowing of a rooster, the yelping of a happy dog just released from a night of captivity.

Bridge yawned and stretched. Billy rose to his feet and shook himself.

"This is the life," said Bridge. "Where you going?"

"To rustle grub," replied Billy. "That's my part o' the sketch."

The other laughed. "Go to it," he said. "I hate it. That's the part that has come nearest making me turn respectable than any other. I hate to ask for a handout."

Billy shrugged. He'd done worse things than that in his life, and off he trudged, whistling. He felt happier than he had for many a day. He never had guessed that the country in the morning could be so beautiful.

Behind him his companion collected the material for a fire, washed himself in the creek, and set the tin can, filled with water, at the edge of the kindling, and waited. There was nothing to cook, so it was useless to light the fire. As he sat there, thinking, his mind reverted to the red mark upon Billy's wrist, and he made a wry face.

Billy approached the farmhouse from which the sounds of awakening still emanated. The farmer saw him coming, and ceasing his activities about the barnyard, leaned across a gate and eyed him, none too hospitably.

"I wanna get something to eat," explained Billy.

"Got any money to pay for it with?" asked the farmer quickly.

"No," said Billy; "but me partner an' me are hungry, an' we gotta eat."

The farmer extended a gnarled forefinger and pointed toward the rear of the house. Billy looked in the direction thus indicated and espied a woodpile. He grinned good naturedly.

Without a word he crossed to the corded wood, picked up an ax which was stuck in a chopping block, and, shedding his coat, went to work. The farmer resumed his chores. Half an hour later he stopped on his way in to breakfast and eyed the growing pile that lay beside Billy.

"You don't hev to chop all the wood in the county to get a meal from Jed Watson," he said.

"I wanna get enough for me partner, too," explained Billy.

"Well, yew've chopped enough fer two meals, son," replied the farmer, and turning toward the kitchen door, he called: "Here, Maw, fix this boy up with suthin' t'eat—enough fer a couple of meals fer two on 'em."

As Billy walked away toward his camp, his arms laden with milk, butter, eggs, a loaf of bread and some cold meat, he grinned rather contentedly.

"A year or so ago," he mused, "I'd a stuck 'em up fer this, an' thought I was smart. Funny how a feller'll change—an' all fer a skirt. A skirt that belongs to somebody else now, too. Hell! what's the difference, anyhow? She'd be glad if she knew, an' it makes me feel better to act like she'd want. That old farmer guy, now. Who'd ever have taken him fer havin' a heart at all? Wen I seen him first I thought he'd like to sic the dog on me, an' there he comes along an' tells 'Maw' to pass me a handout like this! Gee it's a funny world. She used to say that most everybody was decent if you went at 'em right, an' I guess she knew. She knew most everything, anyway. Lord, I wish she'd been born on Grand Ave., or I on Riverside Drive!"

As Billy walked up to his waiting companion, who had touched a match to the firewood as he sighted the numerous packages in the forager's arms, he was repeating, over and over, as though the words held him in the thrall of fascination: "There ain't no sweet Penelope somewhere that's longing much for me."

Bridge eyed the packages as Billy deposited them carefully and one at a time upon the grass beside the fire. The milk was in a clean little graniteware pail, the eggs had been placed in a paper bag, while the other articles were wrapped in pieces of newspaper.

As the opening of each revealed its contents, fresh, clean, and inviting, Bridge closed one eye and cocked the other up at Billy.

"Did he die hard?" he inquired.

"Did who die hard?" demanded the other.

"Why the dog, of course."

"He ain't dead as I know of," replied Billy.

"You don't mean to say, my friend, that they let you get away with all this without sicing the dog on you," said Bridge.

Billy laughed and explained, and the other was relieved—the red mark around Billy's wrist persisted in remaining uppermost in Bridge's mind.

When they had eaten they lay back upon the grass and smoked some more of Bridge's tobacco.

"Well," inquired Bridge, "what's doing now?"

"Let's be hikin'," said Billy.

Bridge rose and stretched. "'My feet are tired and need a change. Come on! It's up to you!'" he quoted.

Billy gathered together the food they had not yet eaten, and made two equal-sized packages of it. He handed one to Bridge.

"We'll divide the pack," he explained, "and here, drink the rest o' this milk, I want the pail."

"What are you going to do with the pail?" asked Bridge.

"Return it," said Billy. "'Maw' just loaned it to me."

Bridge elevated his eyebrows a trifle. He had been mistaken, after all. At the farmhouse the farmer's wife greeted them kindly, thanked Billy for returning her pail—which, if the truth were known, she had not expected to see again—and gave them each a handful of thick, light, golden-brown cookies, the tops of which were encrusted with sugar.

As they walked away Bridge sighed. "Nothing on earth like a good woman," he said.

"'Maw,' or 'Penelope'?" asked Billy.

"Either, or both," replied Bridge. "I have no Penelope, but I did have a mighty fine 'maw.'"

Billy made no reply. He was thinking of the slovenly, blear-eyed woman who had brought him into the world. The memory was far from pleasant. He tried to shake it off.

"'Bridge,'" he said, quite suddenly, and apropos of nothing, in an effort to change the subject. "That's an odd name. I've heard of Bridges and Bridger; but I never heard Bridge before."

"Just a name a fellow gave me once up on the Yukon," explained Bridge. "I used to use a few words he'd never heard before, so he called me 'The

Unabridged,' which was too long. The fellows shortened it to 'Bridge' and it stuck. It has always stuck, and now I haven't any other. I even think of myself, now, as Bridge. Funny, ain't it?"

"Yes," agreed Billy, and that was the end of it. He never thought of asking his companion's true name, any more than Bridge would have questioned him as to his, or of his past. The ethics of the roadside fire and the empty tomato tin do not countenance such impertinences.

For several days the two continued their leisurely way toward Kansas City. Once they rode a few miles on a freight train, but for the most part they were content to plod joyously along the dusty highways. Billy continued to "rustle grub," while Bridge relieved the monotony by an occasional burst of poetry.

"You know so much of that stuff," said Billy as they were smoking by their camp fire one evening, "that I'd think you'd be able to make some up yourself."

"I've tried," admitted Bridge; "but there always seems to be something lacking in my stuff—it don't get under your belt—the divine afflatus is not there. I may start out all right, but I always end up where I didn't expect to go, and where nobody wants to be."

"'Member any of it?" asked Billy.

"There was one I wrote about a lake where I camped once," said Bridge, reminiscently; "but I can only recall one stanza."

"Let's have it," urged Billy. "I bet it has Knibbs hangin' to the ropes."

Bridge cleared his throat, and recited:

> Silver are the ripples,
> Solemn are the dunes,
> Happy are the fishes,
> For they are full of prunes.

He looked up at Billy, a smile twitching at the corners of his mouth. "How's that?" he asked.

Billy scratched his head.

"It's all right but the last line," said Billy, candidly. "There is something wrong with that last line."

"Yes," agreed Bridge, "there is."

"I guess Knibbs is safe for another round at least," said Billy.

Bridge was eying his companion, noting the broad shoulders, the deep chest, the mighty forearm and biceps which the other's light cotton shirt could not conceal.

"It is none of my business," he said presently; "but from your general appearance, from bits of idiom you occasionally drop, and from the way you handled those two boes the night we met I should rather surmise that at some time or other you had been less than a thousand miles from the w.k. roped arena."

"I seen a prize fight once," admitted Billy.

It was the day before they were due to arrive in Kansas City that Billy earned a handout from a restaurant keeper in a small town by doing some odd jobs for the man. The food he gave Billy was wrapped in an old copy of the *Kansas City Star*. When Billy reached camp he tossed the package to Bridge, who, in addition to his honorable post as poet laureate, was also cook. Then Billy walked down to the stream, nearby, that he might wash away the grime and sweat of honest toil from his hands and face.

As Bridge unwrapped the package and the paper unfolded beneath his eyes an article caught his attention—just casually at first; but presently to the exclusion of all else. As he read his eyebrows alternated between a position of considerable elevation to that of a deep frown. Occasionally he nodded knowingly. Finally he glanced up at Billy who was just rising from his ablutions. Hastily Bridge tore from the paper the article that had attracted his interest, folded it, and stuffed it into one of his pockets—he had not had time to finish the reading and he wanted to save the article for a later opportunity for careful perusal.

That evening Bridge sat for a long time scrutinizing Billy through half-closed lids, and often he found his eyes wandering to the red ring about the other's wrist; but whatever may have been within his thoughts he kept to himself.

It was noon when the two sauntered into Kansas City. Billy had a dollar in his pocket—a whole dollar. He had earned it assisting an automobilist out of a ditch.

"We'll have a swell feed," he had confided to Bridge, "an' sleep in a bed just to learn how much nicer it is sleepin' out under the black sky and the shiny little stars."

"You're a profligate, Billy," said Bridge.

"I dunno what that means," said Billy; "but if it's something I shouldn't be I probably am."

The two went to a rooming-house of which Bridge knew, where they could get a clean room with a double bed for fifty cents. It was rather a high price to pay, of course, but Bridge was more or less fastidious, and he admitted to Billy that he'd rather sleep in the clean dirt of the roadside than in the breed of dirt one finds in an unclean bed.

At the end of the hall was a washroom, and toward this Bridge made his way, after removing his coat and throwing it across the foot of the bed. After he had left the room Billy chanced to notice a folded bit of newspaper on the floor beneath Bridge's coat. He picked it up to lay it on the little table which answered the purpose of a dresser when a single word caught his attention. It was a name: Schneider.

Billy unfolded the clipping and as his eyes took in the heading a strange expression entered them—a hard, cold gleam such as had not touched them since the day that he abandoned the deputy sheriff in the woods midway between Chicago and Joliet.

This is what Billy read:

> Billy Byrne, sentenced to life imprisonment in Joliet penitentiary for the murder of Schneider, the old West Side saloon keeper, hurled himself from the train that was bearing him to Joliet yesterday, dragging with him the deputy sheriff to whom he was handcuffed.
>
> The deputy was found a few hours later bound and gagged, lying in the woods along the Santa Fe, not far from Lemont. He was uninjured. He says that Byrne got a good start, and doubtless took advantage of it to return to Chicago, where a man of his stamp could find more numerous and safer retreats than elsewhere.

There was much more—a detailed account of the crime for the commission of which Billy had been sentenced, a full and complete description of Billy, a record of his long years of transgression, and, at last, the mention of a five-hundred-dollar reward that the authorities had offered for information that would lead to his arrest.

When Billy had concluded the reading he refolded the paper and placed it in a pocket of the coat hanging upon the foot of the bed. A moment later Bridge entered the room. Billy caught himself looking often at his companion, and always there came to his mind the termination of the article he had found in Bridge's pocket—the mention of the five-hundred-dollar reward.

"Five hundred dollars," thought Billy, "is a lot o' coin. I just wonder now," and he let his eyes wander to his companion as though he might read upon his face the purpose which lay in the man's heart. "He don't look it; but five hundred dollars is a lot o' coin—fer a bo, and wotinell did he have that article hid in his clothes fer? That's wot I'd like to know. I guess it's up to me to blow."

All the recently acquired content which had been Billy's since he had come upon the poetic Bridge and the two had made their carefree, leisurely way along shaded country roadsides, or paused beside cool brooklets that meandered lazily through sweet-smelling meadows, was dissipated in the instant that he had realized the nature of the article his companion had been carrying and hiding from him.

For days no thought of pursuit or capture had arisen to perplex him. He had seemed such a tiny thing out there amidst the vastness of rolling hills, of woods, and plain that there had been induced within him an unconscious assurance that no one could find him even though they might seek for him.

The idea of meeting a plain clothes man from detective headquarters around the next bend of a peaceful Missouri road was so preposterous and incongruous that Billy had found it impossible to give the matter serious thought.

He never before had been in the country districts of his native land. To him the United States was all like Chicago or New York or Milwaukee, the three cities with which he was most familiar. His experience of unurban localities had been gained amidst the primeval jungles of faraway Yoka. There had been no detective sergeants there—unquestionably there could be none here. Detective sergeants were indigenous to the soil that grew corner saloons and poolrooms, and to none other—as well expect to discover one of Oda Yorimoto's samurai hiding behind a fire plug on Michigan Boulevard, as to look for one of those others along a farm-bordered road.

But here in Kansas City, amidst the noises and odors that meant a large city, it was different. Here the next man he met might be looking for him, or if not then the very first policeman they encountered could arrest him upon a word from Bridge—and Bridge would get five hundred dollars. Just then Bridge burst forth into poetry:

> In a flannel shirt from earth's clean dirt,
> Here, pal, is my calloused hand!
> Oh, I love each day as a rover may,
> Nor seek to understand.
> To enjoy is good enough for me;
> The gypsy of God am I.
> Then here's a hail to—

"Say," he interrupted himself; "what's the matter with going out now and wrapping ourselves around that swell feed you were speaking of?"

Billy rose. It didn't seem possible that Bridge could be going to double-cross him.

> In a flannel shirt from earth's clean dirt,
> Here, pal, is my calloused hand!

Billy repeated the lines half aloud. They renewed his confidence in Bridge, somehow.

"Like them?" asked the latter.

"Yes," said Billy; "s'more of Knibbs?"

"No, Service. Come on, let's go and dine. How about the Midland?" and he grinned at his little joke as he led the way toward the street.

It was late afternoon. The sun already had set; but it still was too light for lamps. Bridge led the way toward a certain eating-place of which he knew where a man might dine well and from a clean platter for two bits. Billy had been keeping his eyes open for detectives. They had passed no uniformed police—that would be the crucial test, thought he—unless Bridge intended tipping off headquarters on the quiet and having the pinch made at night after Billy had gone to bed.

As they reached the little restaurant, which was in a basement, Bridge motioned Billy down ahead of him. Just for an instant he, himself, paused at the head of the stairs and looked about. As he did so a man stepped from the shadow of a doorway upon the opposite side of the street.

If Bridge saw him he apparently gave no sign, for he turned slowly and with deliberate steps followed Billy down into the eating-place.

IV
On the Trail

As they entered the place Billy, who was ahead, sought a table; but as he was about to hang up his cap and seat himself Bridge touched his elbow.

"Let's go to the washroom and clean up a bit," he said, in a voice that might be heard by those nearest.

"Why, we just washed before we left our room," expostulated Billy.

"Shut up and follow me," Bridge whispered into his ear.

Immediately Billy was all suspicion. His hand flew to the pocket in which the gun of the deputy sheriff still rested. They would never take him alive, of that Billy was positive. He wouldn't go back to life imprisonment, not after he had tasted the sweet freedom of the wide spaces—such a freedom as the trammeled city cannot offer.

Bridge saw the movement.

"Cut it," he whispered, "and follow me, as I tell you. I just saw a Chicago dick across the street. He may not have seen you, but it looked almighty like it. He'll be down here in about two seconds now. Come on—we'll beat it through the rear—I know the way."

Billy Byrne heaved a great sigh of relief. Suddenly he was almost reconciled to the thought of capture, for in the instant he had realized that it had not been so much his freedom that he had dreaded to lose as his faith in the companion in whom he had believed.

Without sign of haste the two walked the length of the room and disappeared through the doorway leading into the washroom. Before them was a window opening upon a squalid back yard. The building stood upon a hillside, so that while the entrance to the eating-place was below the level of the street in front, its rear was flush with the ground.

Bridge motioned Billy to climb through the window while he shot the bolt upon the inside of the door leading back into the restaurant. A moment later he followed the fugitive, and then took the lead.

Down narrow, dirty alleys, and through litter-piled back yards he made his way, while Billy followed at his heels. Dusk was gathering, and before they had gone far darkness came.

They neither paused nor spoke until they had left the business portion of the city behind and were well out of the zone of bright lights. Bridge was the first to break the silence.

"I suppose you wonder how I knew," he said.

"No," replied Billy. "I seen that clipping you got in your pocket—it fell out on the floor when you took your coat off in the room this afternoon to go and wash."

"Oh," said Bridge, "I see. Well, as far as I'm concerned that's the end of it—we won't mention it again, old man. I don't need to tell you that I'm for you."

"No, not after tonight," Billy assured him.

They went on again for some little time without speaking, then Billy said:

"I got two things to tell you. The first is that after I seen that newspaper article in your clothes I thought you was figurin' on double-crossin' me an' claimin' the five hun. I ought to of known better. The other is that I didn't kill Schneider. I wasn't near his place that night—an' that's straight."

"I'm glad you told me both," said Bridge. "I think we'll understand each other better after this—we're each runnin' away from something. We'll run together, eh?" and he extended his hand. "In flannel shirt from earth's clean dirt, here, pal, is my calloused hand!" he quoted, laughing.

Billy took the other's hand. He noticed that Bridge hadn't said what *he* was running away from. Billy wondered; but asked no questions.

South they went after they had left the city behind, out into the sweet and silent darkness of the country. During the night they crossed the line into Kansas, and morning found them in a beautiful, hilly country to which all thoughts of cities, crime, and police seemed so utterly foreign that Billy could scarce believe that only a few hours before a Chicago detective had been less than a hundred feet from him.

The new sun burst upon them as they topped a grassy hill. The dew-bespangled blades scintillated beneath the gorgeous rays which would presently sweep them away again into the nothingness from which they had sprung.

Bridge halted and stretched himself. He threw his head back and let the warm sun beat down upon his bronzed face.

There's sunshine in the heart of me,

My blood sings in the breeze;
The mountains are a part of me,
I'm fellow to the trees.
My golden youth I'm squandering,
Sun-libertine am I;
A-wandering, a-wandering,
Until the day I die.

And then he stood for minutes drinking in deep breaths of the pure, sweet air of the new day. Beside him, a head taller, savagely strong, stood Billy Byrne, his broad shoulders squared, his great chest expanding as he inhaled.
"It's great, ain't it?" he said, at last. "I never knew the country was like this, an' I don't know that I ever would have known it if it hadn't been for those poet guys you're always spouting.

"I always had an idea they was sissy fellows," he went on; "but a guy can't be a sissy an' think the thoughts they musta thought to write stuff that sends the blood chasin' through a feller like he'd had a drink on an empty stomach.

"I used to think everybody was a sissy who wasn't a tough guy. I was a tough guy all right, an' I was mighty proud of it. I ain't any more an' haven't been for a long time; but before I took a tumble to myself I'd have hated you, Bridge. I'd a-hated your fine talk, an' your poetry, an' the thing about you that makes you hate to touch a guy for a handout.

"I'd a-hated myself if I'd thought that I could ever talk mushy like I am now. Gee, Bridge, but I was the limit! A girl—a nice girl—called me a mucker once, an' a coward. I was both; but I had the reputation of bein' the toughest guy on the West Side, an' I thought I was a man. I nearly poked her face for her—think of it, Bridge! I nearly did; but something stopped me—something held my hand from it, an' lately I've liked to think that maybe what stopped me was something in me that had always been there—something decent that was really a part of me. I hate to think that I was such a beast at heart as I acted like all my life up to that minute. I began to change then. It was mighty slow, an' I'm still a roughneck; but I'm gettin' on. She helped me most, of course, an' now you're helpin' me a lot, too—you an' your poetry stuff. If some dick don't get me I may get to be a human bein' before I die."

Bridge laughed.

"It *is* odd," he said, "how our viewpoints change with changed environment and the passing of the years. Time was, Billy, when I'd have hated you as much as you would have hated me. I don't know that I should have said hate, for that is not exactly the word. It was more contempt that I felt for men whom I considered as not belonging upon that intellectual or social plane to which I considered I had been born.

"I thought of people who moved outside my limited sphere as 'the great unwashed.' I pitied them, and I honestly believe now that in the bottom of my heart I considered them of different clay than I, and with souls, if they possessed such things, about on a par with the souls of sheep and cows.

"I couldn't have seen the man in you, Billy, then, any more than you could have seen the man in me. I have learned much since then, though I still stick to a part of my original articles of faith—I do believe that all men are not equal; and I know that there are a great many more with whom I would not pal than there are those with whom I would.

"Because one man speaks better English than another, or has read more and remembers it, only makes him a better man in that particular respect. I think none the less of you because you can't quote Browning or Shakespeare—the thing that counts is that you can appreciate, as I do, Service and Kipling and Knibbs.

"Now maybe we are both wrong—maybe Knibbs and Kipling and Service didn't write poetry, and some people will say as much; but whatever it is it gets you and me in the same way, and so in this respect we are equals. Which being the case let's see if we can't rustle some grub, and then find a nice soft spot whereon to pound our respective ears."

Billy, deciding that he was too sleepy to work for food, invested half of the capital that was to have furnished the swell feed the night before in what two bits would purchase from a generous housewife on a nearby farm, and then, stretching themselves beneath the shade of a tree sufficiently far from the road that they might not attract unnecessary observation, they slept until after noon.

But their precaution failed to serve their purpose entirely. A little before noon two filthy, bearded knights of the road clambered laboriously over the fence and headed directly for the very tree under which Billy and Bridge lay sleeping. In the minds of the two was the same thought that had induced Billy Byrne and the poetic Bridge to seek this same secluded spot.

There was in the stiff shuffle of the men something rather familiar. We have seen them before—just for a few minutes it is true; but under circumstances that impressed some of their characteristics upon us. The very last we saw of them they were shuffling away in the darkness along a railroad track, after promising that eventually they would wreak dire vengeance upon Billy, who had just trounced them.

Now as they came unexpectedly upon the two sleepers they did not immediately recognize in them the objects of their recent hate. They just stood looking stupidly down on them, wondering in what way they might turn their discovery to their own advantage.

Nothing in the raiment either of Billy or Bridge indicated that here was any particularly rich field for loot, and, too, the athletic figure of Byrne would rather have discouraged any attempt to roll him without first handing him the "k.o.," as the two would have naively put it.

But as they gazed down upon the features of the sleepers the eyes of one of the tramps narrowed to two ugly slits while those of his companion went wide in incredulity and surprise.

"Do youse know dem guys?" asked the first, and without waiting for a reply he went on: "Dem's de guys dat beat us up back dere de udder side o' K.C. Do youse get 'em?"

"Sure?" asked the other.

"Sure, I'd know dem in a t'ous'n'. Le's hand 'em a couple an' beat it," and he stooped to pick up a large stone that lay near at hand.

"Cut it!" whispered the second tramp. "Youse don't know dem guys at all. Dey may be de guys dat beats us up; but dat big stiff dere is more dan dat. He's wanted in Chi, an' dere's half a t'ou on 'im."

"Who put youse jerry to all dat?" inquired the first tramp, skeptically.

"I was in de still wit 'im—he croaked some guy. He's a lifer. On de way to de pen he pushes dis dick off'n de rattler an' makes his getaway. Dat peter-boy we meets at Quincy slips me an earful about him. Here's w'ere we draws down de five hundred if we're cagey."

"Whaddaya mean, cagey?"

"Why we leaves 'em alone an' goes to de nex' farm an' calls up K.C. an' tips off de dicks, see?"

"Youse don't tink we'll get any o' dat five hun, do youse, wit de dicks in on it?"

The other scratched his head.

"No," he said, rather dubiously, after a moment's deep thought; "dey don't nobody get nothin' dat de dicks see first; but we'll get even with dese blokes, annyway."

"Maybe dey'll pass us a couple bucks," said the other hopefully. "Dey'd orter do dat much."

Detective Sergeant Flannagan of Headquarters, Chicago, slouched in a chair in the private office of the chief of detectives of Kansas City, Missouri. Sergeant Flannagan was sore. He would have said as much himself. He had been sent west to identify a suspect whom the Kansas City authorities had arrested; but had been unable to do so, and had been preparing to return to his home city when the brilliant aureola of an unusual piece of excellent fortune had shone upon him for a moment, and then faded away through the grimy entrance of a basement eating-place.

He had been walking along the street the previous evening thinking of nothing in particular; but with eyes and ears alert as becomes a successful police officer, when he had espied two men approaching upon the opposite sidewalk.

There was something familiar in the swing of the giant frame of one of the men. So, true to years of training, Sergeant Flannagan melted into the shadows of a store entrance and waited until the two should have come closer.

They were directly opposite him when the truth flashed upon him—the big fellow was Billy Byrne, and there was a five-hundred-dollar reward out for him.

And then the two turned and disappeared down the stairway that led to the underground restaurant. Sergeant Flannagan saw Byrne's companion turn and look back just as Flannagan stepped from the doorway to cross the street after them.

That was the last Sergeant Flannagan had seen either of Billy Byrne or his companion. The trail had ceased at the open window of the washroom at the rear of the restaurant, and search as he would be had been unable to pick it up again.

No one in Kansas City had seen two men that night answering the descriptions Flannagan had been able to give—at least no one whom

Flannagan could unearth.

Finally he had been forced to take the Kansas City chief into his confidence, and already a dozen men were scouring such sections of Kansas City in which it seemed most likely an escaped murderer would choose to hide.

Flannagan had been out himself for a while; but now he was in to learn what progress, if any, had been made. He had just learned that three suspects had been arrested and was waiting to have them paraded before him.

When the door swung in and the three were escorted into his presence Sergeant Flannagan gave a snort of disgust, indicative probably not only of despair; but in a manner registering his private opinion of the mental horse power and efficiency of the Kansas City sleuths, for of the three one was a pasty-faced, chestless youth, even then under the influence of cocaine, another was an old, bewhiskered hobo, while the third was unquestionably a Chinaman.

Even professional courtesy could scarce restrain Sergeant Flannagan's desire toward bitter sarcasm, and he was upon the point of launching forth into a vitriolic arraignment of everything west of Chicago up to and including, specifically, the Kansas City detective bureau, when the telephone bell at the chief's desk interrupted him. He had wanted the chief to hear just what he thought, so he waited.

The chief listened for a few minutes, asked several questions and then, placing a fat hand over the transmitter, he wheeled about toward Flannagan.

"Well," he said, "I guess I got something for you at last. There's a bo on the wire that says he's just seen your man down near Shawnee. He wants to know if you'll split the reward with him."

Flannagan yawned and stretched.

"I suppose," he said, ironically, "that if I go down there I'll find he's corraled a nigger," and he looked sorrowfully at the three specimens before him.

"I dunno," said the chief. "This guy says he knows Byrne well, an' that he's got it in for him. Shall I tell him you'll be down—and split the reward?"

"Tell him I'll be down and that I'll treat him right," replied Flannagan, and after the chief had transmitted the message, and hung up the receiver: "Where is this here Shawnee, anyhow?"

"I'll send a couple of men along with you. It isn't far across the line, an' there won't be no trouble in getting back without nobody knowin' anything about it—if you get him."

"All right," said Flannagan, his visions of five hundred already dwindled to a possible one.

It was but a little past one o'clock that a touring car rolled south out of Kansas City with Detective Sergeant Flannagan in the front seat with the driver and two burly representatives of Missouri law in the back.

V
ONE TURN DESERVES ANOTHER

When the two tramps approached the farmhouse at which Billy had purchased food a few hours before the farmer's wife called the dog that was asleep in the summer kitchen and took a shotgun down from its hook beside the door.

From long experience the lady was a reader of character—of hobo character at least—and she saw nothing in the appearance of either of these two that inspired even a modicum of confidence. Now the young fellow who had been there earlier in the day and who, wonder of wonders, had actually paid for the food she gave him, had been of a different stamp. His clothing had proclaimed him a tramp, but, thanks to the razor Bridge always carried, he was clean shaven. His year of total abstinence had given him clear eyes and a healthy skin. There was a freshness and vigor in his appearance and carriage that inspired confidence rather than suspicion.

She had not mistrusted him; but these others she did mistrust. When they asked to use the telephone she refused and ordered them away, thinking it but an excuse to enter the house; but they argued the matter, explaining that they had discovered an escaped murderer hiding nearby—in fact in her own meadow—and that they wished only to call up the Kansas City police.

Finally she yielded, but kept the dog by her side and the shotgun in her hand while the two entered the room and crossed to the telephone upon the opposite side.

From the conversation which she overheard the woman concluded that, after all, she had been mistaken, not only about these two, but about the young man who had come earlier in the day and purchased food from her, for the description the tramp gave of the fugitive tallied exactly with that of the young man.

It seemed incredible that so honest looking a man could be a murderer. The good woman was shocked, and not a little unstrung by the thought that she had been in the house alone when he had come and that if he had wished to he could easily have murdered her.

"I hope they get him," she said, when the tramp had concluded his talk with Kansas City. "It's awful the carryings on they is nowadays. Why a body can't never tell who to trust, and I thought him such a nice young man. And he paid me for what he got, too."

The dog, bored by the inaction, had wandered back into the summer kitchen and resumed his broken slumber. One of the tramps was leaning against the wall talking with the farmer woman. The other was busily engaged in scratching his right shin with what remained of the heel of his left shoe. He supported himself with one hand on a small table upon the top of which was a family Bible.

Quite unexpectedly he lost his balance, the table tipped, he was thrown still farther over toward it, and all in the flash of an eye tramp, table, and family Bible crashed to the floor.

With a little cry of alarm the woman rushed forward to gather up the Holy Book, in her haste forgetting the shotgun and leaving it behind her leaning against the arm of a chair.

Almost simultaneously the two tramps saw the real cause of her perturbation. The large book had fallen upon its back, open; and as several of the leaves turned over before coming to rest their eyes went wide at what was revealed between.

United States currency in denominations of five, ten, and twenty-dollar bills lay snugly inserted between the leaves of the Bible. The tramp who lay on the floor, as yet too surprised to attempt to rise, rolled over and seized the book as a football player seizes the pigskin after a fumble, covering it with his body, his arms, and sticking out his elbows as a further protection to the invaluable thing.

At the first cry of the woman the dog rose, growling, and bounded into the room. The tramp leaning against the wall saw the brute coming—a mongrel hound-dog, bristling and savage.

The shotgun stood almost within the man's reach—a step and it was in his hands. As though sensing the fellow's intentions the dog wheeled from the tramp upon the floor, toward whom he had leaped, and sprang for the other ragged scoundrel.

The muzzle of the gun met him halfway. There was a deafening roar. The dog collapsed to the floor, his chest torn out. Now the woman began to scream for help; but in an instant both the tramps were upon her choking her to silence.

One of them ran to the summer kitchen, returning a moment later with a piece of clothesline, while the other sat astride the victim, his fingers closed about her throat. Once he released his hold and she screamed again. Presently she was secured and gagged. Then the two commenced to rifle the Bible.

Eleven hundred dollars in bills were hidden there, because the woman and her husband didn't believe in banks—the savings of a lifetime. In agony, as she regained consciousness, she saw the last of their little hoard transferred to the pockets of the tramps, and when they had finished they demanded to know where she kept the rest, loosening her gag that she might reply.

She told them that that was all the money she had in the world, and begged them not to take it.

"Youse've got more coin dan dis," growled one of the men, "an' youse had better pass it over, or we'll find a way to make youse."

But still she insisted that that was all. The tramp stepped into the kitchen. A wood fire was burning in the stove. A pair of pliers lay upon the window sill. With these he lifted one of the hot stove-hole covers and returned to the parlor, grinning.

"I guess she'll remember she's got more wen dis begins to woik," he said. "Take off her shoes, Dink."

The other growled an objection.

"Yeh poor boob," he said. "De dicks'll be here in a little while. We'd better be makin' our getaway wid w'at we got."

"Gee!" exclaimed his companion. "I clean forgot all about de dicks," and then after a moment's silence during which his evil face underwent various changes of expression from fear to final relief, he turned an ugly, crooked grimace upon his companion.

"We got to croak her," he said. "Dey ain't no udder way. If dey finds her alive she'll blab sure, an' dey won't be no trouble 'bout gettin' us or identifyin' us neither."

The other shrugged.

"Le's beat it," he whined. "We can't more'n do time fer dis job if we stop now; but de udder'll mean—" and he made a suggestive circle with a grimy finger close to his neck.

"No it won't nothin' of de kind," urged his companion. "I got it all doped out. We got lots o' time before de dicks are due. We'll croak de skirt, an' den we'll beat it up de road *an' meet de dicks*—see?"

The other was aghast.

"Wen did youse go nuts?" he asked.

"I ain't gone nuts. Wait 'til I gets t'rough. We meets de dicks, innocent-like; but first we caches de dough in de woods. We tells 'em we hurried right on to lead 'em to dis Byrne guy, an' wen we gets back here to de farmhouse an' finds wot's happened here we'll be as flabbergasted as dey be."

"Oh, nuts!" exclaimed the other disgustedly. "Youse don't tink youse can put dat over on any wise guy from Chi, do youse? Who will dey tink croaked de old woman an' de ki-yi? Will dey tink dey kilt deyreselves?"

"Dey'll tink Byrne an' his pardner croaked 'em, you simp," replied Crumb.

Dink scratched his head, and as the possibilities of the scheme filtered into his dull brain a broad grin bared his yellow teeth.

"You're dere, pal," he exclaimed, real admiration in his tone. "But who's goin' to do it?"

"I'll do it," said Crumb. "Dere ain't no chanct of gettin' in bad for it, so I jest as soon do the job. Get me a knife, or an ax from de kitchen—de gat makes too much noise."

Something awoke Billy Byrne with a start. Faintly, in the back of his consciousness, the dim suggestion of a loud noise still reverberated. He sat up and looked about him.

"I wonder what that was?" he mused. "It sounded like the report of a gun."

Bridge awoke about the same time, and turned lazily over, raising himself upon an elbow. He grinned at Billy.

"Good morning," he said, and then:

> Says I, "Then let's be on the float. You certainly have got my goat;
> You make me hungry in my throat for seeing things that's new.
> Out there somewhere we'll ride the range a-looking for the new and strange;
> My feet are tired and need a change. Come on! It's up to you!"

"Come on, then," agreed Billy, coming to his feet. As he rose there came, faintly, but distinct, the unmistakable scream of a frightened woman. From the direction of the farmhouse it came—from the farmhouse at which Billy had purchased their breakfast.

Without waiting for a repetition of the cry Billy wheeled and broke into a rapid run in the direction of the little cluster of buildings. Bridge leaped to his feet and followed him, dropping behind though, for he had not had the road work that Billy recently had been through in his training for the battle in which he had defeated the "white hope" that time in New York when Professor Cassidy had wagered his entire pile upon him, nor in vain.

Dink searched about the summer kitchen for an ax or hatchet; but failing to find either rummaged through a table drawer until he came upon a large carving knife. This would do the job nicely. He thumbed the edge as he carried it back into the parlor to Crumb.

The poor woman, lying upon the floor, was quite conscious. Her eyes were wide and rolling in horror. She struggled with her bonds, and tried to force the gag from her mouth with her tongue; but her every effort was useless. She had heard every word that had passed between the two men. She knew that they would carry out the plan they had formulated and that there was no chance that they would be interrupted in their gruesome work, for her husband had driven over to a farm beyond Holliday, leaving before sunrise, and there was little prospect that he would return before milking time in the evening. The detectives from Kansas City could not possibly reach the farm until far too late to save her.

She saw Dink return from the summer kitchen with the long knife. She recalled the day she had bought that knife in town, and the various uses to which she had put it. That very morning she had sliced some bacon with it. How distinctly such little things recurred to her at this frightful moment. And now the hideous creature standing beside her was going to use it to cut her throat.

She saw Crumb take the knife and feel of the blade, running his thumb along it. She saw him stoop, his eyes turned down upon hers. He grasped her chin and forced it upward and back, the better to expose her throat.

Oh, why could she not faint? Why must she suffer all these hideous preliminaries? Why could she not even close her eyes?

Crumb raised the knife and held the blade close above her bared neck. A shudder ran through her, and then the door crashed open and a man sprang into the room. It was Billy Byrne. Through the window he had seen what was passing in the interior.

His hand fell upon Crumb's collar and jerked him backward from his prey. Dink seized the shotgun and turned it upon the intruder; but he was too close. Billy grasped the barrel of the weapon and threw the muzzle up toward the ceiling as the tramp pulled the trigger. Then he wrenched it from the man's hands, swung it once above his head and crashed the stock down upon Dink's skull.

Dink went down and out for the count—for several counts, in fact. Crumb stumbled to his feet and made a break for the door. In the doorway he ran full into Bridge, winded, but ready. The latter realizing that the matted one was attempting to escape, seized a handful of his tangled beard, and, as he had done upon another occasion, held the tramp's head in rigid position while he planted a series of blows in the fellow's face—blows that left Crumb as completely out of battle as was his mildewed comrade.

"Watch 'em," said Billy, handing Bridge the shotgun. Then he turned his attention to the woman. With the carving knife that was to have ended her life he cut her bonds. Removing the gag from her mouth he lifted her in his strong arms and carried her to the little horsehair sofa that stood in one corner of the parlor, laying her upon it very gently.

He was thinking of "Maw" Watson. This woman resembled her just a little—particularly in her comfortable, motherly expansiveness, and she had had a kind word and a cheery goodbye for him that morning as he had departed.

The woman lay upon the sofa, breathing hard, and moaning just a little. The shock had been almost too much even for her stolid nerves. Presently she turned her eyes toward Billy.

"You are a good boy," she said, "and you come just in the nick o' time. They got all my money. It's in their clothes," and then a look of terror overspread her face. For the moment she had forgotten what she had heard about this man—that he was an escaped convict—a convicted murderer. Was she any better off now that she had let him know about the money than she was with the others after they discovered it?

At her words Bridge kneeled and searched the two tramps. He counted the bills as he removed them from their pockets.

"Eleven hundred?" he asked, and handed the money to Billy.

"Eleven hundred, yes," breathed the woman, faintly, her eyes horror-filled and fearful as she gazed upon Billy's face. She didn't care for the money any more—they could have it all if they would only let her live.

Billy turned toward her and held the rumpled green mass out.

"Here," he said; "but that's an awful lot o' coin for a woman to have about de house—an' her all alone. You ought not to a-done it."

She took the money in trembling fingers. It seemed incredible that the man was returning it to her.

"But I knew it," she said finally.

"Knew what?" asked Billy.

"I knew you was a good boy. They said you was a murderer."

Billy's brows contracted, and an expression of pain crossed his face.

"How did they come to say that?" he asked.

"I heard them telephonin' to Kansas City to the police," she replied, and then she sat bolt upright. "The detectives are on their way here now," she almost screamed, "and even if you *are* a murderer I don't care. I won't stand by and see 'em get you after what you have done for me. I don't believe you're a murderer anyhow. You're a good boy. My boy would be about as old and as big as you by now—if he lives. He ran away a long time ago—maybe you've met him. His name's Eddie—Eddie Shorter. I ain't heard from him fer years.

"No," she went on, "I don't believe what they said—you got too good a face; but if you are a murderer you get out now before they come an.' I'll send 'em on a wild-goose chase in the wrong direction."

"But these," said Billy. "We can't leave these here."

"Tie 'em up and give me the shotgun," she said. "I'll bet they don't come any more funny business on me." She had regained both her composure and her nerve by this time.

Together Billy and Bridge trussed up the two tramps. An elephant couldn't have forced the bonds they placed upon them. Then they carried them down cellar and when they had come up again Mrs. Shorter barred the cellar door.

"I reckon they won't get out of there very fast," she said. "And now you two boys run along. Got any money?" and without waiting for a reply she counted twenty-five dollars from the roll she had tucked in the front of her waist and handed them to Billy.

"Nothin' doin'," said he; "but t'anks just the same."

"You got to take it," she insisted. "Let me make believe I'm givin' it to my boy, Eddie—please," and the tears that came to her eyes proved far more effective than her generous words.

"Aw, all right," said Billy. "I'll take it an' pass it along to Eddie if I ever meet him, eh?"

"Now please hurry," she urged. "I don't want you to be caught—even if you are a murderer. I wish you weren't though."

"I'm not," said Billy; "but de law says I am an' what de law says, goes."

He turned toward the doorway with Bridge, calling a goodbye to the woman, but as he stepped out upon the veranda the dust of a fast-moving automobile appeared about a bend in the road a half-mile from the house.

"Too late," he said, turning to Bridge. "Here they come!"

The woman brushed by them and peered up the road.

"Yes," she said, "it must be them. Lordy! What'll we do?"

"I'll duck out the back way, that's what I'll do," said Billy.

"It wouldn't do a mite of good," said Mrs. Shorter, with a shake of her head. "They'll telephone every farmer within twenty mile of here in every direction, an' they'll get you sure. Wait! I got a scheme. Come with me," and she turned and bustled through the little parlor, out of a doorway into something that was half hall and half storeroom. There was a flight of stairs leading to the upper story, and she waddled up them as fast as her legs would carry her, motioning the two men to follow her.

In a rear room was a trapdoor in the ceiling.

"Drag that commode under this," she told them. "Then climb into the attic, and close the trapdoor. They won't never find you there."

Billy pulled the ancient article of furniture beneath the opening, and in another moment the two men were in the stuffy atmosphere of the unventilated loft. Beneath them they heard Mrs. Shorter dragging the commode back to its accustomed place, and then the sound of her footsteps descending the stair.

Presently there came to them the rattling of a motor without, followed by the voices of men in the house. For an hour, half asphyxiated by the closeness of the attic, they waited, and then again they heard the sound of the running engine, diminishing as the machine drew away.

Shortly after, Mrs. Shorter's voice rose to them from below:

"You ken come down now," she said, "they've gone."

When they had descended she led them to the kitchen.

"I got a bite to eat ready for you while they was here," she explained. "When you've done you ken hide in the barn 'til dark, an' after that I'll have my ol' man take you 'cross to Dodson, that's a junction, an' you'd aughter be able to git away easy enough from there. I told 'em you started for Olathe—there's where they've gone with the two tramps.

"My, but I did have a time of it! I ain't much good at story-tellin' but I reckon I told more stories this arternoon than I ever tole before in all my life. I told 'em that they was two of you, an' that the biggest one hed red hair, an' the little one was all pockmarked. Then they said you prob'ly wasn't the man at all, an' my! how they did swear at them two tramps fer gettin' 'em way out here on a wild-goose chase; but they're goin' to look fer you jes' the same in Olathe, only they won't find you there," and she laughed, a bit nervously though.

It was dusk when Mr. Shorter returned from Holliday, but after he had heard his wife's story he said that he'd drive "them two byes" all the way to Mexico, if there wasn't any better plan.

"Dodson's far enough," Bridge assured him, and late that night the grateful farmer set them down at their destination.

An hour later they were speeding south on the Missouri Pacific. Bridge lay back, luxuriously, on the red plush of the smoker seat.

"Some class to us, eh, bo?" asked Billy.

Bridge stretched.

> The tide-hounds race far up the shore—the hunt is on! The breakers roar!
> Her spars are tipped with gold, and o'er her deck the spray is flung;
> The buoys that frolic in the bay, they nod the way, they nod the way!
> The hunt is up! I am the prey! The hunter's bow is strung!

VI
"Baby Bandits"

It was twenty-four hours before Detective Sergeant Flannagan awoke to the fact that something had been put over on him, and that a Kansas farmer's wife had done the putting.

He managed to piece it out finally from the narratives of the two tramps, and when he had returned to the Shorter home and listened to the contradictory and whole-souled improvisations of Shorter *père* and *mère* he was convinced.

Whereupon he immediately telegraphed Chicago headquarters and obtained the necessary authority to proceed upon the trail of the fugitive, Byrne.

And so it was that Sergeant Flannagan landed in El Paso a few days later, drawn thither by various pieces of intelligence he had gathered en route, though with much delay and consequent vexation.

Even after he had quitted the train he was none too sure that he was upon the right trail though he at once repaired to a telegraph office and wired his chief that he was hot on the trail of the fugitive.

As a matter of fact he was much hotter than he imagined, for Billy and Bridge were that very minute not two squares from him, debating as to the future and the best manner of meeting it before it arrived.

"I think," said Billy, "that I'll duck across the border. I won't never be safe in little old U.S., an' with things hoppin' in Mexico the way they have been for the last few years I orter be able to lose myself pretty well."

"Now you're all right, ol' top. You don't have to duck nothin' for you ain't did nothin'. I don't know what you're runnin' away from; but I know it ain't nothin' the police is worryin' about—I can tell that by the way you act—so I guess we'll split here. You'd be a boob to cross if you don't have to, fer if Villa don't get you the Carranzistas will, unless the Zapatistas nab you first.

"Comin' or goin' some greasy-mugged highbinder's bound to croak you if you cross, from what little I've heard since we landed in El Paso.

"We'll feed up together tonight, fer the last time. Then I'll pull my freight." He was silent for a while, and then: "I hate to do it, bo, fer you're the whitest guy I ever struck," which was a great deal for Billy Byrne of Grand Avenue to say.

Bridge finished rolling a brown paper cigarette before he spoke.

"Your words are pure and unadulterated wisdom, my friend," he said. "The chances are scarcely even that two gringo hoboes would last the week out afoot and broke in Viva Mexico; but it has been many years since I followed the dictates of wisdom. Therefore I am going with you."

Billy grinned. He could not conceal his pleasure.

"You're past twenty-one," he said, "an' dry behind the ears. Let's go an' eat. There is still some of that twenty-five left."

Together they entered a saloon which Bridge remembered as permitting a very large consumption of free lunch upon the purchase of a single schooner of beer.

There were round tables scattered about the floor in front of the bar, and after purchasing their beer they carried it to one of these that stood in a far corner of the room close to a rear door.

Here Bridge sat on guard over the foaming open sesame to food while Billy crossed to the free lunch counter and appropriated all that a zealous attendant would permit him to carry off.

When he returned to the table he took a chair with his back to the wall in conformity to a habit of long standing when, as now, it had stood him in good stead to be in a position to see the other fellow at least as soon as the other fellow saw him. The other fellow being more often than not a large gentleman with a bit of shiny metal pinned to his left suspender strap.

"That guy's a tight one," said Billy, jerking his hand in the direction of the guardian of the free lunch. "I scoops up about a good, square meal for a canary bird, an' he makes me cough up half of it. Wants to know if I t'ink I can go into the restaurant business on a fi'-cent schooner of suds."

Bridge laughed.

"Well, you didn't do so badly at that," he said. "I know places where they'd indict you for grand larceny if you took much more than you have here."

"Rotten beer," commented Billy.

"Always is rotten down here," replied Bridge. "I sometimes think they put moth balls in it so it won't spoil."

Billy looked up and smiled. Then he raised his tall glass before him. "Here's to," he started; but he got no further. His eyes traveling past his companion fell upon the figure of a large man entering the low doorway. At the same instant the gentleman's eyes fell upon Billy. Recognition lit those of each simultaneously. The big man started across the room on a run, straight toward Billy Byrne.

The latter leaped to his feet. Bridge, guessing what had happened, rose too.

"Flannagan!" he exclaimed.

The detective was tugging at his revolver, which had stuck in his hip pocket. Byrne reached for his own weapon. Bridge laid a hand on his arm.

"Not that, Billy!" he cried. "There's a door behind you. Here," and he pulled Billy backward toward the doorway in the wall behind them.

Byrne still clung to his schooner of beer, which he had transferred to his left hand as he sought to draw his gun. Flannagan was close to them. Bridge opened the door and strove to pull Billy through; but the latter hesitated just an instant, for he saw that it would be impossible to close and bar the door, provided it had a bar, before Flannagan would be against it with his great shoulders.

The policeman was still struggling to disentangle his revolver from the lining of his pocket. He was bellowing like a bull—yelling at Billy that he was under arrest. Men at the tables were on their feet. Those at the bar had turned around as Flannagan started to run across the floor. Now some of them were moving in the direction of the detective and his prey, but whether from curiosity or with sinister intentions it is difficult to say.

One thing, however, is certain—if all the love that was felt for policemen in general by the men in that room could have been combined in a single individual it still scarcely would have constituted a grand passion.

Flannagan felt rather than saw that others were closing in on him, and then, fortunately for himself, he thought, he managed to draw his weapon. It was just as Billy was fading through the doorway into the room beyond. He saw the revolver gleam in the policeman's hand and then it became evident why Billy had clung so tenaciously to his schooner of beer. Left-handed and hurriedly he threw it; but even Flannagan must have been constrained to admit that it was a good shot. It struck the detective directly in the midst of his features, gave him a nasty cut on the cheek as it broke and filled his eyes full of beer—and beer never was intended as an eye wash.

Spluttering and cursing, Flannagan came to a sudden stop, and when he had wiped the beer from his eyes he found that Billy Byrne had passed through the doorway and closed the door after him.

The room in which Billy and Bridge found themselves was a small one in the center of which was a large round table at which were gathered a half-dozen men at poker. Above the table swung a single arc lamp, casting a garish light upon the players beneath.

Billy looked quickly about for another exit, only to find that besides the doorway through which he had entered there was but a single aperture in the four walls—a small window, heavily barred. The place was a veritable trap.

At their hurried entrance the men had ceased their play, and one or two had risen in profane questioning and protest. Billy ignored them. He was standing with his shoulder against the door trying to secure it against the detective without; but there was neither bolt nor bar.

Flannagan hurtling against the opposite side exerted his noblest efforts to force an entrance to the room; but Billy Byrne's great weight held firm as Gibraltar. His mind revolved various wild plans of escape; but none bade fair to offer the slightest foothold to hope.

The men at the table were clamoring for an explanation of the interruption. Two of them were approaching Billy with the avowed intention of "turning him out," when he turned his head suddenly toward them.

"Can de beef, you poor boobs," he cried. "Dere's a bunch o' dicks out dere—de joint's been pinched."

Instantly pandemonium ensued. Cards, chips, and money were swept as by magic from the board. A dozen dog-eared and filthy magazines and newspapers were snatched from a hiding place beneath the table, and in the fraction of a second the room was transformed from a gambling place to an innocent reading-room.

Billy grinned broadly. Flannagan had ceased his efforts to break down the door, and was endeavoring to persuade Billy that he might as well come out quietly and submit to arrest. Byrne had drawn his revolver again. Now he motioned to Bridge to come to his side.

"Follow me," he whispered. "Don't move 'til I move—then move sudden." Then, turning to the door again, "You big stiff," he cried, "you couldn't take a crip to a hospital, let alone takin' Billy Byrne to the still. Beat it, before I come out an' spread your beezer acrost your map."

If Billy had desired to arouse the ire of Detective Sergeant Flannagan by this little speech he succeeded quite as well as he could have hoped. Flannagan commenced to growl and threaten, and presently again hurled himself against the door.

Instantly Byrne wheeled and fired a single shot into the arc lamp, the shattered carbon rattled to the table with fragments of the globe, and Byrne stepped quickly to one side. The door flew open and Sergeant Flannagan dove headlong into the darkened room. A foot shot out from behind the opened door, and Flannagan, striking it, sprawled upon his face amidst the legs of the literary lights who held dog-eared magazines rightside up or upside down, as they chanced to have picked them up.

Simultaneously Billy Byrne and Bridge dodged through the open doorway, banged the door to behind them, and sped across the barroom toward the street.

As Flannagan shot into their midst the men at the table leaped to their feet and bolted for the doorway; but the detective was up and after them so quickly that only two succeeded in getting out of the room. One of these generously slammed the door in the faces of his fellows, and there they pulled and hauled at each other until Flannagan was among them.

In the pitch darkness he could recognize no one; but to be on the safe side he hit out promiscuously until he had driven them all from the door, then he stood with his back toward it—the inmates of the room his prisoners.

Thus he remained for a moment threatening to shoot at the first sound of movement in the room, and then he opened the door again, and stepping just outside ordered the prisoners to file out one at a time.

As each man passed him Flannagan scrutinized his face, and it was not until they had all emerged and he had reentered the room with a light that he discovered that once again his quarry had eluded him. Detective Sergeant Flannagan was peeved.

The sun smote down upon a dusty road. A heat-haze lay upon the arid land that stretched away upon either hand toward gray-brown hills. A little adobe hut, backed by a few squalid outbuildings, stood out, a screaming highlight in its coat of whitewash, against a background that was garish with light.

Two men plodded along the road. Their coats were off, the brims of their tattered hats were pulled down over eyes closed to mere slits against sun and dust.

One of the men, glancing up at the distant hut, broke into verse:

> Yet then the sun was shining down, a-blazing on the little town,
> A mile or so 'way down the track a-dancing in the sun.
> But somehow, as I waited there, there came a shiver in the air,
> "The birds are flying south," he said. "The winter has begun."

His companion looked up at him who quoted.

"There ain't no track," he said, "an' that 'dobe shack don't look much like a town; but otherwise his Knibbs has got our number all right, all right. We are the birds a-flyin' south, and Flannagan was the shiver in the air. Flannagan is a reg'lar frost. Gee! but I betcha dat guy's sore."

"Why is it, Billy," asked Bridge, after a moment's silence, "that upon occasion you speak king's English after the manner of the boulevard, and again after that of the back alley? Sometimes you say 'that' and 'dat' in the same sentence. Your conversational clashes are numerous. Surely something or someone has cramped your original style."

"I was born and brought up on 'dat,'" explained Billy. "*She* taught me the other line of talk. Sometimes I forget. I had about twenty years of the other and only one of hers, and twenty to one is a long shot—more apt to lose than win."

"'She,' I take it, is *Penelope*," mused Bridge, half to himself. "She must have been a fine girl."

"'Fine' isn't the right word," Billy corrected him. "If a thing's fine there may be something finer, and then something else finest. She was better than finest. She—she was—why, Bridge, I'd have to be a walking dictionary to tell you what she was."

Bridge made no reply, and the two trudged on toward the whitewashed hut in silence for several minutes. Then Bridge broke it:

> And you, my sweet Penelope, out there somewhere you wait
>   for me

With buds of roses in your hair and kisses on your mouth.

Billy sighed and shook his head.

"There ain't no such luck for me," he said. "She's married to another gink now."

They came at last to the hut, upon the shady side of which they found a Mexican squatting puffing upon a cigarette, while upon the doorstep sat a woman, evidently his wife, busily engaged in the preparation of some manner of foodstuff contained in a large, shallow vessel. About them played a couple of half-naked children. A baby sprawled upon a blanket just within the doorway.

The man looked up, suspiciously, as the two approached. Bridge saluted him in fairly understandable Spanish, asking for food, and telling the man that they had money with which to pay for a little—not much, just a little.

The Mexican slowly unfolded himself and arose, motioning the strangers to follow him into the interior of the hut. The woman, at a word from her lord and master, followed them, and at his further dictation brought them frijoles and tortillas.

The price he asked was nominal; but his eyes never left Bridge's hands as the latter brought forth the money and handed it over. He appeared just a trifle disappointed when no more money than the stipulated purchase price was revealed to sight.

"Where you going?" he asked.

"We're looking for work," explained Bridge. "We want to get jobs on one of the American ranches or mines."

"You better go back," warned the Mexican. "I, myself, have nothing against the Americans, señor; but there are many of my countrymen who do not like you. The Americans are all leaving. Some already have been killed by bandits. It is not safe to go farther. Pesita's men are all about here. Even Mexicans are not safe from him. No one knows whether he is for Villa or Carranza. If he finds a Villa ranchero, then Pesita cries Viva Carranza! and his men kill and rob. If, on the other hand, a neighbor of the last victim hears of it in time, and later Pesita comes to him, he assures Pesita that he is for Carranza, whereupon Pesita cries Viva Villa! and falls upon the poor unfortunate, who is lucky if he escapes with his life. But Americans! Ah, Pesita asks them no questions. He hates them all, and kills them all, whenever he can lay his hands upon them. He has sworn to rid Mexico of the gringos."

"Wot's the Dago talkin' about?" asked Billy.

Bridge gave his companion a brief synopsis of the Mexican's conversation.

"Only the gentleman is not an Italian, Billy," he concluded. "He's a Mexican."

"Who said he was an Eyetalian?" demanded Byrne.

As the two Americans and the Mexican conversed within the hut there approached across the dusty flat, from the direction of the nearer hills, a party of five horsemen.

They rode rapidly, coming toward the hut from the side which had neither door nor window, so that those within had no warning of their coming. They were swarthy, ragged ruffians, fully armed, and with an equipment which suggested that they might be a part of a quasi-military organization.

Close behind the hut four of them dismounted while the fifth, remaining in his saddle, held the bridle reins of the horses of his companions. The latter crept stealthily around the outside of the building, toward the door—their carbines ready in their hands.

It was one of the little children who first discovered the presence of the newcomers. With a piercing scream she bolted into the interior and ran to cling to her mother's skirts.

Billy, Bridge, and the Mexican wheeled toward the doorway simultaneously to learn the cause of the girl's fright, and as they did so found themselves covered by four carbines in the hands of as many men.

As his eyes fell upon the faces of the intruders the countenance of the Mexican fell, while his wife dropped to the floor and embraced his knees, weeping.

"Wotinell?" ejaculated Billy Byrne. "What's doin'?"

"We seem to have been made prisoners," suggested Bridge; "but whether by Villistas or Carranzistas I do not know."

Their host understood his words and turned toward the two Americans.

"These are Pesita's men," he said.

"Yes," spoke up one of the bandits, "we are Pesita's men, and Pesita will be delighted, Miguel, to greet you, especially when he sees the sort of company you have been keeping. You know how much Pesita loves the gringos!"

"But this man does not even know us," spoke up Bridge. "We stopped here to get a meal. He never saw us before. We are on our way to the El Orobo Rancho in search of work. We have no money and have broken no laws. Let us go our way in peace. You can gain nothing by detaining us, and as for Miguel here—that is what you called him, I believe—I think from what he said to us that he loves a gringo about as much as your revered chief seems to."

Miguel looked his appreciation of Bridge's defense of him; but it was evident that he did not expect it to bear fruit. Nor did it. The brigand spokesman only grinned sardonically.

"You may tell all this to Pesita himself, señor," he said. "Now come—get a move on—beat it!" The fellow had once worked in El Paso and took great pride in his "higher English" education.

As he started to herd them from the hut Billy demurred. He turned toward Bridge.

"Most of this talk gets by me," he said. "I ain't jerry to all the Dago jabber yet, though I've copped off a little of it in the past two weeks. Put me wise to the gink's lay."

"Elementary, Watson, elementary," replied Bridge. "We are captured by bandits, and they are going to take us to their delightful chief who will doubtless have us shot at sunrise."

"Bandits?" snapped Billy, with a sneer. "Youse don't call dese little runts bandits?"

"Baby bandits, Billy, baby bandits," replied Bridge.

"An' you're goin' to stan' fer lettin' 'em pull off this rough stuff without handin' 'em a comeback?" demanded Byrne.

"We seem to be up against just that very thing," said Bridge. "There are four carbines quite ready for us. It would mean sudden death to resist now. Later we may find an opportunity—I think we'd better act simple and wait." He spoke in a quick, low whisper, for the spokesman of the brigands evidently understood a little English and was on the alert for any trickery.

Billy shrugged, and when their captors again urged them forward he went quietly; but the expression on his face might have perturbed the Mexicans had they known Billy Byrne of Grand Avenue better—he was smiling happily.

Miguel had two ponies in his corral. These the brigands appropriated, placing Billy upon one and Miguel and Bridge upon the other. Billy's great weight rendered it inadvisable to double him up with another rider.

As they were mounting Billy leaned toward Bridge and whispered:

"I'll get these guys, pal—watch me," he said.

"I am with thee, William!—horse, foot, and artillery," laughed Bridge.

"Which reminds me," said Billy, "that I have an ace-in-the-hole—the boobs never frisked me."

"And I am reminded," returned Bridge, as the horses started off to the yank of hackamore ropes in the hands of the brigands who were leading them, "of a touching little thing of Service's:

> Just think! Some night the stars will gleam
> Upon a cold gray stone,
> And trace a name with silver beam,
> And lo! 'twill be your own."

"You're a cheerful guy," was Billy's only comment.

VII
In Pesita's Camp

Pesita was a short, stocky man with a large, dark mustache. He attired himself after his own ideas of what should constitute the uniform of a general—ideas more or less influenced and modified by the chance and caprice of fortune.

At the moment that Billy, Bridge, and Miguel were dragged into his presence his torso was enwrapped in a once resplendent coat covered with yards of gold braid. Upon his shoulders were brass epaulets such as are connected only in one's mind with the ancient chorus ladies of the light operas of fifteen or twenty years ago. Upon his legs were some rusty and ragged overalls. His feet were bare.

He scowled ferociously at the prisoners while his lieutenant narrated the thrilling facts of their capture—thrilling by embellishment.

"You are Americanos?" he asked of Bridge and Billy.

Both agreed that they were. Then Pesita turned toward Miguel.

"Where is Villa?" he asked.

"How should I know, my general?" parried Miguel. "Who am I—a poor man with a tiny rancho—to know of the movements of the great ones of the earth? I did not even know where was the great General Pesita until now I am brought into his gracious presence, to throw myself at his feet and implore that I be permitted to serve him in even the meanest of capacities."

Pesita appeared not to hear what Miguel had said. He turned his shoulder toward the man, and addressed Billy in broken English.

"You were on your way to El Orobo Rancho, eh? Are you acquainted there?" he asked.

Billy replied that they were not—merely looking for employment upon an American-owned ranch or in an American mine.

"Why did you leave your own country?" asked Pesita. "What do you want here in Mexico?"

"Well, ol' top," replied Billy, "you see de birds was flyin' south an' winter was in de air, an a fathead dick from Chi was on me trail—so I ducks."

"Ducks?" queried Pesita, mystified. "Ah, the ducks—they fly south, I see."

"Naw, you poor simp—I blows," explained Billy.

"Ah, yes," agreed Pesita, not wishing to admit any ignorance of plain American even before a despised gringo. "But the large-faced dick—what might that be? I have spend much time in the States, but I do not know that."

"I said 'fathead dick'—dat's a fly cop," Billy elucidated.

"It is he then that is the bird." Pesita beamed at this evidence of his own sagacity. "He fly."

"Flannagan ain't no bird—Flannagan's a dub."

Bridge came to the rescue.

"My erudite friend means," he explained, "that the police chased him out of the United States of America."

Pesita raised his eyebrows. All was now clear to him.

"But why did he not say so?" he asked.

"He tried to," said Bridge. "He did his best."

"Quit yer kiddin'," admonished Billy.

A bright light suddenly burst upon Pesita. He turned upon Bridge.

"Your friend is not then an American?" he asked. "I guessed it. That is why I could not understand him. He speaks the language of the gringo less well even than I. From what country is he?"

Billy Byrne would have asserted with some show of asperity that he was nothing if not American; but Bridge was quick to see a possible loophole for escape for his friend in Pesita's belief that Billy was no gringo, and warned the latter to silence by a quick motion of his head.

"He's from 'Gran' Avenoo,'" he said. "It is not exactly in Germany; but there are a great many Germans there. My friend is a native, so he don't speak German or English either—they have a language of their own in 'Gran' Avenoo."

"I see," said Pesita—"a German colony. I like the Germans—they furnish me with much ammunition and rifles. They are my very good friends. Take Miguel and the gringo away"—this to the soldiers who had brought the prisoners to him—"I will speak further with this man from Granavenoo."

When the others had passed out of hearing Pesita addressed Billy.

"I am sorry, señor," he said, "that you have been put to so much inconvenience. My men could not know that you were not a gringo; but I can make it all right. I will make it all right. You are a big man. The gringos have chased you from their country as they chased me. I hate them. You hate them. But enough of them. You have no business in Mexico except to seek work. I give you work. You are big. You are strong. You are like a bull. You stay with me, señor, and I make you captain. I need men what can talk some English and look like gringo. You do fine. We make much money—you and I. We make it all time while we fight to liberate my poor Mexico. When Mexico liberate we fight some more to liberate her again. The Germans they give me much money to liberate Mexico, and—there are other ways of getting much money when one is riding around through rich country with soldiers liberating his poor, bleeding country. Sabe?"

"Yep, I guess I savvy," said Billy, "an' it listens all right to me's far's you've gone. My pal in on it?"

"Eh?"

"You make my frien' a captain, too?"

Pesita held up his hands and rolled his eyes in holy horror. Take a gringo into his band? It was unthinkable.

"He shot," he cried. "I swear to kill all gringo. I become savior of my country. I rid her of all Americanos."

"Nix on the captain stuff fer me, then," said Billy, firmly. "That guy's a right one. If any big stiff thinks he can croak little ol' Bridge while Billy Byrne's aroun' he's got anudder t'ink comin'. Why, me an' him's just like brudders."

"You like this gringo?" asked Pesita.

"You bet," cried Billy.

Pesita thought for several minutes. In his mind was a scheme which required the help of just such an individual as this stranger—someone who was utterly unknown in the surrounding country and whose presence in a town could not by any stretch of the imagination be connected in any way with the bandit, Pesita.

"I tell you," he said. "I let your friend go. I send him under safe escort to El Orobo Rancho. Maybe he help us there after a while. If you stay I let him go. Otherwise I shoot you both with Miguel."

"Wot you got it in for Mig fer?" asked Billy. "He's a harmless sort o' guy."

"He Villista. Villista with gringos run Mexico—gringos and the church. Just like Huerta would have done it if they'd given him a chance, only Huerta more for church than for gringos."

"Aw, let the poor boob go," urged Billy, "an' I'll come along wit you. Why he's got a wife an' kids—you wouldn't want to leave them without no one to look after them in this Godforsaken country!"

Pesita grinned indulgently.

"Very well, Señor Captain," he said, bowing low. "I let Miguel and your honorable friend go. I send safe escort with them."

"Bully fer you, ol' pot!" exclaimed Billy, and Pesita smiled delightedly in the belief that some complimentary title had been applied to him in the language of "Granavenoo." "I'll go an' tell 'em," said Billy.

"Yes," said Pesita, "and say to them that they will start early in the morning."

As Billy turned and walked in the direction that the soldiers had led Bridge and Miguel, Pesita beckoned to a soldier who leaned upon his gun at a short distance from his "general"—a barefooted, slovenly attempt at a headquarters orderly.

"Send Captain Rozales to me," directed Pesita.

The soldier shuffled away to where a little circle of men in wide-brimmed, metal-encrusted hats squatted in the shade of a tree, chatting, laughing, and rolling cigarettes. He saluted one of these and delivered his message, whereupon the tall, gaunt Captain Rozales arose and came over to Pesita.

"The big one who was brought in today is not a gringo," said Pesita, by way of opening the conversation. "He is from Granavenoo. He can be of great service to us, for he is very friendly with the Germans—yet he looks like a gringo and could pass for one. We can utilize him. Also he is very large and appears to be equally strong. He should make a good fighter and we have none too many. I have made him a captain."

Rozales grinned. Already among Pesita's following of a hundred men there were fifteen captains.

"Where is Granavenoo?" asked Rozales.

"You mean to say, my dear captain," exclaimed Pesita, "that a man of your education does not know where Granavenoo is? I am surprised. Why, it is a German colony."

"Yes, of course. I recall it well now. For the moment it had slipped my mind. My grandfather who was a great traveler was there many times. I have heard him speak of it often."

"But I did not summon you that we might discuss European geography," interrupted Pesita. "I sent for you to tell you that the stranger would not consent to serve me unless I liberated his friend, the gringo, and that sneaking spy of a Miguel. I was forced to yield, for we can use the stranger. So I have promised, my dear captain, that I shall send them upon their road with a safe escort in the morning, and you shall command the guard. Upon your life respect my promise, Rozales; but if some of Villa's cutthroats should fall upon you, and in the battle, while you were trying to defend the gringo and Miguel, both should be slain by the bullets of the Villistas—ah, but it would be deplorable, Rozales, but it would not be your fault. Who, indeed, could blame you who had fought well and risked your men and yourself in the performance of your sacred duty? Rozales, should such a thing occur what could I do in token of my great pleasure other than make you a colonel?"

"I shall defend them with my life, my general," cried Rozales, bowing low.

"Good!" cried Pesita. "That is all."

Rozales started back toward the ring of smokers.

"Ah, Captain!" cried Pesita. "Another thing. Will you make it known to the other officers that the stranger from Granavenoo is a captain and that it is my wish that he be well treated, but not told so much as might injure him, or his usefulness, about our sacred work of liberating poor, bleeding unhappy Mexico."

Again Rozales bowed and departed. This time he was not recalled.

Billy found Bridge and Miguel squatting on the ground with two dirty-faced peons standing guard over them. The latter were some little distance away. They made no objection when Billy approached the prisoners though they had looked in mild surprise when they saw him crossing toward them without a guard.

Billy sat down beside Bridge, and broke into a laugh.

"What's the joke?" asked Bridge. "Are we going to be hanged instead of being shot?"

"We ain't goin' to be either," said Billy, "an' I'm a captain. Whaddaya know about that?"

He explained all that had taken place between himself and Pesita while Bridge and Miguel listened attentively to his every word.

"I t'ought it was about de only way out fer us," said Billy. "We were in worse than I t'ought."

"Can the Bowery stuff, Billy," cried Bridge, "and talk like a white man. You can, you know."

"All right, bo," cried Billy, good-naturedly. "You see I forget when there is anything pressing like this, to chew about. Then I fall back into the old lingo. Well, as I was saying, I didn't want to do it unless you would stay too, but he wouldn't have you. He has it in for all gringos, and that bull you passed him about me being from a foreign country called Grand Avenue! He fell for it like a rube for the tapped-wire stuff. He said if I wouldn't stay and help him he'd croak the bunch of us."

"How about that ace-in-the-hole, you were telling me about?" asked Bridge.

"I still got it," and Billy fondled something hard that swung under his left arm beneath his shirt; "but, Lord, man! what could I do against the whole bunch? I might get a few of them; but they'd get us all in the end. This other way is better, though I hate to have to split with you, old man."

He was silent then for a moment, looking hard at the ground. Bridge whistled, and cleared his throat.

"I've always wanted to spend a year in Rio," he said. "We'll meet there, when you can make your getaway."

"You've said it," agreed Byrne. "It's Rio as soon as we can make it. Pesita's promised to set you both loose in the morning and send you under safe escort—Miguel to his happy home, and you to El Orobo Rancho. I guess the old stiff isn't so bad after all."

Miguel had pricked up his ears at the sound of the word *escort*. He leaned far forward, closer to the two Americans, and whispered.

"Who is to command the escort?" he asked.

"I dunno," said Billy. "What difference does it make?"

"It makes all the difference between life and death for your friend and for me," said Miguel. "There is no reason why I should need an escort. I know my way throughout all Chihuahua as well as Pesita or any of his cutthroats. I have come and gone all my life without an escort. Of course your friend is different. It might be well for him to have company to El Orobo. Maybe it is all right; but wait until we learn who commands the escort. I know Pesita well. I know his methods. If Rozales rides out with us tomorrow morning you may say goodbye to your friend forever, for you will never see him in Rio, or elsewhere. He and I will be dead before ten o'clock."

"What makes you think that, bo?" demanded Billy.

"I do not think, señor," replied Miguel; "I know."

"Well," said Billy, "we'll wait and see."

"If it is Rozales, say nothing," said Miguel. "It will do no good; but we may then be on the watch, and if possible you might find the means to obtain a couple of revolvers for us. In which case—" he shrugged and permitted a faint smile to flex his lips.

As they talked a soldier came and announced that they were no longer prisoners—they were to have the freedom of the camp; "but," he concluded, "the general requests that you do not pass beyond the limits of the camp. There are many desperadoes in the hills and he fears for your safety, now that you are his guests."

The man spoke Spanish, so that it was necessary that Bridge interpret his words for the benefit of Billy, who had understood only part of what he said.

"Ask him," said Byrne, "if that stuff goes for me, too."

"He says no," replied Bridge after questioning the soldier, "that the captain is now one of them, and may go and come as do the other officers. Such are Pesita's orders."

Billy arose. The messenger had returned to his post at headquarters. The guard had withdrawn, leaving the three men alone.

"So long, old man," said Billy. "If I'm goin' to be of any help to you and Mig the less I'm seen with you the better. I'll blow over and mix with the Dago bunch, an' practice sittin' on my heels. It seems to be the right dope down here, an' I got to learn all I can about bein' a greaser seein' that I've turned one."

"Goodbye Billy, remember Rio," said Bridge.

"And the revolvers, señor," added Miguel.

"You bet," replied Billy, and strolled off in the direction of the little circle of cigarette smokers.

As he approached them Rozales looked up and smiled. Then, rising, extended his hand.

"Señor Captain," he said, "we welcome you. I am Captain Rozales." He hesitated waiting for Billy to give his name.

"My monacker's Byrne," said Billy. "Pleased to meet you, Cap."

"Ah, Captain Byrne," and Rozales proceeded to introduce the newcomer to his fellow-officers.

Several, like Rozales, were educated men who had been officers in the army under former regimes; but had turned bandit as the safer alternative to suffering immediate death at the hands of the faction then in power. The others, for the most part, were pure-blooded Indians whose adult lives had been spent in outlawry and brigandage. All were small of stature beside the giant, Byrne. Rozales and two others spoke English. With those Billy conversed. He tried to learn from them the name of the officer who was to command the escort that was to accompany Bridge and Miguel into the valley on the morrow; but Rozales and the others assured him that they did not know.

When he had asked the question Billy had been looking straight at Rozales, and he had seen the man's pupils contract and noticed the slight backward movement of the body which also denotes determination. Billy knew, therefore, that Rozales was lying. He did know who was to command the escort, and there was something sinister in that knowledge or the fellow would not have denied it.

The American began to consider plans for saving his friend from the fate which Pesita had outlined for him. Rozales, too, was thinking rapidly. He was no fool. Why had the stranger desired to know who was to command the escort? He knew none of the officers personally. What difference then, did it make to him who rode out on the morrow with his friend? Ah, but Miguel knew that it would make a difference. Miguel had spoken to the new captain, and aroused his suspicions.

Rozales excused himself and rose. A moment later he was in conversation with Pesita, unburdening himself of his suspicions, and outlining a plan.

"Do not send me in charge of the escort," he advised. "Send Captain Byrne himself."

Pesita pooh-poohed the idea.

"But wait," urged Rozales. "Let the stranger ride in command, with a half-dozen picked men who will see that nothing goes wrong. An hour before dawn I will send two men—they will be our best shots—on ahead. They will stop at a place we both know, and about noon the Captain Byrne and his escort will ride back to camp and tell us that they were attacked by a troop of Villa's men, and that both our guests were killed. It will be sad; but it will not be our fault. We will swear vengeance upon Villa, and the Captain Byrne will hate him as a good Pesitista should."

"You have the cunning of the Coyote, my captain," cried Pesita. "It shall be done as you suggest. Go now, and I will send for Captain Byrne, and give him his orders for the morning."

As Rozales strolled away a figure rose from the shadows at the side of Pesita's tent and slunk off into the darkness.

VIII
BILLY'S FIRST COMMAND

And so it was that having breakfasted in the morning Bridge and Miguel started downward toward the valley protected by an escort under Captain Billy Byrne. An old service jacket and a wide-brimmed hat, both donated by brother officers, constituted Captain Byrne's uniform. His mount was the largest that the picket line of Pesita's forces could produce. Billy loomed large amongst his men.

For an hour they rode along the trail, Billy and Bridge conversing upon various subjects, none of which touched upon the one uppermost in the mind of each. Miguel rode, silent and preoccupied. The evening before he had whispered something to Bridge as he had crawled out of the darkness to lie close to the American, and during a brief moment that morning Bridge had found an opportunity to relay the Mexican's message to Billy Byrne.

The latter had but raised his eyebrows a trifle at the time, but later he smiled more than was usual with him. Something seemed to please him immensely.

Beside him at the head of the column rode Bridge and Miguel. Behind them trailed the six swarthy little troopers—the picked men upon whom Pesita could depend.

They had reached a point where the trail passes through a narrow dry arroyo which the waters of the rainy season had cut deep into the soft, powdery soil. Upon either bank grew cacti and mesquite, forming a sheltering screen behind which a regiment might have hidden. The place was ideal for an ambuscade.

"Here, Señor Capitan," whispered Miguel, as they neared the entrance to the trap.

A low hill shut off from their view all but the head of the cut, and it also hid them from the sight of any possible enemy which might have been lurking in wait for them farther down the arroyo.

At Miguel's words Byrne wheeled his horse to the right away from the trail which led through the bottom of the waterway and around the base of the hill, or rather in that direction, for he had scarce deviated from the direct way before one of the troopers spurred to his side, calling out in Spanish that he was upon the wrong trail.

"Wot's this guy chewin' about?" asked Billy, turning to Miguel.

"He says you must keep to the arroyo, Señor Capitan," explained the Mexican.

"Tell him to go back into his stall," was Byrne's laconic rejoinder, as he pushed his mount forward to pass the brigand.

The soldier was voluble in his objections. Again he reined in front of Billy, and by this time his five fellows had spurred forward to block the way.

"This is the wrong trail," they cried. "Come this other way, Capitan. Pesita has so ordered it."

Catching the drift of their remarks, Billy waved them to one side.

"I'm bossin' this picnic," he announced. "Get out o' the way, an' be quick about it if you don't want to be hurted."

Again he rode forward. Again the troopers interposed their mounts, and this time their leader cocked his carbine. His attitude was menacing. Billy was close to him. Their ponies were shoulder to shoulder, that of the bandit almost broadside of the trail.

Now Billy Byrne was more than passing well acquainted with many of the fundamental principles of sudden brawls. It is safe to say that he had never heard of Van Bibber; but he knew, as well as Van Bibber knew, that it is well to hit first.

Without a word and without warning he struck, leaning forward with all the weight of his body behind his blow, and catching the man full beneath the chin he lifted him as neatly from his saddle as though a battering ram had struck him.

Simultaneously Bridge and Miguel drew revolvers from their shirts and as Billy wheeled his pony toward the remaining five they opened fire upon them.

The battle was short and sweet. One almost escaped but Miguel, who proved to be an excellent revolver shot, brought him down at a hundred yards. He then, with utter disregard for the rules of civilized warfare, dispatched those who were not already dead.

"We must let none return to carry false tales to Pesita," he explained.

Even Billy Byrne winced at the ruthlessness of the cold-blooded murders; but he realized the necessity which confronted them though he could not have brought himself to do the things which the Mexican did with such sangfroid and even evident enjoyment.

"Now for the others!" cried Miguel, when he had assured himself that each of the six were really quite dead.

Spurring after him Billy and Bridge ran their horses over the rough ground at the base of the little hill, and then parallel to the arroyo for a matter of a hundred yards, where they espied two Indians, carbines in hand, standing in evident consternation because of the unexpected fusillade of shots which they had just heard and which they were unable to account for.

At the sight of the three the sharpshooters dropped behind cover and fired. Billy's horse stumbled at the first report, caught himself, reared high upon his hind legs and then toppled over, dead.

His rider, throwing himself to one side, scrambled to his feet and fired twice at the partially concealed men. Miguel and Bridge rode in rapidly to close quarters, firing as they came. One of the two men Pesita had sent to assassinate his "guests" dropped his gun, clutched at his breast, screamed, and sank back behind a clump of mesquite. The other turned and leaped over the edge of the bank into the arroyo, rolling and tumbling to the bottom in a cloud of dry dust.

As he rose to his feet and started on a run up the bed of the dry stream, dodging a zigzag course from one bit of scant cover to another Billy Byrne stepped to the edge of the washout and threw his carbine to his shoulder. His face was flushed, his eyes sparkled, a smile lighted his regular features.

"This is the life!" he cried, and pulled the trigger.

The man beneath him, running for his life like a frightened jackrabbit, sprawled forward upon his face, made a single effort to rise and then slumped limply down, forever.

Miguel and Bridge, dismounted now, came to Byrne's side. The Mexican was grinning broadly.

"The captain is one grand fighter," he said. "How my dear general would admire such a man as the captain. Doubtless he would make him a colonel. Come with me Señor Capitan and your fortune is made."

"Come where?" asked Billy Byrne.

"To the camp of the liberator of poor, bleeding Mexico—to General Francisco Villa."

"Nothin' doin'," said Billy. "I'm hooked up with this Pesita person now, an' I guess I'll stick. He's given me more of a run for my money in the last twenty-four hours than I've had since I parted from my dear old friend, the Lord of Yoka."

"But Señor Capitan," cried Miguel, "you do not mean to say that you are going back to Pesita! He will shoot you down with his own hand when he has learned what has happened here."

"I guess not," said Billy.

"You'd better go with Miguel, Billy," urged Bridge. "Pesita will not forgive you this. You've cost him eight men today and he hasn't any more men than he needs at best. Besides you've made a monkey of him and unless I miss my guess you'll have to pay for it."

"No," said Billy, "I kind o' like this Pesita gent. I think I'll stick around with him for a while yet. Anyhow until I've had a chance to see his face after I've made my report to him. You guys run along now and make your getaway good, an' I'll beat it back to camp."

He crossed to where the two horses of the slain marksmen were hidden, turned one of them loose and mounted the other.

"So long, boes!" he cried, and with a wave of his hand wheeled about and spurred back along the trail over which they had just come.

Miguel and Bridge watched him for a moment, then they, too, mounted and turned away in the opposite direction. Bridge recited no verse for the balance of that day. His heart lay heavy in his bosom, for he missed Billy Byrne, and was fearful of the fate which awaited him at the camp of the bandit.

Billy, blithe as a lark, rode gaily back along the trail to camp. He looked forward with unmixed delight to his coming interview with Pesita, and to the wild, half-savage life which association with the bandit promised. All his life had Billy Byrne fed upon excitement and adventure. As gangster, thug, holdup man and second-story artist Billy had found food for his appetite within the dismal, sooty streets of Chicago's great West Side, and then Fate had flung him upon the savage shore of Yoka to find other forms of adventure where the best that is in a strong man may be brought out in the stern battle for existence against primeval men and conditions. The West Side had developed only Billy's basest characteristics. He might have slipped back easily into the old ways had it not been for *her* and the recollection of that which he had read in her eyes. Love had been there; but greater than that to hold a man into the straight and narrow path of decency and honor had been respect and admiration. It had seemed incredible to Billy that a goddess should feel such things for him—for the same man her scornful lips once had branded as coward and mucker; yet he had read the truth aright, and since then Billy Byrne had done his best according to the light that had been given him to deserve the belief she had in him.

So far there had crept into his consciousness no disquieting doubts as to the consistency of his recent action in joining the force of a depredating Mexican outlaw. Billy knew nothing of the political conditions of the republic. Had Pesita told him that he was president of Mexico, Billy could not have disputed the statement from any knowledge of facts which he possessed. As a matter of fact about all Billy had ever known of Mexico was that it had some connection with an important place called Juarez where running meets were held.

To Billy Byrne, then, Pesita was a real general, and Billy, himself, a bona fide captain. He had entered an army which was at war with some other army. What they were warring about Billy knew not, nor did he care. There should be fighting and he loved that—that much he knew. The ethics of Pesita's warfare troubled him not. He had heard that some great American general had said: "War is hell." Billy was willing to take his word for it, and accept anything which came in the guise of war as entirely proper and as it should be.

The afternoon was far gone when Billy drew rein in the camp of the outlaw band. Pesita with the bulk of his raiders was out upon some excursion to the north. Only half a dozen men lolled about, smoking or sleeping away the hot day. They looked at Billy in evident surprise when they saw him riding in alone; but they asked no questions and Billy offered no explanation—his report was for the ears of Pesita only.

The balance of the day Billy spent in acquiring further knowledge of Spanish by conversing with those of the men who remained awake, and asking innumerable questions. It was almost sundown when Pesita rode in. Two riderless horses were led by troopers in the rear of the little column and three men swayed painfully in their saddles and their clothing was stained with blood.

Evidently Pesita had met with resistance. There was much voluble chattering on the part of those who had remained behind in their endeavors to extract from their returning comrades the details of the day's enterprise.

By piecing together the various scraps of conversation he could understand Billy discovered that Pesita had ridden far to demand tribute from a wealthy ranchero, only to find that word of his coming had preceded him and brought a large detachment of Villa's regulars who concealed themselves about the house and outbuildings until Pesita and his entire force were well within close range.

"We were lucky to get off as well as we did," said an officer.

Billy grinned inwardly as he thought of the pleasant frame of mind in which Pesita might now be expected to receive the news that eight of his troopers had been killed and his two "guests" safely removed from the sphere of his hospitality.

And even as his mind dwelt delightedly upon the subject a ragged Indian carrying a carbine and with heavy silver spurs strapped to his bare feet approached and saluted him.

"General Pesita wishes Señor Capitan Byrne to report to him at once," said the man.

"Sure Mike!" replied Billy, and made his way through the pandemonium of the camp toward the headquarters tent.

As he went he slipped his hand inside his shirt and loosened something which hung beneath his left arm.

"Li'l ol' ace-in-the-hole," he murmured affectionately.

He found Pesita pacing back and forth before his tent—an energetic bundle of nerves which no amount of hard riding and fighting could tire or discourage.

As Billy approached Pesita shot a quick glance at his face, that he might read, perhaps, in his new officer's expression whether anger or suspicion had been aroused by the killing of his American friend, for Pesita never dreamed but that Bridge had been dead since mid-forenoon.

"Well," said Pesita, smiling, "you left Señor Bridge and Miguel safely at their destination?"

"I couldn't take 'em all the way," replied Billy, "cause I didn't have no more men to guard 'em with; but I seen 'em past the danger I guess an' well on their way."

"You had no men?" questioned Pesita. "You had six troopers."

"Oh, they was all croaked before we'd been gone two hours. You see it happens like this: We got as far as that dry arroyo just before the trail drops down into the valley, when up jumps a bunch of this here Villa's guys and commenced takin' pot shots at us.

"Seein' as how I was sent to guard Bridge an' Mig, I makes them dismount and hunt cover, and then me an' my men wades in and cleans up the bunch. They was only a few of them but they croaked the whole bloomin' six o' mine.

"I tell you it was some scrap while it lasted; but I saved your guests from gettin' hurted an' I know that that's what you sent me to do. It's too bad about the six men we lost but, leave it to me, we'll get even with that Villa guy yet. Just lead me to 'im."

As he spoke Billy commenced scratching himself beneath the left arm, and then, as though to better reach the point of irritation, he slipped his hand inside his shirt. If Pesita noticed the apparently innocent little act, or interpreted it correctly may or may not have been the fact. He stood looking straight into Byrne's eyes for a full minute. His face denoted neither baffled rage nor contemplated revenge. Presently a slow smile raised his heavy mustache and revealed his strong, white teeth.

"You have done well, Captain Byrne," he said. "You are a man after my own heart," and he extended his hand.

A half-hour later Billy walked slowly back to his own blankets, and to say that he was puzzled would scarce have described his mental state.

"I can't quite make that gink out," he mused. "Either he's a mighty good loser or else he's a deep one who'll wait a year to get me the way he wants to get me."

And Pesita a few moments later was saying to Captain Rozales:

"I should have shot him if I could spare such a man; but it is seldom I find one with the courage and effrontery he possesses. Why think of it, Rozales, he kills eight of my men, and lets my prisoners escape, and then dares to come back and tell me about it when he might easily have gotten away. Villa would have made him an officer for this thing, and Miguel must have told him so. He found out in some way about your little plan and he turned the tables on us. We can use him, Rozales, but we must watch him. Also, my dear captain, watch his right hand and when he slips it into his shirt be careful that you do not draw on him—unless you happen to be behind him."

Rozales was not inclined to take his chief's view of Byrne's value to them. He argued that the man was guilty of disloyalty and therefore a menace. What he thought, but did not advance as an argument, was of a different nature. Rozales was filled with rage to think that the newcomer had outwitted him, and beaten him at his own game, and he was jealous, too, of the man's ascendancy in the esteem of Pesita; but he hid his personal feelings beneath a cloak of seeming acquiescence in his chief's views, knowing that some day his time would come when he might rid himself of the danger of this obnoxious rival.

"And tomorrow," continued Pesita, "I am sending him to Cuivaca. Villa has considerable funds in bank there, and this stranger can learn what I want to know about the size of the detachment holding the town, and the habits of the garrison."

IX
Barbara in Mexico

The manager of El Orobo Rancho was an American named Grayson. He was a tall, wiry man whose education had been acquired principally in the cow camps of Texas, where, among other things one does *not* learn to love nor trust a greaser. As a result of this early training Grayson was peculiarly unfitted in some respects to manage an American ranch in Mexico; but he was a just man, and so if his vaqueros did not love him, they at least respected him, and everyone who was or possessed the latent characteristics of a wrongdoer feared him.

Perhaps it is not fair to say that Grayson was in any way unfitted for the position he held, since as a matter of fact he was an ideal ranch foreman, and, if the truth be known, the simple fact that he was a gringo would have been sufficient to have won him the hatred of the Mexicans who worked under him—not in the course of their everyday relations; but when the fires of racial animosity were fanned to flame by some untoward incident upon either side of the border.

Today Grayson was particularly rabid. The more so because he could not vent his anger upon the cause of it, who was no less a person than his boss.

It seemed incredible to Grayson that any man of intelligence could have conceived and then carried out the fool thing which the boss had just done, which was to have come from the safety of New York City to the hazards of warring Mexico, bringing—and this was the worst feature of it—his daughter with him. And at such a time! Scarce a day passed without its rumors or reports of new affronts and even atrocities being perpetrated upon American residents of Mexico. Each day, too, the gravity of these acts increased. From mere insult they had run of late to assault and even to murder. Nor was the end in sight.

Pesita had openly sworn to rid Mexico of the gringo—to kill on sight every American who fell into his hands. And what could Grayson do in case of a determined attack upon the rancho? It is true he had a hundred men— laborers and vaqueros; but scarce a dozen of these were Americans, and the rest would, almost without exception, follow the inclinations of consanguinity in case of trouble.

To add to Grayson's irritability he had just lost his bookkeeper, and if there was one thing more than any other that Grayson hated it was pen and ink. The youth had been a "lunger" from Iowa, a fairly nice little chap, and entirely suited to his duties under any other circumstances than those which prevailed in Mexico at that time. He was in mortal terror of his life every moment that he was awake, and at last had given in to the urge of cowardice and resigned. The day previous he had been bundled into a buckboard and driven over to the Mexican Central which, at that time, still was operating trains—occasionally—between Chihuahua and Juarez.

His mind filled with these unpleasant thoughts, Grayson sat at his desk in the office of the ranch trying to unravel the riddle of a balance sheet which would not balance. Mixed with the blue of the smoke from his briar was the deeper azure of a spirited monologue in which Grayson was engaged.

A girl was passing the building at the moment. At her side walked a gray-haired man—one of those men whom you just naturally fit into a mental picture of a director's meeting somewhere along Wall Street.

"Sich langwidge!" cried the girl, with a laugh, covering her ears with her palms.

The man at her side smiled.

"I can't say that I blame him much, Barbara," he replied. "It was a very foolish thing for me to bring you down here at this time. I can't understand what ever possessed me to do it."

"Don't blame yourself, dear," remonstrated the girl, "when it was all my fault. I begged and begged and begged until you had to consent, and I'm not sorry either—if nothing happens to you because of our coming. I couldn't stay in New York another minute. Everyone was so snoopy, and I could just tell that they were dying to ask questions about Billy and me."

"I can't get it through my head yet, Barbara," said the man, "why in the world you broke with Billy Mallory. He's one of the finest young men in New York City today—just my ideal of the sort of man I'd like my only daughter to marry."

"I tried, Papa," said the girl in a low voice; "but I couldn't—I just couldn't."

"Was it because—" the man stopped abruptly. "Well, never mind dear, I shan't be snoopy too. Here now, you run along and do some snooping yourself about the ranch. I want to stop in and have a talk with Grayson."

Down by one of the corrals where three men were busily engaged in attempting to persuade an unbroken pony that a spade bit is a pleasant thing to wear in one's mouth, Barbara found a seat upon a wagon box which commanded an excellent view of the entertainment going on within the corral. As she sat there experiencing a combination of admiration for the agility and courage of the men and pity for the horse the tones of a pleasant masculine voice broke in upon her thoughts.

> "Out there somewhere!" says I to me. "By Gosh, I guess, thats poetry!
> Out there somewhere—Penelope—with kisses on her mouth!"
> And then, thinks I, "O college guy! your talk it gets me in the eye,
> The north is creeping in the air; the birds are flying south."

Barbara swung around to view the poet. She saw a slender man astride a fagged Mexican pony. A ragged coat and ragged trousers covered the man's nakedness. Indian moccasins protected his feet, while a torn and shapeless felt hat sat upon his well-shaped head. *American* was written all over him. No one could have imagined him anything else. Apparently he was a tramp as well—his apparel proclaimed him that; but there were two discordant notes in the otherwise harmonious ensemble of your typical bo. He was clean shaven and he rode a pony. He rode erect, too, with the easy seat of an army officer.

At sight of the girl he raised his battered hat and swept it low to his pony's shoulder as he bent in a profound bow.

"I seek the majordomo, señorita," he said.

"Mr. Grayson is up at the office, that little building to the left of the ranchhouse," replied the girl, pointing.

The newcomer had addressed her in Spanish, and as he heard her reply, in pure and liquid English, his eyes widened a trifle; but the familiar smile with which he had greeted her left his face, and his parting bow was much more dignified though no less profound than its predecessor.

> And you, my sweet Penelope, out there somewhere you wait for me,

With buds of roses in your hair and kisses on your mouth.

Grayson and his employer both looked up as the words of Knibbs' poem floated in to them through the open window.

"I wonder where that blew in from," remarked Grayson, as his eyes discovered Bridge astride the tired pony, looking at him through the window. A polite smile touched the stranger's lips as his eyes met Grayson's, and then wandered past him to the imposing figure of the Easterner.

"Good evening, gentlemen," said Bridge.

"Evenin'," snapped Grayson. "Go over to the cookhouse and the Chink'll give you something to eat. Turn your pony in the lower pasture. Smith'll show you where to bunk tonight, an' you kin hev your breakfast in the mornin'. S'long!" The ranch superintendent turned back to the paper in his hand which he had been discussing with his employer at the moment of the interruption. He had volleyed his instructions at Bridge as though pouring a rain of lead from a machine gun, and now that he had said what he had to say the incident was closed in so far as he was concerned.

The hospitality of the Southwest permitted no stranger to be turned away without food and a night's lodging. Grayson having arranged for these felt that he had done all that might be expected of a host, especially when the uninvited guest was so obviously a hobo and doubtless a horse thief as well, for who ever knew a hobo to own a horse?

Bridge continued to sit where he had reined in his pony. He was looking at Grayson with what the discerning boss judged to be politely concealed enjoyment.

"Possibly," suggested the boss in a whisper to his aide, "the man has business with you. You did not ask him, and I am sure that he said nothing about wishing a meal or a place to sleep."

"Huh?" grunted Grayson, and then to Bridge, "Well, what the devil *do* you want?"

"A job," replied Bridge, "or, to be more explicit, I need a job—far be it from me to *wish* one."

The Easterner smiled. Grayson looked a bit mystified—and irritated.

"Well, I hain't got none," he snapped. "We don't need nobody now unless it might be a good puncher—one who can rope and ride."

"I can ride," replied Bridge, "as is evidenced by the fact that you now see me astride a horse."

"I said *ride*," said Grayson. "Any fool can *sit* on a horse. *No*, I hain't got nothin', an' I'm busy now. Hold on!" he exclaimed as though seized by a sudden inspiration. He looked sharply at Bridge for a moment and then shook his head sadly. "No, I'm afraid you couldn't do it—a guy's got to be eddicated for the job I got in mind."

"Washing dishes?" suggested Bridge.

Grayson ignored the playfulness of the other's question.

"Keepin' books," he explained. There was a finality in his tone which said: "As you, of course, cannot keep books the interview is now over. Get out!"

"I could try," said Bridge. "I can read and write, you know. Let me try." Bridge wanted money for the trip to Rio, and, too, he wanted to stay in the country until Billy was ready to leave.

"Savvy Spanish?" asked Grayson.

"I read and write it better than I speak it," said Bridge, "though I do the latter well enough to get along anywhere that it is spoken."

Grayson wanted a bookkeeper worse than he could ever recall having wanted anything before in all his life. His better judgment told him that it was the height of idiocy to employ a ragged bum as a bookkeeper; but the bum was at least as much of a hope to him as is a straw to a drowning man, and so Grayson clutched at him.

"Go an' turn your cayuse in an' then come back here," he directed, "an' I'll give you a tryout."

"Thanks," said Bridge, and rode off in the direction of the pasture gate.

"'Fraid he won't never do," said Grayson, ruefully, after Bridge had passed out of earshot.

"I rather imagine that he will," said the boss. "He is an educated man, Grayson—you can tell that from his English, which is excellent. He's probably one of the great army of down-and-outers. The world is full of them—poor devils. Give him a chance, Grayson, and anyway he adds another American to our force, and each one counts."

"Yes, that's right; but I hope you won't need 'em before you an' Miss Barbara go," said Grayson.

"I hope not, Grayson; but one can never tell with conditions here such as they are. Have you any hope that you will be able to obtain a safe conduct for us from General Villa?"

"Oh, Villa'll give us the paper all right," said Grayson; "but it won't do us no good unless we don't meet nobody but Villa's men on the way out. This here Pesita's the critter I'm leery of. He's got it in for all Americans, and especially for El Orobo Rancho. You know we beat off a raid of his about six months ago—killed half a dozen of his men, an' he won't never forgive that. Villa can't spare a big enough force to give us safe escort to the border and he can't assure the safety of the train service. It looks mighty bad, sir—I don't see what in hell you came for."

"Neither do I, Grayson," agreed the boss; "but I'm here and we've got to make the best of it. All this may blow over—it has before—and we'll laugh at our fears in a few weeks."

"This thing that's happenin' now won't never blow over 'til the stars and stripes blow over Chihuahua," said Grayson with finality.

A few moments later Bridge returned to the office, having unsaddled his pony and turned it into the pasture.

"What's your name?" asked Grayson, preparing to enter it in his time book.

"Bridge," replied the new bookkeeper.

"'Nitials," snapped Grayson.

Bridge hesitated. "Oh, put me down as L. Bridge," he said.

"Where from?" asked the ranch foreman.

"El Orobo Rancho," answered Bridge.

Grayson shot a quick glance at the man. The answer confirmed his suspicions that the stranger was probably a horse thief, which, in Grayson's estimation, was the worst thing a man could be.

"Where did you get that pony you come in on?" he demanded. "I ain't sayin' nothin' of course, but I jest want to tell you that we ain't got no use for horse thieves here."

The Easterner, who had been a listener, was shocked by the brutality of Grayson's speech; but Bridge only laughed.

"If you must know," he said, "I never bought that horse, an' the man he belonged to didn't give him to me. I just took him."

"You got your nerve," growled Grayson. "I guess you better git out. We don't want no horse thieves here."

"Wait," interposed the boss. "This man doesn't act like a horse thief. A horse thief, I should imagine, would scarcely admit his guilt. Let's have his story before we judge him."

"All right," said Grayson; "but he's just admitted he stole the horse."

Bridge turned to the boss. "Thanks," he said; "but really I did steal the horse."

Grayson made a gesture which said: "See, I told you so."

"It was like this," went on Bridge. "The gentleman who owned the horse, together with some of his friends, had been shooting at me and my friends. When it was all over there was no one left to inform us who were the legal heirs of the late owners of this and several other horses which were left upon our hands, so I borrowed this one. The law would say, doubtless, that I had stolen it; but I am perfectly willing to return it to its rightful owners if someone will find them for me."

"You been in a scrap?" asked Grayson. "Who with?"

"A party of Pesita's men," replied Bridge.

"When?"

"Yesterday."

"You see they are working pretty close," said Grayson, to his employer, and then to Bridge: "Well, if you took that cayuse from one of Pesita's bunch you can't call that stealin'. Your room's in there, back of the office, an' you'll find some clothes there that the last man forgot to take with him. You ken have 'em, an' from the looks o' yourn you need 'em."

"Thank you," replied Bridge. "My clothes are a bit rusty. I shall have to speak to James about them," and he passed through into the little bedroom off the office, and closed the door behind him.

"James?" grunted Grayson. "Who the devil does he mean by James? I hain't seen but one of 'em."

The boss was laughing quietly.

"The man's a character," he said. "He'll be worth all you pay him—if you can appreciate him, which I doubt, Grayson."

"I ken appreciate him if he ken keep books," replied Grayson. "That's all I ask of him."

When Bridge emerged from the bedroom he was clothed in white duck trousers, a soft shirt, and a pair of tennis shoes, and such a change had they wrought in his appearance that neither Grayson nor his employer would have known him had they not seen him come from the room into which they had sent him to make the exchange of clothing.

"Feel better?" asked the boss, smiling.

"Clothes are but an incident with me," replied Bridge. "I wear them because it is easier to do so than it would be to dodge the weather and the police. Whatever I may have upon my back affects in no way what I have within my head. No, I cannot say that I feel any better, since these clothes are not as comfortable as my old ones. However if it pleases Mr. Grayson that I should wear a pink kimono while working for him I shall gladly wear a pink kimono. What shall I do first, sir?" The question was directed toward Grayson.

"Sit down here an' see what you ken make of this bunch of trouble," replied the foreman. "I'll talk with you again this evenin'."

As Grayson and his employer quitted the office and walked together toward the corrals the latter's brow was corrugated by thought and his facial expression that of one who labors to fasten upon a baffling and illusive recollection.

"It beats all, Grayson," he said presently; "but I am sure that I have known this new bookkeeper of yours before. The moment he came out of that room dressed like a human being I knew that I had known him; but for the life of me I can't place him. I should be willing to wager considerable, however, that his name is not Bridge."

"S'pect you're right," assented Grayson. "He's probably one o' them eastern dude bank clerks what's gone wrong and come down here to hide. Mighty fine place to hide jest now, too.

"And say, speakin' of banks," he went on, "what'll I do 'bout sendin' over to Cuivaca fer the pay tomorrow. Next day's pay day. I don't like to send this here bum, I can't trust a greaser no better, an' I can't spare none of my white men thet I ken trust."

"Send him with a couple of the most trustworthy Mexicans you have," suggested the boss.

"There ain't no sich critter," replied Grayson; "but I guess that's the best I ken do. I'll send him along with Tony an' Benito—they hate each other too much to frame up anything together, an' they both hate a gringo. I reckon they'll hev a lovely trip."

"But they'll get back with the money, eh?" queried the boss.

"If Pesita don't get 'em," replied Grayson.

X
Billy Cracks a Safe

Billy Byrne, captain, rode into Cuivaca from the south. He had made a wide detour in order to accomplish this; but under the circumstances he had thought it wise to do so. In his pocket was a safe conduct from one of Villa's generals farther south—a safe conduct taken by Pesita from the body of one of his recent victims. It would explain Billy's presence in Cuivaca since it had been intended to carry its rightful possessor to Juarez and across the border into the United States.

He found the military establishment at Cuivaca small and ill commanded. There were soldiers upon the streets; but the only regularly detailed guard was stationed in front of the bank. No one questioned Billy. He did not have to show his safe conduct.

"This looks easy," thought Billy. "A reg'lar skinch."

He first attended to his horse, turning him into a public corral, and then sauntered up the street to the bank, which he entered, still unquestioned. Inside he changed a bill of large denomination which Pesita had given him for the purpose of an excuse to examine the lay of the bank from the inside. Billy took a long time to count the change. All the time his eyes wandered about the interior while he made mental notes of such salient features as might prove of moment to him later. The money counted Billy slowly rolled a cigarette.

He saw that the bank was roughly divided into two sections by a wire and wood partition. On one side were the customers, on the other the clerks and a teller. The latter sat behind a small wicket through which he received deposits and cashed checks. Back of him, against the wall, stood a large safe of American manufacture. Billy had had business before with similar safes. A doorway in the rear wall led into the yard behind the building. It was closed by a heavy door covered with sheet iron and fastened by several bolts and a thick, strong bar. There were no windows in the rear wall. From that side the bank appeared almost impregnable to silent assault.

Inside everything was primitive and Billy found himself wondering how a week passed without seeing a bank robbery in the town. Possibly the strong rear defenses and the armed guard in front accounted for it. Satisfied with what he had learned he passed out onto the sidewalk and crossed the street to a saloon. Some soldiers and citizens were drinking at little tables in front of the bar. A couple of card games were in progress, and through the open rear doorway Billy saw a little gathering encircling a cock fight.

In none of these things was Billy interested. What he had wished in entering the saloon was merely an excuse to place himself upon the opposite side of the street from the bank that he might inspect the front from the outside without arousing suspicion.

Having purchased and drunk a bottle of poor beer, the temperature of which had probably never been below eighty since it left the bottling department of the Texas brewery which inflicted it upon the ignorant, he sauntered to the front window and looked out.

There he saw that the bank building was a two-story affair, the entrance to the second story being at the left side of the first floor, opening directly onto the sidewalk in full view of the sentry who paced to and fro before the structure.

Billy wondered what the second floor was utilized for. He saw soiled hangings at the windows which aroused a hope and a sudden inspiration. There was a sign above the entrance to the second floor; but Billy's knowledge of the language had not progressed sufficiently to permit him to translate it, although he had his suspicions as to its meaning. He would learn if his guess was correct.

Returning to the bar he ordered another bottle of beer, and as he drank it he practiced upon the bartender some of his recently acquired Spanish and learned, though not without considerable difficulty, that he might find lodgings for the night upon the second floor of the bank building.

Much elated, Billy left the saloon and walked along the street until he came to the one general store of the town. After another heart rending scrimmage with the language of Ferdinand and Isabella he succeeded in making several purchases—two heavy sacks, a brace, two bits, and a keyhole saw. Placing the tools in one of the sacks he wrapped the whole in the second sack and made his way back to the bank building.

Upon the second floor he found the proprietor of the rooming-house and engaged a room in the rear of the building, overlooking the yard. The layout was eminently satisfactory to Captain Byrne and it was with a feeling of great self-satisfaction that he descended and sought a restaurant.

He had been sent by Pesita merely to look over the ground and the defenses of the town, that the outlaw might later ride in with his entire force and loot the bank; but Billy Byrne, out of his past experience in such matters, had evolved a much simpler plan for separating the enemy from his wealth.

Having eaten, Billy returned to his room. It was now dark and the bank closed and unlighted showed that all had left it. Only the sentry paced up and down the sidewalk in front.

Going at once to his room Billy withdrew his tools from their hiding place beneath the mattress, and a moment later was busily engaged in boring holes through the floor at the foot of his bed. For an hour he worked, cautiously and quietly, until he had a rough circle of holes enclosing a space about two feet in diameter. Then he laid aside the brace and bit, and took the keyhole saw, with which he patiently sawed through the wood between contiguous holes, until, the circle completed, he lifted out a section of the floor leaving an aperture large enough to permit him to squeeze his body through when the time arrived for him to pass into the bank beneath.

While Billy had worked three men had ridden into Cuivaca. They were Tony, Benito, and the new bookkeeper of El Orobo Rancho. The Mexicans, after eating, repaired at once to the joys of the cantina; while Bridge sought a room in the building to which his escort directed him.

As chance would have it, it was the same building in which Billy labored and the room lay upon the rear side of it overlooking the same yard. But Bridge did not lie awake to inspect his surroundings. For years he had not ridden as many miles as he had during the past two days, so that long unused muscles cried out for rest and relaxation. As a result, Bridge was asleep almost as soon as his head touched the pillow, and so profound was his slumber that it seemed that nothing short of a convulsion of nature would arouse him.

As Bridge lay down upon his bed Billy Byrne left his room and descended to the street. The sentry before the bank paid no attention to him, and Billy passed along, unhindered, to the corral where he had left his horse. Here, as he was saddling the animal, he was accosted, much to his disgust, by the proprietor.

In broken English the man expressed surprise that Billy rode out so late at night, and the American thought that he detected something more than curiosity in the other's manner and tone—suspicion of the strange gringo.

It would never do to leave the fellow in that state of mind, and so Billy leaned close to the other's ear, and with a broad grin and a wink whispered: "Señorita," and jerked his thumb toward the south. "I'll be back by mornin'," he added.

The Mexican's manner altered at once. He laughed and nodded, knowingly, and poked Billy in the ribs. Then he watched him mount and ride out of the corral toward the south—which was also in the direction of the bank, to the rear of which Billy rode without effort to conceal his movements.

There he dismounted and left his horse standing with the bridle reins dragging upon the ground, while he removed the lariat from the pommel of the saddle, and, stuffing it inside his shirt, walked back to the street on which the building stood, and so made his way past the sentry and to his room.

Here he pushed back the bed which he had drawn over the hole in the floor, dropped his two sacks through into the bank, and tying the brace to one end of the lariat lowered it through after the sacks.

Looping the middle of the lariat over a bedpost Billy grasped both strands firmly and lowered himself through the aperture into the room beneath. He made no more noise in his descent than he had made upon other similar occasions in his past life when he had practiced the gentle art of porch-climbing along Ashland Avenue and Washington Boulevard.

Having gained the floor he pulled upon one end of the lariat until he had drawn it free of the bedpost above, when it fell into his waiting hands. Coiling it carefully Billy placed it around his neck and under one arm. Billy, acting as a professional, was a careful and methodical man. He always saw that every little detail was properly attended to before he went on to the next phase of his endeavors. Because of this ingrained caution Billy had long since secured the tops of the two sacks together, leaving only a sufficient opening to permit of their each being filled without delay or inconvenience.

Now he turned his attention to the rear door. The bar and bolts were easily shot from their seats from the inside, and Billy saw to it that this was attended to before he went further with his labors. It were well to have one's retreat assured at the earliest possible moment. A single bolt Billy left in place that he might not be surprised by an intruder; but first he had tested it and discovered that it could be drawn with ease.

These matters satisfactorily attended to Billy assaulted the combination knob of the safe with the metal bit which he had inserted in the brace before lowering it into the bank.

The work was hard and progressed slowly. It was necessary to withdraw the bit often and lubricate it with a piece of soap which Billy had brought along in his pocket for the purpose; but eventually a hole was bored through into the tumblers of the combination lock.

From without Billy could hear the footsteps of the sentry pacing back and forth within fifty feet of him, all unconscious that the bank he was guarding was being looted almost beneath his eyes. Once a corporal came with another soldier and relieved the sentry. After that Billy heard the footfalls no longer, for the new sentry was barefoot.

The boring finished, Billy drew a bit of wire from an inside pocket and inserted it in the hole. Then, working the wire with accustomed fingers, he turned the combination knob this way and that, feeling with the bit of wire until the tumblers should all be in line.

This, too, was slow work; but it was infinitely less liable to attract attention than any other method of safe cracking with which Billy was familiar.

It was long past midnight when Captain Byrne was rewarded with success—the tumblers clicked into position, the handle of the safe door turned and the bolts slipped back.

To swing open the door and transfer the contents of the safe to the two sacks was the work of but a few minutes. As Billy rose and threw the heavy burden across a shoulder he heard a challenge from without, and then a parley. Immediately after the sound of footsteps ascending the stairway to the rooming-house came plainly to his ears, and then he had slipped the last bolt upon the rear door and was out in the yard beyond.

Now Bridge, sleeping the sleep of utter exhaustion that the boom of a cannon might not have disturbed, did that inexplicable thing which every one of us has done a hundred times in our lives. He awakened, with a start, out of a sound sleep, though no disturbing noise had reached his ears. Something impelled him to sit up in bed, and as he did so he could see through the window beside him into the yard at the rear of the building. There in the moonlight he saw a man throwing a sack across the horn of a saddle. He saw the man mount, and he saw him wheel his horse around about and ride away toward the north. There seemed to Bridge nothing unusual about the man's act, nor had there been any indication either of stealth or haste to arouse the American's suspicions. Bridge lay back again upon his pillows and sought to woo the slumber which the sudden awakening seemed to have banished for the remainder of the night.

And up the stairway to the second floor staggered Tony and Benito. Their money was gone; but they had acquired something else which appeared much more difficult to carry and not so easily gotten rid of.

Tony held the key to their room. It was the second room upon the right of the hall. Tony remembered that very distinctly. He had impressed it upon his mind before leaving the room earlier in the evening, for Tony had feared some such contingency as that which had befallen.

Tony fumbled with the handle of a door, and stabbed vainly at an elusive keyhole.

"Wait," mumbled Benito. "This is not the room. It was the second door from the stairway. This is the third."

Tony lurched about and staggered back. Tony reasoned: "If that was the third door the next behind me must be the second, and on the right;" but Tony took not into consideration that he had reversed the direction of his erratic wobbling. He lunged across the hall—not because he wished to but because the spirits moved him. He came in contact with a door. "This, then, must be the second door," he soliloquized, "and it is upon my right. Ah, Benito, this is the room!"

Benito was skeptical. He said as much; but Tony was obdurate. Did he not know a second door when he saw one? Was he, furthermore, not a grown man and therefore entirely capable of distinguishing between his left hand and his right? Yes! Tony was all of that, and more, so Tony inserted the key in the lock—it would have turned any lock upon the second floor—and, lo! the door swung inward upon its hinges.

"Ah! Benito," cried Tony. "Did I not tell you so? See! This is our room, for the key opens the door."

The room was dark. Tony, carried forward by the weight of his head, which had long since grown unaccountably heavy, rushed his feet rapidly forward that he might keep them within a few inches of his center of equilibrium.

The distance which it took his feet to catch up with his head was equal to the distance between the doorway and the foot of the bed, and when Tony reached that spot, with Benito meandering after him, the latter, much to his astonishment, saw in the diffused moonlight which pervaded the room, the miraculous disappearance of his former enemy and erstwhile friend. Then from the depths below came a wild scream and a heavy thud.

The sentry upon the beat before the bank heard both. For an instant he stood motionless, then he called aloud for the guard, and turned toward the bank door. But this was locked and he could but peer in through the windows. Seeing a dark form within, and being a Mexican he raised his rifle and fired through the glass of the doors.

Tony, who had dropped through the hole which Billy had used so quietly, heard the zing of a bullet pass his head, and the impact as it sploshed into the adobe wall behind him. With a second yell Tony dodged behind the safe and besought *Mary* to protect him.

From above Benito peered through the hole into the blackness below. Down the hall came the barefoot landlord, awakened by the screams and the shot. Behind him came Bridge, buckling his revolver belt about his hips as he ran. Not having been furnished with pajamas Bridge had not thought it necessary to remove his clothing, and so he had lost no time in dressing.

When the two, now joined by Benito, reached the street they found the guard there, battering in the bank doors. Benito, fearing for the life of Tony, which if anyone took should be taken by him, rushed upon the sergeant of the guard, explaining with both lips and hands the remarkable accident which had precipitated Tony into the bank.

The sergeant listened, though he did not believe, and when the doors had fallen in, he commanded Tony to come out with his hands above his head. Then followed an investigation which disclosed the looting of the safe, and the great hole in the ceiling through which Tony had tumbled.

The bank president came while the sergeant and the landlord were in Billy's room investigating. Bridge had followed them.

"It was the gringo," cried the excited Boniface. "This is his room. He has cut a hole in my floor which I shall have to pay to have repaired."

A captain came next, sleepy-eyed and profane. When he heard what had happened and that the wealth which he had been detailed to guard had been taken while he slept, he tore his hair and promised that the sentry should be shot at dawn.

By the time they had returned to the street all the male population of Cuivaca was there and most of the female.

"One-thousand dollars," cried the bank president, "to the man who stops the thief and returns to me what the villain has stolen."

A detachment of soldiers was in the saddle and passing the bank as the offer was made.

"Which way did he go?" asked the captain. "Did no one see him leave?"

Bridge was upon the point of saying that he had seen him and that he had ridden north, when it occurred to him that a thousand dollars—even a thousand dollars Mex—was a great deal of money, and that it would carry both himself and Billy to Rio and leave something for pleasure beside.

Then up spoke a tall, thin man with the skin of a coffee bean.

"I saw him, Señor Capitan," he cried. "He kept his horse in my corral, and at night he came and took it out saying that he was riding to visit a señorita. He fooled me, the scoundrel; but I will tell you—he rode south. I saw him ride south with my own eyes."

"Then we shall have him before morning," cried the captain, "for there is but one place to the south where a robber would ride, and he has not had sufficient start of us that he can reach safety before we overhaul him. Forward! March!" and the detachment moved down the narrow street. "Trot! March!" And as they passed the store: "Gallop! March!"

Bridge almost ran the length of the street to the corral. His pony must be rested by now, and a few miles to the north the gringo whose capture meant a thousand dollars to Bridge was on the road to liberty.

"I hate to do it," thought Bridge; "because, even if he is a bank robber, he's an American; but I need the money and in all probability the fellow is a scoundrel who should have been hanged long ago."

Over the trail to the north rode Captain Billy Byrne, secure in the belief that no pursuit would develop until after the opening hour of the bank in the morning, by which time he would be halfway on his return journey to Pesita's camp.

"Ol' man Pesita'll be some surprised when I show him what I got for him," mused Billy. "Say!" he exclaimed suddenly and aloud, "Why the devil should I take all this swag back to that yellow-faced yegg? Who pulled this thing off anyway? Why me, of course, and does anybody think Billy Byrne's boob enough to split with a guy that didn't have a hand in it at all. Split! Why the nut'll take it all!

"Nix! Me for the border. I couldn't do a thing with all this coin down in Rio, an' Bridgie'll be along there most any time. We can hit it up some in lil' ol' Rio on this bunch o' dough. Why, say kid, there must be a million here, from the weight of it."

A frown suddenly clouded his face. "Why did I take it?" he asked himself. "Was I crackin' a safe, or was I pullin' off something fine fer poor, bleedin' Mexico? If I was a-doin' that they ain't nothin' criminal in what I done—except to the guy that owned the coin. If I was just plain crackin' a safe on my own hook why then I'm a crook again an' I can't be that—no, not with that face of yours standin' out there so plain right in front of me, just as though you were there yourself, askin' me to remember an' be decent. God! Barbara—why wasn't I born for the likes of you, and not just a measly, ornery mucker like I am. Oh, hell! what is that that Bridge sings of Knibbses:

> There ain't no sweet Penelope somewhere that's longing much for me,
> But I can smell the blundering sea, and hear the rigging hum;
> And I can hear the whispering lips that fly before the outbound ships,
> And I can hear the breakers on the sand a-calling "Come!"

Billy took off his hat and scratched his head.

"Funny," he thought, "how a girl and poetry can get a tough nut like me. I wonder what the guys that used to hang out in back of Kelly's 'ud say if they seen what was goin' on in my bean just now. They'd call me Lizzy, eh? Well, they wouldn't call me Lizzy more'n once. I may be gettin' soft in the head, but I'm all to the good with my dukes."

Speed is not conducive to sentimental thoughts and so Billy had unconsciously permitted his pony to drop into a lazy walk. There was no need for haste anyhow. No one knew yet that the bank had been robbed, or at least so Billy argued. He might, however, have thought differently upon the subject of haste could he have had a glimpse of the horseman in his rear—two miles behind him, now, but rapidly closing up the distance at a keen gallop, while he strained his eyes across the moonlit flat ahead in eager search for his quarry.

So absorbed was Billy Byrne in his reflections that his ears were deaf to the pounding of the hoofs of the pursuer's horse upon the soft dust of the dry road until Bridge was little more than a hundred yards from him. For the last half-mile Bridge had had the figure of the fugitive in full view and his mind had been playing rapidly with seductive visions of the one-thousand dollars reward—one-thousand dollars Mex, perhaps, but still quite enough to excite pleasant thoughts. At the first glimpse of the horseman ahead Bridge had reined his mount down to a trot that the noise of his approach might thereby be lessened. He had drawn his revolver from its holster, and was upon the point of putting spurs to his horse for a sudden dash upon the fugitive when the man ahead, finally attracted by the noise of the other's approach, turned in his saddle and saw him.

Neither recognized the other, and at Bridge's command of, "Hands up!" Billy, lightning-like in his quickness, drew and fired. The bullet raked Bridge's hat from his head but left him unscathed.

Billy had wheeled his pony around until he stood broadside toward Bridge. The latter fired scarce a second after Billy's shot had pinged so perilously close—fired at a perfect target but fifty yards away.

At the sound of the report the robber's horse reared and plunged, then, wheeling and tottering high upon its hind feet, fell backward. Billy, realizing that his mount had been hit, tried to throw himself from the saddle; but until the very moment that the beast toppled over the man was held by his cartridge belt which, as the animal first lunged, had caught over the high horn of the Mexican saddle.

The belt slipped from the horn as the horse was falling, and Billy succeeded in throwing himself a little to one side. One leg, however, was pinned beneath the animal's body and the force of the fall jarred the revolver from Billy's hand to drop just beyond his reach.

His carbine was in its boot at the horse's side, and the animal was lying upon it. Instantly Bridge rode to his side and covered him with his revolver.

"Don't move," he commanded, "or I'll be under the painful necessity of terminating your earthly endeavors right here and now."

"Well, for the love o' Mike!" cried the fallen bandit. "You?"

Bridge was off his horse the instant that the familiar voice sounded in his ears.

"Billy!" he exclaimed. "Why—Billy—was it you who robbed the bank?" Even as he spoke Bridge was busy easing the weight of the dead pony from Billy's leg.

"Anything broken?" he asked as the bandit struggled to free himself.

"Not so you could notice it," replied Billy, and a moment later he was on his feet. "Say, bo," he added, "it's a mighty good thing you dropped little pinto here, for I'd a sure got you my next shot. Gee! it makes me sweat to think of it. But about this bank robbin' business. You can't exactly say that I robbed a bank. That money was the enemy's resources, an' I just nicked their resources. That's war. That ain't robbery. I ain't takin' it for myself— it's for the cause—the cause o' poor, bleedin' Mexico," and Billy grinned a large grin.

"You took it for Pesita?" asked Bridge.

"Of course," replied Billy. "I won't get a jitney of it. I wouldn't take none of it, Bridge, honest. I'm on the square now."

"I know you are, Billy," replied the other; "but if you're caught you might find it difficult to convince the authorities of your highmindedness and your disinterestedness."

"Authorities!" scoffed Billy. "There ain't no authorities in Mexico. One bandit is just as good as another, and from Pesita to Carranza they're all bandits at heart. They ain't a one of 'em that gives two whoops in hell for poor, bleedin' Mexico—unless they can do the bleedin' themselves. It's dog eat dog here. If they caught me they'd shoot me whether I'd robbed their bank or not. What's that?" Billy was suddenly alert, straining his eyes back in the direction of Cuivaca.

"They're coming, Billy," said Bridge. "Take my horse—quick! You must get out of here in a hurry. The whole post is searching for you. I thought that they went toward the south, though. Some of them must have circled."

"What'll you do if I take your horse?" asked Billy.

"I can walk back," said Bridge, "it isn't far to town. I'll tell them that I had come only a short distance when my horse threw me and ran away. They'll believe it for they think I'm a rotten horseman—the two vaqueros who escorted me to town I mean."

Billy hesitated. "I hate to do it, Bridge," he said.

"You must, Billy," urged the other.

"If they find us here together it'll merely mean that the two of us will get it, for I'll stick with you, Billy, and we can't fight off a whole troop of cavalry out here in the open. If you take my horse we can both get out of it, and later I'll see you in Rio. Goodbye, Billy, I'm off for town," and Bridge turned and started back along the road on foot.

Billy watched him in silence for a moment. The truth of Bridge's statement of fact was so apparent that Billy was forced to accept the plan. A moment later he transferred the bags of loot to Bridge's pony, swung into the saddle, and took a last backward look at the diminishing figure of the man swinging along in the direction of Cuivaca.

"Say," he muttered to himself; "but you're a right one, bo," and wheeling to the north he clapped his spurs to his new mount and loped easily off into the night.

XI
Barbara Releases a Conspirator

It was a week later, yet Grayson still was growling about the loss of "that there Brazos pony." Grayson, the boss, and the boss's daughter were sitting upon the veranda of the ranchhouse when the foreman reverted to the subject.

"I knew I didn't have no business hirin' a man thet can't ride," he said. "Why thet there Brazos pony never did stumble, an' if he'd of stumbled he'd a-stood aroun' a year waitin' to be caught up agin. I jest cain't figger it out no ways how thet there tenderfoot bookkeeper lost him. He must a-shooed him away with a stick. An' saddle an' bridle an' all gone too. Doggone it!"

"I'm the one who should be peeved," spoke up the girl with a wry smile. "Brazos was my pony. He's the one you picked out for me to ride while I am here; but I am sure poor Mr. Bridge feels as badly about it as anyone, and I know that he couldn't help it. We shouldn't be too hard on him. We might just as well attempt to hold him responsible for the looting of the bank and the loss of the payroll money."

"Well," said Grayson, "I give him thet horse 'cause I knew he couldn't ride, an' thet was the safest horse in the cavvy. I wisht I'd given him Santa Anna instid—I wouldn't a-minded losin' him. There won't no one ride him anyhow he's thet ornery."

"The thing that surprises me most," remarked the boss, "is that Brazos doesn't come back. He was foaled on this range, and he's never been ridden anywhere else, has he?"

"He was foaled right here on this ranch," Grayson corrected him, "and he ain't never been more'n a hundred mile from it. If he ain't dead or stolen he'd a-ben back afore the bookkeeper was. It's almighty queer."

"What sort of bookkeeper is Mr. Bridge?" asked the girl.

"Oh, he's all right I guess," replied Grayson grudgingly. "A feller's got to be some good at something. He's probably one of these here paper-collar, cracker-fed college dudes thet don't know nothin' else 'cept writin' in books."

The girl rose, smiled, and moved away.

"I like Mr. Bridge, anyhow," she called back over her shoulder, "for whatever he may not be he is certainly a well-bred gentleman," which speech did not tend to raise Mr. Bridge in the estimation of the hard-fisted ranch foreman.

"Funny them greasers don't come in from the north range with thet bunch o' steers. They ben gone all day now," he said to the boss, ignoring the girl's parting sally.

Bridge sat tip-tilted against the front of the office building reading an ancient magazine which he had found within. His day's work was done and he was but waiting for the gong that would call him to the evening meal with the other employees of the ranch. The magazine failed to rouse his interest. He let it drop idly to his knees and with eyes closed reverted to his never-failing source of entertainment.

> And then that slim, poetic guy he turned and looked me in the eye,
> ".... It's overland and overland and overseas to—where?"
> "Most anywhere that isn't here," I says. His face went kind of queer.
> "The place we're in is always here. The other place is there."

Bridge stretched luxuriously. "'There,'" he repeated. "I've been searching for *there* for many years; but for some reason I can never get away from *here*. About two weeks of any place on earth and that place is just plain *here* to me, and I'm longing once again for *there*."

His musings were interrupted by a sweet feminine voice close by. Bridge did not open his eyes at once—he just sat there, listening.

> As I was hiking past the woods, the cool and sleepy summer woods,
> I saw a guy a-talking to the sunshine in the air;
> Thinks I, "He's going to have a fit—I'll stick around and watch a bit;"
> But he paid no attention, hardly knowing I was there.

Then the girl broke into a merry laugh and Bridge opened his eyes and came to his feet.

"I didn't know you cared for that sort of stuff," he said. "Knibbs writes man-verse. I shouldn't have imagined that it would appeal to a young lady."

"But it does, though," she replied; "at least to me. There's a swing to it and a freedom that 'gets me in the eye.'"

Again she laughed, and when this girl laughed, harder-headed and much older men than Mr. L. Bridge felt strange emotions move within their breasts.

For a week Barbara had seen a great deal of the new bookkeeper. Aside from her father he was the only man of culture and refinement of which the rancho could boast, or, as the rancho would have put it, be ashamed of.

She had often sought the veranda of the little office and lured the new bookkeeper from his work, and on several occasions had had him at the ranchhouse. Not only was he an interesting talker; but there was an element of mystery about him which appealed to the girl's sense of romance.

She knew that he was a gentleman born and reared, and she often found herself wondering what tragic train of circumstances had set him adrift among the flotsam of humanity's wreckage. Too, the same persistent conviction that she had known him somewhere in the past that possessed her father clung to her mind; but she could not place him.

"I overheard your dissertation on *here* and *there*," said the girl. "I could not very well help it—it would have been rude to interrupt a conversation." Her eyes sparkled mischievously and her cheeks dimpled.

"You wouldn't have been interrupting a conversation," objected Bridge, smiling; "you would have been turning a monologue into a conversation."

"But it was a conversation," insisted the girl. "The wanderer was conversing with the bookkeeper. You are a victim of wanderlust, Mr. L. Bridge—don't deny it. You hate bookkeeping, or any other such prosaic vocation as requires permanent residence in one place."

"Come now," expostulated the man. "That is hardly fair. Haven't I been here a whole week?"

They both laughed.

"What in the world can have induced you to remain so long?" cried Barbara. "How very much like an old timer you must feel—one of the oldest inhabitants."

"I am a regular aborigine," declared Bridge; but his heart would have chosen another reply. It would have been glad to tell the girl that there was a very real and a very growing inducement to remain at El Orobo Rancho. The man was too self-controlled, however, to give way to the impulses of his heart.

At first he had just liked the girl, and been immensely glad of her companionship because there was so much that was common to them both—a love for good music, good pictures, and good literature—things Bridge hadn't had an opportunity to discuss with another for a long, long time.

And slowly he had found delight in just sitting and looking at her. He was experienced enough to realize that this was a dangerous symptom, and so from the moment he had been forced to acknowledge it to himself he had been very careful to guard his speech and his manner in the girl's presence.

He found pleasure in dreaming of what might have been as he sat watching the girl's changing expression as different moods possessed her; but as for permitting a hope, even, of realization of his dreams—ah, he was far too practical for that, dreamer though he was.

As the two talked Grayson passed. His rather stern face clouded as he saw the girl and the new bookkeeper laughing there together.

"Ain't you got nothin' to do?" he asked Bridge.

"Yes, indeed," replied the latter.

"Then why don't you do it?" snapped Grayson.

"I am," said Bridge.

"Mr. Bridge is entertaining me," interrupted the girl, before Grayson could make any rejoinder. "It is my fault—I took him from his work. You don't mind, do you, Mr. Grayson?"

Grayson mumbled an inarticulate reply and went his way.

"Mr. Grayson does not seem particularly enthusiastic about me," laughed Bridge.

"No," replied the girl, candidly; "but I think it's just because you can't ride."

"Can't ride!" ejaculated Bridge. "Why, haven't I been riding ever since I came here?"

"Mr. Grayson doesn't consider anything in the way of equestrianism riding unless the ridden is perpetually seeking the life of the rider," explained Barbara. "Just at present he is terribly put out because you lost

Brazos. He says Brazos never stumbled in his life, and even if you had fallen from his back he would have stood beside you waiting for you to remount him. You see he was the kindest horse on the ranch—especially picked for me to ride. However in the world *did* you lose him, Mr. Bridge?" The girl was looking full at the man as she propounded her query. Bridge was silent. A faint flush overspread his face. He had not before known that the horse was hers. He couldn't very well tell her the truth, and he wouldn't lie to her, so he made no reply.

Barbara saw the flush and noted the man's silence. For the first time her suspicions were aroused, yet she would not believe that this gentle, amiable drifter could be guilty of any crime greater than negligence or carelessness. But why his evident embarrassment now? The girl was mystified. For a moment or two they sat in silence, then Barbara rose.

"I must run along back now," she explained. "Papa will be wondering what has become of me."

"Yes," said Bridge, and let her go. He would have been glad to tell her the truth; but he couldn't do that without betraying Billy. He had heard enough to know that Francisco Villa had been so angered over the bold looting of the bank in the face of a company of his own soldiers that he would stop at nothing to secure the person of the thief once his identity was known. Bridge was perfectly satisfied with the ethics of his own act on the night of the bank robbery. He knew that the girl would have applauded him, and that Grayson himself would have done what Bridge did had a like emergency confronted the ranch foreman; but to have admitted complicity in the escape of the fugitive would have been to have exposed himself to the wrath of Villa, and at the same time revealed the identity of the thief. "Nor," thought Bridge, "would it get Brazos back for Barbara."

It was after dark when the vaqueros Grayson had sent to the north range returned to the ranch. They came empty-handed and slowly for one of them supported a wounded comrade on the saddle before him. They rode directly to the office where Grayson and Bridge were going over some of the business of the day, and when the former saw them his brow clouded for he knew before he heard their story what had happened.

"Who done it?" he asked, as the men filed into the office, half carrying the wounded man.

"Some of Pesita's followers," replied Benito.

"Did they git the steers, too?" inquired Grayson.

"Part of them—we drove off most and scattered them. We saw the Brazos pony, too," and Benito looked from beneath heavy lashes in the direction of the bookkeeper.

"Where?" asked Grayson.

"One of Pesita's officers rode him—an Americano. Tony and I saw this same man in Cuivaca the night the bank was robbed, and today he was riding the Brazos pony." Again the dark eyes turned toward Bridge.

Grayson was quick to catch the significance of the Mexican's meaning. The more so as it was directly in line with suspicions which he himself had been nursing since the robbery.

During the colloquy the boss entered the office. He had heard the returning vaqueros ride into the ranch and noting that they brought no steers with them had come to the office to hear their story. Barbara, spurred by curiosity, accompanied her father.

"You heard what Benito says?" asked Grayson, turning toward his employer.

The latter nodded. All eyes were upon Bridge.

"Well," snapped Grayson, "what you gotta say fer yourself? I ben suspectin' you right along. I knew derned well that that there Brazos pony never run off by hisself. You an' that other crook from the States framed this whole thing up pretty slick, didn'tcha? Well, we'll—"

"Wait a moment, wait a moment, Grayson," interrupted the boss. "Give Mr. Bridge a chance to explain. You're making a rather serious charge against him without any particularly strong proof to back your accusation."

"Oh, that's all right," exclaimed Bridge, with a smile. "I have known that Mr. Grayson suspected me of implication in the robbery; but who can blame him—a man who can't ride might be guilty of almost anything."

Grayson sniffed. Barbara took a step nearer Bridge. She had been ready to doubt him herself only an hour or so ago; but that was before he had been accused. Now that she found others arrayed against him her impulse was to come to his defense.

"You didn't do it, did you, Mr. Bridge?" Her tone was almost pleading.

"If you mean robbing the bank," he replied; "I did not, Miss Barbara. I knew no more about it until after it was over than Benito or Tony—in fact they were the ones who discovered it while I was still asleep in my room above the bank."

"Well, how did the robber git thet there Brazos pony then?" demanded Grayson savagely. "Thet's what I want to know."

"You'll have to ask him, Mr. Grayson," replied Bridge.

"Villa'll ask him, when he gits holt of him," snapped Grayson; "but I reckon he'll git all the information out of you thet he wants first. He'll be in Cuivaca tomorrer, an' so will you."

"You mean that you are going to turn me over to General Villa?" asked Bridge. "You are going to turn an American over to that butcher knowing that he'll be shot inside of twenty-four hours?"

"Shootin's too damned good fer a horse thief," replied Grayson.

Barbara turned impulsively toward her father. "You won't let Mr. Grayson do that?" she asked.

"Mr. Grayson knows best how to handle such an affair as this, Barbara," replied her father. "He is my superintendent, and I have made it a point never to interfere with him."

"You will let Mr. Bridge be shot without making an effort to save him?" she demanded.

"We do not know that he will be shot," replied the ranch owner. "If he is innocent there is no reason why he should be punished. If he is guilty of implication in the Cuivaca bank robbery he deserves, according to the rules of war, to die, for General Villa, I am told, considers that a treasonable act. Some of the funds upon which his government depends for munitions of war were there—they were stolen and turned over to the enemies of Mexico."

"And if we interfere we'll turn Villa against us," interposed Grayson. "He ain't any too keen for Americans as it is. Why, if this fellow was my brother I'd hev to turn him over to the authorities."

"Well, I thank God," exclaimed Bridge fervently, "that in addition to being shot by Villa I don't have to endure the added disgrace of being related to you, and I'm not so sure that I shall be hanged by Villa," and with that he wiped the oil lamp from the table against which he had been leaning, and leaped across the room for the doorway.

Barbara and her father had been standing nearest the exit, and as the girl realized the bold break for liberty the man was making, she pushed her father to one side and threw open the door.

Bridge was through it in an instant, with a parting, "God bless you, little girl!" as he passed her. Then the door was closed with a bang. Barbara turned the key, withdrew it from the lock and threw it across the darkened room.

Grayson and the unwounded Mexicans leaped after the fugitive only to find their way barred by the locked door. Outside Bridge ran to the horses standing patiently with lowered heads awaiting the return of their masters. In an instant he was astride one of them, and lashing the others ahead of him with a quirt he spurred away into the night.

By the time Grayson and the Mexicans had wormed their way through one of the small windows of the office the new bookkeeper was beyond sight and earshot.

As the ranch foreman was saddling up with several of his men in the corral to give chase to the fugitive the boss strolled in and touched him on the arm.

"Mr. Grayson," he said, "I have made it a point never to interfere with you; but I am going to ask you now not to pursue Mr. Bridge. I shall be glad if he makes good his escape. Barbara was right—he is a fellow-American. We cannot turn him over to Villa, or any other Mexican to be murdered."

Grumblingly Grayson unsaddled. "Ef you'd seen what I've seen around here," he said, "I guess you wouldn't be so keen to save this feller's hide."

"What do you mean?" asked the boss.

"I mean that he's ben tryin' to make love to your daughter."

The older man laughed. "Don't be a fool, Grayson," he said, and walked away.

An hour later Barbara was strolling up and down before the ranchhouse in the cool and refreshing air of the Chihuahua night. Her mind was occupied with disquieting reflections of the past few hours. Her pride was immeasurably hurt by the part impulse had forced her to take in the affair at the office. Not that she regretted that she had connived in the escape of Bridge; but it was humiliating that a girl of her position should have been compelled to play so melodramatic a part before Grayson and his Mexican vaqueros.

Then, too, was she disappointed in Bridge. She had looked upon him as a gentleman whom misfortune and wanderlust had reduced to the lowest stratum of society. Now she feared that he belonged to that substratum which lies below the lowest which society recognizes as a part of itself, and which is composed solely of the criminal class.

It was hard for Barbara to realize that she had associated with a thief—just for a moment it was hard, until recollection forced upon her the unwelcome fact of the status of another whom she had known—to whom she had given her love. The girl did not wince at the thought—instead she squared her shoulders and raised her chin.

"I am proud of him, whatever he may have been," she murmured; but she was not thinking of the new bookkeeper. When she did think again of Bridge it was to be glad that he had escaped—"for he is an American, like myself."

"Well!" exclaimed a voice behind her. "You played us a pretty trick, Miss Barbara."

The girl turned to see Grayson approaching. To her surprise he seemed to hold no resentment whatsoever. She greeted him courteously.

"I couldn't let you turn an American over to General Villa," she said, "no matter what he had done."

"I liked your spirit," said the man. "You're the kind o' girl I ben lookin' fer all my life—one with nerve an' grit, an' you got 'em both. You liked thet bookkeepin' critter, an' he wasn't half a man. I like you an' I am a man, ef I do say so myself."

The girl drew back in astonishment.

"Mr. Grayson!" she exclaimed. "You are forgetting yourself."

"No I ain't," he cried hoarsely. "I love you an' I'm goin' to have you. You'd love me too ef you knew me better."

He took a step forward and grasped her arm, trying to draw her to him. The girl pushed him away with one hand, and with the other struck him across the face.

Grayson dropped her arm, and as he did so she drew herself to her full height and looked him straight in the eyes.

"You may go now," she said, her voice like ice. "I shall never speak of this to anyone—provided you never attempt to repeat it."

The man made no reply. The blow in the face had cooled his ardor temporarily, but had it not also served another purpose?—to crystallize it into a firm and inexorable resolve.

When he had departed Barbara turned and entered the house.

XII
Billy to the Rescue

It was nearly ten o'clock the following morning when Barbara, sitting upon the veranda of the ranchhouse, saw her father approaching from the direction of the office. His face wore a troubled expression which the girl could not but note.

"What's the matter, Papa?" she asked, as he sank into a chair at her side.

"Your self-sacrifice of last evening was all to no avail," he replied. "Bridge has been captured by Villistas."

"What?" cried the girl. "You can't mean it—how did you learn?"

"Grayson just had a phone message from Cuivaca," he explained. "They only repaired the line yesterday since Pesita's men cut it last month. This was our first message. And do you know, Barbara, I can't help feeling sorry. I had hoped that he would get away."

"So had I," said the girl.

Her father was eyeing her closely to note the effect of his announcement upon her; but he could see no greater concern reflected than that which he himself felt for a fellow-man and an American who was doomed to death at the hands of an alien race, far from his own land and his own people.

"Can nothing be done?" she asked.

"Absolutely," he replied with finality. "I have talked it over with Grayson and he assures me that an attempt at intervention upon our part might tend to antagonize Villa, in which case we are all as good as lost. He is none too fond of us as it is, and Grayson believes, and not without reason, that he would welcome the slightest pretext for withdrawing the protection of his favor. Instantly he did that we should become the prey of every marauding band that infests the mountains. Not only would Pesita swoop down upon us, but those companies of freebooters which acknowledge nominal loyalty to Villa would be about our ears in no time. No, dear, we may do nothing. The young man has made his bed, and now I am afraid that he will have to lie in it alone."

For awhile the girl sat in silence, and presently her father arose and entered the house. Shortly after she followed him, reappearing soon in riding togs and walking rapidly to the corrals. Here she found an American cowboy busily engaged in whittling a stick as he sat upon an upturned cracker box and shot accurate streams of tobacco juice at a couple of industrious tumble bugs that had had the great impudence to roll their little ball of provender within the whittler's range.

"O Eddie!" she cried.

The man looked up, and was at once electrified into action. He sprang to his feet and whipped off his sombrero. A broad smile illumined his freckled face.

"Yes, miss," he answered. "What can I do for you?"

"Saddle a pony for me, Eddie," she explained. "I want to take a little ride."

"Sure!" he assured her cheerily. "Have it ready in a jiffy," and away he went, uncoiling his riata, toward the little group of saddle ponies which stood in the corral against necessity for instant use.

In a couple of minutes he came back leading one, which he tied to the corral bars.

"But I can't ride that horse," exclaimed the girl. "He bucks."

"Sure," said Eddie. "I'm a-goin' to ride him."

"Oh, are you going somewhere?" she asked.

"I'm goin' with you, miss," announced Eddie, sheepishly.

"But I didn't ask you, Eddie, and I don't want you—today," she urged.

"Sorry, miss," he threw back over his shoulder as he walked back to rope a second pony; "but them's orders. You're not to be allowed to ride no place without a escort. 'Twouldn't be safe neither, miss," he almost pleaded, "an' I won't hinder you none. I'll ride behind far enough to be there ef I'm needed."

Directly he came back with another pony, a sad-eyed, gentle-appearing little beast, and commenced saddling and bridling the two.

"Will you promise," she asked, after watching him in silence for a time, "that you will tell no one where I go or whom I see?"

"Cross my heart hope to die," he assured her.

"All right, Eddie, then I'll let you come with me, and you can ride beside me, instead of behind."

Across the flat they rode, following the windings of the river road, one mile, two, five, ten. Eddie had long since been wondering what the purpose of so steady a pace could be. This was no pleasure ride which took the boss's daughter—"heifer," Eddie would have called her—ten miles up river at a hard trot. Eddie was worried, too. They had passed the danger line, and were well within the stamping ground of Pesita and his retainers. Here each little adobe dwelling, and they were scattered at intervals of a mile or more along the river, contained a rabid partisan of Pesita, or it contained no one—Pesita had seen to this latter condition personally.

At last the young lady drew rein before a squalid and dilapidated hut. Eddie gasped. It was José's, and José was a notorious scoundrel whom old age alone kept from the active pursuit of the only calling he ever had known—brigandage. Why should the boss's daughter come to José? José was hand in glove with every cutthroat in Chihuahua, or at least within a radius of two hundred miles of his abode.

Barbara swung herself from the saddle, and handed her bridle reins to Eddie.

"Hold him, please," she said. "I'll be gone but a moment."

"You're not goin' in there to see old José alone?" gasped Eddie.

"Why not?" she asked. "If you're afraid you can leave my horse and ride along home."

Eddie colored to the roots of his sandy hair, and kept silent. The girl approached the doorway of the mean hovel and peered within. At one end sat a bent old man, smoking. He looked up as Barbara's figure darkened the doorway.

"José!" said the girl.

The old man rose to his feet and came toward her.

"Eh? Señorita, eh?" he cackled.

"You are José?" she asked.

"*Si*, señorita," replied the old Indian. "What can poor old José do to serve the beautiful señorita?"

"You can carry a message to one of Pesita's officers," replied the girl. "I have heard much about you since I came to Mexico. I know that there is not another man in this part of Chihuahua who may so easily reach Pesita as you." She raised her hand for silence as the Indian would have protested. Then she reached into the pocket of her riding breeches and withdrew a handful of silver which she permitted to trickle, tinklingly, from one palm to the other. "I wish you to go to the camp of Pesita," she continued, "and carry word to the man who robbed the bank at Cuivaca—he is an American—that his friend, Señor Bridge has been captured by Villa and is being held for execution in Cuivaca. You must go at once—you must get word to Señor Bridge's friend so that help may reach Señor Bridge before dawn. Do you understand?"

The Indian nodded assent.

"Here," said the girl, "is a payment on account. When I know that you delivered the message in time you shall have as much more. Will you do it?"

"I will try," said the Indian, and stretched forth a clawlike hand for the money.

"Good!" exclaimed Barbara. "Now start at once," and she dropped the silver coins into the old man's palm.

It was dusk when Captain Billy Byrne was summoned to the tent of Pesita. There he found a weazened, old Indian squatting at the side of the outlaw.

"José," said Pesita, "has word for you."

Billy Byrne turned questioningly toward the Indian.

"I have been sent, Señor Capitan," explained José, "by the beautiful señorita of El Orobo Rancho to tell you that your friend, Señor Bridge, has been captured by General Villa, and is being held at Cuivaca, where he will doubtless be shot—if help does not reach him before tomorrow morning."

Pesita was looking questioningly at Byrne. Since the gringo had returned from Cuivaca with the loot of the bank and turned the last penny of it over to him the outlaw had looked upon his new captain as something just short of superhuman. To have robbed the bank thus easily while Villa's soldiers paced back and forth before the doorway seemed little short of an indication of miraculous powers, while to have turned the loot over intact to his chief, not asking for so much as a peso of it, was absolutely incredible.

Pesita could not understand this man; but he admired him greatly and feared him, too. Such a man was worth a hundred of the ordinary run of humanity that enlisted beneath Pesita's banners. Byrne had but to ask a favor to have it granted, and now, when he called upon Pesita to furnish him with a suitable force for the rescue of Bridge the brigand enthusiastically acceded to his demands.

"I will come," he exclaimed, "and all my men shall ride with me. We will take Cuivaca by storm. We may even capture Villa himself."

"Wait a minute, bo," interrupted Billy Byrne. "Don't get excited. I'm lookin' to get my pal outen' Cuivaca. After that I don't care who you capture; but I'm goin' to get Bridgie out first. I ken do it with twenty-five men—if it ain't too late. Then, if you want to, you can shoot up the town. Lemme have the twenty-five, an' you hang around the edges with the rest of 'em 'til I'm done. Whaddaya say?"

Pesita was willing to agree to anything, and so it came that half an hour later Billy Byrne was leading a choice selection of some two dozen cutthroats down through the hills toward Cuivaca. While a couple of miles in the rear followed Pesita with the balance of his band.

Billy rode until the few remaining lights of Cuivaca shone but a short distance ahead and they could hear plainly the strains of a grating graphophone from beyond the open windows of a dance hall, and the voices of the sentries as they called the hour.

"Stay here," said Billy to a sergeant at his side, "until you hear a hoot owl cry three times from the direction of the barracks and guardhouse, then charge the opposite end of the town, firing off your carbines like hell an' yellin' yer heads off. Make all the racket you can, an' keep it up 'til you get 'em comin' in your direction, see? Then turn an' drop back slowly, eggin' 'em on, but holdin' 'em to it as long as you can. Do you get me, bo?"

From the mixture of Spanish and English and Granavenooish the sergeant gleaned enough of the intent of his commander to permit him to salute and admit that he understood what was required of him.

Having given his instructions Billy Byrne rode off to the west, circled Cuivaca and came close up upon the southern edge of the little village. Here he dismounted and left his horse hidden behind an outbuilding, while he crept cautiously forward to reconnoiter.

He knew that the force within the village had no reason to fear attack. Villa knew where the main bodies of his enemies lay, and that no force could approach Cuivaca without word of its coming reaching the garrison many hours in advance of the foe. That Pesita, or another of the several bandit chiefs in the neighborhood would dare descend upon a garrisoned town never for a moment entered the calculations of the rebel leader.

For these reasons Billy argued that Cuivaca would be poorly guarded. On the night he had spent there he had seen sentries before the bank, the guardhouse, and the barracks in addition to one who paced to and fro in front of the house in which the commander of the garrison maintained his headquarters. Aside from these the town was unguarded.

Nor were conditions different tonight. Billy came within a hundred yards of the guardhouse before he discovered a sentinel. The fellow lolled upon his gun in front of the building—an adobe structure in the rear of the barracks. The other three sides of the guardhouse appeared to be unwatched.

Billy threw himself upon his stomach and crawled slowly forward stopping often. The sentry seemed asleep. He did not move. Billy reached the shadow at the side of the structure and some fifty feet from the soldier without detection. Then he rose to his feet directly beneath a barred window.

Within Bridge paced back and forth the length of the little building. He could not sleep. Tomorrow he was to be shot! Bridge did not wish to die. That very morning General Villa in person had examined him. The general had been exceedingly wroth—the sting of the theft of his funds still irritated him; but he had given Bridge no inkling as to his fate. It had remained for a fellow-prisoner to do that. This man, a deserter, was to be shot, so he said, with Bridge, a fact which gave him an additional twenty-four hours of life, since, he asserted, General Villa wished to be elsewhere than in Cuivaca when an American was executed. Thus he could disclaim responsibility for the act.

The general was to depart in the morning. Shortly after, Bridge and the deserter would be led out and blindfolded before a stone wall—if there was such a thing, or a brick wall, or an adobe wall. It made little difference to the deserter, or to Bridge either. The wall was but a trivial factor. It might go far to add romance to whomever should read of the affair later; but in so far as Bridge and the deserter were concerned it meant nothing. A billboard, thought Bridge, bearing the slogan: "Eventually! Why not now?" would have been equally as efficacious and far more appropriate.

The room in which he was confined was stuffy with the odor of accumulated filth. Two small barred windows alone gave means of ventilation. He and the deserter were the only prisoners. The latter slept as soundly as though the morrow held nothing more momentous in his destiny than any of the days that had preceded it. Bridge was moved to kick the fellow into consciousness of his impending fate. Instead he walked to the south window to fill his lungs with the free air beyond his prison pen, and gaze sorrowfully at the starlit sky which he should never again behold. In a low tone Bridge crooned a snatch of the poem that he and Billy liked best:

> And you, my sweet Penelope, out there somewhere you wait
>   for me,
> With buds of roses in your hair and kisses on your mouth.

Bridge's mental vision was concentrated upon the veranda of a white-walled ranchhouse to the east. He shook his head angrily.

"It's just as well," he thought. "She's not for me."

Something moved upon the ground beyond the window. Bridge became suddenly intent upon the thing. He saw it rise and resolve itself into the figure of a man, and then, in a low whisper, came a familiar voice:

"There ain't no roses in my hair, but there's a barker in my shirt, an' another at me side. Here's one of 'em. They got kisses beat a city block. How's the door o' this thing fastened?" The speaker was quite close to the window now, his face but a few inches from Bridge's.

"Billy!" ejaculated the condemned man.

"Surest thing you know; but about the door?"

"Just a heavy bar on the outside," replied Bridge.

"Easy," commented Billy, relieved. "Get ready to beat it when I open the door. I got a pony south o' town that'll have to carry double for a little way tonight."

"God bless you, Billy!" whispered Bridge, fervently.

"Lay low a few minutes," said Billy, and moved away toward the rear of the guardhouse.

A few minutes later there broke upon the night air the dismal hoot of an owl. At intervals of a few seconds it was repeated twice. The sentry before the guardhouse shifted his position and looked about, then he settled back, transferring his weight to the other foot, and resumed his bovine meditations.

The man at the rear of the guardhouse moved silently along the side of the structure until he stood within a few feet of the unsuspecting sentinel, hidden from him by the corner of the building. A heavy revolver dangled from his right hand. He held it loosely by the barrel, and waited.

For five minutes the silence of the night was unbroken, then from the east came a single shot, followed immediately by a scattering fusillade and a chorus of hoarse cries.

Billy Byrne smiled. The sentry resumed indications of quickness From the barracks beyond the guardhouse came sharp commands and the sounds of men running. From the opposite end of the town the noise of battle welled up to ominous proportions.

Billy heard the soldiers stream from their quarters and a moment later saw them trot up the street at the double. Everyone was moving toward the opposite end of the town except the lone sentinel before the guardhouse. The moment seemed propitious for his attempt.

Billy peered around the corner of the guardhouse. Conditions were just as he had pictured they would be. The sentry stood gazing in the direction of the firing, his back toward the guardhouse door and Billy.

With a bound the American cleared the space between himself and the unsuspecting and unfortunate soldier. The butt of the heavy revolver fell, almost noiselessly, upon the back of the sentry's head, and the man sank to the ground without even a moan.

Turning to the door Billy knocked the bar from its place, the door swung in and Bridge slipped through to liberty.

"Quick!" said Billy. "Follow me," and turned at a rapid run toward the south edge of the town. He made no effort now to conceal his movements. Speed was the only essential, and the two covered the ground swiftly and openly without any attempt to take advantage of cover.

They reached Billy's horse unnoticed, and a moment later were trotting toward the west to circle the town and regain the trail to the north and safety.

To the east they heard the diminishing rifle fire of the combatants as Pesita's men fell steadily back before the defenders, and drew them away from Cuivaca in accordance with Billy's plan.

"Like takin' candy from a baby," said Billy, when the flickering lights of Cuivaca shone to the south of them, and the road ahead lay clear to the rendezvous of the brigands.

"Yes," agreed Bridge; "but what I'd like to know, Billy, is how you found out I was there."

"Penelope," said Byrne, laughing.

"Penelope!" queried Bridge. "I'm not at all sure that I follow you, Billy."

"Well, seein' as you're sittin' on behind you can't be leadin' me," returned Billy; "but cuttin' the kid it was a skirt tipped it off to me where you was—the beautiful señorita of El Orobo Rancho, I think José called her. Now are you hep?"

Bridge gave an exclamation of astonishment. "God bless her!" he said. "She did that for me?"

"She sure did," Billy assured him, "an' I'll bet an iron case she's a-waitin' for you there with buds o' roses in her hair an' kisses on her mouth, you old son-of-a-gun, you." Billy laughed happily. He was happy anyway at having rescued Bridge, and the knowledge that his friend was in love and that the girl reciprocated his affection—all of which Billy assumed as the only explanation of her interest in Bridge—only added to his joy. "She ain't a greaser is she?" he asked presently.

"I should say not," replied Bridge. "She's a perfect queen from New York City; but, Billy, she's not for me. What she did was prompted by a generous heart. She couldn't care for me, Billy. Her father is a wealthy man—he could have the pick of the land—of many lands—if she cared to marry. You don't think for a minute she'd want a hobo, do you?"

"You can't most always tell," replied Billy, a trifle sadly. "I knew such a queen once who would have chosen a mucker, if he'd a-let her. You're stuck on her, ol' man?"

"I'm afraid I am, Billy," Bridge admitted; "but what's the use? Let's forget it. Oh, say, is this the horse I let you take the night you robbed the bank?"

"Yes," said Billy; "same little pony, an' a mighty well-behaved one, too. Why?"

"It's hers," said Bridge.

"An' she wants it back?"

"She didn't say so; but I'd like to get it to her some way," said Bridge.

"You ride it back when you go," suggested Billy.

"But I can't go back," said Bridge; "it was Grayson, the foreman, who made it so hot for me I had to leave. He tried to arrest me and send me to Villa."

"What for?" asked Billy.

"He didn't like me, and wanted to get rid of me." Bridge wouldn't say that his relations with Billy had brought him into trouble.

"Oh, well, I'll take it back myself then, and at the same time I'll tell Penelope what a regular fellow you are, and punch in the foreman's face for good luck."

"No, you mustn't go there. They know you now. It was some of El Orobo's men you shot up day before yesterday when you took their steers from them. They recognized the pony, and one of them had seen you in Cuivaca the night of the robbery. They would be sure to get you, Billy."

Shortly the two came in touch with the retreating Pesitistas who were riding slowly toward their mountain camp. Their pursuers had long since given up the chase, fearing that they might be being lured into the midst of a greatly superior force, and had returned to Cuivaca.

It was nearly morning when Bridge and Billy threw themselves down upon the latter's blankets, fagged.

"Well, well," murmured Billy Byrne; "li'l ol' Bridgie's found his Penelope," and fell asleep.

XIII
BARBARA AGAIN

Captain Billy Byrne rode out of the hills the following afternoon upon a pinto pony that showed the whites of its eyes in a wicked rim about the iris and kept its ears perpetually flattened backward.

At the end of a lariat trailed the Brazos pony, for Billy, laughing aside Bridge's pleas, was on his way to El Orobo Rancho to return the stolen horse to its fair owner.

At the moment of departure Pesita had asked Billy to ride by way of José's to instruct the old Indian that he should bear word to one Esteban that Pesita required his presence.

It is a long ride from the retreat of the Pesitistas to José's squalid hut, especially if one be leading an extra horse, and so it was that darkness had fallen long before Billy arrived in sight of José's. Dismounting some distance from the hut, Billy approached cautiously, since the world is filled with dangers for those who are beyond the law, and one may not be too careful.

Billy could see a light showing through a small window, and toward this he made his way. A short distance from José's is another, larger structure from which the former inhabitants had fled the wrath of Pesita. It was dark and apparently tenantless; but as a matter of fact a pair of eyes chanced at the very moment of Billy's coming to be looking out through the open doorway.

The owner turned and spoke to someone behind him.

"José has another visitor," he said. "Possibly this one is less harmless than the other. He comes with great caution. Let us investigate."

Three other men rose from their blankets upon the floor and joined the speaker. They were all armed, and clothed in the nondescript uniforms of Villistas. Billy's back was toward them as they sneaked from the hut in which they were intending to spend the night and crept quietly toward him.

Billy was busily engaged in peering through the little window into the interior of the old Indian's hovel. He saw an American in earnest conversation with José. Who could the man be? Billy did not recognize him; but presently José answered the question.

"It shall be done as you wish, Señor Grayson," he said.

"Ah!" thought Billy; "the foreman of El Orobo. I wonder what business he has with this old scoundrel—and at night."

What other thoughts Billy might have had upon the subject were rudely interrupted by four energetic gentlemen in his rear, who leaped upon him simultaneously and dragged him to the ground. Billy made no outcry; but he fought none the less strenuously for his freedom, and he fought after the manner of Grand Avenue, which is not a pretty, however effective, way it may be.

But four against one when all the advantages lie with the four are heavy odds, and when Grayson and José ran out to investigate, and the ranch foreman added his weight to that of the others Billy was finally subdued. That each of his antagonists would carry mementos of the battle for many days was slight compensation for the loss of liberty. However, it was some.

After disarming their captive and tying his hands at his back they jerked him to his feet and examined him.

"Who are you?" asked Grayson. "What you doin' sneakin' 'round spyin' on me, eh?"

"If you wanna know who I am, bo," replied Billy, "go ask de Harlem Hurricane, an' as fer spyin' on youse, I wasn't; but from de looks I guess youse need spyin, yuh tin-horn."

A pony whinnied a short distance from the hut.

"That must be his horse," said one of the Villistas, and walked away to investigate, returning shortly after with the pinto pony and Brazos.

The moment Grayson saw the latter he gave an exclamation of understanding.

"I know him now," he said. "You've made a good catch, Sergeant. This is the fellow who robbed the bank at Cuivaca. I recognize him from the descriptions I've had of him, and the fact that he's got the Brazos pony makes it a cinch. Villa oughter promote you for this."

"Yep," interjected Billy, "he orter make youse an admiral at least; but youse ain't got me home yet, an' it'll take more'n four Dagos an' a tin-horn to do it."

"They'll get you there all right, my friend," Grayson assured him. "Now come along."

They bundled Billy into his own saddle, and shortly after the little party was winding southward along the river in the direction of El Orobo Rancho, with the intention of putting up there for the balance of the night where their prisoner could be properly secured and guarded. As they rode away from the dilapidated hut of the Indian the old man stood silhouetted against the rectangle of dim light which marked the open doorway, and shook his fist at the back of the departing ranch foreman.

"*El cochino!*" he cackled, and turned back into his hut.

At El Orobo Rancho Barbara walked to and fro outside the ranchhouse. Within her father sat reading beneath the rays of an oil lamp. From the quarters of the men came the strains of guitar music, and an occasional loud laugh indicated the climax of some of Eddie Shorter's famous Kansas farmer stories.

Barbara was upon the point of returning indoors when her attention was attracted by the approach of a half-dozen horsemen. They reined into the ranchyard and dismounted before the office building. Wondering a little who came so late, Barbara entered the house, mentioning casually to her father that which she had just seen.

The ranch owner, now always fearful of attack, was upon the point of investigating when Grayson rode up to the veranda and dismounted. Barbara and her father were at the door as he ascended the steps.

"Good news!" exclaimed the foreman. "I've got the bank robber, and Brazos, too. Caught the sneakin' coyote up to—up the river a bit." He had almost said "José's;" but caught himself in time. "Someone's been cuttin' the wire at the north side of the north pasture, an' I was ridin' up to see ef I could catch 'em at it," he explained.

"He is an American?" asked the boss.

"Looks like it; but he's got the heart of a greaser," replied Grayson. "Some of Villa's men are with me, and they're a-goin' to take him to Cuivaca tomorrow."

Neither Barbara nor her father seemed to enthuse much. To them an American was an American here in Mexico, where every hand was against their race. That at home they might have looked with disgust upon this same man did not alter their attitude here, that no American should take sides against his own people. Barbara said as much to Grayson.

"Why this fellow's one of Pesita's officers," exclaimed Grayson. "He don't deserve no sympathy from us nor from no other Americans. Pesita has sworn to kill every American that falls into his hands, and this fellow's with him to help him do it. He's a bad un."

"I can't help what he may do," insisted Barbara. "He's an American, and I for one would never be a party to his death at the hands of a Mexican, and it will mean death to him to be taken to Cuivaca."

"Well, miss," said Grayson, "you won't hev to be responsible—I'll take all the responsibility there is and welcome. I just thought you'd like to know we had him." He was addressing his employer. The latter nodded, and Grayson turned and left the room. Outside he cast a sneering laugh back over his shoulder and swung into his saddle.

In front of the men's quarters he drew rein again and shouted Eddie's name. Shorter came to the door.

"Get your six-shooter an' a rifle, an' come on over to the office. I want to see you a minute."

Eddie did as he was bid, and when he entered the little room he saw four Mexicans lolling about smoking cigarettes while Grayson stood before a chair in which sat a man with his arms tied behind his back. Grayson turned to Eddie.

"This party here is the slick un that robbed the bank, and got away on thet there Brazos pony thet miserable bookkeepin' dude giv him. The sergeant here an' his men are a-goin' to take him to Cuivaca in the mornin'. You stand guard over him 'til midnight, then they'll relieve you. They gotta get a little sleep first, though, an' I gotta get some supper. Don't stand fer no funny business now, Eddie," Grayson admonished him, and was on the point of leaving the office when a thought occurred to him. "Say, Shorter," he said, "they ain't no way of gettin' out of the little bedroom in back there except through this room. The windows are too small fer a big man to get through. I'll tell you what, we'll lock him up in there an' then you won't hev to worry none an' neither will we. You can jest spread out them Navajos there and go to sleep right plump ag'in the door, an' there won't nobody hev to relieve you all night."

"Sure," said Eddie, "leave it to me—I'll watch the slicker."

Satisfied that their prisoner was safe for the night the Villistas and Grayson departed, after seeing him safely locked in the back room.

At the mention by the foreman of his guard's names—Eddie and Shorter—Billy had studied the face of the young American cowpuncher, for the two names had aroused within his memory a tantalizing suggestion that they should be very familiar. Yet he could connect them in no way with anyone he had known in the past and he was quite sure that he never before had set eyes upon this man.

Sitting in the dark with nothing to occupy him Billy let his mind dwell upon the identity of his jailer, until, as may have happened to you, nothing in the whole world seemed equally as important as the solution of the mystery. Even his impending fate faded into nothingness by comparison with the momentous question as to where he had heard the name Eddie Shorter before.

As he sat puzzling his brain over the inconsequential matter something stirred upon the floor close to his feet, and presently he jerked back a booted foot that a rat had commenced to gnaw upon.

"Helluva place to stick a guy," mused Billy, "in wit a bunch o' man-eatin' rats. Hey!" and he turned his face toward the door. "You, Eddie! Come here!"

Eddie approached the door and listened.

"Wot do you want?" he asked. "None o' your funny business, you know. I'm from Shawnee, Kansas, I am, an' they don't come no slicker from nowhere on earth. You can't fool me."

Shawnee, Kansas! Eddie Shorter! The whole puzzle was cleared in Billy's mind in an instant.

"So you're Eddie Shorter of Shawnee, Kansas, are you?" called Billy. "Well I know your maw, Eddie, an' ef I had such a maw as you got I wouldn't be down here wastin' my time workin' alongside a lot of Dagos; but that ain't what I started out to say, which was that I want a light in here. The damned rats are tryin' to chaw off me kicks an' when they're done wit them they'll climb up after me an' old man Villa'll be sore as a pup."

"You know my maw?" asked Eddie, and there was a wistful note in his voice. "Aw shucks! you don't know her—that's jest some o' your funny, slicker business. You wanna git me in there an' then you'll try an' git aroun' me some sort o' way to let you escape; but I'm too slick for that."

"On the level Eddie, I know your maw," persisted Billy. "I ben in your maw's house jest a few weeks ago. 'Member the horsehair sofa between the windows? 'Member the Bible on the little marble-topped table? Eh? An' Tige? Well, Tige's croaked; but your maw an' your paw ain't an' they want you back, Eddie. I don't care ef you believe me, son, or not; but your maw was mighty good to me, an' you promise me you'll write her an' then go back home as fast as you can. It ain't everybody's got a swell maw like that, an' them as has ought to be good to 'em."

Beyond the closed door Eddie's jaw was commencing to tremble. Memory was flooding his heart and his eyes with sweet recollections of an ample breast where he used to pillow his head, of a big capable hand that was wont to smooth his brow and stroke back his red hair. Eddie gulped.

"You ain't joshin' me?" he asked. Billy Byrne caught the tremor in the voice.

"I ain't kiddin' you son," he said. "Wotinell do you take me fer—one o' these greasy Dagos? You an' I're Americans—I wouldn't string a home guy down here in this here Godforsaken neck o' the woods."

Billy heard the lock turn, and a moment later the door was cautiously opened revealing Eddie safely ensconced behind two six-shooters.

"That's right, Eddie," said Billy, with a laugh. "Don't you take no chances, no matter how much sob stuff I hand you, fer, I'll give it to you straight, ef I get the chanct I'll make my getaway; but I can't do it wit my flippers trussed, an' you wit a brace of gats sittin' on me. Let's have a light, Eddie. That won't do nobody any harm, an' it may discourage the rats."

Eddie backed across the office to a table where stood a small lamp. Keeping an eye through the door on his prisoner he lighted the lamp and carried it into the back room, setting it upon a commode which stood in one corner.

"You really seen maw?" he asked. "Is she well?"

"Looked well when I seen her," said Billy; "but she wants her boy back a whole lot. I guess she'd look better still ef he walked in on her some day."

"I'll do it," cried Eddie. "The minute they get money for the pay I'll hike. Tell me your name. I'll ask her ef she remembers you when I get home. Gee! but I wish I was walkin' in the front door now."

"She never knew my name," said Billy; "but you tell her you seen the bo that mussed up the two yeggmen who rolled her an' were tryin' to croak her wit a butcher knife. I guess she ain't fergot. Me an' my pal were beatin' it—he was on the square but the dicks was after me an' she let us have money to make our getaway. She's all right, kid."

There came a knock at the outer office door. Eddie sprang back into the front room, closing and locking the door after him, just as Barbara entered.

"Eddie," she asked, "may I see the prisoner? I want to talk to him."

"You want to talk with a bank robber?" exclaimed Eddie. "Why you ain't crazy are you, Miss Barbara?"

"No, I'm not crazy; but I want to speak with him alone for just a moment, Eddie—please."

Eddie hesitated. He knew that Grayson would be angry if he let the boss's daughter into that back room alone with an outlaw and a robber, and the boss himself would probably be inclined to have Eddie drawn and quartered; but it was hard to refuse Miss Barbara anything.

"Where is he?" she asked.

Eddie jerked a thumb in the direction of the door. The key still was in the lock.

"Go to the window and look at the moon, Eddie," suggested the girl. "It's perfectly gorgeous tonight. Please, Eddie," as he still hesitated.

Eddie shook his head and moved slowly toward the window.

"There can't nobody refuse you nothin', miss," he said; "'specially when you got your heart set on it."

"That's a dear, Eddie," purred the girl, and moved swiftly across the room to the locked door.

As she turned the key in the lock she felt a little shiver of nervous excitement run through her. "What sort of man would he be—this hardened outlaw and robber—this renegade American who had cast his lot with the avowed enemies of his own people?" she wondered.

Only her desire to learn of Bridge's fate urged her to attempt so distasteful an interview; but she dared not ask another to put the question for her, since should her complicity in Bridge's escape—provided of course that he had escaped—become known to Villa the fate of the Americans at El Orobo would be definitely sealed.

She turned the knob and pushed the door open, slowly. A man was sitting in a chair in the center of the room. His back was toward her. He was a big man. His broad shoulders loomed immense above the back of the rude chair. A shock of black hair, rumpled and tousled, covered a well-shaped head.

At the sound of the door creaking upon its hinges he turned his face in her direction, and as his eyes met hers all four went wide in surprise and incredulity.

"Billy!" she cried.

"Barbara!—you?" and Billy rose to his feet, his bound hands struggling to be free.

The girl closed the door behind her and crossed to him.

"You robbed the bank, Billy?" she asked. "It was you, after the promises you made me to live straight always—for my sake?" Her voice trembled with emotion. The man could see that she suffered, and yet he felt his own anguish, too.

"But you are married," he said. "I saw it in the papers. What do you care, now, Barbara? I'm nothing to you."

"I'm not married, Billy," she cried. "I couldn't marry Mr. Mallory. I tried to make myself believe that I could; but at last I knew that I did not love him and never could, and I wouldn't marry a man I didn't love.

"I never dreamed that it was you here, Billy," she went on. "I came to ask you about Mr. Bridge. I wanted to know if he escaped, or if—if—oh, this awful country! They think no more of human life here than a butcher thinks of the life of the animal he dresses."

A sudden light illumined Billy's mind. Why had it not occurred to him before? This was Bridge's Penelope! The woman he loved was loved by his best friend. And she had sent a messenger to him, to Billy, to save her lover. She had come here to the office tonight to question a stranger—a man she thought an outlaw and a robber—because she could not rest without word from the man she loved. Billy stiffened. He was hurt to the bottom of his heart; but he did not blame Bridge—it was fate. Nor did he blame Barbara because she loved Bridge. Bridge was more her kind anyway. He was a college guy. Billy was only a mucker.

"Bridge got away all right," he said. "And say, he didn't have nothin' to do with pullin' off that safe crackin'. I done it myself. He didn't know I was in town an' I didn't know he was there. He's the squarest guy in the world, Bridge is. He follered me that night an' took a shot at me, thinkin' I was the robber all right but not knowin' I was me. He got my horse, an' when he found it was me, he made me take your pony an' make my getaway, fer he knew Villa's men would croak me sure if they caught me. You can't blame him fer that, can you? Him an' I were good pals—he couldn't do nothin' else. It was him that made me bring your pony back to you. It's in the corral now, I reckon. I was a-bringin' it back when they got me. Now you better go. This ain't no place fer you, an' I ain't had no sleep fer so long I'm most dead." His tones were cool. He appeared bored by her company; though as a matter of fact his heart was breaking with love for her—love that he believed unrequited—and he yearned to tear loose his bonds and crush her in his arms.

It was Barbara's turn now to be hurt. She drew herself up.

"I am sorry that I have disturbed your rest," she said, and walked away, her head in the air; but all the way back to the ranchhouse she kept repeating over and over to herself: "Tomorrow they will shoot him! Tomorrow they will shoot him! Tomorrow they will shoot him!"

XIV
'Twixt Love and Duty

For an hour Barbara Harding paced the veranda of the ranchhouse, pride and love battling for the ascendency within her breast. She could not let him die, that she knew; but how might she save him?

The strains of music and the laughter from the bunkhouse had ceased. The ranch slept. Over the brow of the low bluff upon the opposite side of the river a little party of silent horsemen filed downward to the ford. At the bluff's foot a barbed-wire fence marked the eastern boundary of the ranch's enclosed fields. The foremost horseman dismounted and cut the strands of wire, carrying them to one side from the path of the feet of the horses which now passed through the opening he had made.

Down into the river they rode following the ford even in the darkness with an assurance which indicated long familiarity. Then through a fringe of willows out across a meadow toward the ranch buildings the riders made their way. The manner of their approach, their utter silence, the hour, all contributed toward the sinister.

Upon the veranda of the ranchhouse Barbara Harding came to a sudden halt. Her entire manner indicated final decision, and determination. A moment she stood in thought and then ran quickly down the steps and in the direction of the office. Here she found Eddie dozing at his post. She did not disturb him. A glance through the window satisfied her that he was alone with the prisoner. From the office building Barbara passed on to the corral. A few horses stood within the enclosure, their heads drooping dejectedly. As she entered they raised their muzzles and sniffed suspiciously, ears a-cock, and as the girl approached closer to them they moved warily away, snorting, and passed around her to the opposite side of the corral. As they moved by her she scrutinized them and her heart dropped, for Brazos was not among them. He must have been turned out into the pasture.

She passed over to the bars that closed the opening from the corral into the pasture and wormed her way between two of them. A hackamore with a piece of halter rope attached to it hung across the upper bar. Taking it down she moved off across the pasture in the direction the saddle horses most often took when liberated from the corral.

If they had not crossed the river she felt that she might find and catch Brazos, for lumps of sugar and bits of bread had inspired in his equine soul a wondrous attachment for his temporary mistress.

Down the beaten trail the animals had made to the river the girl hurried, her eyes penetrating the darkness ahead and to either hand for the looming bulks that would be the horses she sought, and among which she might hope to discover the gentle little Brazos.

The nearer she came to the river the lower dropped her spirits, for as yet no sign of the animals was to be seen. To have attempted to place a hackamore upon any of the wild creatures in the corral would have been the height of foolishness—only a well-sped riata in the hands of a strong man could have captured one of these.

Closer and closer to the fringe of willows along the river she came, until, at their very edge, there broke upon her already taut nerves the hideous and uncanny scream of a wildcat. The girl stopped short in her tracks. She felt the chill of fear creep through her skin, and a twitching at the roots of her hair evidenced to her the extremity of her terror. Should she turn back? The horses might be between her and the river, but judgment told her that they had crossed. Should she brave the nervous fright of a passage through that dark, forbidding labyrinth of gloom when she knew that she should not find the horses within reach beyond?

She turned to retrace her steps. She must find another way! But was there another way? And "Tomorrow they will shoot him!" She shuddered, bit her lower lip in an effort to command her courage, and then, wheeling, plunged into the thicket.

Again the cat screamed—close by—but the girl never hesitated in her advance, and a few moments later she broke through the willows a dozen paces from the river bank. Her eyes strained through the night; but no horses were to be seen.

The trail, cut by the hoofs of many animals, ran deep and straight down into the swirling water. Upon the opposite side Brazos must be feeding or resting, just beyond reach.

Barbara dug her nails into her palms in the bitterness of her disappointment. She followed down to the very edge of the water. It was black and forbidding. Even in the daytime she would not have been confident of following the ford—by night it would be madness to attempt it. She choked down a sob. Her shoulders drooped. Her head bent forward. She was the picture of disappointment and despair.

"What can I do?" she moaned. "Tomorrow they will shoot him!"

The thought seemed to electrify her.

"They shall not shoot him!" she cried aloud. "They shall not shoot him while I live to prevent it!"

Again her head was up and her shoulders squared. Tying the hackamore about her waist, she took a single deep breath of reassurance and stepped out into the river. For a dozen paces she found no difficulty in following the ford. It was broad and straight; but toward the center of the river, as she felt her way along a step at a time, she came to a place where directly before her the ledge upon which she crossed shelved off into deep water. She turned upward, trying to locate the direction of the new turn; but here too there was no footing. Down river she felt solid rock beneath her feet. Ah! this was the way, and boldly she stepped out, the water already above her knees. Two, three steps she took, and with each one her confidence and hope arose, and then the fourth step—and there was no footing. She felt herself lunging into the stream, and tried to draw back and regain the ledge; but the force of the current was too much for her, and, so suddenly it seemed that she had thrown herself in, she was in the channel swimming for her life.

The trend of the current there was back in the direction of the bank she had but just quitted, yet so strong was her determination to succeed for Billy Byrne's sake that she turned her face toward the opposite shore and fought to reach the seemingly impossible goal which love had set for her. Again and again she was swept under by the force of the current. Again and again she rose and battled, not for her own life; but for the life of the man she once had loathed and whom she later had come to love. Inch by inch she won toward the shore of her desire, and inch by inch of her progress she felt her strength failing. Could she win? Ah! if she were but a man, and with the thought came another: Thank God that I am a woman with a woman's love which gives strength to drive me into the clutches of death for his sake!

Her heart thundered in tumultuous protest against the strain of her panting lungs. Her limbs felt cold and numb; but she could not give up even though she was now convinced that she had thrown her life away uselessly.

They would find her body; but no one would ever guess what had driven her to her death. Not even *he* would know that it was for his sake. And then she felt the tugging of the channel current suddenly lessen, an eddy carried her gently inshore, her feet touched the sand and gravel of the bottom. Gasping for breath, staggering, stumbling, she reeled on a few paces and then slipped down clutching at the river's bank. Here the water was shallow, and here she lay until her strength returned. Then she urged herself up and onward, climbed to the top of the bank with success at last within reach.

To find the horses now required but a few minutes' search. They stood huddled in a black mass close to the barbed-wire fence at the extremity of the pasture. As she approached them they commenced to separate slowly, edging away while they faced her in curiosity. Softly she called: "Brazos! Come, Brazos!" until a unit of the moving mass detached itself and came toward her, nickering.

"Good Brazos!" she cooed. "That's a good pony," and walked forward to meet him.

The animal let her reach up and stroke his forehead, while he muzzled about her for the expected tidbit. Gently she worked the hackamore over his nose and above his ears, and when it was safely in place she breathed a deep sigh of relief and throwing her arms about his neck pressed her cheek to his.

"You dear old Brazos," she whispered.

The horse stood quietly while the girl wriggled herself to his back, and then at a word and a touch from her heels moved off at a walk in the direction of the ford. The crossing this time was one of infinite ease, for Barbara let the rope lie loose and Brazos take his own way.

Through the willows upon the opposite bank he shouldered his path, across the meadow still at a walk, lest they arouse attention, and through a gate which led directly from the meadow into the ranchyard. Here she tied him to the outside of the corral, while she went in search of saddle and bridle. Whose she took she did not know, nor care, but that the saddle was enormously heavy she was perfectly aware long before she had dragged it halfway to where Brazos stood.

Three times she essayed to lift it to his back before she succeeded in accomplishing the Herculean task, and had it been any other horse upon the ranch than Brazos the thing could never have been done; but the kindly little pony stood in statuesque resignation while the heavy Mexican tree was banged and thumped against his legs and ribs, until a lucky swing carried it to his withers.

Saddled and bridled Barbara led him to the rear of the building and thus, by a roundabout way, to the back of the office building. Here she could see a light in the room in which Billy was confined, and after dropping the bridle reins to the ground she made her way to the front of the structure.

Creeping stealthily to the porch she peered in at the window. Eddie was stretched out in cramped though seeming luxury in an office chair. His feet were cocked up on the desk before him. In his lap lay his six-shooter ready for any emergency. Another reposed in its holster at his belt.

Barbara tiptoed to the door. Holding her breath she turned the knob gently. The door swung open without a sound, and an instant later she stood within the room. Again her eyes were fixed upon Eddie Shorter. She saw his nerveless fingers relax their hold upon the grip of his revolver. She saw the weapon slip farther down into his lap. He did not move, other than to the deep and regular breathing of profound slumber.

Barbara crossed the room to his side.

Behind the ranchhouse three figures crept forward in the shadows. Behind them a matter of a hundred yards stood a little clump of horses and with them were the figures of more men. These waited in silence. The other three crept toward the house. It was such a ranchhouse as you might find by the scores or hundreds throughout Texas. Grayson, evidently, or some other Texan, had designed it. There was nothing Mexican about it, nor anything beautiful. It stood two storied, verandaed and hideous, a blot upon the soil of picturesque Mexico.

To the roof of the veranda clambered the three prowlers, and across it to an open window. The window belonged to the bedroom of Miss Barbara Harding. Here they paused and listened, then two of them entered the room. They were gone for but a few minutes. When they emerged they showed evidences, by their gestures to the third man who had awaited outside, of disgust and disappointment.

Cautiously they descended as they had come and made their way back to those other men who had remained with the horses. Here there ensued a low-toned conference, and while it progressed Barbara Harding reached forth a steady hand which belied the terror in her soul and plucked the revolver from Eddie Shorter's lap. Eddie slept on.

Again on tiptoe the girl recrossed the office to the locked door leading into the back room. The key was in the lock. Gingerly she turned it, keeping a furtive eye upon the sleeping guard, and the muzzle of his own revolver leveled menacingly upon him. Eddie Shorter stirred in his sleep and raised a hand to his face. The heart of Barbara Harding ceased to beat while she stood waiting for the man to open his eyes and discover her; but he did nothing of the kind. Instead his hand dropped limply at his side and he resumed his regular breathing.

The key turned in the lock beneath the gentle pressure of her fingers, the bolt slipped quietly back and she pushed the door ajar. Within, Billy Byrne turned inquiring eyes in the direction of the opening door, and as he saw who it was who entered surprise showed upon his face; but he spoke no word for the girl held a silencing finger to her lips.

Quickly she came to his side and motioned him to rise while she tugged at the knots which held the bonds in place about his arms. Once she stopped long enough to recross the room and close the door which she had left open when she entered.

It required fully five minutes—the longest five minutes of Barbara Harding's life, she thought—before the knots gave to her efforts; but at last the rope fell to the floor and Billy Byrne was free.

He started to speak, to thank her, and, perhaps, to scold her for the rash thing she had undertaken for him; but she silenced him again, and with a whispered, "Come!" turned toward the door.

As she opened it a crack to reconnoiter she kept the revolver pointed straight ahead of her into the adjoining room. Eddie, however, still slept on in peaceful ignorance of the trick which was being played upon him.

Now the two started forward for the door which opened from the office upon the porch, and as they did so Barbara turned again toward Billy to caution him to silence for his spurs had tinkled as he moved. For a moment their eyes were not upon Eddie Shorter and Fate had it that at that very moment Eddie awoke and opened his own eyes.

The sight that met them was so astonishing that for a second the Kansan could not move. He saw Barbara Harding, a revolver in her hand, aiding the outlaw to escape, and in the instant that surprise kept him motionless Eddie saw, too, another picture—the picture of a motherly woman in a little farmhouse back in Kansas, and Eddie realized that this man, this outlaw, had been the means of arousing within him a desire and a determination to return again to those loving arms. Too, the man had saved his mother from injury, and possible death.

Eddie shut his eyes quickly and thought hard and fast. Miss Barbara had always been kind to him. In his boyish heart he had loved her, hopelessly of course, in a boyish way. She wanted the outlaw to escape. Eddie realized that he would do anything that Miss Barbara wanted, even if he had to risk his life at it.

The girl and the man were at the door. She pushed him through ahead of her while she kept the revolver leveled upon Eddie, then she passed out after him and closed the door, while Eddie Shorter kept his eyes tightly closed and prayed to his God that Billy Byrne might get safely away.

Outside and in the rear of the office building Barbara pressed the revolver upon Billy.

"You will need it," she said. "There is Brazos—take him. God bless and guard you, Billy!" and she was gone.

Billy swallowed bard. He wanted to run after her and take her in his arms; but he recalled Bridge, and with a sigh turned toward the patient Brazos. Languidly he gathered up the reins and mounted, and then unconcernedly as though he were an honored guest departing by daylight he rode out of the ranchyard and turned Brazos' head north up the river road.

And as Billy disappeared in the darkness toward the north Barbara Harding walked slowly toward the ranchhouse, while from a little group of men and horses a hundred yards away three men detached themselves and crept toward her, for they had seen her in the moonlight as she left Billy outside the office and strolled slowly in the direction of the house.

They hid in the shadow at the side of the house until the girl had turned the corner and was approaching the veranda, then they ran quickly forward and as she mounted the steps she was seized from behind and dragged backward. A hand was clapped over her mouth and a whispered threat warned her to silence.

Half dragging and half carrying her the three men bore her back to where their confederates awaited them. A huge fellow mounted his pony and Barbara was lifted to the horn of the saddle before him. Then the others mounted and as silently as they had come they rode away, following the same path.

Barbara Harding had not cried out nor attempted to, for she had seen very shortly after her capture that she was in the hands of Indians and she judged from what she had heard of the little band of Pimans who held forth in the mountains to the east that they would as gladly knife her as not. José was a Piman, and she immediately connected José with the perpetration, or at least the planning of her abduction. Thus she felt assured that no harm would come to her, since José had been famous in his time for the number and size of the ransoms he had collected.

Her father would pay what was demanded, she would be returned and, aside from a few days of discomfort and hardship, she would be none the worse off for her experience. Reasoning thus it was not difficult to maintain her composure and presence of mind.

As Barbara was borne toward the east, Billy Byrne rode steadily northward. It was his intention to stop at José's hut and deliver the message which Pesita had given him for the old Indian. Then he would disappear into the mountains to the west, join Pesita and urge a new raid upon some favored friend of General Francisco Villa, for Billy had no love for Villa.

He should have been glad to pay his respects to El Orobo Rancho and its foreman; but the fact that Anthony Harding owned it and that he and Barbara were there was sufficient effectually to banish all thoughts of revenge along that line.

"Maybe I can get his goat later," he thought, "when he's away from the ranch. I don't like that stiff, anyhow. He orter been a harness bull."

It was four o'clock in the morning when Billy dismounted in front of José's hut. He pounded on the door until the man came and opened it.

"Eh!" exclaimed José as he saw who his early morning visitor was, "you got away from them. Fine!" and the old man chuckled. "I send word to Pesita two, four hours ago that Villistas capture Capitan Byrne and take him to Cuivaca."

"Thanks," said Billy. "Pesita wants you to send Esteban to him. I didn't have no chance to tell you last night while them pikers was stickin' aroun', so I stops now on my way back to the hills."

"I will send Esteban tonight if I can get him; but I do not know. Esteban is working for the pig, Grayson."

"Wot's he doin' fer Grayson?" asked Billy. "And what was the Grayson guy doin' up here with you, José? Ain't you gettin' pretty thick with Pesita's enemies?"

"José good friends everybody," and the old man grinned. "Grayson have a job he want good men for. José furnish men. Grayson pay well. Job got nothin' do Pesita, Villa, Carranza, revolution—just private job. Grayson want señorita. He pay to get her. That all."

"Oh," said Billy, and yawned. He was not interested in Mr. Grayson's amours. "Why didn't the poor boob go get her himself?" he inquired disinterestedly. "He must be a yap to hire a bunch o' guys to go cop off a siwash girl fer him."

"It is not a siwash girl, Señor Capitan," said José. "It is one beautiful señorita—the daughter of the owner of El Orobo Rancho."

"What?" cried Billy Byrne. "What's that you say?"

"Yes, Señor Capitan, what of it?" inquired José. "Grayson he pay me furnish the men. Esteban he go with his warriors. I get Esteban. They go tonight take away the señorita; but not for Grayson," and the old fellow laughed. "I can no help can I? Grayson pay me money get men. I get them. I no help if they keep girl," and he shrugged.

"They're comin' for her tonight?" cried Billy.

"*Si*, señor," replied José. "Doubtless they already take her."

"Hell!" muttered Billy Byrne, as he swung Brazos about so quickly that the little pony pivoted upon his hind legs and dashed away toward the south over the same trail he had just traversed.

XV
AN INDIAN'S TREACHERY

The Brazos pony had traveled far that day but for only a trifle over ten miles had he carried a rider upon his back. He was, consequently, far from fagged as he leaped forward to the lifted reins and tore along the dusty river trail back in the direction of Orobo.

Never before had Brazos covered ten miles in so short a time, for it was not yet five o'clock when, reeling with fatigue, he stopped, staggered and fell in front of the office building at El Orobo.

Eddie Shorter had sat in the chair as Barbara and Billy had last seen him waiting until Byrne should have an ample start before arousing Grayson and reporting the prisoner's escape. Eddie had determined that he would give Billy an hour. He grinned as he anticipated the rage of Grayson and the Villistas when they learned that their bird had flown, and as he mused and waited he fell asleep.

It was broad daylight when Eddie awoke, and as he looked up at the little clock ticking against the wall, and saw the time he gave an exclamation of surprise and leaped to his feet. Just as he opened the outer door of the office he saw a horseman leap from a winded pony in front of the building. He saw the animal collapse and sink to the ground, and then he recognized the pony as Brazos, and another glance at the man brought recognition of him, too.

"You?" cried Eddie. "What are you doin' back here? I gotta take you now," and he started to draw his revolver; but Billy Byrne had him covered before ever his hand reached the grip of his gun.

"Put 'em up!" admonished Billy, "and listen to me. This ain't no time fer gunplay or no such foolishness. I ain't back here to be took—get that out o' your nut. I'm tipped off that a bunch o' siwashes was down here last night to swipe Miss Harding. Come! We gotta go see if she's here or not, an' don't try any funny business on me, Eddie. I ain't a-goin' to be taken again, an' whoever tries it gets his, see?"

Eddie was down off the porch in an instant, and making for the ranchhouse.

"I'm with you," he said. "Who told you? And who done it?"

"Never mind who told me; but a siwash named Esteban was to pull the thing off for Grayson. Grayson wanted Miss Harding an' he was goin' to have her stolen for him."

"The hound!" muttered Eddie.

The two men dashed up onto the veranda of the ranchhouse and pounded at the door until a Chinaman opened it and stuck out his head, inquiringly.

"Is Miss Harding here?" demanded Billy.

"Mlissy Hardie kleep," snapped the servant. "Wally wanee here flo blekfas?," and would have shut the door in their faces had not Billy intruded a heavy boot. The next instant he placed a large palm over the celestial's face and pushed the man back into the house. Once inside he called Mr. Harding's name aloud.

"What is it?" asked the gentleman a moment later as he appeared in a bedroom doorway off the living-room clad in his pajamas. "What's the matter? Why, gad man, is that you? Is this really Billy Byrne?"

"Sure," replied Byrne shortly; "but we can't waste any time chinnin'. I heard that Miss Barbara was goin' to be swiped last night—I heard that she had been. Now hurry and see if she is here."

Anthony Harding turned and leaped up the narrow stairway to the second floor four steps at a time. He hadn't gone upstairs in that fashion in forty years. Without even pausing to rap he burst into his daughter's bedroom. It was empty. The bed was unruffled. It had not been slept in. With a moan the man turned back and ran hastily to the other rooms upon the second floor—Barbara was nowhere to be found. Then he hastened downstairs to the two men awaiting him.

As he entered the room from one end Grayson entered it from the other through the doorway leading out upon the veranda. Billy Byrne had heard footsteps upon the boards without and he was ready, so that as Grayson entered he found himself looking straight at the business end of a six-shooter. The foreman halted, and stood looking in surprise first at Billy Byrne, and then at Eddie Shorter and Mr. Harding.

"What does this mean?" he demanded, addressing Eddie. "What you doin' here with your prisoner? Who told you to let him out, eh?"

"Can the chatter," growled Billy Byrne. "Shorter didn't let me out. I escaped hours ago, and I've just come back from José's to ask you where Miss Harding is, you low-lived cur, you. Where is she?"

"What has Mr. Grayson to do with it?" asked Mr. Harding. "How should he know anything about it? It's all a mystery to me—you here, of all men in the world, and Grayson talking about you as the prisoner. I can't make it out. Quick, though, Byrne, tell me all you know about Barbara."

Billy kept Grayson covered as he replied to the request of Harding.

"This guy hires a bunch of Pimans to steal Miss Barbara," he said. "I got it straight from the fellow he paid the money to for gettin' him the right men to pull off the job. He wants her it seems," and Billy shot a look at the ranch foreman that would have killed if looks could. "She can't have been gone long. I seen her after midnight, just before I made my getaway, so they can't have taken her very far. This thing here can't help us none neither, for he don't know where she is any more'n we do. He thinks he does; but he don't. The siwashes framed it on him, an' they've doubled-crossed him. I got that straight too; but, Gawd! I don't know where they've taken her or what they're goin' to do with her."

As he spoke he turned his eyes for the first time away from Grayson and looked full in Anthony Harding's face. The latter saw beneath the strong character lines of the other's countenance the agony of fear and doubt that lay heavy upon his heart.

In the brief instant that Billy's watchful gaze left the figure of the ranch foreman the latter saw the opportunity he craved. He was standing directly in the doorway—a single step would carry him out of range of Byrne's gun, placing a wall between it and him, and Grayson was not slow in taking that step.

When Billy turned his eyes back the Texan had disappeared, and by the time the former reached the doorway Grayson was halfway to the office building on the veranda of which stood the four soldiers of Villa grumbling and muttering over the absence of their prisoner of the previous evening.

Billy Byrne stepped out into the open. The ranch foreman called aloud to the four Mexicans that their prisoner was at the ranchhouse and as they looked in that direction they saw him, revolver in hand, coming slowly toward them. There was a smile upon his lips which they could not see because of the distance, and which, not knowing Billy Byrne, they would not have interpreted correctly; but the revolver they did understand, and at sight of it one of them threw his carbine to his shoulder. His finger, however, never closed upon the trigger, for there came the sound of a shot from beyond Billy Byrne and the Mexican staggered forward, pitching over the edge of the porch to the ground.

Billy turned his head in the direction from which the shot had come and saw Eddie Shorter running toward him, a smoking six-shooter in his right hand.

"Go back," commanded Byrne; "this is my funeral."

"Not on your life," replied Eddie Shorter. "Those greasers don't take no white man off'n El Orobo, while I'm here. Get busy! They're comin'."

And sure enough they were coming, and as they came their carbines popped and the bullets whizzed about the heads of the two Americans. Grayson, too, had taken a hand upon the side of the Villistas. From the bunkhouse other men were running rapidly in the direction of the fight, attracted by the first shots.

Billy and Eddie stood their ground, a few paces apart. Two more of Villa's men went down. Grayson ran for cover. Then Billy Byrne dropped the last of the Mexicans just as the men from the bunkhouse came panting upon the scene. There were both Americans and Mexicans among them. All were armed and weapons were ready in their hands.

They paused a short distance from the two men. Eddie's presence upon the side of the stranger saved Billy from instant death, for Eddie was well liked by both his Mexican and American fellow-workers.

"What's the fuss?" asked an American.

Eddie told them, and when they learned that the boss's daughter had been spirited away and that the ranch foreman was at the bottom of it the anger of the Americans rose to a dangerous pitch.

"Where is he?" someone asked. They were gathered in a little cluster now about Billy Byrne and Shorter.

"I saw him duck behind the office building," said Eddie.

"Come on," said another. "We'll get him."

"Someone get a rope." The men spoke in low, ordinary tones—they appeared unexcited. Determination was the most apparent characteristic of the group. One of them ran back toward the bunkhouse for his rope. The others walked slowly in the direction of the rear of the office building. Grayson was not there. The search proceeded. The Americans were in advance. The Mexicans kept in a group by themselves a little in rear of the others—it was not their trouble. If the gringos wanted to lynch another gringo, well and good—that was the gringos' business. They would keep out of it, and they did.

Down past the bunkhouse and the cookhouse to the stables the searchers made their way. Grayson could not be found. In the stables one of the men made a discovery—the foreman's saddle had vanished. Out in the corrals they went. One of the men laughed—the bars were down and the saddle horses gone. Eddie Shorter presently pointed out across the pasture and the river to the skyline of the low bluffs beyond. The others looked. A horseman was just visible urging his mount upward to the crest, the two stood in silhouette against the morning sky pink with the new sun.

"That's him," said Eddie.

"Let him go," said Billy Byrne. "He won't never come back and he ain't worth chasin'. Not while we got Miss Barbara to look after. My horse is down there with yours. I'm goin' down to get him. Will you come, Shorter? I may need help—I ain't much with a rope yet."

He started off without waiting for a reply, and all the Americans followed. Together they circled the horses and drove them back to the corral. When Billy had saddled and mounted he saw that the others had done likewise.

"We're goin' with you," said one of the men. "Miss Barbara b'longs to us."

Billy nodded and moved off in the direction of the ranchhouse. Here he dismounted and with Eddie Shorter and Mr. Harding commenced circling the house in search of some manner of clue to the direction taken by the abductors. It was not long before they came upon the spot where the Indians' horses had stood the night before. From there the trail led plainly down toward the river. In a moment ten Americans were following it, after Mr. Harding had supplied Billy Byrne with a carbine, another six-shooter, and ammunition.

Through the river and the cut in the barbed-wire fence, then up the face of the bluff and out across the low mesa beyond the trail led. For a mile it was distinct, and then disappeared as though the riders had separated.

"Well," said Billy, as the others drew around him for consultation, "they'd be goin' to the hills there. They was Pimans—Esteban's tribe. They got her up there in the hills somewheres. Let's split up an' search the hills for her. Whoever comes on 'em first'll have to do some shootin' and the rest of us can close in an' help. We can go in pairs—then if one's killed the other can ride out an' lead the way back to where it happened."

The men seemed satisfied with the plan and broke up into parties of two. Eddie Shorter paired off with Billy Byrne.

"Spread out," said the latter to his companions. "Eddie an' I'll ride straight ahead—the rest of you can fan out a few miles on either side of us. S'long an' good luck," and he started off toward the hills, Eddie Shorter at his side.

Back at the ranch the Mexican vaqueros lounged about, grumbling. With no foreman there was nothing to do except talk about their troubles. They had not been paid since the looting of the bank at Cuivaca, for Mr. Harding had been unable to get any silver from elsewhere until a few days since. He now had assurances that it was on the way to him; but whether or not it would reach El Orobo was a question.

"Why should we stay here when we are not paid?" asked one of them.

"Yes, why?" chorused several others.

"There is nothing to do here," said another. "We will go to Cuivaca. I, for one, am tired of working for the gringos."

This met with the unqualified approval of all, and a few moments later the men had saddled their ponies and were galloping away in the direction of sunbaked Cuivaca. They sang now, and were happy, for they were as little boys playing hooky from school—not bad men; but rather irresponsible children.

Once in Cuivaca they swooped down upon the drinking-place, where, with what little money a few of them had left they proceeded to get drunk.

Later in the day an old, dried-up Indian entered. He was hot and dusty from a long ride.

"Hey, José!" cried one of the vaqueros from El Orobo Rancho; "you old rascal, what are you doing here?"

José looked around upon them. He knew them all—they represented the Mexican contingent of the riders of El Orobo. José wondered what they were all doing here in Cuivaca at one time. Even upon a pay day it never had been the rule of El Orobo to allow more than four men at a time to come to town.

"Oh, José come to buy coffee and tobacco," he replied. He looked about searchingly. "Where are the others?" he asked, "—the gringos?"

"They have ridden after Esteban," explained one of the vaqueros. "He has run off with Señorita Harding."

José raised his eyebrows as though this was all news. "And Señor Grayson has gone with them?" he asked. "He was very fond of the señorita."

"Señor Grayson has run away," went on the other speaker. "The other gringos wished to hang him, for it is said he has bribed Esteban to do this thing."

Again José raised his eyebrows. "Impossible!" he ejaculated. "And who then guards the ranch?" he asked presently.

"Señor Harding, two Mexican house servants, and a Chinaman," and the vaquero laughed.

"I must be going," José announced after a moment. "It is a long ride for an old man from my poor home to Cuivaca, and back again."

The vaqueros were paying no further attention to him, and the Indian passed out and sought his pony; but when he had mounted and ridden from town he took a strange direction for one whose path lies to the east, since he turned his pony's head toward the northwest.

José had ridden far that day, since Billy had left his humble hut. He had gone to the west to the little rancho of one of Pesita's adherents who had dispatched a boy to carry word to the bandit that his Captain Byrne had escaped the Villistas, and then José had ridden into Cuivaca by a circuitous route which brought him up from the east side of the town.

Now he was riding once again for Pesita; but this time he would bear the information himself. He found the chief in camp and after begging tobacco and a cigarette paper the Indian finally reached the purpose of his visit.

"José has just come from Cuivaca," he said, "and there he drank with all the Mexican vaqueros of El Orobo Rancho—*all*, my general, you understand. It seems that Esteban has carried off the beautiful señorita of El Orobo Rancho, and the vaqueros tell José that *all* the American vaqueros have ridden in search of her—*all*, my general, you understand. In such times of danger it is odd that the gringos should leave El Orobo thus unguarded. Only the rich Señor Harding, two house servants, and a Chinaman remain."

A man lay stretched upon his blankets in a tent next to that occupied by Pesita. At the sound of the speaker's voice, low though it was, he raised his head and listened. He heard every word, and a scowl settled upon his brow.

Barbara stolen! Mr. Harding practically alone upon the ranch! And Pesita in possession of this information!

Bridge rose to his feet. He buckled his cartridge belt about his waist and picked up his carbine, then he crawled under the rear wall of his tent and walked slowly off in the direction of the picket line where the horses were tethered.

"Ah, Señor Bridge," said a pleasant voice in his ear; "where to?"

Bridge turned quickly to look into the smiling, evil face of Rozales.

"Oh," he replied, "I'm going out to see if I can't find some shooting. It's awfully dull sitting around here doing nothing."

"*Si*, señor," agreed Rozales; "I, too, find it so. Let us go together—I know where the shooting is best."

"I don't doubt it," thought Bridge; "probably in the back;" but aloud he said: "Certainly, that will be fine," for he guessed that Rozales had been set to watch his movements and prevent his escape, and, perchance, to be the sole witness of some unhappy event which should carry Señor Bridge to the arms of his fathers.

Rozales called a soldier to saddle and bridle their horses and shortly after the two were riding abreast down the trail out of the hills. Where it was necessary that they ride in single file Bridge was careful to see that Rozales rode ahead, and the Mexican graciously permitted the American to fall behind.

If he was inspired by any other motive than simple espionage he was evidently content to bide his time until chance gave him the opening he desired, and it was equally evident that he felt as safe in front of the American as behind him.

At a point where a ravine down which they had ridden debauched upon a mesa Rozales suggested that they ride to the north, which was not at all the direction in which Bridge intended going. The American demurred.

"But there is no shooting down in the valley," urged Rozales.

"I think there will be," was Bridge's enigmatical reply, and then, with a sudden exclamation of surprise he pointed over Rozales' shoulder. "What's that?" he cried in a voice tense with excitement.

The Mexican turned his head quickly in the direction Bridge's index finger indicated.

"I see nothing," said Rozales, after a moment.

"You do now, though," replied Bridge, and as the Mexican's eyes returned in the direction of his companion he was forced to admit that he did see something—the dismal, hollow eye of a six-shooter looking him straight in the face.

"Señor Bridge!" exclaimed Rozales. "What are you doing? What do you mean?"

"I mean," said Bridge, "that if you are at all solicitous of your health you'll climb down off that pony, not forgetting to keep your hands above your head when you reach the ground. Now climb!"

Rozales dismounted.

"Turn your back toward me," commanded the American, and when the other had obeyed him, Bridge dismounted and removed the man's weapons from his belt. "Now you may go, Rozales," he said, "and should you ever have an American in your power again remember that I spared your life when I might easily have taken it—when it would have been infinitely safer for me to have done it."

The Mexican made no reply, but the black scowl that clouded his face boded ill for the next gringo who should be so unfortunate as to fall into his hands. Slowly he wheeled about and started back up the trail in the direction of the Pesita camp.

"I'll be halfway to El Orobo," thought Bridge, "before he gets a chance to tell Pesita what happened to him," and then he remounted and rode on down into the valley, leading Rozales' horse behind him.

It would never do, he knew, to turn the animal loose too soon, since he would doubtless make his way back to camp, and in doing so would have to pass Rozales who would catch him. Time was what Bridge wanted—to be well on his way to Orobo before Pesita should learn of his escape.

Bridge knew nothing of what had happened to Billy, for Pesita had seen to it that the information was kept from the American. The latter had, nevertheless, been worrying not a little at the absence of his friend for he knew that he had taken his liberty and his life in his hands in riding down to El Orobo among avowed enemies.

Far to his rear Rozales plodded sullenly up the steep trail through the mountains, revolving in his mind various exquisite tortures he should be delighted to inflict upon the next gringo who came into his power.

XVI
Eddie Makes Good

Billy Byrne and Eddie Shorter rode steadily in the direction of the hills. Upon either side and at intervals of a mile or more stretched the others of their party, occasionally visible; but for the most part not. Once in the hills the two could no longer see their friends or be seen by them.

Both Byrne and Eddie felt that chance had placed them upon the right trail for a well-marked and long-used path wound upward through a canyon along which they rode. It was an excellent location for an ambush, and both men breathed more freely when they had passed out of it into more open country upon a narrow tableland between the first foothills and the main range of mountains.

Here again was the trail well marked, and when Eddie, looking ahead, saw that it appeared to lead in the direction of a vivid green spot close to the base of the gray brown hills he gave an exclamation of assurance.

"We're on the right trail all right, old man," he said. "They's water there," and he pointed ahead at the green splotch upon the gray. "That's where they'd be havin' their village. I ain't never been up here so I ain't familiar with the country. You see we don't run no cattle this side the river—the Pimans won't let us. They don't care to have no white men pokin' round in their country; but I'll bet a hat we find a camp there."

Onward they rode toward the little spot of green. Sometimes it was in sight and again as they approached higher ground, or wound through gullies and ravines it was lost to their sight; but always they kept it as their goal. The trail they were upon led to it—of that there could be no longer the slightest doubt. And as they rode with their destination in view black, beady eyes looked down upon them from the very green oasis toward which they urged their ponies—tiring now from the climb.

A lithe, brown body lay stretched comfortably upon a bed of grasses at the edge of a little rise of ground beneath which the riders must pass before they came to the cluster of huts which squatted in a tiny natural park at the foot of the main peak. Far above the watcher a spring of clear, pure water bubbled out of the mountainside, and running downward formed little pools among the rocks which held it. And with this water the Pimans irrigated their small fields before it sank from sight again into the earth just below their village. Beside the brown body lay a long rifle. The man's eyes watched, unblinking, the two specks far below him whom he knew and had known for an hour were gringos.

Another brown body wormed itself forward to his side and peered over the edge of the declivity down upon the white men. He spoke a few words in a whisper to him who watched with the rifle, and then crawled back again and disappeared. And all the while, onward and upward came Billy Byrne and Eddie Shorter, each knowing in his heart that if not already, then at any moment a watcher would discover them and a little later a bullet would fly that would find one of them, and they took the chance for the sake of the American girl who lay hidden somewhere in these hills, for in no other way could they locate her hiding place more quickly. Any one of the other eight Americans who rode in pairs into the hills at other points to the left and right of Billy Byrne and his companion would have and was even then cheerfully taking the same chances that Eddie and Billy took, only the latter were now assured that to one of them would fall the sacrifice, for as they had come closer Eddie had seen a thin wreath of smoke rising from among the trees of the oasis. Now, indeed, were they sure that they had chanced upon the trail to the Piman village.

"We gotta keep our eyes peeled," said Eddie, as they wound into a ravine which from its location evidently led directly up to the village. "We ain't far from 'em now, an' if they get us they'll get us about here."

As though to punctuate his speech with the final period a rifle cracked above them. Eddie jumped spasmodically and clutched his breast.

"I'm hit," he said, quite unemotionally.

Billy Byrne's revolver had answered the shot from above them, the bullet striking where Billy had seen a puff of smoke following the rifle shot. Then Billy turned toward Eddie.

"Hit bad?" he asked.

"Yep, I guess so," said Eddie. "What'll we do? Hide up here, or ride back after the others?"

Another shot rang out above them, although Billy had been watching for a target at which to shoot again—a target which he had been positive he would get when the man rose to fire again. And Billy did see the fellow at last—a few paces from where he had first fired; but not until the other had dropped Eddie's horse beneath him. Byrne fired again, and this time he had the satisfaction of seeing a brown body rise, struggle a moment, and then roll over once upon the grass before it came to rest.

"I reckon we'll stay here," said Billy, looking ruefully at Eddie's horse.

Eddie rose and as he did so he staggered and grew very white. Billy dismounted and ran forward, putting an arm about him. Another shot came from above and Billy Byrne's pony grunted and collapsed.

"Hell!" exclaimed Byrne. "We gotta get out of this," and lifting his wounded comrade in his arms he ran for the shelter of the bluff from the summit of which the snipers had fired upon them. Close in, hugging the face of the perpendicular wall of tumbled rock and earth, they were out of range of the Indians; but Billy did not stop when he had reached temporary safety. Farther up toward the direction in which lay the village, and halfway up the side of the bluff Billy saw what he took to be excellent shelter. Here the face of the bluff was less steep and upon it lay a number of large boulders, while others protruded from the ground about them.

Toward these Billy made his way. The wounded man across his shoulder was suffering indescribable agonies; but he bit his lip and stifled the cries that each step his comrade took seemed to wrench from him, lest he attract the enemy to their position.

Above them all was silence, yet Billy knew that alert, red foemen were creeping to the edge of the bluff in search of their prey. If he could but reach the shelter of the boulders before the Pimans discovered them!

The minutes that were consumed in covering the hundred yards seemed as many hours to Billy Byrne; but at last he dragged the fainting cowboy between two large boulders close under the edge of the bluff and found himself in a little, natural fortress, well adapted to defense.

From above they were protected from the fire of the Indians upon the bluff by the height of the boulder at the foot of which they lay, while another just in front hid them from possible marksmen across the canyon. Smaller rocks scattered about gave promise of shelter from flank fire, and as soon as he had deposited Eddie in the comparative safety of their retreat Byrne commenced forming a low breastwork upon the side facing the village—the direction from which they might naturally expect attack. This done he turned his attention to the opening upon the opposite side and soon had a similar defense constructed there, then he turned his attention to

Eddie, though keeping a watchful eye upon both approaches to their stronghold.

The Kansan lay upon his side, moaning. Blood stained his lips and nostrils, and when Billy Byrne opened his shirt and found a gaping wound in his right breast he knew how serious was his companion's injury. As he felt Billy working over him the boy opened his eyes.

"Do you think I'm done for?" he asked in a tortured whisper.

"Nothin' doin'," lied Billy cheerfully. "Just a scratch. You'll be all right in a day or two."

Eddie shook his head wearily. "I wish I could believe you," he said. "I ben figgerin' on goin' back to see maw. I ain't thought o' nothin' else since you told me 'bout how she missed me. I ken see her right now just like I was there. I'll bet she's scrubbin' the kitchen floor. Maw was always a-scrubbin' somethin'. Gee! but it's tough to cash in like this just when I was figgerin' on goin' home."

Billy couldn't think of anything to say. He turned to look up and down the canyon in search of the enemy.

"Home!" whispered Eddie. "Home!"

"Aw, shucks!" said Billy kindly. "You'll get home all right, kid. The boys must a-heard the shootin' an' they'll be along in no time now. Then we'll clean up this bunch o' coons an' have you back to El Orobo an' nursed into shape in no time."

Eddie tried to smile as he looked up into the other's face. He reached a hand out and laid it on Billy's arm.

"You're all right, old man," he whispered. "I know you're lyin' an' so do you; but it makes me feel better anyway to have you say them things."

Billy felt as one who has been caught stealing from a blind man. The only adequate reply of which he could think was, "Aw, shucks!"

"Say," said Eddie after a moment's silence, "if you get out o' here an' ever go back to the States promise me you'll look up maw and paw an' tell 'em I was comin' home—to stay. Tell 'em I died decent, too, will you—died like paw was always a-tellin' me my granddad died, fightin' Injuns 'round Fort Dodge somewheres."

"Sure," said Billy; "I'll tell 'em. Gee! Look who's comin' here," and as he spoke he flattened himself to the ground just as a bullet pinged against the rock above his head and the report of a rifle sounded from up the canyon. "That guy most got me. I'll have to be 'tendin' to business better'n this."

He drew himself slowly up upon his elbows, his carbine ready in his hand, and peered through a small aperture between two of the rocks which composed his breastwork. Then he stuck the muzzle of the weapon through, took aim and pulled the trigger.

"Didje get him?" asked Eddie.

"Yep," said Billy, and fired again. "Got that one too. Say, they're tough-lookin' guys; but I guess they won't come so fast next time. Those two were right in the open, workin' up to us on their bellies. They must a-thought we was sleepin'."

For an hour Billy neither saw nor heard any sign of the enemy, though several times he raised his hat above the breastwork upon the muzzle of his carbine to draw their fire.

It was mid-afternoon when the sound of distant rifle fire came faintly to the ears of the two men from somewhere far below them.

"The boys must be comin'," whispered Eddie Shorter hopefully.

For half an hour the firing continued and then silence again fell upon the mountains. Eddie began to wander mentally. He talked much of Kansas and his old home, and many times he begged for water.

"Buck up, kid," said Billy; "the boys'll be along in a minute now an' then we'll get you all the water you want."

But the boys did not come. Billy was standing up now, stretching his legs, and searching up and down the canyon for Indians. He was wondering if he could chance making a break for the valley where they stood some slight chance of meeting with their companions, and even as he considered the matter seriously there came a staccato report and Billy Byrne fell forward in a heap.

"God!" cried Eddie. "They got him now, they got him."

Byrne stirred and struggled to rise.

"Like'll they got me," he said, and staggered to his knees.

Over the breastwork he saw a half-dozen Indians running rapidly toward the shelter—he saw them in a haze of red that was caused not by blood but by anger. With an oath Billy Byrne leaped to his feet. From his knees up his whole body was exposed to the enemy; but Billy cared not. He was in a berserker rage. Whipping his carbine to his shoulder he let drive at the advancing Indians who were now beyond hope of cover. They must come on or be shot down where they were, so they came on, yelling like devils and stopping momentarily to fire upon the rash white man who stood so perfect a target before them.

But their haste spoiled their marksmanship. The bullets zinged and zipped against the rocky little fortress, they nicked Billy's shirt and trousers and hat, and all the while he stood there pumping lead into his assailants— not hysterically; but with the cool deliberation of a butcher slaughtering beeves.

One by one the Pimans dropped until but a single Indian rushed frantically upon the white man, and then the last of the assailants lunged forward across the breastwork with a bullet from Billy's carbine through his forehead.

Eddie Shorter had raised himself painfully upon an elbow that he might witness the battle, and when it was over he sank back, the blood welling from between his set teeth.

Billy turned to look at him when the last of the Pimans was disposed of, and seeing his condition kneeled beside him and took his head in the hollow of an arm.

"You orter lie still," he cautioned the Kansan. "Tain't good for you to move around much."

"It was worth it," whispered Eddie. "Say, but that was some scrap. You got your nerve standin' up there against the bunch of 'em; but if you hadn't they'd have rushed us and some of 'em would a-got in."

"Funny the boys don't come," said Billy.

"Yes," replied Eddie, with a sigh; "it's milkin' time now, an' I figgered on goin' to Shawnee this evenin'. Them's nice cookies, maw. I—"

Billy Byrne was bending low to catch his feeble words, and when the voice trailed out into nothingness he lowered the tousled red head to the hard earth and turned away.

Could it be that the thing which glistened on the eyelid of the toughest guy on the West Side was a tear?

The afternoon waned and night came, but it brought to Billy Byrne neither renewed attack nor succor. The bullet which had dropped him momentarily had but creased his forehead. Aside from the fact that he was blood covered from the wound it had inconvenienced him in no way, and now that darkness had fallen he commenced to plan upon leaving the shelter.

First he transferred Eddie's ammunition to his own person, and such valuables and trinkets as he thought "maw" might be glad to have, then he removed the breechblock from Eddie's carbine and stuck it in his pocket that the weapon might be valueless to the Indians when they found it.

"Sorry I can't bury you old man," was Billy's parting comment, as he climbed over the breastwork and melted into the night.

Billy Byrne moved cautiously through the darkness, and he moved not in the direction of escape and safety but directly up the canyon in the way that the village of the Pimans lay.

Soon he heard the sound of voices and shortly after saw the light of cook fires playing upon bronzed faces and upon the fronts of low huts. Some women were moaning and wailing. Billy guessed that they mourned for those whom his bullets had found earlier in the day. In the darkness of the night, far up among the rough, forbidding mountains it was all very weird and uncanny.

Billy crept closer to the village. Shelter was abundant. He saw no sign of sentry and wondered why they should be so lax in the face of almost certain attack. Then it occurred to him that possibly the firing he and Eddie had heard earlier in the day far down among the foothills might have meant the extermination of the Americans from El Orobo.

"Well, I'll be next then," mused Billy, and wormed closer to the huts. His eyes were on the alert every instant, as were his ears; but no sign of that which he sought rewarded his keenest observation.

Until midnight he lay in concealment and all that time the mourners continued their dismal wailing. Then, one by one, they entered their huts, and silence reigned within the village.

Billy crept closer. He eyed each hut with longing, wondering gaze. Which could it be? How could he determine? One seemed little more promising than the others. He had noted those to which Indians had retired. There were three into which he had seen none go. These, then, should be the first to undergo his scrutiny.

The night was dark. The moon had not yet risen. Only a few dying fires cast a wavering and uncertain light upon the scene. Through the shadows Billy Byrne crept closer and closer. At last he lay close beside one of the huts which was to be the first to claim his attention.

For several moments he lay listening intently for any sound which might come from within; but there was none. He crawled to the doorway and peered within. Utter darkness shrouded and hid the interior.

Billy rose and walked boldly inside. If he could see no one within, then no one could see him once he was inside the door. Therefore, so reasoned Billy Byrne, he would have as good a chance as the occupants of the hut, should they prove to be enemies.

He crossed the floor carefully, stopping often to listen. At last he heard a rustling sound just ahead of him. His fingers tightened upon the revolver he carried in his right hand, by the barrel, clublike. Billy had no intention of making any more noise than necessary.

Again he heard a sound from the same direction. It was not at all unlike the frightened gasp of a woman. Billy emitted a low growl, in fair imitation of a prowling dog that has been disturbed.

Again the gasp, and a low: "Go away!" in liquid feminine tones—and in English!

Billy uttered a low: "S-s-sh!" and tiptoed closer. Extending his hands they presently came in contact with a human body which shrank from him with another smothered cry.

"Barbara!" whispered Billy, bending closer.

A hand reached out through the darkness, found him, and closed upon his sleeve.

"Who are you?" asked a low voice.

"Billy," he replied. "Are you alone in here?"

"No, an old woman guards me," replied the girl, and at the same time they both heard a movement close at hand, and something scurried past them to be silhouetted for an instant against the path of lesser darkness which marked the location of the doorway.

"There she goes!" cried Barbara. "She heard you and she has gone for help."

"Then come!" said Billy, seizing the girl's arm and dragging her to her feet; but they had scarce crossed half the distance to the doorway when the cries of the old woman without warned them that the camp was being aroused.

Billy thrust a revolver into Barbara's hand. "We gotta make a fight of it, little girl," he said. "But you'd better die than be here alone."

As they emerged from the hut they saw warriors running from every doorway. The old woman stood screaming in Piman at the top of her lungs. Billy, keeping Barbara in front of him that he might shield her body with his own, turned directly out of the village. He did not fire at first hoping that they might elude detection and thus not draw the fire of the Indians upon them; but he was doomed to disappointment, and they had taken scarcely a dozen steps when a rifle spoke above the noise of human voices and a bullet whizzed past them.

Then Billy replied, and Barbara, too, from just behind his shoulder. Together they backed away toward the shadow of the trees beyond the village and as they went they poured shot after shot into the village.

The Indians, but just awakened and still half stupid from sleep, did not know but that they were attacked by a vastly superior force, and this fear held them in check for several minutes—long enough for Billy and Barbara to reach the summit of the bluff from which Billy and Eddie had first been fired upon.

Here they were hidden from the view of the Indians, and Billy broke at once into a run, half carrying the girl with a strong arm about her waist.

"If we can reach the foothills," he said, "I think we can dodge 'em, an' by goin' all night we may reach the river and El Orobo by morning. It's a long hike, Barbara, but we gotta make it—we gotta, for if daylight finds us in the Piman country we won't never make it. Anyway," he concluded optimistically, "it's all down hill."

"We'll make it, Billy," she replied, "if we can get past the sentry."

"What sentry?" asked Billy. "I didn't see no sentry when I come in."

"They keep a sentry way down the trail all night," replied the girl. "In the daytime he is nearer the village—on the top of this bluff, for from here he can see the whole valley; but at night they station him farther away in a narrow part of the trail."

"It's a mighty good thing you tipped me off," said Billy; "for I'd a-run right into him. I thought they was all behind us now."

After that they went more cautiously, and when they reached the part of the trail where the sentry might be expected to be found, Barbara warned Billy of the fact. Like two thieves they crept along in the shadow of the canyon wall. Inwardly Billy cursed the darkness of the night which hid from view everything more than a few paces from them; yet it may have been this very darkness which saved them, since it hid them as effectually from an enemy as it hid the enemy from them. They had reached the point where Barbara was positive the sentry should be. The girl was clinging tightly to Billy's left arm. He could feel the pressure of her fingers as they sunk into his muscles, sending little tremors and thrills through his giant frame. Even in the face of death Billy Byrne could sense the ecstasies of personal contact with this girl—the only woman he ever had loved or ever would.

And then a black shadow loomed before them, and a rifle flashed in their faces without a word or a sign of warning.

XVII
"You Are My Girl!"

Mr. Anthony Harding was pacing back and forth the length of the veranda of the ranchhouse at El Orobo waiting for some word of hope from those who had ridden out in search of his daughter, Barbara. Each swirling dust devil that eddied across the dry flat on either side of the river roused hopes within his breast that it might have been spurred into activity by the hoofs of a pony bearing a messenger of good tidings; but always his hopes were dashed, for no horseman emerged from the heat haze of the distance where the little dust devils raced playfully among the cacti and the greasewood.

But at last, in the northwest, a horseman, unheralded by gyrating dust column, came into sight. Mr. Harding shook his head sorrowfully. It had not been from this direction that he had expected word of Barbara, yet he kept his eyes fastened upon the rider until the latter reined in at the ranchyard and loped a tired and sweating pony to the foot of the veranda steps. Then Mr. Harding saw who the newcomer was.

"Bridge!" he exclaimed. "What brings you back here? Don't you know that you endanger us as well as yourself by being seen here? General Villa will think that we have been harboring you."

Bridge swung from the saddle and ran up onto the veranda. He paid not the slightest attention to Anthony Harding's protest.

"How many men you got here that you can depend on?" he asked.

"None," replied the Easterner. "What do you mean?"

"None!" cried Bridge, incredulity and hopelessness showing upon his countenance. "Isn't there a Chinaman and a couple of faithful Mexicans?"

"Oh, yes, of course," assented Mr. Harding; "but what are you driving at?"

"Pesita is on his way here to clean up El Orobo. He can't be very far behind me. Call the men you got, and we'll get together all the guns and ammunition on the ranch, and barricade the ranchhouse. We may be able to stand 'em off. Have you heard anything of Miss Barbara?"

Anthony Harding shook his head sadly.

"Then we'll have to stay right here and do the best we can," said Bridge. "I was thinking we might make a run for it if Miss Barbara was here; but as she's not we must wait for those who went out after her."

Mr. Harding summoned the two Mexicans while Bridge ran to the cookhouse and ordered the Chinaman to the ranchhouse. Then the erstwhile bookkeeper ransacked the bunkhouse for arms and ammunition. What little he found he carried to the ranchhouse, and with the help of the others barricaded the doors and windows of the first floor.

"We'll have to make our fight from the upper windows," he explained to the ranch owner. "If Pesita doesn't bring too large a force we may be able to stand them off until you can get help from Cuivaca. Call up there now and see if you can get Villa to send help—he ought to protect you from Pesita. I understand that there is no love lost between the two."

Anthony Harding went at once to the telephone and rang for the central at Cuivaca.

"Tell it to the operator," shouted Bridge who stood peering through an opening in the barricade before a front window; "they are coming now, and the chances are that the first thing they'll do is cut the telephone wires."

The Easterner poured his story and appeal for help into the ears of the girl at the other end of the line, and then for a few moments there was silence in the room as he listened to her reply.

"Impossible!" and "My God! it can't be true," Bridge heard the older man ejaculate, and then he saw him hang up the receiver and turn from the instrument, his face drawn and pinched with an expression of utter hopelessness.

"What's wrong?" asked Bridge.

"Villa has turned against the Americans," replied Harding, dully. "The operator evidently feels friendly toward us, for she warned me not to appeal to Villa and told me why. Even now, this minute, the man has a force of twenty-five hundred ready to march on Columbus, New Mexico. Three Americans were hanged in Cuivaca this afternoon. It's horrible, sir! It's horrible! We are as good as dead this very minute. Even if we stand off Pesita we can never escape to the border through Villa's forces."

"It looks bad," admitted Bridge. "In fact it couldn't look much worse; but here we are, and while our ammunition holds out about all we can do is stay here and use it. Will you men stand by us?" he addressed the Chinaman and the two Mexicans, who assured him that they had no love for Pesita and would fight for Anthony Harding in preference to going over to the enemy.

"Good!" exclaimed Bridge, "and now for upstairs. They'll be howling around here in about five minutes, and we want to give them a reception they won't forget."

He led the way to the second floor, where the five took up positions near the front windows. A short distance from the ranchhouse they could see the enemy, consisting of a detachment of some twenty of Pesita's troopers riding at a brisk trot in their direction.

"Pesita's with them," announced Bridge, presently. "He's the little fellow on the sorrel. Wait until they are close up, then give them a few rounds; but go easy on the ammunition—we haven't any too much."

Pesita, expecting no resistance, rode boldly into the ranchyard. At the bunkhouse and the office his little force halted while three or four troopers dismounted and entered the buildings in search of victims. Disappointed there they moved toward the ranchhouse.

"Lie low!" Bridge cautioned his companions. "Don't let them see you, and wait till I give the word before you fire."

On came the horsemen at a slow walk. Bridge waited until they were within a few yards of the house, then he cried: "Now! Let 'em have it!" A rattle of rifle fire broke from the upper windows into the ranks of the Pesitistas. Three troopers reeled and slipped from their saddles. Two horses dropped in their tracks. Cursing and yelling, the balance of the horsemen wheeled and galloped away in the direction of the office building, followed by the fire of the defenders.

"That wasn't so bad," cried Bridge. "I'll venture a guess that Mr. Pesita is some surprised—and sore. There they go behind the office. They'll stay there a few minutes talking it over and getting up their courage to try it again. Next time they'll come from another direction. You two," he continued, turning to the Mexicans, "take positions on the east and south sides of the house. Sing can remain here with Mr. Harding. I'll take the north side facing the office. Shoot at the first man who shows his head. If we can hold them off until dark we may be able to get away. Whatever happens don't let one of them get close enough to fire the house. That's what they'll try for."

It was fifteen minutes before the second attack came. Five dismounted troopers made a dash for the north side of the house; but when Bridge dropped the first of them before he had taken ten steps from the office building and wounded a second the others retreated for shelter.

Time and again as the afternoon wore away Pesita made attempts to get men close up to the house; but in each instance they were driven back, until at last they desisted from their efforts to fire the house or rush it, and contented themselves with firing an occasional shot through the windows opposite them.

"They're waiting for dark," said Bridge to Mr. Harding during a temporary lull in the hostilities, "and then we're goners, unless the boys come back from across the river in time."

"Couldn't we get away after dark?" asked the Easterner.

"It's our only hope if help don't reach us," replied Bridge.

But when night finally fell and the five men made an attempt to leave the house upon the side away from the office building they were met with the flash of carbines and the ping of bullets. One of the Mexican defenders fell, mortally wounded, and the others were barely able to drag him within and replace the barricade before the door when five of Pesita's men charged close up to their defenses. These were finally driven off and again there came a lull; but all hope of escape was gone, and Bridge reposted the defenders at the upper windows where they might watch every approach to the house.

As the hours dragged on the hopelessness of their position grew upon the minds of all. Their ammunition was almost gone—each man had but a few rounds remaining—and it was evident that Pesita, through an inordinate desire for revenge, would persist until he had reduced their fortress and claimed the last of them as his victim.

It was with such cheerful expectations that they awaited the final assault which would see them without ammunition and defenseless in the face of a cruel and implacable foe.

It was just before daylight that the anticipated rush occurred. From every side rang the reports of carbines and the yells of the bandits. There were scarcely more than a dozen of the original twenty left; but they made up for their depleted numbers by the rapidity with which they worked their firearms and the loudness and ferocity of their savage cries.

And this time they reached the shelter of the veranda and commenced battering at the door.

At the report of the rifle so close to them Billy Byrne shoved Barbara quickly to one side and leaped forward to close with the man who barred their way to liberty.

That they had surprised him even more than he had them was evidenced by the wildness of his shot which passed harmlessly above their heads as well as by the fact that he had permitted them to come so close before engaging them.

To the latter event was attributable his undoing, for it permitted Billy Byrne to close with him before the Indian could reload his antiquated weapon. Down the two men went, the American on top, each striving for a death-hold; but in weight and strength and skill the Piman was far outclassed by the trained fighter, a part of whose daily workouts had consisted in wrestling with proficient artists of the mat.

Barbara Harding ran forward to assist her champion but as the men rolled and tumbled over the ground she could find no opening for a blow that might not endanger Billy Byrne quite as much as it endangered his antagonist; but presently she discovered that the American required no assistance. She saw the Indian's head bending slowly forward beneath the resistless force of the other's huge muscles, she heard the crack that announced the parting of the vertebrae and saw the limp thing which had but a moment before been a man, pulsing with life and vigor, roll helplessly aside—a harmless and inanimate lump of clay.

Billy Byrne leaped to his feet, shaking himself as a great mastiff might whose coat had been ruffled in a fight.

"Come!" he whispered. "We gotta beat it now for sure. That guy's shot'll lead 'em right down to us," and once more they took up their flight down toward the valley, along an unknown trail through the darkness of the night.

For the most part they moved in silence, Billy holding the girl's arm or hand to steady her over the rough and dangerous portions of the path. And as they went there grew in Billy's breast a love so deep and so resistless that he found himself wondering that he had ever imagined that his former passion for this girl was love.

This new thing surged through him and over him with all the blind, brutal, compelling force of a mighty tidal wave. It battered down and swept away the frail barriers of his newfound gentleness. Again he was the Mucker—hating the artificial wall of social caste which separated him from this girl; but now he was ready to climb the wall, or, better still, to batter it down with his huge fists. But the time was not yet—first he must get Barbara to a place of safety.

On and on they went. The night grew cold. Far ahead there sounded the occasional pop of a rifle. Billy wondered what it could mean and as they approached the ranch and he discovered that it came from that direction he hastened their steps to even greater speed than before.

"Somebody's shootin' up the ranch," he volunteered. "Wonder who it could be."

"Suppose it is your friend and general?" asked the girl.

Billy made no reply. They reached the river and as Billy knew not where the fords lay he plunged in at the point at which the water first barred their progress and dragging the girl after him, plowed bull-like for the opposite shore. Where the water was above his depth he swam while Barbara clung to his shoulders. Thus they made the passage quickly and safely.

Billy stopped long enough to shake the water out of his carbine, which the girl had carried across, and then forged ahead toward the ranchhouse from which the sounds of battle came now in increased volume.

And at the ranchhouse "hell was popping." The moment Bridge realized that some of the attackers had reached the veranda he called the surviving Mexican and the Chinaman to follow him to the lower floor where they might stand a better chance to repel this new attack. Mr. Harding he persuaded to remain upstairs.

Outside a dozen men were battering to force an entrance. Already one panel had splintered, and as Bridge entered the room he could see the figures of the bandits through the hole they had made. Raising his rifle he fired through the aperture. There was a scream as one of the attackers dropped; but the others only increased their efforts, their oaths, and their threats of vengeance.

The three defenders poured a few rounds through the sagging door, then Bridge noted that the Chinaman ceased firing.

"What's the matter?" he asked.

"Allee gonee," replied Sing, pointing to his ammunition belt.

At the same instant the Mexican threw down his carbine and rushed for a window on the opposite side of the room. His ammunition was exhausted and with it had departed his courage. Flight seemed the only course remaining. Bridge made no effort to stop him. He would have been glad to fly, too; but he could not leave Anthony Harding, and he was sure that the older man would prove unequal to any sustained flight on foot.

"You better go, too, Sing," he said to the Chinaman, placing another bullet through the door; "there's nothing more that you can do, and it may be that they are all on this side now—I think they are. You fellows have fought splendidly. Wish I could give you something more substantial than thanks; but that's all I have now and shortly Pesita won't even leave me that much."

"Allee light," replied Sing cheerfully, and a second later he was clambering through the window in the wake of the loyal Mexican.

And then the door crashed in and half a dozen troopers followed by Pesita himself burst into the room.

Bridge was standing at the foot of the stairs, his carbine clubbed, for he had just spent his last bullet. He knew that he must die; but he was determined to make them purchase his life as dearly as he could, and to die in defense of Anthony Harding, the father of the girl he loved, even though hopelessly.

Pesita saw from the American's attitude that he had no more ammunition. He struck up the carbine of a trooper who was about to shoot Bridge down.

"Wait!" commanded the bandit. "Cease firing! His ammunition is gone. Will you surrender?" he asked of Bridge.

"Not until I have beaten from the heads of one or two of your friends," he replied, "that which their egotism leads them to imagine are brains. No, if you take me alive, Pesita, you will have to kill me to do it."

Pesita shrugged. "Very well," he said, indifferently, "it makes little difference to me—that stairway is as good as a wall. These brave defenders of the liberty of poor, bleeding Mexico will make an excellent firing squad. Attention, my children! Ready! Aim!"

Eleven carbines were leveled at Bridge. In the ghastly light of early dawn the sallow complexions of the Mexicans took on a weird hue. The American made a wry face, a slight shudder shook his slender frame, and then he squared his shoulders and looked Pesita smilingly in the face.

The figure of a man appeared at the window through which the Chinaman and the loyal Mexican had escaped. Quick eyes took in the scene within the room.

"Hey!" he yelled. "Cut the rough stuff!" and leaped into the room.

Pesita, surprised by the interruption, turned toward the intruder before he had given the command to fire. A smile lit his features when he saw who it was.

"Ah!" he exclaimed, "my dear Captain Byrne. Just in time to see a traitor and a spy pay the penalty for his crimes."

"Nothin' doin'," growled Billy Byrne, and then he threw his carbine to his shoulder and took careful aim at Pesita's face.

How easy it would have been to have hesitated a moment in the window before he made his presence known—just long enough for Pesita to speak the single word that would have sent eleven bullets speeding into the body of the man who loved Barbara and whom Billy believed the girl loved. But did such a thought occur to Billy Byrne of Grand Avenue? It did not. He forgot every other consideration beyond his loyalty to a friend. Bridge and Pesita were looking at him in wide-eyed astonishment.

"Lay down your carbines!" Billy shot his command at the firing squad. "Lay 'em down or I'll bore Pesita. Tell 'em to lay 'em down, Pesita. I gotta bead on your beezer."

Pesita did as he was bid, his yellow face pasty with rage.

"Now their cartridge belts!" snapped Billy, and when these had been deposited upon the floor he told Bridge to disarm the bandit chief.

"Is Mr. Harding safe?" he asked of Bridge, and receiving an affirmative he called upstairs for the older man to descend.

As Mr. Harding reached the foot of the stairs Barbara entered the room by the window through which Billy had come—a window which opened upon the side veranda.

"Now we gotta hike," announced Billy. "It won't never be safe for none of you here after this, not even if you do think Villa's your friend—which he ain't the friend of no American."

"We know that now," said Mr. Harding, and repeated to Billy that which the telephone operator had told him earlier in the day.

Marching Pesita and his men ahead of them Billy and the others made their way to the rear of the office building where the horses of the bandits were tethered. They were each armed now from the discarded weapons of the raiders, and well supplied with ammunition. The Chinaman and the loyal Mexican also discovered themselves when they learned that the tables had been turned upon Pesita. They, too, were armed and all were mounted, and when Billy had loaded the remaining weapons upon the balance of the horses the party rode away, driving Pesita's livestock and arms ahead of them.

"I imagine," remarked Bridge, "that you've rather discouraged pursuit for a while at least;" but pursuit came sooner than they had anticipated.

They had reached a point on the river not far from José's when a band of horsemen appeared approaching from the west. Billy urged his party to greater speed that they might avoid a meeting if possible; but it soon became evident that the strangers had no intention of permitting them to go unchallenged, for they altered their course and increased their speed so that they were soon bearing down upon the fugitives at a rapid gallop.

"I guess," said Billy, "that we'd better open up on 'em. It's a cinch they ain't no friends of ours anywhere in these parts."

"Hadn't we better wait a moment," said Mr. Harding; "we do not want to chance making any mistake."

"It ain't never a mistake to shoot a Dago," replied Billy. His eyes were fastened upon the approaching horsemen, and he presently gave an exclamation of recognition. "There's Rozales," he said. "I couldn't mistake that beanpole nowheres. We're safe enough in takin' a shot at 'em if Rosie's with 'em. He's Pesita's head guy," and he drew his revolver and took a single shot in the direction of his former comrades. Bridge followed his example. The oncoming Pesitistas reined in. Billy returned his revolver to its holster and drew his carbine.

"You ride on ahead," he said to Mr. Harding and Barbara. "Bridge and I'll bring up the rear."

Then he stopped his pony and turning took deliberate aim at the knot of horsemen to their left. A bandit tumbled from his saddle and the fight was on.

Fortunately for the Americans Rozales had but a handful of men with him and Rozales himself was never keen for a fight in the open.

All morning he hovered around the rear of the escaping Americans; but neither side did much damage to the other, and during the afternoon Billy noticed that Rozales merely followed within sight of them, after having dispatched one of his men back in the direction from which they had come.

"After reinforcements," commented Byrne.

All day they rode without meeting with any roving bands of soldiers or bandits, and the explanation was all too sinister to the Americans when coupled with the knowledge that Villa was to attack an American town that night.

"I wish we could reach the border in time to warn 'em," said Billy; "but they ain't no chance. If we cross before sunup tomorrow morning we'll be doin' well."

He had scarcely spoken to Barbara Harding all day, for his duties as rear guard had kept him busy; nor had he conversed much with Bridge, though he had often eyed the latter whose gaze wandered many times to the slender, graceful figure of the girl ahead of them.

Billy was thinking as he never had thought before. It seemed to him a cruel fate that had so shaped their destinies that his best friend loved the girl Billy loved. That Bridge was ignorant of Billy's infatuation for her the latter well knew. He could not blame Bridge, nor could he, upon the other hand, quite reconcile himself to the more than apparent adoration which marked his friend's attitude toward Barbara.

As daylight waned the fugitives realized from the shuffling gait of their mounts, from drooping heads and dull eyes that rest was imperative. They themselves were fagged, too, and when a ranchhouse loomed in front of them they decided to halt for much-needed recuperation.

Here they found three Americans who were totally unaware of Villa's contemplated raid across the border, and who when they were informed of it were doubly glad to welcome six extra carbines, for Barbara not only was armed but was eminently qualified to expend ammunition without wasting it.

Rozales and his small band halted out of range of the ranch; but they went hungry while their quarry fed themselves and their tired mounts.

The Clark brothers and their cousin, a man by the name of Mason, who were the sole inhabitants of the ranch counseled a long rest—two hours at least, for the border was still ten miles away and speed at the last moment might be their sole means of salvation.

Billy was for moving on at once before the reinforcements, for which he was sure Rozales had dispatched his messenger, could overtake them. But the others were tired and argued, too, that upon jaded ponies they could not hope to escape and so they waited, until, just as they were ready to continue their flight, flight became impossible.

Darkness had fallen when the little party commenced to resaddle their ponies and in the midst of their labors there came a rude and disheartening interruption. Billy had kept either the Chinaman or Bridge constantly upon watch toward the direction in which Rozales' men lolled smoking in the dark, and it was the crack of Bridge's carbine which awoke the Americans to the fact that though the border lay but a few miles away they were still far from safety.

As he fired Bridge turned in his saddle and shouted to the others to make for the shelter of the ranchhouse.

"There are two hundred of them," he cried. "Run for cover!"

Billy and the Clark brothers leaped to their saddles and spurred toward the point where Bridge sat pumping lead into the advancing enemy. Mason and Mr. Harding hurried Barbara to the questionable safety of the ranchhouse. The Mexican followed them, and Bridge ordered Sing back to assist in barricading the doors and windows, while he and Billy and the Clark boys held the bandits in momentary check.

Falling back slowly and firing constantly as they came the four approached the house while Pesita and his full band advanced cautiously after them. They had almost reached the house when Bridge lunged forward from his saddle. The Clark boys had dismounted and were leading their ponies inside the house. Billy alone noted the wounding of his friend. Without an instant's hesitation he slipped from his saddle, ran back to where Bridge lay and lifted him in his arms. Bullets were pattering thick about them. A horseman far in advance of his fellows galloped forward with drawn saber to cut down the gringos.

Billy, casting an occasional glance behind, saw the danger in time to meet it—just, in fact, as the weapon was cutting through the air toward his head. Dropping Bridge and dodging to one side he managed to escape the cut, and before the swordsman could recover Billy had leaped to his pony's side and seizing the rider about the waist dragged him to the ground.

"Rozales!" he exclaimed, and struck the man as he had never struck another in all his life, with the full force of his mighty muscles backed by his great weight, with clenched fist full in the face.

There was a spurting of blood and a splintering of bone, and Captain Guillermo Rozales sank senseless to the ground, his career of crime and rapine ended forever.

Again Billy lifted Bridge in his arms and this time he succeeded in reaching the ranchhouse without opposition though a little crimson stream trickled down his left arm to drop upon the face of his friend as he deposited Bridge upon the floor of the house.

All night the Pesitistas circled the lone ranchhouse. All night they poured their volleys into the adobe walls and through the barricaded windows. All night the little band of defenders fought gallantly for their lives; but as day approached the futility of their endeavors was borne in upon them, for of the nine one was dead and three wounded, and the numbers of their assailants seemed undiminished.

Billy Byrne had been lying all night upon his stomach before a window firing out into the darkness at the dim forms which occasionally showed against the dull, dead background of the moonless desert.

Presently he leaped to his feet and crossed the floor to the room in which the horses had been placed.

"Everybody fire toward the rear of the house as fast as they can," said Billy. "I want a clear space for my getaway."

"Where you goin?" asked one of the Clark brothers.

"North," replied Billy, "after some of Funston's men on the border."

"But they won't cross," said Mr. Harding. "Washington won't let them."

"They gotta," snapped Billy Byrne, "an' they will when they know there's an American girl here with a bunch of Dagos yappin' around."

"You'll be killed," said Price Clark. "You can't never get through."

"Leave it to me," replied Billy. "Just get ready an' open that back door when I give the word, an' then shut it again in a hurry when I've gone through."

He led a horse from the side room, and mounted it.

"Open her up, boes!" he shouted, and "S'long everybody!"

Price Clark swung the door open. Billy put spurs to his mount and threw himself forward flat against the animal's neck. Another moment he was through and a rattling fusillade of shots proclaimed the fact that his bold feat had not gone unnoted by the foe.

The little Mexican pony shot like a bolt from a crossbow out across the level desert. The rattling of carbines only served to add speed to its frightened feet. Billy sat erect in the saddle, guiding the horse with his left hand and working his revolver methodically with his right.

At a window behind him Barbara Harding stood breathless and spellbound until he had disappeared into the gloom of the early morning darkness to the north, then she turned with a weary sigh and resumed her place beside the wounded Bridge whose head she bathed with cool water, while he tossed in the delirium of fever.

The first streaks of daylight were piercing the heavens, the Pesitistas were rallying for a decisive charge, the hopes of the little band of besieged were at low ebb when from the west there sounded the pounding of many hoofs.

"Villa," moaned Westcott Clark, hopelessly. "We're done for now, sure enough. He must be comin' back from his raid on the border."

In the faint light of dawn they saw a column of horsemen deploy suddenly into a long, thin line which galloped forward over the flat earth, coming toward them like a huge, relentless engine of destruction.

The Pesitistas were watching too. They had ceased firing and sat in their saddles forgetful of their contemplated charge.

The occupants of the ranchhouse were gathered at the small windows.

"What's them?" cried Mason—"them things floating over 'em."

"They're guidons!" exclaimed Price Clark "—the guidons of the United States cavalry regiment. See 'em! See 'em? God! but don't they look good?"

There was a wild whoop from the lungs of the advancing cavalrymen. Pesita's troops answered it with a scattering volley, and a moment later the Americans were among them in that famous revolver charge which is now history.

Daylight had come revealing to the watchers in the ranchhouse the figures of the combatants. In the thick of the fight loomed the giant figure of a man in nondescript garb which more closely resembled the apparel of the Pesitistas than it did the uniforms of the American soldiery, yet it was with them he fought. Barbara's eyes were the first to detect him.

"There's Mr. Byrne," she cried. "It must have been he who brought the troops."

"Why, he hasn't had time to reach the border yet," remonstrated one of the Clark boys, "much less get back here with help."

"There he is though," said Mr. Harding. "It's certainly strange. I can't understand what American troops are doing across the border—especially under the present administration."

The Pesitistas held their ground for but a moment then they wheeled and fled; but not before Pesita himself had forced his pony close to that of Billy Byrne.

"Traitor!" screamed the bandit. "You shall die for this," and fired point-blank at the American.

Billy felt a burning sensation in his already wounded left arm; but his right was still good.

"For poor, bleeding Mexico!" he cried, and put a bullet through Pesita's forehead.

"What was that you said?" asked an officer reining in beside Billy.

"Every time I croak a Mexican," said Billy, "I feel like I'd done just that much more to make Mexico a decent place to live in."

Under escort of the men of the Thirteenth Cavalry who had pursued Villa's raiders into Mexico and upon whom Billy Byrne had stumbled by chance, the little party of fugitives came safely to United States soil, where all but one breathed sighs of heartfelt relief.

Bridge was given first aid by members of the hospital corps, who assured Billy that his friend would not die. Mr. Harding and Barbara were taken in by the wife of an officer, and it was at the quarters of the latter that Billy Byrne found her alone in the sitting-room.

The girl looked up as he entered, a sad smile upon her face. She was about to ask him of his wound; but he gave her no opportunity.

"I've come for you," he said. "I gave you up once when I thought it was better for you to marry a man in your own class. I won't give you up again. You're mine—you're my girl, and I'm goin' to take you with me. Were goin' to Galveston as fast as we can, and from there we're goin' to Rio. You belonged to me long before Bridge saw you. He can't have you. Nobody can have you but me, and if anyone tries to keep me from taking you they'll get killed."

He took a step nearer that brought him close to her. She did not shrink—only looked up into his face with wide eyes filled with wonder. He seized her roughly in his arms.

"You are my girl!" he cried hoarsely. "Kiss me!"

"Wait!" she said. "First tell me what you meant by saying that Bridge couldn't have me. I never knew that Bridge wanted me, and I certainly have never wanted Bridge. O Billy! Why didn't you do this long ago? Months ago in New York I wanted you to take me; but you left me to another man whom I didn't love. I thought you had ceased to care, Billy, and since we have been together here—since that night in the room back of the office—you have made me feel that I was nothing to you. Take me, Billy! Take me anywhere in the world that you go. I love you and I'll slave for you—anything just to be with you."

"Barbara!" cried Billy Byrne, and then his voice was smothered by the pressure of warm, red lips against his own.

A half hour later Billy stepped out into the street to make his way to the railroad station that he might procure transportation for three to Galveston. Anthony Harding was going with them. He had listened to Barbara's pleas, and had finally volunteered to back Billy Byrne's flight from the jurisdiction of the law, or at least to a place where, under a new name, he could start life over again and live it as the son-in-law of old Anthony Harding should live.

Among the crowd viewing the havoc wrought by the raiders the previous night was a large man with a red face. It happened that he turned suddenly about as Billy Byrne was on the point of passing behind him. Both men started as recognition lighted their faces and he of the red face found himself looking down the barrel of a six-shooter.

"Put it up, Byrne," he admonished the other coolly. "I didn't know you were so good on the draw."

"I'm good on the draw all right, Flannagan," said Billy, "and I ain't drawin' for amusement neither. I gotta chance to get away and live straight, and have a little happiness in life, and, Flannagan, the man who tries to crab my game is goin' to get himself croaked. I'll never go back to stir alive. See?"

"Yep," said Flannagan, "I see; but I ain't tryin' to crab your game. I ain't down here after you this trip. Where you been, anyway, that you don't know the war's over? Why Coke Sheehan confessed a month ago that it was him that croaked Schneider, and the governor pardoned you about ten days ago."

"You stringin' me?" asked Billy, a vicious glint in his eyes.

"On the level," Flannagan assured him. "Wait, I gotta clippin' from the *Trib* in my clothes somewheres that gives all the dope."

He drew some papers from his coat pocket and handed one to Billy.

"Turn your back and hold up your hands while I read," said Byrne, and as Flannagan did as he was bid Billy unfolded the soiled bit of newspaper and read that which set him a-trembling with nervous excitement.

A moment later Detective Sergeant Flannagan ventured a rearward glance to note how Byrne was receiving the joyful tidings which the newspaper article contained.

"Well, I'll be!" ejaculated the sleuth, for Billy Byrne was already a hundred yards away and breaking all records in his dash for the sitting-room he had quitted but a few minutes before.

It was a happy and contented trio who took the train the following day on their way back to New York City after bidding Bridge goodbye in the improvised hospital and exacting his promise that he would visit them in New York in the near future.

It was a month later spring was filling the southland with new, sweet life. The joy of living was reflected in the song of birds and the opening of buds. Beside a slow-moving stream a man squatted before a tiny fire. A battered tin can, half filled with water stood close to the burning embers. Upon a sharpened stick the man roasted a bit of meat, and as he watched it curling at the edges as the flame licked it he spoke aloud though there was none to hear:

> Just for a con I'd like to know (yes, he crossed over long ago;
> And he was right, believe me, bo!) if somewhere in the South,
> Down where the clouds lie on the sea, he found his sweet
>   Penelope
> With buds of roses in her hair and kisses on her mouth.

"Which is what they will be singing about me one of these days," he commented.